DAPHNE DU M**

By the same authors

LANDSCAPES OF DESIRE: Metaphors in Modern
Women's Fiction

Daphne du Maurier

Writing, Identity and the Gothic Imagination

Avril Horner

and

Sue Zlosnik

palgrave

First published in Great Britain 1998 by
MACMILLAN PRESS LTD
Houndmills, Basingstoke, Hampshire RG21 6XS and London
Companies and representatives throughout the world

A catalogue record for this book is available from the British Library.

ISBN 0–333–64333–X hardcover
ISBN 0–333–64334–8 paperback

First published in the United States of America 1998 by
ST. MARTIN'S PRESS, INC.,
Scholarly and Reference Division,
175 Fifth Avenue, New York, N.Y. 10010

ISBN 0–312–21146–5

Library of Congress Cataloging-in-Publication Data
Horner, Avril, 1947–
Daphne du Maurier : writing, identity, and the gothic imagination
/ Avril Horner and Sue Zlosnik.
p. cm.
Includes bibliographical references (p.   ) and index.
ISBN 0–312–21146–5
1. Du Maurier, Daphne, Dame, 1907–   —Criticism and
interpretation.   2. Psychological fiction, English—History and
criticism.   3. Women and literature—England—History—20th century.
4. Horror tales, English—History and criticism.   5. Gothic revival
(Literature)—Great Britain.   6. Identity (Psychology) in
literature.   I. Zlosnik, Sue, 1949–   .   II. Title.
PR6007.U47Z67 1998
823'.912—dc21   97–31890
                                                              CIP

This book is printed on paper suitable for recycling and made from fully managed and sustained forest sources.

Printed & Bound by Antony Rowe Ltd, Eastbourne
Transferred to digital printing 2002

This book is dedicated with love and affection to Avril's father, James Harry Lowe, and Sue's mother, Elsie Wealleans Peters, who both know a good story when they read one.

Contents

Contents

Acknowledgements

The seed for this book was planted many years ago when we taught *Rebecca* as a set text on a course entitled 'Female Gothic' for the Extra-Mural Department of Manchester University. It has taken some time to bring our developing ideas about Daphne du Maurier to fruition and we are grateful to many people for their lively interest in our work. In particular, Oriel Malet has been a responsive and generous correspondent; her memories of Daphne du Maurier as a close friend and her independent views on her writing have been a useful touchstone for our own critical opinions. We remember, with pleasure and gratitude, a beautiful late autumn day spent at her house in northern France. Christian (Kits) Browning, Daphne du Maurier's son, has also encouraged us in the writing of this book, patiently answering queries and following its progress with interest. We would like to thank him and his wife, Hacker, for their hospitality during our visit to Ferryside in April, 1995. Thanks, too, to David and Clint of Fowey for some practical help.

We also wish to thank the following colleagues who have encouraged us in the project and who who have offered expertise in particular areas: Mike Cohen, Paul Callick, Angus Easson, Clare Hanson, Michael Parker, Terry Phillips, Susan Rowland and Ella Westland. Scott McCracken deserves special thanks, not only for offering constructive criticism on first drafts of some chapters, but for persuading us in the book's early days that we should 'go with the Gothic'. We are particularly indebted to Mary Eagleton, whose astute reading of the final manuscript version prompted some last minute improvements. Any errors or infelicities that remain are, of course, entirely our own.

Certain sections of this book started life as conference papers and appear in slightly altered versions elsewhere. We are grateful to the editors and publishers of *BELLS (Barcelona English Language and Literature Studies)* 'Literature and Culture' Issue, No. 7 (1996), for permission to reprint, in altered and condensed form within Chapter 4, '"Those Curious Sloping Letters": Reading the Writing of du Maurier's *Rebecca*'. This article was based on a paper given at the second conference of the European Society for the Study of English, held in Bordeaux in September 1993. We also wish to thank the editors and publishers of *Prose Studies*, 'Correspondences: A Special Issue on Letters', Vol. 19, No. 2 (1996) for permission to reprint parts of 'A "Disembodied Spirit": The Letters and Fiction of Daphne du Maurier' within the first part of Chapter 1. This article was based on a paper given at a conference entitled 'Correspondences' held at the University of Groningen, The Netherlands, in November 1994. The second part of Chapter 6 is based on a conference paper given at the second conference of The International Gothic Association, held at the University of Stirling in the summer of 1995. This paper will be published in its original form in the conference proceedings to be edited by David Punter and published by Macmillan in 1998. Similarly, the second part of Chapter 5 is based on a conference paper given at the third conference of the European Society for the Study of English which took place in Glasgow in September 1995. This paper will be published in its original form in the conference proceedings to be edited by Richard Todd and published by Rodopi Press, Amsterdam.

The recent revival of interest in the life and work of Daphne du Maurier has resulted in publications without which our own book could not have been written. In particular, Alison Light's pioneering academic study of du Maurier's work in *Forever England: Femininity, Literature and Conservatism Between the Wars* (Routledge, 1991) and Margaret Forster's biography of du Maurier, published by Chatto & Windus in 1993, proved invaluable resources. Readers will quickly become aware that although we do not always agree with Forster's reading of du Maurier's life or with Light's interpretation of du Maurier's novels, their work has been the catalyst for our argument concerning the Gothic element in du Maurier's fiction and its relation to her writing identity. (In this connection, Ellen Violett, the daughter of Ellen Doubleday, has asked us to point out that the source of Margaret Forster's quotations from the correspondence between Daphne du Maurier and Ellen M. Doubleday is the Ellen McCarter Doubleday Collection at Princeton University, represented by Ellen McCarter Violett, family curator.) Jane Blackstock, of Victor Gollancz Ltd, kindly allowed us access to letters and documents associated with the publication of *Rebecca*. We are grateful to Curtis Brown, literary agents for the Estate of Daphne du Maurier, for permission to quote from both published and unpublished letters by Daphne du Maurier.

We wish to thank the English Department of the University of Salford for granting Avril Horner a semester's study leave during the academic year 1995-6 and the Research Committee of Liverpool Hope University College for the award of a grant to Sue Zlosnik which facilitated visits to London and Cornwall. Thanks are due too to Salford University's European Studies Research Institute, which encouraged the project and funded conference travel for Avril Horner, and to John Elford, Pro-Rector of Liverpool Hope, whose Cornish background led to his taking a particular interest and to the loan of several useful books. We would also like to thank the many students at both these institutions whose enthusiasm for du Maurier's work constantly reaffirmed our own opinion of her as undervalued writer. Charmian Hearne's early interest in a book on Daphne du Maurier gave us confidence to proceed with the project. As our editor she has, throughout its writing, offered good advice and much support.

Finally, we wish to thank our families which, added together, comprise six sons in various stages of adolescence and young adulthood, one young delinquent labrador, one elderly sweet-tempered mongrel, three cats and one bad-tempered cockatiel - not forgetting, of course, John and Howard. They all (with the possible exception of the cockatiel) viewed the project with interest and good-humour and have sustained us through the inevitable periods of exhaustion and doubt with a mixture of comforting words, phlegmatic good sense and the occasional bad joke. Cups of coffee or tea and glasses of wine always seemed to appear at just the right moment.

AVRIL HORNER
SUE ZLOSNIK

1

A 'Disembodied Spirit': Writing, Identity and the Gothic Imagination

Daphne du Maurier's public identity as a romantic novelist and a story-teller who can spin a good yarn has eclipsed for too long her versatility and skill as a writer. In her published works, which span the years 1931 to 1989, she experimented with several genres including the family saga, biography, women's romantic fiction, the Gothic novel, and the short story. Her writing career was therefore long and varied. Critical interpretation of her work, however, often seems to 'freeze' her within a certain mode of writing or within a certain period of her life. Prompted by the Penguin reprint of seven du Maurier novels, Ronald Bryden, for example, produced one of the first articles to assess her work seriously in relation to the literary canon; this appeared in *The Spectator* in 1962. Recognizing 'Miss du Maurier...[as]... one of the world's great literary phenomena' and noting that her novels 'have been read by millions of people in scores of languages', Bryden nevertheless dismissed her as a superficial romantic novelist who, like her father and grandfather before her, revelled in nostalgia and was capable of producing only 'a glossy brand of entertaining nonsense'.[1] This perception of du Maurier as more an entertainer than a serious writer is frequently echoed today. Writing in The *Observer* in August 1996, Neil Spencer admitted that he would be taking du Maurier's novels with him when holidaying in Cornwall, 'less for their middlebrow yarns than for their evocation of Cornwall's mysterious, history-sodden landscape'.[2] The inclusion of du Maurier as an important writer in the Royal Mail's 'great twentieth-century women' series of stamps, released in August 1996, brought protests from many. Quentin Bell said he thought du Maurier an obscure choice – 'She was an agreeable writer of agreeable fiction, but not a great or serious author' – and Carmen Callil, founder of Virago Press, commented 'As much as I love du Maurier, I

1

wouldn't have chosen her. I could think of 500 others'.[3] This
general tendency to damn du Maurier's writing with faint praise
is inflected rather differently in academic critiques. For example,
Alison Light, in *Forever England: Femininity, Literature and Conservatism Between the Wars* (1991) concentrates, as did Bryden, on du
Maurier's inter-war novels. Whilst usefully linking the problemati-
zation of masculinity and femininity offered by du Maurier's
novels with the broader cultural changes which took place after
World War One, Light constructs her as a conservative woman
writer and emphasizes what she sees as the element of nostalgia
in her work. She is, however, forced into making 'conservatism'
and 'nostalgia' internally fissured and contradictory categories
in order to accommodate this reading. More recently, Margaret
Forster's biographical study of du Maurier, published in 1993, offers
a fresh portrait of du Maurier as writer and woman. Containing
extracts from previously unpublished letters between du Maurier
and Ellen Doubleday, Forster's biography intimates that the novelist's life as a happily married wife and mother was something of a
pretence. Reviews of Forster's book were dominated by specul-
ations concerning du Maurier's 'real' sexual identity, yet the
opportunity for reading the novels afresh in the light of the letters
was neglected. There is now a danger that interest in du Maurier's
writing might be eclipsed by interest in her life.

It is the aim of this book to provide a fresh assessment of Daphne
du Maurier's work and of her status as a writer. Our interest in du
Maurier is based on the belief that her best novels and short stories
offer particularly interesting examples of how Gothic writing is
inflected by both personal and broader cultural values and
anxieties. *Daphne du Maurier: Writing, Identity and the Gothic Imagination* is therefore structured through an attempt to relate du
Maurier's work to generic traditions and conventions (in particular,
those of Gothic fiction), cultural moment and the author's 'writing'
of her own identity. We agree with Margaret Anne Doody that 'The
works of any artist represent the meeting of three histories: the life
of the individual, the cultural life of the surrounding society, and
the tradition of the chosen art'.[4] As Doody's fine study of Frances
Burney's life and work demonstrates, the correspondence between
these 'histories' is not, however, a simple one. Many recent theorists of autobiography argue that all literature is to some extent
autobiographical and that the generic boundaries between
letters, fiction and autobiography can no longer be regarded as

unproblematic.[5] No longer working with the simple assumption that the 'life' can be read through the fiction – or vice versa – the contemporary reader can, instead, see the works as integral to the author's construction of his or her identity. The critic is thereby freed to read autobiographical writings as quasi-fictions and fictions as aspects of autobiography. To read du Maurier's work in relation to her life and times is, in the words of Janice Morgan:

> to be made aware of the evolving self as an endless negotiation between event and illusion, the actual and the imaginary, where myth, allegory, and lived experience combine in complex, inter-dependent patterns to form what Michel Leiris calls the 'authenticity' of the self.[6]

Du Maurier's letters are of much interest in this respect, since they reveal an intriguing story of the writer's identity in process, especially in relation to what Judith Kegan Gardiner has defined as 'the area of self-concept'. This, she claims, is 'especially troubled for women' and its dissonances are often reflected in women's writing. Such dissonances are, she suggests, communicated through paradoxes of sameness and difference – 'from other women, especially their mothers; from men; and from social injunctions for what women should be, including those inscribed in the literary canon'.[7] Much of what Gardiner says about female identity and its relation to writing by women continues to provide a sensible starting point for analysis of a woman author's work. For example:

> we can approach a text with the hypothesis that its female author is engaged in a process of testing and defining various aspects of identity chosen from many imaginative possibilities. That is, the woman writer uses her text, particularly one centering on a female hero, as part of a continuing process involving her own self-definition and her empathic identification with her character. Thus the text and its female hero begin as narcissistic extensions of the author.[8]

Daphne du Maurier's fiction is not autobiographical in any obvious way and early critics tended to see it, as did Ronald Bryden, as escapist make-believe. This book will argue, however, that the use of Gothic conventions in du Maurier's work enables her to explore the anxieties of identity at their deepest level. An ambivalence concerning the 'self' is also reflected in her letters, written over many years, which deal more overtly with such anxieties; a consideration of them offers a useful prologue to discussion of the fictional texts.

WRITING, GENDER AND ANXIETY

Daphne du Maurier appears to have been keenly aware of her father's desire for a son to carry on the family artistic tradition. Her father, Gerald du Maurier, a famous actor-manager of the London stage, was himself the son of George du Maurier, Punch cartoonist and novelist who, in his most famous work, *Trilby* (1894), created the sinister Svengali. As is clear from Margaret Forster's biography, Daphne du Maurier's relationship with her father was emotionally very intense. Muriel du Maurier gave birth to three daughters but not the son her husband dearly wished for; Daphne, the middle child (born in 1907), became her father's favourite, no doubt partly because he saw in her a continuation of his own father's literary talents.[9] Perhaps not surprisingly, then, Daphne du Maurier grew up wishing that she had been born a boy; in an early letter to the family governess, known as Tod, she states, 'If only I was a man'.[10] As a child she bonded closely with her father and created an idealized masculine *alter ego* called Eric Avon, a character who was all action and bravado and who was drawn from the boys' adventure stories she had read. Du Maurier recalls this character in *Myself When Young* which was published in 1977; there were, she writes, 'no psychological depths to Eric Avon. He just shone at everything'.[11] However, she was not close to her mother, whom she thought of as 'the Snow Queen in disguise'.[12] In a letter written at the age of 53 to Oriel Malet, she comments that her mother was a 'very basic type of woman' and that she had inherited only 'the normal thing of a woman wanting to be married from her, and from Daddy's mother, also a basic type'.[13] Indeed, du Maurier was prone as a child to fantasizing a 'better' mother, as she later recognized.[14] Forster points out that the young Daphne bore a startling resemblance to the actress Gladys Cooper and that she used to imagine that she was really her daughter, 'smuggled at birth into Mummy's care (except that Mummy would never have stood for it)'.[15] As an adult she created substitute mothers both in life (Forster claims that 'Ferdy', 'Tod' and Ellen Doubleday were all mother replacements[16]) and in fiction (the character of the mother, Stella Martyn, in the play *September Tide* – originally entitled *Mother* – was based on Ellen Doubleday, the wife of her American publisher[17]).

Daphne du Maurier matured into an adult woman who seemed, superficially at least, to follow the conventional pattern expected of women of her class. In 1932, at the age of twenty-five, she married Major 'Boy' Browning. During a period of his active service in the Second World War, she took their three children to live in a cottage in Cornwall, moving in 1943 to Menabilly, which became the family home. It was here she found the space and tranquillity she needed to write during her married life. This surface conformity, however, hid a complex personality, which Forster's biography has attempted to explore. In spite of living an apparently conventional and happy life as wife, mother and successful novelist, du Maurier continued to experience anxiety and ambivalence about her identity as a woman writer. For much of her life she felt that part of herself was a 'disembodied spirit', a phrase she uses in two separate letters to Ellen Doubleday. She uses it first in a letter dated December 1947 (written in a parodic fairy-tale manner), to describe what we would now call a sense of split subjectivity:

> And then the boy realised he had to grow up and not be a boy any longer, so he turned into a girl, and not an unattractive one at that, and the boy was locked in a box forever. D. du M. wrote her books, and had young men, and later a husband, and children, and a lover, and life was sometimes lovely and sometimes rather sad, but when she found Menabilly and lived in it alone, she opened up the box sometimes and let the phantom, who was neither girl nor boy but disembodied spirit, dance in the evening when there was no one to see...[18]

In a letter to Ellen written almost a year later in September 1948, reflecting on her husband's reliance on her money-earning capacity as a best-selling novelist, she uses the phrase in a slightly different way:

> I mean, really, women should not have careers. It's people like me who have careers who really have bitched up the old relationship between men and women. Women ought to be soft and gentle and dependent. Disembodied spirits like myself are all *wrong*.[19]

In the first letter, she describes a masculine dimension of her being which, while 'locked' away, undergoes a metamorphosis into the 'disembodied spirit' which is androgynous and suggestive of a more authentic 'self'. Such a creative spirit, associated as it is in this letter with her life at Menabilly, is intrinsic to her life as a writer. However, the second letter suggests that while acknowledging her career as that of author, she felt ill-at-ease as a successful *woman* writer in the wider world; this is confirmed by another letter to Ellen Doubleday written in October 1948, in which she confesses to seeing her work as having given her 'a masculine approach to life'.[20] Later, having become intrigued by the work of Jung and Adler during the winter of 1954, she explains her 'disembodied' self by reference to Jung's vocabulary of duality and identifies her writing persona as having sprung from a repressed 'No. 2' masculine side. In a letter to her 17-year-old daughter in the same year she explains, 'When I get madly boyish No. 2 is in charge, and then, after a bit, the situation is reversed...No. 2 can come to the surface and be helpful...he certainly has a lot to do with my writing'.[21] While such a 'disembodied spirit' was containable, while it could be put back in the box, it could do no harm; when, however, du Maurier perceived it as taking over – when she referred to *herself* as the 'disembodied spirit' – then she believed it to be socially destructive. Thus du Maurier perceived her *writing* identity as masculine; it is no coincidence that of the eight novels which have a first person narrator (a device she favoured), only three of them, *Rebecca* and *The King's General* and *The Glass Blowers*, have a female narrator. Arguably, it was this anxiety concerning the 'other' contained within the 'self' which gave Jung's work particular resonance for her. Du Maurier's life-long interest in the figure of the transgressive double (explored most famously in *Rebecca*) is a manifestation of an anxiety which drew her continually back to the Gothic mode of writing.

However, the letters to Oriel Malet, edited by the recipient and published in 1993, tell a rather different story from those to Ellen Doubleday. Malet's collection spans the period between the early 1950s and 1981, although the friendship appears, from her account, to have lasted until du Maurier's death in 1989. Thus many of the letters were written after du Maurier's intense relationships with Ellen Doubleday and the actress Gertrude Lawrence.[22] The Malet letters demonstrate that, having come to see herself as a 'disembodied spirit', du Maurier was, over the following years, able to deal more positively with her sense of split subjectivity. The author's letters to this younger woman writer, to whom she constantly offers professional advice and encouragement, inscribe an identity which acknowledges the creative power of the imagination whilst seeking to .circumscribe its role in everyday life. They suggest that du Maurier had, to some extent, come to terms with a more fractured earlier self, a resolution also suggested by a letter of 1957 to Maureen Baker-Munton (cited in full as an appendix in Margaret Forster's biography), in which du Maurier is able to accept that a multiplicity of 'selves' might constitute her identity. In contrast with those to Ellen Doubleday, the Malet letters represent one side of a dialogue with someone who is herself a writer and are, perhaps, the more significant because du Maurier lived a fairly secluded life in Cornwall and was not part of a literary circle in which writing was regularly discussed. Thus they concern themselves with the problems of writing and with a continuing interest in the relationship between fiction and the 'real' world; difficulties and enthusiasms are shared, the lives and work of Katherine Mansfield and the Brontës acting as frequent reference points for both women writers, for example. In these letters, du Maurier's reading of Jung's work is alluded to in a way which suggests that it continued to have a significant influence on her understanding of her imaginative life as a writer. In a letter from the early 1950s, she makes clear her preference for Jung's work over that of Freud or Adler and writes:

> He tells one about one's subconscious self, but is not saying that *all* one wants is endless bed like Freud. Only he does say that the ordinary life of an artist or writer can never be satisfactory, because of this awful creating thing that goes on inside them all the time, making them Gondal – so I am deeply interested. Try and get some of his books.[23]

The Malet letters are characterised by an easy use of du Maurier slang terms: the verb 'to Gondal', for example, derives from du Maurier's interest in the Brontës and signifies the constant process of make-believe which characterizes her own interior life. (In her introduction to *Wuthering Heights*, published by Macdonald & Co. in 1955, du Maurier stresses how important the dream world of Gondal was for Emily Brontë who, she claims, alone of all the Brontës, continued to revel 'in its glory' and live 'with it forever'.[24])

Such an interior life, however, needs stimulation and further letters to Oriel Malet indicate that 'Gondalling' often required a 'Peg'. A 'Peg' is glossed by Malet as 'someone whom one momentarily invests with romantic glamour, but more particularly as the inspiration for a fictional character'[25] (it may also convey the idea of using someone as a peg on which to hang one's own 'new' or experimental identity[26]). In 1964, some ten years after the letter concerning Jung, du Maurier writes to Oriel Malet:

> The Peg made an interest, and one's dream life (which you and I, as imaginative writers, have) centred around this Peg, although one's reason told one that it was non-adult and absurd. It must be a lot mixed up with sex because now I don't feel I need Peg any more, but before C. of L. my Peg images were very strong. Looking back now, although they served beautifully as characters in books, it was awfully silly, *au fond*, pegging them as *people*. I learnt my lesson, and I have told you this before, when having pegged Gertrude (bits of Maria in *Parasites*, bit of *Rachel* etc.) and then she died – I was quite *bouleversée* by the death; *not* because how sad, a friend had died, but how bottomless – a peg had vanished! A fabric that one had built disintegrated![27]

Many of the letters to Malet reveal such informal self-analysis. The 'self-concept' is different from that evident in earlier correspondence and reveals a resolution of the anxiety concerning the split subjectivity expressed by the 'boy-in-the box' trope. The above quotation suggests that the dimming of female sexuality aided this resolution and allowed a degree of detachment and objectivity not available to the younger woman writer ('C. of L.' refers to the 'change of life'). Such detachment enables the older du Maurier to see that the relationships with both Ellen and Gertrude involved 'Gondalling' about 'Pegs'; in retrospect, Gertrude is seen as '*not* a person who had filled my whole life ... but a Peg, and a lovely illusion',[28] and the fascination with Ellen is put into perspective:

> when I had that (to me, rather silly, now!) 'thing' about Ellen, which was pure Gondal, it was only making up *My Cousin Rachel*, and pegging the Rachel woman on to her, and making her die, that I was able to rid myself of it. For writers, the only way we can do it, is to *write* them out.[29]

To a certain extent this reading of her past is anticipated in the letter to Maureen Baker-Munton written in 1957. Here du Maurier tries to explain how 'my obsessions – you can only call them that – for poor old Ellen D and Gertrude – were all part of a nervous breakdown going on *inside myself*, partly to do with my muddled troubles, and writing and a fear of facing reality'.[30] Interestingly, in a letter written in August 1958 to console Oriel Malet on the loss of her much-loved godmother, du Maurier reflects on the significance of what she called her 'women "pegs"' and reconstructs both Ellen Doubleday and Gertrude Lawrence as mother-figures:

> It's strange that, in your last MS...I still saw the struggle of the non-adult you, the child who protests 'Don't let the world and "them" hurt me'... You have to stand alone, and not a bitter, Doomed alone, but independent of the Mother. Because really that is what she has been, and a Peg too, in a great deep sense of the mother that went before, and the eternal one that we carry inside us. For some, this dependence is stronger than others. I've carried it about for years, because of missing it, hence my 'women' pegs.[31]

Here, aged fifty one, and writing as the mother of three children aged twenty-five, twenty-one and eighteen, du Maurier can be seen re-assessing the significance of the mother's role in the development of the writer's identity and preoccupations. This late acknowledgement of the mother's importance in what Freudians would term the 'family romance' does not necessarily contradict her rather pejorative comments on her mother as a 'basic type' (made in a letter to Oriel Malet two years later). Rather, it suggests that as an older woman, and a mother herself, she has become aware of the *symbolic* importance of the mother: perhaps for du Maurier, as for Frances Burney, 'the experience of mothering meant a consoling psychic return of the absent mother, now reembodied in herself'.[32] This realization coincides with her perception that those earlier relationships with women 'pegs', which had caused such inner turmoil were, seen through the lens of time, intrinsic to her psychological development as an individual and therefore to her life *as a writer*. This insight seems to result in a greater self-assurance and, indeed, some peace of mind; a new understanding of the workings of the unconscious (gained, presumably through her reading of Jung) allows her to be kinder to her younger self and enables her to grant an 'authenticity' to her feminine, as well as her masculine, 'selves'. Looking back, at the age of forty-eight, on the 'vaguely dissatisfied and unhappy' early days of her marriage, she notes that 'I didn't know about the unconscious... and thought I was being disloyal to Moper, who was being a very loving husband, and I got guilt. It's the things we *don't* know about ourselves that are the nuisance'.[33] Later, in 1958, she comments:

> I *do* know how artists and writers can have these friendships with people, with women, with girls, and in a way it's a sort of blend of attraction and imagination, and all the things wrapped up, and they like it that way.... I am all *for* Pegs, having lived on them for most of my life, and got them out of my system with books, but my God, you have to be jolly careful when you bring them into practical living issues. They either explode like bubbles and vanish, or else turn catastrophic.[34]

Another way of reading this self-assessment during the middle years, however, is to view it as an attempt by du Maurier to retrieve the bisexual elements of her past identity into a more orthodox heterosexual identity for her middle age; the nature of her friendship with Oriel Malet may have provoked a particular kind of reconstruction of the self in du Maurier's letters to the younger writer.[35] This interpretation relies, in its turn, however, on the acceptance of Forster's assumption in her biography of du Maurier that the 'boy-in-the-box' signified either a repressed sexual desire for women or a hidden bisexual nature. Du Maurier does in fact refer to herself in a letter as a 'half-breed'[36] and this could be seen as an acknowledgement of bisexuality. However, Forster occasionally seems to construe the author's ambivalence concerning her sexual identity as indicative of repressed lesbian desire:

> The fury she felt at being thought a lesbian was because she truly did not see herself as such... In many ways, she reflected the sexual judgements of her era. During the twenties and thirties, when she was growing up, women who were lesbians were thought of as women who should have been born men... Today a lesbian would define her sexuality differently; a man is precisely what she would not wish to be. A lesbian is now simply a woman who loves women, and to whom intimacy with a man is abhorrent.[37]

Forster's representation of du Maurier's sexual identity is constructed through her reading of the letters between du Maurier and Ellen Doubleday – but these are quoted only in extract form. Since these letters are currently sealed in Princeton University Library, there is no way, at present, of checking the extracts used by Forster against either the context of whole letters or the backdrop of the whole correspondence.[38] In discussing the fiction, therefore, we need to remain aware that reference to the life entails working with conflicting constructions of the author both by others (Forster's biography and Malet's edited collection of letters give quite different senses of du Maurier's 'identity') and by herself. However, we do not intend to offer here an alternative or 'authoritative' biographical reading; rather, we are concerned with two issues: the manner in which du Maurier's work focuses on questions of identity and the use of writing (particularly Gothic writing) in order to negotiate aspects of identity.

Interestingly, it was during this period of later middle age that du Maurier was to write three successful novels, each with a male narrator: *The Scapegoat* (1957), *The Flight of the Falcon* (1965) and *The House on the Strand* (1969). This period also produced a number of successful short stories, most notably 'Don't Look Now', which is told from the point of view of its central male character.[39] The creative tension generated by her anxiety over her identity as a woman writer is thus complicated by an exploration of masculine identities in her work; the later fiction, therefore, represents not a further rewriting of the anxiety of female authorship, evident in texts such as *Rebecca* (written by the young army wife with two small children), but a departure into new and varied masculine identities which constitute what Alison Light has described as 'a language of a developing selfhood'.[40] Authorship is now accepted as a state of freedom which allows her to explore other 'selves'. By 1963 she recognized her 'Gondalling' and the need for 'Pegs' as an essential part of this freedom:

> If you look back into my life, since you knew me – and before that, when you didn't – it has always been fundamentally rather monotonous and uneventful, from a worldly point of view. Just being a person down here, Moper coming at weekends, and the children at school; the Main events, my books being written, and leading a queer Gondal imaginary life. If I had *not* written, and *not* Gondalled, I should probably have gone raving mad, or

taken to looking out for some sort of menace, to make an interest![41]

Significantly, of the five novels with male narrators (*I'll Never be
Young Again, My Cousin Rachel, The Scapegoat, The Flight of the Falcon*
and *The House on the Strand*), the last three have narrators whose
social identity is also precarious in some way: John is forced to
assume the identity of his look-alike, Jean de Gué; Beo returns to
Ruffano as a stranger with another name; and, most dramatically of
all, Richard is transported back through time into a life in which he
can be only a passive and invisible observer. The device of the male
narrator in these later works is used to probe the problematic
nature of masculinity; interestingly, each of them is in some way
dislocated from his environment, whether it be through the time
slip of *The House on the Strand*, or through the exchange of identity
with another in *The Scapegoat*. Indeed, in *The Flight of the Falcon* it is
the narrator himself, Armino Fabbio (Beo), who, returning to his
home city of Ruffano for the first time since the War (when he left it
in the company of his mother and her German commandant lover)
describes himself as 'a disembodied spirit'.[42] These characters are
far removed from the 'Eric Avon' fantasy figure of du Maurier's
youth, but in *Myself When Young* du Maurier acknowledges that he
surfaced in an oblique manner in those novels which have male
narrators:

> their personalities can be said to be undeveloped, inadequate,
> sharing a characteristic that had never been Eric's, who had
> dominated his Dampier brother friends. For each of my five
> narrators depended, for reassurance, on a male friend older than
> himself... if there was an Eric Avon struggling to escape from
> my feminine unconscious through the years, he certainly suc-
> ceeded in the imagination, however different from his prototype,
> for I would identify with my series of inadequate narrators,
> plunge into their escapades with relish and excitement, then
> banish them from memory until the next one emerged![43]

By the time she wrote these lines at the age of seventy, du Maurier
had displaced the notion of the 'disembodied spirit' onto the fictional characters themselves and recognizes that her writing has
been an externalisation of anxiety concerning her own identity.
This recognition acknowledged an identity which could accom-

modate or, indeed, was built upon, conflicting identifications: we might remember here Diana Fuss's claim that 'identification is the detour through the other that defines a self'.[44] In exploring 'otherness' in texts such as *Rebecca* and *The Scapegoat*, du Maurier had been, she later realized, playing out her own internal conflicts concerning gender, creativity and desire. She had managed, in the words of Mary Mason, the 'evolution and delineation of an identity by way of alterity'[45] partly *through fiction itself*. The letters to Oriel Malet show that increasing years gave her a more affirmative sense of the writing self: she realizes that she has become what she is through having lived much of her life in the imagination. Thus, prompted by her correspondence with the younger writer, she undertakes an interrogation of the writing process and comes to see that identity is not a 'given' to be discovered, but a dynamic process of construction. The correspondences with Ellen Doubleday and Oriel Malet show a writer moving away from what Jonathan Dollimore has described as an 'essentialist quest in the name of an authentic self' (the 'depth' model of identity) to an awareness that fiction can offer competing representations of 'self' such that identity is perpetually rewritten (the 'surface' model of identity).[46] Judith Butler's argument, in *Gender Trouble*, that gender is a continuous performative act, rather than an essential aspect of identity, might also be used to illuminate du Maurier's changing attitude to her 'self':

> *gender* is not a noun, but neither is it a set of free-floating attributes, for we have seen that the substantive effect of gender is performatively produced and compelled by the regulatory practices of gender coherence. Hence, within the inherited discourse of the metaphysics of substance, gender proves to be performative – that is, constituting the identity it is purported to be. In this sense, gender is always a doing, though not a doing by a subject who might be said to preexist the deed.[47]

If, as Butler claims, 'The unity of the subject is thus already potentially contested by the distinction that permits of gender as a multiple interpretation of sex',[48] then du Maurier's description of herself as a 'disembodied spirit' might well be an attempt to express a sense of fractured subjectivity. It also expresses a desire to reject the determining role of the sexed body in creating social identity. The rejection of embodiment itself, however, is accommodated only by the discourses of religious faith and the Gothic.

In du Maurier's play *September Tide*, published in 1948, a young artist tells his mother-in-law that the portrait he has painted of her represents not her past selves, but 'the complete person that you are now. The Stella of today'. Stella replies ('with humility' according to the stage direction), 'Is anyone ever final and complete?'[49] It seems probable that du Maurier, like her character (and like Julia Kristeva), believed that a person's identity is never 'finished'. Indeed, her letters suggest that writers 'make' their own identities as much through the imagination as anything else; in this lies such 'authenticity' as they may achieve. In this respect, she anticipated the recent theoretical surmise that writing is 'a continuous process of self-integration, one that can never be completed' and that 'fictional identifications of various kinds are certainly among the many ways we use (however mysteriously) to construct our own identities'.[50]

SEXUALITY, HISTORICAL MOMENT AND IDENTITY

As we have seen, phrases that du Maurier uses to express her sense of self during the 1940s – a 'disembodied spirit', 'half-breed' – suggest an anxiety concerning sexuality, gender and identity. Such an anxiety and such language are not, however, free-floating, but belong to a particular historical moment: du Maurier's attitude to her own identity surely derives in part from the contradictions and tensions to be found within late nineteenth- and early twentieth-century discursive formations of sexuality. She was an adolescent and young woman during a period when ideas about female sexuality and identity were undergoing a radical shift and moving towards a more rigid categorization. Lillian Faderman, in *Surpassing the Love of Men: Romantic Friendship and Love between Women from the Renaissance to the Present* (1981), argues that the term 'romantic friendship' signified, until the early twentieth century, a relationship which was based on spiritual and emotional love between two women and which was usually, though not always, asexual. Martha Vicinus, in her essay 'Distance and Desire: English Boarding School Friendships, 1870–1920', traces the way in which life in English boarding schools of the period 'encouraged an idealized love for an older, publicly successful woman'; she suggests that some of these relationships may have had a sexual dimension whilst others did not.[51] Such friendships, accepted as a normal part of growing up during the late nineteenth century, were, however, being presented as dangerous to women by the 1920s. Like Vicinus, Faderman sees the twentieth century's 'passion for categorizing love'[52] as deriving from the work of the early sexologists such as Krafft-Ebing and Havelock Ellis (who were publishing towards the end of the nineteenth century) and that of Freud, whose ideas had superseded theirs by the 1920s. The work of these men produced a new language and resulted in a new discourse of female sexuality. This, however, was a mixed blessing for women, since as well as providing a vocabulary in which women could express their desires for other women (the most famous example, perhaps, being Radclyffe Hall's adoption of the concept of 'inversion' in *The Well of Loneliness*, published in 1928), it also led to the 'morbidification' of female friendships.[53] Richard von Krafft-Ebing's work of the 1880s categorized lesbians into four types which ranged from the feminine-looking lesbian to the woman who looks, to all external appearances, like a man. A girl's predilection for boys' games and pastimes was seen by Krafft-Ebing to indicate a congenital condition and as symptomatic of an unhealthy desire for gender reversal. In his eyes, Esther Newton argues, 'any gender-crossing or aspiration to male privilege was probably a symptom of lesbianism'.[54] His work, together with that of Karl Heinrich Ulrich, also gave rise to the idea of a 'masculine' soul 'trapped' in a woman's body: 'The masculine soul, heaving in the female bosom, finds pleasure in the pursuit of manly sports, and in manifestations of courage and bravado'.[55] This language soon found its way into the popular fiction of the early twentieth century: Lillian Faderman cites as an example Sherwood Anderson's *Poor White*, published in 1920, in which a character called Kate Chancellor 'had the body of a woman' but 'was in her nature a man'.[56]

Havelock Ellis, writing in the 1890s, 'refined' Krafft-Ebing's categories. He argued that as well as 'congenital inverts' (i.e. full lesbians, or true 'inverts'), there was a type of woman he referred to as the 'intermediate sex'; this woman was only potentially lesbian, but could be 'seduced' by congenital inverts in the sort of 'unwholesome' environment which excluded male company – for example, that of single-sex boarding schools or women's clubs. The 'true' 'female invert', however, was presented as sexually rapacious and socially dangerous; in popular fiction of the early twentieth century she was occasionally represented as a vampire.[57] 'By the 1920s', according to Carroll Smith-Rosenberg, 'charges of lesbianism had become a common way to discredit women professionals, reformers, and educators...'.[58] Many women internalized such evaluations and felt themselves to be freakish; Hall's *The Well of Loneliness*, as Newton notes, 'explores the self-hatred and doubt inherent in defining oneself as a "sexual deviant"'.[59] For some modernist women writers of the first few decades of the twentieth century, however, such a language and the subject position it created offered a transgressive identity that was attractive. Hence writers such as Gertrude Stein and Djuna Barnes lived their lives as 'mannish' lesbians, whilst Virginia Woolf, a modernist of ambiguous sexual identity, used tropes of cross-dressing and transformation in *Orlando* (1928) in order to express what Sandra Gilbert has described as a 'gleeful skepticism'[60] towards gender categories. 'For many women of Radclyffe Hall's generation' writes Esther Newton, 'sexuality – for itself and as a symbol of female autonomy – became a preoccupation'.[61] By the time du Maurier was writing in the 1930s, Freud's theories of sexuality, far more sophisticated than those of Krafft-Ebing or Havelock Ellis, were percolating through popular culture.[62] However, although Freud rejected the notion of a man's soul 'trapped' in a woman's body, his essay 'The Psychogenesis of a Case of Homosexuality in a Woman' (published in 1920) suggested that love between women was no more than a stage of arrested development (a judgement we see reflected perhaps in du Maurier's letter to Oriel Malet in which she describes her relationship with Ellen Doubleday as, in retrospect, a 'rather silly..."thing"'[63]). Further, his conservative notion of gender led him to define his subject's mental acuity as 'masculine'. In fact, Freud had dealt far more subtly with male 'inversion' in his 1905 work, *Three Essays on the Theory of Sexuality*, in which, as Ed Cohen notes, discussion of 'the "female invert" is largely obscured'.[64]

By the 1920s, then, the work of Krafft-Ebing and Havelock Ellis had resulted in women's friendships and schoolgirl crushes being seen as dangerous. The du Maurier sisters were certainly aware of this; recalling her years at school, Angela du Maurier (Daphne du Maurier's sister), born in 1904, laments:

I have never been able to understand the suspicious attitude in schools directed to friendships made between students of different ages, and from different forms. I know when I was young and at the few schools I did attend it was considered 'unhealthy' to form attachments with people of other ages. What a ridiculous term to use – unhealthy.[65]

This complaint corroborates Martha Vicinus's view that 'The public discourse on sexuality had clearly altered by the 1920s'; she goes on to note that in 1921 'an attempt to amend the Criminal Law Amendment Act to make lesbianism (like male homosexuality) illegal was defeated on the grounds that women might learn something they knew nothing about'.[66] Lesbianism had entered the language of sexuality as a distinct category and, through Freud's work, the notion of bisexuality had become absorbed into discussions of sexual identity. Historically, then, there was a link between this more rigid categorization of gender and increasingly conservative attitudes towards the role of women in the social sphere. Both were exacerbated by the loss of political feminism's impetus during the inter-war years. Only a few feminist magazines celebrated the career woman; in the general media, however, much emphasis was given to the idea that a woman's proper place was in the home – and that a woman who wished for a life other than that of housewife and mother was somehow perverse: 'flappers, career women, spinsters and lesbians were all portrayed as highly undesirable stereotypes, to be rejected at all costs', according to Deirdre Beddoe.[67] Several popular novels of the 1920s, including A.S.M.Hutchinson's *This Freedom* (1922) and Storm Jameson's *Three Kingdoms* (1926), explored the conflict between the demands of work and home for women; the former 'became a by-word for the danger to home, family and to women themselves of women taking up careers'.[68] Feminism itself was seen by some as both an aspect of, and conducive to, social degeneracy. In a book published in 1920, Arabella Kenealy, a member of the Eugenic Society, claimed that:

Feminism disrupts [the] complementarity of the sexes. The result of women's competition with men was the development of 'mixed type', more or less degenerate, structurally, functionally and mentally, which imperil the race.[69]

Although by the 1930s there were more positive images of the career woman to be found in both American and British films, the type-casting of actresses such as Mae West and Jean Harlow as sex-symbols resulted in role models whose open expression of hetero-sexual desire was aligned with the 'bad' women of Hollywood. Conversely, the 'good' woman was presented as content with her domestic lot as wife and mother; middle-class women in particular were expected to present role models of maternal femininity. Indeed, the middle-class woman was more constrained by inter-war notions of behaviour 'proper' to women than her working-class counterpart, and magazines aimed at the middle-class reader suggest that 'a very high standard of housekeeping was expected during the inter-war years'.[70]

This is the background against which we should place du Maurier's life as an adolescent in the 1920s and as a young woman writer in the 1930s. Certainly, her theatrical family, with its literary and slightly bohemian background, was not hidebound by conventional bourgeois attitudes; Gerald du Maurier kept what his family referred to as a 'stable' of young women admirers throughout his married years, and Daphne du Maurier had a sexual liaison (with the director Carol Reed) before she married 'Boy' Browning.[71] Nevertheless, the conflicts she felt about her sexual identity and her role as a successful woman writer undoubtedly owed much to conventional attitudes towards female sexuality and to conservative ideas concerning women and work which were circulating at the time. Forster's biography has given us one narrative of du Maurier's life: a sexual desire for other women, repressed until middle age when it finds expression in the relationships with Ellen Doubleday and Gertrude Lawrence. However, du Maurier's early sense of herself as 'really' a boy, to which Forster draws attention, may have been simply a resistance to the social construction of femininity as essentially passive and/or domestic (there is plenty of evidence in both Forster's biography and Malet's book that du Maurier hated shopping, cleaning and cooking[72]). In *Myself When Young* she writes, 'Why wasn't I born a boy? They did all the brave things. Fought all the battles'.[73] Janet Sayers gives several examples of women who expressed similar longings: Simone de Beauvoir identified with the masculinity of her father; Olive Schreiner, in her novel *From Man to Man*, has her heroine dream 'How nice it would be to be a man', since political activity would then be open to her; Maya Angelou has confessed how, as a child, she 'wished my soul that I had been born a boy'.[74] In summarising points made by Joan Riviere in her 1929 essay, 'Womanliness as Masquerade', Judith Butler notes that:

the rivalry with the father is not over the desire of the mother, as one might expect, but over the place of the father in public discourse as speaker, lecturer, writer – that is, as a user of signs rather than a sign-object, an item of exchange.[75]

Thus neither du Maurier's early sense of herself as 'really' masculine, nor her adolescent 'crush' on her teacher Mlle Fernande Yvon ('Ferdy'), necessarily 'prove' that she was lesbian. Neither was du Maurier's habit of wearing trousers necessarily indicative of 'mythic mannish' lesbianism, as some tabloid responses to Forster's biography suggested; her love of wearing trousers was perfectly consonant both with the late 1920s vogue for tailored trousers for women[76] and with du Maurier's own liking for 'jam-along' (meaning easy and informal) clothes. However, nor can du Maurier's passionate outburst against lesbianism in a letter to Ellen Doubleday (written in December 1947) – 'by God and by Christ if anyone should call that sort of love by that unattractive word that begins with "L", I'd tear their guts out'[77] – be taken as 'proof' that she was *not* bisexual or lesbian. Given the discursive construction of lesbianism during the 1920s as something abhorrent (and the way in which bisexuality tended, until recently, to be collapsed into lesbianism or homosexuality), it is not surprising that many women rejected the word 'lesbian' as self-descriptive at that time. Indeed, Forster suggests at the end of her biography that it may have been the very virulence of such discursive formations that induced du Maurier to 'hide' her 'real' feelings for women.[78]

As we have seen, in later life in letters to Oriel Malet, du Maurier constructs the 'crush' on Ellen as a 'silly' 'thing'; retrospectively it is construed as a 'stage' through which she had to pass in order to reach psychological maturity. Du Maurier's own narrative of 'self' in these letters conflicts, therefore, with Forster's story of a suppressed lesbian identity, although, of course, that does not necessarily make it 'true', particularly as she was known within her family to have a chameleon-like ability to appear as different things to different people.[79] Her frequent adoption of the male narrator figure during this later period of her life, at which time she was consciously constructing a heterosexual identity, may, in fact, have been a way of pursuing gender indeterminacy during a time when her surface life was becoming more trammelled. After the intense relationships with both Ellen Doubleday (written out through the characters of Stella in *September Tide* and Rachel in *My Cousin*

Rachel) and Gertrude Lawrence had died down, du Maurier seems, superficially at least, to have assumed an unproblematic heterosexual identity. Arguably, though, the fiction allowed her to continue to express that side of herself culturally designated as 'masculine' at a time when she was reconstructing her own life along more conventional gender lines. Characters such as Beo in *The Flight of the Falcon* (1965) and Dick in *The House on the Strand* (1969), although inadequate in many ways, enjoy a freedom of movement through both space and time and a sense of autonomy which du Maurier perhaps still associated with masculinity rather than femininity. Interestingly, their relationships with women are, in various ways, troubled.[80]

There are thus several ways of understanding du Maurier's sexual identity: as a heterosexual woman (an identity constructed by du Maurier in her letters to Oriel Malet) who formed occasional intense, romantic friendships with women; as a heterosexual who retrieved some previous bisexual episodes into a more orthodox identity for middle age; as a bisexual who chose to conform to a more conventional gender identity as she grew older; and as a repressed lesbian (Forster's implied reading). Like that of many women authors, du Maurier's sexual identity 'defies easy, quick, or simplistic categorization'.[81] Certainly the words 'half-breed' and 'disembodied spirit', as du Maurier uses them in her letters to Ellen Doubleday, betray a sense of being out of role sometimes both sexually and socially, a feeling exacerbated perhaps by the fact that she was an author from a family in which writing had been part of a quasi-bohemian *masculine* tradition.[82] Such complexities in the life were, until the publication of Forster's biography, hidden from general view and du Maurier's 'identity' presented itself unproblematically. However, the publication of extracts from du Maurier's letters to Ellen Doubleday which express such anguish over their love and friendship, have given us a much more complex sense of her identity. The resulting tendency to define her as *either* heterosexual, *or* bisexual, *or* lesbian, reveals more about our century's need to categorize gendered behaviour through a sexed body than it does about du Maurier's protean sense of 'self'. Du Maurier's own representation of her identity (and its relationship with her writing), as articulated in her letters, is more rich and complex than her critics and biographers allow. This may be because many find gender indeterminacy unsettling, perhaps because it exposes an inherent instability in the construction of sexual difference. It can appear threatening because it seems to destabilize the very idea of identity itself; in Judith Butler's words:

> the very notion of 'the person' is called into question by the cultural emergence of those 'incoherent' or 'discontinuous' gendered beings who appear to be persons but who fail to conform to the gendered norms of cultural intelligibility by which persons are defined.[83]

Conversely, du Maurier's use of a masculine narrator, or the focalization of experience through a male character in her fiction, is – for most readers – entirely unproblematic since the writer is traditionally allowed licence, through the imagination, to transgress gender boundaries. Such transgression, so long as it is confined to fictional strategies, is not perceived as in any way threatening. However, we shall argue that du Maurier's complicated sense of gender identity is related to her use of the double, the representation of split subjectivity, and an invocation of the uncanny in her work. Forster's biography narrates a life characterized by the rejection of a unitary sexual identity; this book is concerned with the way in which such a rejection also informs the fiction. Whereas du Maurier's autobiographical works, *Myself When Young* and *The Rebecca Notebook and Other Memories*, present the 'self' in a rational and often light-hearted way, du Maurier's Gothic writings use the grotesque and the sinister to explore shifting anxieties concerning the nature of identity. In this respect, du Maurier's novels and short stories which have a Gothic element arguably give us a clearer sense of 'the person who is Me'[84] as an evolving self than do the autobiographical writings.

DU MAURIER AND THE GOTHIC: DISEMBODIED SPIRITS?

Critical work on du Maurier's skill as a Gothic novelist and writer of short stories has hardly begun. Recently, Andrew Michael Roberts has claimed that the most remarkable thing about du Maurier's work is 'its concern with neo-Gothic motifs and the thin line which divides psychological obsession from supernatural possibilities'; in his obituary of du Maurier, Richard Kelly asserts that the best of her works 'stand out...as landmarks in the development of the modern Gothic tale'.[85] Yet at the time of writing, there are only two studies of du Maurier's novel, *Rebecca*, that explore its Gothic elements with any subtlety (by contrast, there are several on Hitchcock's film of *Rebecca*[86]). The first of these is a chapter by Michelle A. Massé in her book *In the Name of Love: Women, Masochism and the Gothic* (1992). Massé argues that du Maurier's most famous novel re-enacts the beating fantasy to be found at the heart of many Gothic texts. In this Freudian reading, the quest of the nameless narrator is for the position of power (which includes knowledge of sexual relations) which will enable her to become the beater, not the beaten. Allan Lloyd-Smith's sophisticated reading of *Rebecca* as a Gothic text, which also appeared in 1992,[87] uses psychoanalytic theory developed by Nicolas Abraham and Maria Torok in order to argue that the writing process, signified by Rebecca's script in du Maurier's novel, is itself uncanny.

In choosing to focus on du Maurier as a Gothic writer we diverge from the approach adopted by the most well-known critics of her work, who have not fully recognized its Gothic power. The pioneering analyses of both Roger Bromley and Alison Light were informed by both cultural studies and socialist theory (Bromley's essay was influenced by Gramscian thought and Light writes as a materialist feminist).[88] Although they established du Maurier's work as a worthwhile subject for study, we feel that it is time to break away from these class-centred analyses which have dominated the academic critical reception of du Maurier's writing in Britain since the mid-1980s, particularly since they have sometimes been based on mistaken versions of du Maurier's own class position. For example, in her 1985 article, '"Returning to Manderley": romance fiction, female sexuality and class', Alison Light describes du Maurier as 'a displaced aristocrat';[89] in her later work, *Forever England: Femininity, Literature and Conservatism between the Wars*, she accuses du Maurier of 'a romantic Toryism'.[90] This perception of du Maurier's social position and political leaning clearly influences the way Light interprets *Rebecca* in relation to the dynamics of class. In her book, Light corrects her earlier mistaken assumptions about du Maurier's social background, however, noting that the author was 'more than happy to find her "roots" in solid bourgeois pride and an entrepreneurial, mercantile family'.[91] Nonetheless, in the same chapter she draws on 'the image of du Maurier herself as the wife of a general who in later years was privy to the royal household' and from this slips into describing du Maurier's work as structured by 'themes dear to the Tory imagination in its vision of a lost past to be contrasted with a lack-lustre present'.[92] These statements imply that Light assumes that du Maurier herself was Tory in politics and conservative in values. In fact, du Maurier, like many people, was a complex mixture of the radical and the reactionary. She sent her children to private school, loathed caravan sites, employed cooks and housekeepers and in many ways led a very privileged life. She was not, however, the stereotypical Tory lady that this description might seem to imply: she was uninterested in clothes and material things for herself (although no small portion of the money she earned as an author funded her husband's love of boats); she did not like socializing; for much of her life she was a Labour supporter (she greatly admired Harold Wilson who, with his wife, used to call in at Menabilly on his way to the Scilly Isles[93]). Letters written to Victor Gollancz in the 1930s express interest in his left-wing politics and one asks if she might accompany him to a political meeting. The correspondence with Oriel Malet in later years reveals that du Maurier continued to think of herself as left-wing: a letter written in March 1956 declares an early sympathy with the IRA ('It's my natural thing about hating authority!'); one dated 2 November 1970 refers to 'Those idiotic Tories [who] have helped all the tycoons with their mini-budget, and the poor people are poorer than ever' and finishes 'I shall turn Communist!'.[94] Oriel Malet also records how, on hearing her elderly cousin Dora describe local Cornish people as 'yokels' and members of 'the lower orders', du Maurier (always proud of her Republican French ancestors) muttered fiercely, 'A la lanterne!'[95] By the early 1970s, however, according to Margaret Forster, du Maurier 'had lost faith in her pin-up boy, Harold Wilson, and was in favour of Edward Heath'.[96]

Positioning du Maurier rather differently in the social hierarchy, Malcolm Kelsall describes her in a 1993 publication as an 'upwardly mobile writer' whose description of the overgrown grounds of Manderley (seen by the narrator in a dream) communicates the author's 'fear of the proletariat'.[97] Du Maurier's ancestors did, indeed, demonstrate a desire for upward mobility: the family name, as the author herself discovered in researching her family background, derived from the fact that during the eighteenth century a French ancestor, Robert Mathurin Busson, tacked 'du Maurier' – the name of a family property – on to their

surname in order to give it social cachet. However, du Maurier
herself was certainly no social climber: she was a very reclusive
figure, even when young, and found the occasional visits of the
royal family to Menabilly (made in connection with her husband's
position in late middle age as Treasurer to the Duke of Edinburgh)
a social nightmare. A letter written to Oriel Malet in 1962 reads:
'Another awful fussing thing is that we have suddenly been
warned that the Queen wants to come here on 23 July – to Mena
– to tea! She will be visiting Cornwall, and wants to come to Fowey
in the Royal Yacht. It is the Doom of all time... It means a com-
motion, and all her entourage, and policemen and chauffeurs –
how *shall* we manage? It has ruined my summer!'[98] Moreover,
neither du Maurier nor her ancestors were ever members of the
aristocracy: her father's title came with a knighthood earned in
1922 and her own title of 'Lady Browning' derived from her
marriage to Major 'Boy' Browning. Nor were the du Mauriers ever
excessively rich: the rather bohemian lifestyle of her grandfather
devolved into the extravagant and slightly unconventional way of
life adopted by her father who, although well-off as an actor
manager for most of his career, spent the last few years of his life
(after the death of his business manager, Tom Vaughan) worrying
about the money he owed the Inland Revenue.[99] Neither George
nor Gerald du Maurier could be defined as aristocratic or typical of
the bourgeoisie, any more than could Daphne herself; yet such
misconceptions have frequently coloured critical readings of her
work. Less concerned with class than earlier critics, we have chosen
to adopt an eclectic critical approach to du Maurier's writing. Our
book is informed by recent work on the Gothic (in particular the
debate concerning the Female Gothic), concepts of sexuality and
identity current in cultural studies, and deconstructive–psychoanalytic feminist theory. We have found the writings of Julia
Kristeva (in particular her concept of the abject) and Luce Irigaray
(in particular her work on cultural matricide) of especial value.

Du Maurier's career as a Gothic writer falls into three phases.
The first of these is a search for 'authenticity' (in both the life and
the work) which is dominated by the belief that there is an
'authentic' self to be discovered via, for example, family history
or sense of place (a belief abandoned in later works). This phase
involves anxieties which include the possibly incestuous nature of
desire within the family and the mismatch between an 'authentic'
self (which may be androgynous or bisexual) and a surface self

(which is unmistakably feminine and heterosexual). The second phase is marked by an anxiety concerning female authorship: writing is seen as an empowering, masculinizing process which threatens to disrupt the nature of female identity as well as the social fabric (the key text here is *Rebecca*). The third phase involves experimental identities via male narration, or focalization through a male character (a strategy used early on in *I'll Never Be Young Again*, abandoned until *My Cousin Rachel* in 1951 and then used increasingly in the later fiction). Fears explored in this later phase include a fear of identity itself as something fragile and precarious (with the consequent threat of social dislocation) and a horror of the ageing process and its threat to an identity constructed with reference to a younger self. This phase is also characterized by a pre-occupation with the symbolic importance of the mother which manifests itself through the narration of plots which enact matricide.

Du Maurier's Gothic fiction could be described as typical of Female Gothic writing in so far as it does not, finally, demand a suspension of disbelief. Sinister characters such as the Vicar of Altarnun, Rebecca and the dwarf woman of 'Don't Look Now' are not 'disembodied' spirits in a paranormal sense, but flesh and blood people who threaten, or have threatened, the life of the protagonist and the fabric of social order. In du Maurier's work the supernatural often appears to be retrieved into the world of the real, as in the novels of Ann Radcliffe. For example, Rebecca is only a ghost in so far as she is a powerful memory for the novel's characters; the Vicar of Altarnun, whatever his delusions, is an unscrupulous smuggler rather than a son of Satan, and his 'strangeness' is human, rather than supernatural. However, du Maurier's works which employ the Gothic mode never completely exorcise the sinister: Rebecca continues to function as a haunting presence for both characters and readers despite the burning down of Manderley, and the plot resolution of 'Don't Look Now' does not explain the time slip which enables John to 'see' his own funeral. Nor is the disturbing nature of the Vicar of Altarnun entirely explained by his albino appearance and the incongruity of a rural vicar masterminding criminal activities. The sinister remains as a trace of fear in these texts: fear of the unknown (or what is deemed be culturally 'unknowable'/transgressive) and, essentially, of how far the unknown might radically reconstitute or destroy the 'self'. As in many classic Gothic texts, what is simultaneously feared, desired, and 'unknowable' is often embodied in du Maurier's work in a double or *alter ego*. In her letter of 1957 to Maureen Baker-Munton, Daphne du Maurier wrote of herself and her husband, 'We are both doubles. So is everyone. Every one of us has his, or her dark side. Which is to overcome the other?'[100] This fascination with the double resonates interestingly with the issue of gender and identity for, as Judith Butler argues:

> If prohibition creates the 'fundamental divide' of sexuality, and if this 'divide' is shown to be duplicitous precisely because of the artificiality of its division, then there must be a division that *resists* division, a psychic doubleness or inherent bisexuality that comes to undermine every effort of severing.[101]

Such 'psychic doubleness or inherent bisexuality', which resists definition through binary oppositions and breaks down the boundaries between 'masculine' and 'feminine', offers a way of reinventing the 'self'[102] through an encounter with an 'other' who stands, in Gothic writing, for the Other. Du Maurier's Gothic texts, whilst probing the boundaries which separate 'masculine' from 'feminine', heterosexual from homosexual desire, sexual desire from familial love, also explore the fear accompanying the loss of such boundaries. For the textual 'other', as well as being an object of desire, can become a terrifying force who may well invade and destroy the 'self': the Vicar of Altarnun in *Jamaica Inn*, Rebecca, and Jean in *The Scapegoat* all, in their own ways, threaten this.

Despite her skill and range as a Gothic writer, du Maurier is often categorized primarily as a writer of romantic fiction for women, especially in relation to the 'Cornish' novels, *Jamaica Inn*, *Rebecca*, *Frenchman's Creek* and *My Cousin Rachel*. Indeed, surveys such as Joseph McAleer's *Popular Reading and Publishing in Britain 1914–1950* (1992) confirm that du Maurier's novels have been broadly perceived as books for women readers.[103] Publishers of the 'Cornish' novels, in particular, have adopted marketing strategies which target women readers through, for example, jacket design and 'blurb' definitions aimed at a female, rather than a male, readership.[104] It may, of course, be the case that the fears and anxieties most powerfully explored in du Maurier's novels are fears still shared by many women in modern society: this might explain why her work continues to be popular among women readers and why it has a strong cross-cultural appeal despite the regional setting of her most famous novels and despite their assumption that the reader is familiar with the English class system. Nonetheless, such categorization has impeded a full appreciation of du Maurier's achievement as a writer since it has confined her novels – with the exception of *Rebecca* – to a single generic category and a gendered readership. Du Maurier's short stories, on the other hand, are usually marketed for a mixed readership and the element of horror consequently played up (words such as 'chilling, 'subtle', 'sinister' and 'terrifying' feature strongly on their covers). Even her best-known short stories, however, such as 'The Birds' and 'Don't Look Now', have received little attention from literary critics. Conversely the film versions of both stories have generated a great deal of critical analysis. Most book-length analyses of Hitchcock's work, for example, include some discussion of his 1963 film version of du Maurier's 'The Birds', published in 1952. Interestingly, in her recent book on Gothic horror, Judith Halberstam offers a fascinating reading of what she describes as 'Alfred Hitchcock's classic horror film', yet she omits to mention that du Maurier wrote the short story upon which the director based his work.[105]

Our particular interest in du Maurier as a writer of the Gothic who probes the boundaries of identity, including sexual identity, inevitably brings us into the debate which originated in the 1970s and which concerns the nature of 'Female Gothic', a phrase coined by Ellen Moers in *Literary Women* (1976). The debate over whether the Female Gothic can be identified as a separate literary genre has continued since, with an impressive list of contributors including Joanna Russ, Margaret Anne Doody, Coral Ann Howells, Sandra Gilbert and Susan Gubar, Claire Kahane, Tania Modleski, Juliann E. Fleenor, Frances L. Restuccia, Kate Ellis, Eugenia C. DeLamotte, Michelle A. Massé, Susan Wolstenholme, Jacqueline Howard and, most recently, Anne Williams.[106] As Elaine Showalter has suggested, the move to theorize a Female Gothic was probably itself a result of 'the change in consciousness that came out of the women's liberation movement of the late 1960s'; critics consequently focused on the Female Gothic 'as a genre that expressed women's dark protests, fantasies, and fear'.[107] As she notes (citing Claire Kahane), in the 1970s it was fashionable to read the Female Gothic as a confrontation with mothering and the problems of femininity. In the mid-1980s, however, critics influenced by poststructuralism and the work of Lacan saw the Female Gothic as a mode of writing which corresponded to 'the feminine, the romantic, the transgressive, and the revolutionary'.[108] Since then, critics have tended to confine themselves to study of the Female Gothic within a particular period (Ellis and DeLamotte focus on eighteenth- and nineteenth-century texts respectively, for instance) and have drawn on the work of particular theorists in order to make their arguments (for example, Jacqueline Howard's work is influenced by Bakhtinian theory, Anne Williams' by that of Kristeva and a recent publication by Robert Miles uses Foucauldian theories of discourse to analyse the novels of Ann Radcliffe[109]).

We have found much of this work extremely useful for our own project. We have been influenced by DeLamotte's work on boundaries in Gothic texts, and how they relate to the boundaries of the 'self' and, in particular, by her insistence that 'the problem of the boundaries of the self was a crucial issue for women in some special ways – ways that sometimes manifest themselves even in a woman's portrayal of a male protagonist'.[110] Anne Williams' recent book, which speculates on, among other things, the way Gothic romance inscribes the 'family romance' and on what constitutes 'The Female Plot of Gothic Fiction', has been an invaluable and stimulating resource. These works and many others have provided paradigms of Female Gothic writing against which to test our reading of du Maurier's novels and short stories. Inevitably, however, we found ourselves questioning some of the assertions made in such studies. For example, both DeLamotte and Williams agree that the Female Gothic resists unhappy or ambiguous closure, the former noting that 'Gothic by women is almost always happy ... Such endings reveal women's Gothic to be deeply conservative' and the latter claiming that whereas the Male Gothic has a tragic plot:

> The female formula demands a happy ending, the conventional marriage of Western comedy. This plot is ... affirmative of the power of the Symbolic. It celebrates ... a marriage of mind and nature, though from the female perspective, the successful 'marriage' is a wedding to culture. ... The Female Gothic heroine experiences a rebirth. She is awakened to a world in which love is not only possible but available; she acquires in marriage a new name and, most important, a new identity.[111]

This 'formula' may be appropriate when applied to eighteenth-century Gothic novels by women or to what are often rather loosely described as 'popular Gothic novels' (including mid- twentieth-century American Female Gothic – sometimes referred to as 'drugstore' Gothic – or 'Gothic romances'[112]), but it does not work when applied to Charlotte Brontë's *Villette*, Jean Rhys's *Wide Sargasso Sea*, du Maurier's *Rebecca* or Fay Weldon's *The Life and Loves of a She Devil* – all of which often appear on courses entitled 'Female Gothic'. There is, perhaps, still a critical confusion concerning the differences (if there are any) between Gothic romances of the best-selling pulp fiction variety which are written for women readers and a gendered genre entitled 'Female Gothic' which may (or may not) encompass the work of writers as diverse as Charlotte Brontë and Victoria Holt. Williams also claims that 'Male Gothic differs from the female formula in narrative technique, in its assumptions about the supernatural, and in plot'.[113] Again, this is problematic when we look at du Maurier's work, which does not clearly separate itself off as Female Gothic in line with Williams' formulae, according to which, for example, Female Gothic 'explains the ghosts' (whereas Male Gothic does not), Male Gothic is 'uncertain' in its narrative closure (whereas Female Gothic is not), and 'Female Gothic is organized around the resources of terror' (whereas 'Male Gothic specializes in horror').[114] Although for some critics, Female Gothic can be written only by women, Williams sees Female Gothic as defined through its delineation of 'the "female" position in a patriarchal culture. Therefore it is most likely to emerge through the writing of women, but it is not necessarily limited to them'.[115] The subversiveness of Female Gothic resides, for Williams, in readings which release 'alternatives to the Father's Law' by, for example, reconstruing the meaning of 'the heroine's passivity and intermittent helplessness, and the dubious satisfactions of a plot resolved in marriage'. Such readings can only emerge, she notes, from a 'new perspective', one which derives from 'an unconscious secret shared between female writers and readers'.[116]

Where do such recent critical pronouncements leave us when considering the nature of du Maurier's Gothic fiction? Du Maurier's work initially seems to use what *might* be called the standard Female Gothic plot formula in novels such as *Jamaica Inn* and *Rebecca* (the heroine confined to a mysterious or sinister building and dominated by a powerful, older man), although even in these texts closure can hardly be described as 'affirmative'. But her varying use of Gothic conventions (*The Scapegoat* and 'Don't

Look Now' clearly develop her interest in the double, which is explored only implicitly in *Jamaica Inn* and *Rebecca*, for example) and her tendency to move between male and female narrators (and therefore between 'masculine' and 'feminine' subject positions) mean that her work defies categorization according to the formulae established by critics such as DeLamotte and Williams. This raises a number of questions. Does du Maurier's Gothic work, written from both 'masculine' and 'feminine' subject positions, expose such formulae as too reductive or too mechanistic? Or does it lead us to conclude that the complexity of du Maurier's sexual identity enabled her to write both Male and Female Gothic fiction? Indeed, *can* the Gothic text itself be said to have a specific gendered identity, depending on the perspective it seems to adopt in relation to 'the Law of the Father'? Or is such a perspective only realized by the reader, rather than being implicit in the text? And is it released only, as Williams suggests, through the alliance of a particular reader with a particular text (an alliance based, moreover, on 'an unconscious secret shared between female writers and readers')? In which case, does that not render the application of Male or Female Gothic formulae, or criteria, to individual texts a redundant critical act (since these imply that the genre can be gendered by formal features inherent *within* the text)? This book sets out to engage with these questions in its evaluation of du Maurier's Gothic writing; we hope to further the debate even if we cannot supply all the answers.

2
Family Gothic

In this chapter we shall examine Daphne du Maurier's early novels. These works, which concentrate heavily on self and family, show du Maurier's imagination beginning to engage with the Gothic. Their particular emphases also point to matters which will continue to inform du Maurier's writing throughout her career: *The Loving Spirit* (1931) sets up Cornwall as an important and appropriate landscape for her subject matter; *I'll Never Be Young Again* (1932) deals with a sexually fragmented subject; *The Progress of Julius* (1933) explores the 'other' through the 'foreign'. These early works are clear evidence of the author's interest in the relation between the 'self' and the 'other', which manifests itself in the later fiction as a doppelgänger or *alter ego* figure. The 'difference' between the 'self' and the 'other' may manifest itself through age, gender, social class, 'foreignness', or any combination of these. In Elisabeth Bronfen's words, 'For the subject, the function of the other is to reaffirm and guarantee the stability of its position in the world, a sense of self-identity and self-centredness'.[1] In the Gothic text, however, this relationship is marked by restless anxiety and, as William Patrick Day suggests, is one invariably 'defined by the struggle between the impulse to domination and the impulse to submission'.[2] Moreover, in du Maurier's Gothic texts, as in most Gothic writing, the boundaries which separate the 'self' from the 'other' are frequently seen to be permeable and unstable. The relation of the subject to the 'other' in the Gothic world is further complicated by the fact that the 'other', often representing what is lacking in the 'self', may be an object of both fear and desire.[3] The 'other' may therefore be exotically attractive *because* it defies the social regulation of identity and so offers the chance to create/ interact with a new, transgressive 'self'. 'The Gothic', in Judith Halberstam's words, 'inspires fear and desire at the same time – fear of and desire for the other, fear of and desire for the possibly latent perversity lurking within the reader herself'.[4]

The construction of the 'other' – and therefore of the 'self' – is, of course, always inflected by contemporary cultural values, for which the family (amongst other institutions) acts as a mediator. In its moulding of bourgeois sensibility, the family power structure (at least from the mid-eighteenth century onwards) helped mediate distinctions based on nationality, class, 'race', gender and region; in so doing, it aided the creation of the modern, fragmented subject.[5] In her early work, du Maurier explores the desires and murderous hatreds of the family romance; although they cannot be described as full Gothic texts, these novels draw on a sense of the uncanny in their portraits of tortured selves and split subjectivities.[6] Du Maurier's early novels, like those of many writers, show an obsessive interest in the family romance. However, their naturalistic representation of the domestic sphere reveals how, and in what ways, it is inflected by the historical process. Du Maurier's interest as a young author in the psychological dynamics of family life was undoubtedly influenced by her own 'family romance' in which her father was a charismatic presence. The relationship between Gerald du Maurier and his daughter Daphne during her adolescence and early womanhood was itself influenced by a long history of father/daughter 'romancing',[7] a moment of which is represented by du Maurier's portrait of Aunt May in her biography of her father, *Gerald* (published in 1934). In this text, du Maurier constructs her aunt Marie Louise (known to the family as 'May') as the daughter who had a 'special' relationship with her father, George du Maurier. (There were five children in the family, three of whom were girls: Beatrix, known as 'Trixie', Guy, Sylvia, Marie Louise and Gerald). Du Maurier describes her aunt May as having 'a flaming devotion' to her grandfather and as being 'the true daughter of his dreams';[8] later she refers to her grandfather's 'spiritual longings' as 'all mixed up inexplicably with his deep attachment to May' (*Gerald*, p. 65). This aunt, who, du Maurier claims, had 'a better brain' (*Gerald*, p. 57) than any of her siblings (including du Maurier's own father), was, it seems, heartbroken when her father died in 1896: 'no one thought she would ever be the same again' (*Gerald*, p. 79). Within a short period, however, Aunt May became engaged to a likeable young man named Edward Coles whom she soon married; this daughter felt herself free to marry, it seems, only after her father died. May's 'special' relationship with her father, George du Maurier, is typical of a relationship we can detect in many eighteenth- and nineteenth-century texts, but particularly in the sentimental literature of the late eighteenth century where we find it, in Janet Todd's words, 'shorn of its social and economic problems and...marvellously extolled'.[9] It was one built on a sentimentalized bond, often supposedly founded on likeness of temperament and consolidated by shared interests, and it offered distinct subject positions for both father and daughter whilst simultaneously rendering the line between erotic and familial love somewhat indistinct. Margaret Anne Doody sees this father/daughter romance as having its origin in cultural and social shifts during the eighteenth century:

> It took the eighteenth century (when in fact the old structures were crumbling, and kings and fathers actually had less authority than previously) to insist on the high emotive content of parental–filial relations. The child (especially a daughter) should not only *be* obedient, but *feel* the oozy luxury of obedience; and the father, while making demands, could (especially to a daughter) give expression to soft, tender (not to say gushing) emotion. Close relations between father and daughter were insisted on as never before...If the daughter is charmingly childlike in trust, devotion, submissiveness, the father is also permitted to be familiar, soft, and tender. In fact, the father is to gain authority (even authority to destroy) through tenderness; a sort of emotional blackmail is substituted for more straightforward authoritarianism.[10]

Literature offers many instances of such father–daughter romancing: Evelina's relationship with her guardian and surrogate father, Mr Villars, in Frances Burney's *Evelina*; Amelia Sedley and her father in Thackeray's *Vanity Fair*; Eppie and her adoptive father in George Eliot's *Silas Marner*; old Mr Dorrit and his daughter in Dickens's *Little Dorrit*; Eleanor Bold and her father, Septimus Harding, in Trollope's *Barchester Towers*. Fictional examples such as these provide evidence of the persistence of the cultural construct well into the nineteenth century. Du Maurier's biography of her father, *Gerald: A Portrait*, which was published in 1934, provides proof that the father–daughter dynamic described by Margaret Anne Doody still continued as a narrative within the family romance during the twentieth century. If du Maurier's Aunt May was her grandfather's 'chosen' daughter, Daphne seems to have been her father's favourite, partly because they were very alike: 'There was an empathy between the two of them which was quite unmistakable'[11] claims Margaret Forster. As she grew older and developed relationships with young men, however, her father's possessiveness signalled an almost sexual jealousy. Forster records how he would spy on Carol Reed kissing Daphne when he brought her home and would pry into what they had been up to sexually – and how, apparently, he 'burst into tears and cried that it was not fair' on hearing of his daughter's decision to marry Major Tommy ('Boy') Browning.[12] In du Maurier's own record of her father's life she describes how 'he would watch in the passage for his own daughter to return, and question her hysterically, like one demented, if the hands of the stable clock stood at half past two' (*Gerald*, p. 215). Such behaviour illustrates how the eighteenth-century sentimentalization of the family romance set up a powerful paradigm of the father–daughter bond in which paternal love could easily become inflected by a jealous possessiveness more usually associated with sexual desire.[13] Both Daphne du Maurier's own relationship with her father and her fictional representations of the 'family romance' should, then, be placed within the broader historical framework of the evolution of the family.

Anne Williams, drawing on the work of Stephen Greenblatt, sees 'a new assertion of power by the family (and by a state operating according to the implicit rules of patriarchy)' as clashing 'with a new impulse' towards 'self-fashioning' during the early modern period. The resulting internal conflict within the family, she argues, produces 'the materials of which eighteenth-century Gothic is made' and is reflected in Gothic fiction: 'Gothic romance *is* family romance'[14] [our italics]. Such conflict informs du Maurier's early writing which focuses relentlessly on the individual struggle to attain a 'self-fashioned' identity within the confines of the family. Du Maurier's first four works, published within four years of each other, show us an apprentice novelist experimenting with different prose genres and one who is yet to recognize and develop her talent for the Gothic. *The Loving Spirit* (1931) is a family saga and to some extent a regional novel; *I'll Never Be Young Again* (1932) (focalized through a male narrator) is perhaps best described as a Künstlerroman (albeit a portrait of an artist who fails); *The Progress of Julius* (1933) is a Bildungsroman; *Gerald: A Portrait* (1934) is a biography of her father. The different generic conventions of these forms produce differently inflected various of the family romance narrative. They all, however, have at their heart the parent–child relationship and the family situation, despite the fact that the three novels seem to have plots superficially propelled by the search for a heterosexual partner and the quest for success.[15] Furthermore, all are marked by a tentative use of the uncanny. It is, of course, possible to analyse both du Maurier's relationship with her father and her early novels through Freudian theory. In this reading, the intensity of the parent–child relationship would derive from and be structured by a repressed sexual desire and this, in turn, would be seen as the latent content, or subtext, of the novels. However, we agree with Anne Williams that Freudian readings of Gothic texts tend to be circular and unsatisfactory, since both Freud and the Gothic writer are in effect telling the same story. The Gothic plot is, like Freud's account of the psyche, 'overdetermined' by the rules of the family.[16] According to Williams, the patriarchal family is 'the *mythos* or structure informing (the) Gothic category of "otherness"', just as for Freud 'the mind's secret "structures" and dynamics, conform to the patriarchal version of "reality" – the Symbolic – even as he questions it'.[17] Not surprisingly, then, both discourses use the same spatial metaphors to represent the unconscious: it is that uncanny space on the margins of consciousness. To visit the repressed is to explore the dark dungeons, labyrinths and cellars or the unvisited sinister attic of the otherwise well-lit house of the Enlightenment. Those who do so may not like what they find there and will come back changed. In Freud's work, as in much male Gothic writing, the feminine is the dark 'other' associated with the passive, the unknowable, the irrational and the potentially hysterical. And, as in the classic Gothic text, the 'secrets' of Freud's family romance are those concerning sex and violence. The proprieties of the family and of civilization itself are structured against such secrets: 'The price of civilization is a certain discontent within'.[18] Indeed, Williams suggests that:

the similarities between the Freudian model of the psyche and the conventions of Gothic fiction are best understood as parallel expressions of an Enlightenment frame of mind...The very word 'Enlightenment' creates a necessity for darkness; to celebrate, even to recognize the known implies that there must be mysteries also. As Michel Foucault has repeatedly shown, Enlightenment thought characteristically ordered and organized by creating institutions to enforce distinctions between society and its other, whether it resides in madness, illness, criminality, or sexuality. Like the haunted Gothic castle, the Freudian discourse of the self *creates* the haunted, dark, mysterious space even as it attempts to organize or control it.[19]

This perhaps explains why Freudian readings of the Gothic often seem reductive and, at their worst, resemble what Williams calls 'a kind of Freudian Easter Egg Hunt'.[20] It also explains the uncanny sense of *déja vu* experienced by many readers of psychoanalytic accounts of Gothic tales. As Jerrold E. Hogle observes:

> It seems as though one or another psychoanalytic plot were nearly always the essential Gothic plot, however much the Gothic precedes psychoanalysis in history and whatever the basis of the Gothic's psychological schemes in a larger cultural project of enacting and disguising social inequities and anxieties.[21]

Yet psychoanalytic discourse has given us a vocabulary and a useful set of concepts which enable us to analyse Gothic texts with economy and which do provide some insights into the nature of desire in Gothic writing. How, then, to recuperate it in such a way as to prevent the uncanny duplication between the one and the other? How to link it to the broader cultural framework and historical moment from which the Gothic text emerges and with which it engages? The most fruitful recent work in this respect has taken the reworkings of Freudian thought that we find in, for example, the writings of Kristeva and Irigaray, and used them to bridge the gap between psychoanalysis and culture/history. Both Anne Williams and Jerrold E. Hogle, for instance, use Kristevan theory to explore how representations of the abject in certain Gothic texts relate to certain discourses and cultural values at a particular historical moment. This approach, as Jerrold E. Hogle points out, allows us to 'connect psychological repression with the cultural ways of constructing coherent senses of "self" that initially made and still make the very concept of repression conceivable'.[22] It thus avoids the collapse of the story (of both life and text) into the atemporal mythos of Freud's family romance (which re-locates its significance in the subjective world of the dream) and enables us to relate the creation of individual identity to the formation of group identities based on gender, class, nation or 'race' (whilst retrieving the cultural and historical contexts). Kristeva's concept of the abject thereby becomes a concept which enables critics of the Gothic to

define how shared constructions of 'otherness' are predicated upon
shared cultural values: you may know a culture by what it 'throws
off'. Oral abjection, one of the three broad categories of the abject, is
perhaps the most clearly marked by cultural difference through
social taboo.[23] The frogs' legs and snails that provide a delicious
appetiser for the French palate may well provoke only nausea and
disgust in the English eater: the abject itself, then, is in part culturally constructed. Thus Kristeva uses psychoanalysis to interpret
the structural binaries of, for example, edible–inedible and clean–
unclean, established by anthropologists. When analysed with this
in mind, the Gothic text gives up its ghost of history and cultural
context. As Jerrold E. Hogle has argued, the struggle in the Gothic
text is the tension between different possibilities for the 'self' that
Gothic protagonists, authors, and readers 'want to face *and* deny in
order to re-enact their self-definitions'.[24] Abjection within the
Gothic text, then, frequently signifies both fear concerning the
breakdown of culturally constructed boundaries of identity at a
particular historical moment, and an attempt to shore them up.
Read in this way, du Maurier's Gothic writing suggests a search for
identity in perpetual tension with culturally endorsed definitions
of what it means to be 'oneself'.

CORNISH BEGINNINGS: *THE LOVING SPIRIT*

Du Maurier's first novel, *The Loving Spirit*, published in 1931, tells
the story of the Coombe family. Based on research into a Cornish
family, the Slades, it embraces elements of the family saga and
romantic fiction; it is also heavily influenced by Emily Brontë's
Wuthering Heights, as the title (taken from a Brontë poem)
intimates.[25] In particular, the emotional pull on the characters of
the sea and the Cornish landscape, and their desire to be absorbed
by and dissolved in them, derives from the relationship between
landscape and character in Emily Brontë's fictional world. This
itself was influenced by Romantic notions of the sublime and the
Methodist discourse of dissolution and consummation.[26] *The
Loving Spirit* does not, however, manage to evoke a sense of
regionalism and domestic detail as realistically as does Brontë's
work. Indeed, the attempt to reproduce Cornish dialect is heavy-
handed compared with Brontë's scrupulous transcription of West
Yorkshire speech and at times, as Forster comments, verges on the

'ludicrous'.[27] A novel which celebrates a particular place (Plyn, based on Polruan, near Fowey), *The Loving Spirit* represents Cornwall with sub-Brontëesque intensity and mysticism; the London scenes are, however, rendered more realistically and more wittily (Forster rightly describes these as written 'in the *Kipps* style of H.G.Wells, full of social observation and detail'[28]). This may have been partly because du Maurier knew London better (she had, after all, been brought up there); she was also trying to re-create a Cornwall of the past whilst focusing on a social class different from her own (the Coombes are boat-builders). The novel romanticizes the Cornish landscape and characterizes the Cornish themselves as sea-loving people who are passionate and restless by nature. Ella Westland argues that such romanticization has its roots in Romanticism's late eighteenth-century representations of the 'wilder' parts of Britain and that it continues to influence the writing of popular fiction set in the area.[29] This latter type of romance is distinguished by its plot which focuses on a relationship of passionate love taking place in a wild and 'romantic' landscape. *The Loving Spirit*, falling into this category, clearly demonstrates the influence of the earlier tradition on du Maurier's first novel. In literary terms, it is an apprentice work, yet its obsessive interest in how far the family romance and a sense of place contribute to the formation of identity signal what were to become enduring interests for du Maurier.

Read as a romance text, *The Loving Spirit* is an example of family saga writing which traces the fortunes of four generations – Janet Coombe, her son Joseph, his son Christopher, and Christopher's daughter Jennifer. All four characters suffer from various constraints and embark on a restless search for freedom and self-fulfilment. 'The loving spirit' can only smile, as the last page intimates, when, like Heathcliff and Cathy on the moors, it is 'free'.[30] In the case of Janet Coombe, born in 1811, who wishes for an active life at sea, the constraint is marriage and child-bearing, the destiny of most women of her class. As a child she senses that her authentic 'self' is masculine rather than feminine, although she inhabits a female body. Like Mary Yellan of *Jamaica Inn* (published five years later in 1936), she feels that society, with its laws and expectations concerning women's roles, has cheated her out of the life most suited to her, and that conventional marriage will only constrain her further: 'It seemed to her that she was scarce grown from a child to a girl, but that she must change into a woman – and forever. No more could she lift her skirts and run about the rocks, nor wander amongst the sheep on the hills' (*Loving Spirit*, p.15). Both her marriage to her cousin, Thomas Coombe, and the resulting pregnancy, only exacerbate this sense of alienation: she looks 'strange' to herself in the mirror on her wedding-day (*Loving Spirit*, p. 18) and, when pregnant, she sees her body as 'ugly' and 'misshapen' and bows 'her head in her hands for shame that she had been born a woman' (*Loving Spirit*, p. 47). Janet, then, suffers from a split sense of self:

> Janet still stood on the hilltop and watched the sea, and it seemed that there were two sides of her; one that wanted to be the wife of a man, and to care for him and love him tenderly, and one that asked only to be part of a ship, part of the seas and the sky above, with the glad free ways of a gull. (*Loving Spirit*, p. 16)

She resolves this feeling of fragmentation by identifying increasingly with her son, Joseph, who grows up to be a sea captain and whom she sees as 'her second self'; through him she can experience 'all the things which had been denied her because of her sex' (*Loving Spirit*, p. 66). She feels that her rightful place is by the side of Joseph, at sea, and in a strange and uncanny twist of plot, this desire is granted her: upon being made a Master in the Merchant Service, Joseph has his mother's likeness made into a figurehead for the ship which he will command. The likeness, everyone agrees, is striking but Janet Coombe herself dies of heart failure at the moment the ship is launched. Her soul, we are told, passes 'into the breathing, living ship' (*Loving Spirit*, p. 100): Janet Coombe may be dead, but a more authentic 'self' is born in the figurehead which is given a ghostly anthropomorphized role in the rest of the novel, benignly seeing over and directing the destinies of her descendants. Empowered only through death, Janet Coombe's translation into a ship's figurehead becomes emblematic of a common fantasy for women writers and readers – deliverance from the woman's domestic role through voyage and the transcendence of time, although as Alison Light wryly points out, 'No doubt (du Maurier) recognised, however, that such fortunate transfigurations are not the lot of us all'.[31]

Four generations on, Janet's great grand-daughter, Jennifer Coombe, is able to deal more actively with similar dissatisfactions – or English society has changed sufficiently for them to be at least partially resolved. Born in Plyn in 1906, the only daughter of Christopher Coombe (Janet's grandson) and his wife, Bertha, she is particularly close to her father. Jennifer, like her great-grandmother, loves the sea and cannot imagine life without it. However, after the death of her father who, as a member of the local life-boat crew, drowns trying to save the *Janet Coombe* from being wrecked during a stormy night, Jennifer, her two brothers and her mother move to London, her mother's original home. Here she grows up, attending school and experiencing the deaths of both her brothers in the First World War. The summer of 1923 sees Jennifer working for her living (she becomes a kennel-maid, shop-assistant, waitress and typist over the next two years) and enjoying (like Clarissa Dalloway's daughter in Woolf's *Mrs Dalloway*) a freedom of movement across London offered by the urban network of tubes and buses. She experiences a liberty only dreamt of by her great-grandmother and reminds her mother that 'the war had changed everything' (*Loving Spirit*, p. 290). However, she sees that her freedom is very superficial and comments to her grandmother that, apart from being able to work and travel independently, her life is very much like her mother's had been. She is restless for change; like her great-grandmother, her first love is the sea and she longs to return to Cornwall which promises to grant fulfilment of self. On reaching nineteen years of age she decides she is tired of living in a city 'overcrowded with girls wanting to be typists' (*Loving Spirit*, p. 298) and she returns to Plyn. The final twenty pages take the reader briskly through a series of exciting and melodramatic events which culminate in Jennifer being rescued from her uncle's burning house by John Stevens, a distant cousin on her father's side, whom she marries. The novel closes, sentimentally, with Jennifer happily married and holding her two-year old son in her arms; on the outside wall of his nursery the figurehead of the 'Janet Coombe' is fixed to a beam of the house, 'her eyes gazing towards the sea' (*Loving Spirit*, p. 351). The Coombe boat-building business has been revived and John and Jennifer can look forward to a financially secure future. The novel thus uses marriage, motherhood and the benign 'presence' of Janet Coombe to suggest a moment of emotional, sexual and personal fulfilment for Jennifer in its closing pages. This is the closure of Domestic Romance, identified by Lyn Pykett as 'the restitution of family fortunes, the restoration of disrupted stability, and intimations of protracted domestic bliss in the protected space of the ideal nuclear family'.[32]

However, as in most of du Maurier's novels, closure here functions only superficially since it is haunted by unresolved desires. Jennifer's childhood 'horror of growing up' results from the fear of the constraints that adult femininity will bring: of having to forget 'to pretend you are a boy, walking dully instead of slashing at trees with your sword' (*Loving Spirit*, p. 285). Like her great-grandmother, Jennifer feels that her authentic 'self' is a boy, not a girl; even as a young woman being 'courted' by John Stevens, she still perceives her body as boyish. This is at odds with John's image of her, and he tells her that she is 'a bloody fool' for thinking that she does not look like a girl (*Loving Spirit*, p. 332). Jennifer's restless 'masculine' energy can, however, be contained by the closure offered by Domestic Romance partly because society is seen to have changed since 1830. The novel presents positively the freedoms allowed to women like Jennifer in the twentieth century and Jennifer's enactment of a revenge plot on the manipulative and mean-spirited Uncle Philip allows her a more active, shaping role in family history and politics than that accorded to her great-grand-mother, doomed to live her life through vicarious emotional fulfilment. To this extent, as Alison Light has suggested, *The Loving Spirit* 'has absorbed the feminist protest of the late Victorian and Edwardian years and can now offer it to readers as a kind of common sense'.[33] However, the novel's agenda concerning women's struggle for fulfilment is riven with contradictions. Jennifer, as a fourth-generation woman of the Coombe family, may be more active in shaping family history than her great-grand-mother but her story moves towards traditional closure for women characters in that she is rescued from a burning house by her cousin who is also, arguably, 'rescuing' her from what was often perceived as the restless and empty life of spinsterhood offered by the twentieth-century workplace, now open to women.[34] It is never quite clear why Jennifer, who is as passionate and resourceful a character as her great-grandmother, and who loves the sea and the landscape of Cornwall with a similar intensity, should be perfectly content with the role of wife and mother whereas Janet Coombe was not. Jennifer's marriage to John veils, rather than solves, her crisis of identity and this explains why the novel's 'domestic' closure seems sentimental and unconvincing. This ambivalence concerning a 'modern' identity for women is, however, as Christine Bridgwood argues, typical of the family saga, in which there is often a contradiction:

between the opening out with the third generation to a more independent, self-determining lifestyle for women (albeit within marriage) and the undercutting of any social change by the discourse of fate and cyclical repetition which frames the text and operates powerfully within it.[35]

Thus, claims Bridgwood, history is always 'a double-edged discourse' in the family saga:

> it is at once the sharp nudge of awareness of historical progress
> ...and the soothing balm of an ideology of stoical acceptance
> which naturalizes the social and sexual status quo, and is ultimately dependent upon essentialist categories of femininity.[36]

Despite its happy ending, then, *The Loving Spirit* opens up several ideological contradictions concerning the family, identity and sexuality. Moreover, the novel's conservative agenda is offset by its *unheimlich*, or uncanny, aspects, which signal subversive and unresolved desires. These are presented most obviously in Janet Coombe's intense relationship with her son Joseph, whom she sees as her 'second self'. Like many young boys, Joseph as a child fantasizes that his mother will be his future partner; unlike most young boys, however, he never grows out of this fantasy.[37] His letters to her, when he goes away as a young man, are 'strange' and 'passionate' (*Loving Spirit*, p. 85); it is his mother who remains 'the woman of my heart' (*Loving Spirit*, p. 86). We see that as a young man Joseph finds the scent of women 'disturbing' (*Loving Spirit*, p. 108) and is confused by his ambiguous feelings towards them. One night in Hamburg he is drawn to a prostitute who uncannily reminds him 'of someone – of something; she was like a clue to an invisible secret, and then it was gone again' (*Loving Spirit*, p. 109). Although the significance of this eludes Joseph, a verbal link subtextually informs the reader that it signals repressed desire for the mother. Overwhelmed with homesickness for Plyn, Joseph returns to his ship and seems to hear the figurehead, modelled on his mother, whisper to him 'Open your heart, Joseph, an' come to me. There is no fear, no ugliness, no death...I'm alive an' free, an' loving you as of old – Joseph – Joseph' (*Loving Spirit*, p. 111); these words resonate tellingly with Joseph's last sight of the prostitute as 'a bent figure encased in ugly stiff corsets, drawing on a pair of long black stockings' (*Loving Spirit*, p. 110), which acts as a prohibition against sexual involvement with other women. Joseph's ambivalence about adult female sexuality is thus illustrated by this episode. Freud links such ambivalence with a perception of the female genitals as uncanny and explains this in terms of a repressed desire for the mother:

> It often happens that male patients declare that they feel there is something uncanny about the female genital organs. This *unheimlich* place, however, is the entrance to the former *heim* [home] of all human beings, to the place where everyone dwelt once upon a time and in the beginning. There is a humorous saying: 'Love is homesickness'; and whenever a man dreams of a place or a country and says to himself, still in the dream, 'this place is familiar to me, I have been there before', we may interpret the place as being his mother's genitals or her body. In this case, too, the *unheimlich* is what was once *heimisch*, home-like, familiar; the prefix 'un' is the token of repression.[38]

The intrusion of the *unheimlich* into *The Loving Spirit* hints, then, at what Shoshana Felman describes as 'womb nostalgia, a nostalgia for the woman as a familial and familiar essence, a nostalgia for femininity as snug and canny, *heimlich*, that is, according to Freud's definition, "belonging to the *house* or to the *family*," "tame, companionable to man"'.[39] Such a nostalgia, Felman argues, 'turns out to be a deluded, murderous narcissistic fantasy that in reality represses femininity as difference, kills the real woman'.[40] The 'natural' deaths of both Joseph's wives take on a sinister symbolic significance in the light of such an insight. However, in seeing his mother as his unrequited love *and* his uncanny double, Joseph is disturbed by the feminine within himself and this destabilizes his masculine identity. The feminine, Joseph finally discovers (as does Henri de Marsay in Balzac's tale, according to Shoshana Felman), 'is not *outside* the masculine, its reassuring canny *opposite*, it is *inside* the masculine, its uncanny *difference from itself*'.[41] Joseph's descent into madness in *The Loving Spirit* may, then, be read as a response to the fissuring of his 'masculine' 'self'. *The Loving Spirit* thus intimates du Maurier's early interest in both the role of sexual desire within the family romance and the use of Gothic literary conventions which would allow her to explore the condition of the fragmented subject.

A similar closeness is traced between a parent and child in the third and fourth generations of the Coombe family: Jennifer Coombe is her father's favourite child and, after his premature death, Jennifer nurtures her memory of him as 'the most perfect man in the world' (*Loving Spirit*, p. 331). In the broader romance of the family, Christopher Coombe (Joseph's son by his marriage to Susan Collins) functions as a link between Janet and Joseph in the nineteenth century and Jennifer in the twentieth century, thereby ensuring the survival of a powerful familial identity:

> Janet – Joseph – Christopher – Jennifer, *all bound together in some strange and thwarted love* for one another, handing down this strain of restlessness and suffering, this intolerable longing for beauty and freedom; all searching for the nameless things, the untrodden ways, but finding peace only in Plyn and in each other; each one torn apart from his beloved by the physical separation of death, yet remaining part of them for ever, bound by countless links that none could break, uniting in one another the living presence of a wise and loving spirit.
>
> (*Loving Spirit*, p. 309; our italics)

Arguably, it is only Christopher's early death which saves his daughter from developing the sort of emotional ambivalence to the 'opposite' sex that her grandfather, Joseph, exhibited in his life. John Stevens, Jennifer's husband, comes close to articulating this notion, suggesting to Jennifer that her relations' happiness was soured by the intensity of the parent-child bond. Ironically, John Stevens, an idealized wise and protective character, is himself transparently a father-figure for Jennifer although he is only five years older. This dynamic is repeated in *Rebecca*: Maxim, who is roughly twenty years older than his wife, comments to the narrator that 'A husband is not so very different from a father after all'.[42]

There is, then, a strong tension between the 'realist' elements of *The Loving Spirit* and its Gothic strain. Whereas the former, orchestrated by the conventions of the family saga, move the novel towards the happy ending of Domestic Romance, the latter undermines the validity of that ending by continually foregrounding incestuous love as the desired, yet forbidden, resolution of familial love. Here lie the seeds of Gothic fantasy, in that desire for the 'other', perceived as needed to complete the 'self', is transgressive desire which leads to self-destruction. In her first novel, then, we see du Maurier beginning to explore the discontents of the fragmented subject. The novel's closure is unconvincing because it forecloses on this fragmentation. *The Loving Spirit* provides us with an interesting example of textual repression: inside this fat family saga there is a lean Gothic novel struggling to get out.

THE 'SPLIT SUBJECT': *I'LL NEVER BE YOUNG AGAIN*

In her second novel, *I'll Never Be Young Again* (1932), du Maurier uses a male narrator in order to explore vexed familial relationships solely from the perspective of the fragmented masculine subject. The novel itself falls sharply into two distinct halves. The first half represents a masculine world of sea-faring and adventure and is dominated by an intense relationship between Dick, the hero, and Jake, an older man. The second half is set largely in the bohemian world of Paris in the 1930s, where Dick's initially satisfying relationship with a young woman called Hesta fails because of his inability to accept her increasingly active female sexuality. Thus the bifurcated nature of the novel reflects its hero's state of split subjectivity. The only way Dick can finally resolve his psychic sexual fragmentation is to embrace the celibate lifestyle of the 'confirmed bachelor', a choice culturally endorsed for men well into the twentieth century.

The first chapter presents the reader with a young man of twenty-one who is about to commit suicide. He is saved from plunging into the Thames, however, by a stranger named Jake, who takes Richard (or Dick, as the older man calls him) under his wing. Dick's inadequate parenting, by an emotionally remote mother and an intimidating and aloof father ('I had a poet for a father, and my mother was his slave'[43]), is atoned for by Jake's protection of and loving care for the young man. Whereas his father is a great writer whose literary fame oppresses Dick – 'My father was a legend . . . something changeless and immortal like some saga whispered from generation to generation' (*Never Young*, p. 20) – Jake, a sailor, seems to come from nowhere and asks for nothing. Wishing to become an author, Dick has found himself creatively impotent in his father's sight, unable to write or make anything of his life. (The representation of Dick's difficult relationship with his author father might well reflect both the emotional distance between du Maurier and her mother and the anxiety of influence she felt in the face of her paternal literary inheritance.) Before leaving home for the last time, Dick's final stand against his father had been to thrust some quasi-porno-graphic writing under his nose. As we shall see, the pornographic text functions in the novel as a signifier of a broad cultural misogyny through which masculine identity defines itself within a patriarchal society; indeed, Dick's behaviour here might be read as an attempt to assert a crude adult masculinity in the face of the father. Writing, then, is implicated in Dick's struggle for sexual identity, as it was for du Maurier herself. Jake, who is six or seven years older than Dick, offers him both paternal love and a role model for adulthood. Both active in the traditional masculine sense (he is a prize fighter and has travelled widely) and strangely meditative (he is well read and, significantly, *Hamlet* is one of his favourite works), he becomes the father figure the younger man has craved; together they travel to Norway and Sweden, Jake gradually restoring Dick's sense of faith in himself. Jake's ideas on sexual ethics are, however, quaintly idealistic for a man who has roamed the world; it is revealed that he has killed a man (and consequently spent seven years in prison) because the man's seduction of a virgin led to her moral 'degeneracy' and eventual death. Alison Light argues that the novel expresses a revolt 'against post-war "promiscuity"'[44] but even granted that, *I'll Never Be Young Again* seems punctuated to an unusual degree by a revulsion from heterosexuality: Jake's life is one of sexual abstinence (he is described at one stage by his young companion as 'damned sexless' [*Never Young*, p. 44]) and Dick refers several times to sexual appetite as something 'filthy', particularly when it occurs in women. Against the complex and troubled world of heterosexual relations, then, Richard's relationship with Jake appears initially pure, healing and uncomplicated. Their sea voyages and trips into the fjords and mountains bring them close together through a form of male bonding which excludes the feminine, the domestic and the expressive: 'Jake and I had entered into a strange intimacy where silence meant more to us than words' (*Never Young*, p. 50); 'it was good, this atmosphere of not thinking nor caring, and of men without women' (*Never Young*, p. 110). The only note of discord is that introduced by Dick through his relationship with an American woman called Carrie, whom he meets on board a ship to Gud-vangen and with whom, after a brief flirtation, he has intercourse. Her femininity (she has 'big eyes' and puts on 'a baby voice' [*Never*

Young, p. 85]) disturbs and seduces him. His subsequent disgust
with himself and his contempt for Carrie is displaced on to 'ugly'
German women, 'their dresses bursting across their large breasts'
and their leering male partners (*Never Young*, pp. 88/9); Carrie
herself, who is singing with the Germans, suddenly looks 'like a
clown at a circus' (*Never Young*, p. 89), a description which signals
du Maurier's early awareness of gender identity as masquerade.
For Dick, sex with Carrie results in a feeling of 'inexpiable degradation' (*Never Young*, p. 91) and, far from reaffirming his masculine
identity, threatens it: 'I was the sham one with no measure of
reality and no quality of truth' (*Never Young*, p. 91). Discussing the
liaison with Jake, Dick describes sexual intercourse as 'pretty damn
filthy' (*Never Young*, p. 94), although Jake reassures him that it is
different if the man loves the woman.

Significantly, then, one of the most vivid and convincing scenes
in the novel, written in a prose style like Hemingway's as Alison
Light has noted,[45] describes a fight in a Stockholm café in which
Dick and Jake get involved. Dick experiences a strange sense of
euphoria ('strange' at least to the woman reader) which the text
evokes with 'masculine' terseness: 'this is all right, I thought, this is
all right' (*Never Young*, p. 116). He feels more 'authentic', in fact,
fighting side by side with Jake, than he does when embracing
Carrie. The fight itself borders on violent embrace:

> they were my hands that fastened themselves round the throat of
> a man, and my feet that kicked something lying on the ground.
> For this was flesh against my flesh, and teeth that broke with my
> fist and the warm blood of a man I hated, and his cry of pain –
> crying because of me.   (*Never Young*, p. 116)

However, whilst it reaffirms particular notions of masculinity,
Dick's relationship with Jake simultaneously replays a troubled
phase of the family romance since the 'enemy' (in reality some
Swedish thugs) also represents the Father who has to be chall-
enged. In du Maurier's version of the Oedipal tale, the son flees
the father and the replacement father dies in his stead; Jake
becomes a scapegoat for the sins of the Father. Having been
'healed' by Jake's surrogate fathering, Dick feels as if he 'had been
re-born with a new strength and a new understanding' (*Never
Young*, p. 50). However, despite Jake's comment that he does not
want Dick 'to grow up' (*Never Young*, p. 108), Dick's sexual

initiation has already signalled the end of their emotional intimacy.
The two men flee the scene of the fight in a boat bound for Nantes,
the rough macho life at sea – 'living in a hell, filthy and unwashed,
hungry and tired, blaspheming to a heedless sky' (*Never Young*, p.
120) – offering another form of male bonding. Such male bonding is
re-enacted in Dick's unconscious so as to effect a fantasy merging
of the ideal and the real fathers. In a dream he sees:

> Jake walk through the open window, and touch my father on the
> shoulder, and they smiled as though they had known each other
> for a long while, and their faces seemed incredibly alike – mer-
> ging finally into one.   (*Never Young*, p. 131)

The ship, however, sinks off the coast of France in the Baie des
Trépassés (the Bay of the Dead) and Jake drowns in a quasi-
mystical moment, 'his splendour, unbroken and immortal' (*Never
Young*, p. 133). Dick's sense of terror, 'calling to him, and he was
not there' (*Never Young*, p. 133) reenacts that of the abandoned
child: Jake's death is presented as the sacrifice of the father that
the child might live; like a guilty child, Dick blames himself for
Jake's death.

Part Two of the novel sees Dick leaving Brittany for Paris. Alone
and unhappy, Dick vows that he will succeed and prove himself as
an author, without trading on his father's fame. He therefore takes
a series of jobs and begins to write in his spare time. The act of
writing seems suddenly to reaffirm his sense of identity: 'writing
was my thing' (*Never Young*, p. 159). Having finally identified with
his father as a writer, Dick sends him a long letter in the hope that
it will put the relationship on a better footing. The desired response
does not, however, materialize; instead, he receives a cheque for
£500. It is at this moment of emotional rejection by his father that he
meets and falls in love with a young pianist called Hesta. Hesta is a
distinctively modern figure whose bohemian identity is marked by
the wearing of a striking orange beret.[46] Obsessed by her, he
persuades her to share his flat and to give up her studies and
promising career as a concert pianist. Meanwhile, he is becoming
more and more engrossed in writing a play; the fact that he
acknowledges Oscar Wilde's influence perhaps signals sexual
ambivalence, despite his liaison with Hesta. Margaret Forster, commenting on the intensity of Dick's bond with Jake, has suggested
that 'There is an implicit, though never realized, homosexual

relationship between the two men, but there is also more than a hint that they are each a half of the same man'.[47]

In a much later work, *The Scapegoat* (1957), du Maurier was to repeat, with more success, the strategy of presenting two male characters as 'each a half of the same man'. Occasional disturbing memories of Jake cloud the relationship between Dick and Hesta; at one point, after making love to Hesta, Dick sees Jake's face looking at him expressing horror and fear. He also finds that sex has become like a drug, the intoxicating effects of which have begun to pall. Hesta, on the other hand, now enjoys their intimacy and displays a frankness about her sexual desire that Dick finds 'filthy': 'it's the beginning of degradation, the loss of everything that's perfect and lovely in you' (*Never Young*, p. 267). His lust is no longer for Hesta (who is by now merely part of the background) but for 'this power of writing, more dangerous than adventure, more satisfying than love' (*Never Young*, p. 218). However, a trip to London to meet his father's publisher, to whom he shows his play and recently completed novel, dashes his hopes: the publisher, whilst praising his father's most recent work (a long poem entitled 'Conflict') dismisses Dick's writing as only 'a grotesque resemblance' of his father's (*Never Young*, p. 256). Dick's reaction to this disappointment is to invest his relationship with Hesta with greater significance; he will, he decides, ask her to marry him. He returns to Paris, however, only to find that she has left him for a fellow musician. Hesta, who has found a modern feminine identity in the sexually permissive climate of Europe after the First World War, no longer entertains notions of love and marriage. Dick shortly receives a telegram, informing him of his father's death and he returns to England for good. The novel closes with a picture of Dick's London life where he lives alone in a comfortable flat: he has become a banker in the city and dines at his club most evenings. Instead of being part of his father's literary world, he has embraced a version of the masculine society which has all along dictated the romances and values of his life; thus only now does he feel 'peace and contentment' (*Never Young*, p. 281). The initiation into this society means leaving behind the 'phases' of youth – he will 'never be young again' – but its rewards, in terms of material comfort and status, are great. Above all, such a lifestyle offers a secure identity rooted in the nineteenth-century figure of the bachelor, albeit one achieved through the negation of sexual desire.

Dick's retreat from heterosexuality is aligned with his rejection of homosexual identification, signalled obliquely several times in the text: at one point, for example, he parries the question '"Are you a sodomite?"' with the joky reply, '"No, I haven't sufficient rhythm"' (*Never Young*, p. 150). Unable to form an identity founded on heterosexuality, homosexuality or bisexuality, Dick enters what Eve Kosofsky Sedgwick has defined as a state of 'sexual anesthesia'. She applies this phrase to the work of several writers, including that of George du Maurier, du Maurier's grandfather and author of *Trilby* (1894) (a novel which presents a somewhat sentimental celebration of bachelor life):

> In the work of such writers as du Maurier, Barrie, and James, among others, male homosexual panic was acted out as a sometimes agonized sexual anesthesia that was damaging to both its male subjects and its female non-objects.[48]

Daphne du Maurier's bachelor anti-hero is, however, finally spared both the agony and the pain of unrequited desire. What Kosofsky Sedgwick describes as 'the development of the bachelor taxonomy'[49] has removed him from the Gothic plot although, as we shall see, du Maurier chooses later to revive the Gothic tradition in characters such as the Vicar of Altarnun whose ambiguous sexual identity is related to the threatening and the sinister. The broken-backed nature of du Maurier's second novel might suggest not only the inexperience of the apprentice writer but also an attempt to reflect the bifurcated nature of Western masculinity itself. According to Jonathan Dollimore, this is a masculinity that, built upon an intense identification with the male, can easily slip into homoeroticism.[50] Such a masculinity necessarily defines itself *against* the culturally 'feminine' and derogates it, yet at the same time insists on male desire *for* the 'feminine' as an essential component of that masculinity. Dick comes to regard himself as 'an ordinary man' (*Never Young*, p. 260); part of the novel's shock for the woman reader is how far such 'ordinariness', in what du Maurier constructs as the masculine subject, is dependent upon the notion that women are contemptible. Authenticity of self, it would seem, depends on derogation of the feminine, if one is a man. (Much later, du Maurier was to describe – in relation to *My Cousin Rachel* – such values as 'a kind of gentlemanly misogyny'.[51]) This is communicated not only by the elevation of the Jake/Dick friendship into a quasi-mystical communion, but also through the novel's constant return to the pornographic text which represents the female subject as object. Dick, we remember, asserted his difference from his hated father by flinging his own 'pornographic' poems at him; later, in a strange episode in a Parisian café Dick recites some of these earlier pieces to a group of English listeners, one of whom buys them for a hundred and fifty francs; in addition, the boat sailing to Nantes offers a form of male bonding which represents adult female sexuality through crude pornographic drawings and camp parodies of heterosexual relationships. The resulting impasse for Dick (he finds women repellent and degenerate if they are sexually active but neither can he accept a homosexual or bisexual identity) forces him to choose a state of sexual anesthesia; the novel eschews marriage as closure and, instead, concludes with a bachelor living a life of sexual abstinence in the company of other men.

It is Jake's uncanny presence in the novel which, like that of Janet Coombe in *The Loving Spirit*, both gestures towards the Gothic and signals the fragmentation of unitary identity. Whatever the reader may think, Dick construes his adoring love for Jake as proper and unimpeachable; in contrast, both his desire for Esther and her liberal attitude to female sexuality he expresses in terms of 'filth'. For Dick, Hesta's sexuality falls into the third category of the abject: horror of the signs of sexual difference. Her body, as the site of menstrual blood and potential maternity, presumably threatens his masculine identity by signifying the corporeal link to the mother, a debt, according to Irigaray, which is culturally suppressed (and one textually indicated, perhaps, by the shadowy presence of Dick's mother in his imagination as compared with what he perceives as the overbearing presence of his father). By the time Dick has come to terms with what seems an instinctive revulsion from the female (although this is, in fact, culturally constructed) and wishes to marry Hesta, it is too late: she has found herself another 'dick'. The homosocial code, it seems, *makes* the reproductive female body into a site of the abject. Published in 1932, *I'll Never Be Young Again* reflects a masculine nervousness about female sexuality which goes far beyond disapproval of post-war promiscuity. Unable to understand or articulate fully his own identity crisis, Dick can progress no further as a writer and is 'blocked' in more ways than one. His use of pornographic texts as both a challenge to his father and as an assertion of his own creative potency clearly signal the fragility of his masculine identity. Ostensibly a Künstlerroman, the novel's shadowy Gothic elements reveal a young man's attempts to shore up a stable 'self' against the threat of fragmentation inevitably induced by the social structures which form his identity.

It is important, finally, to place this novel in the wider context of both *fin de siècle* male 'romance' writing and late nineteenth/early twentieth-century cultural anxiety concerning the survival of masculine 'authenticity'. 'Manliness' (and with it, the future of the Empire) was, during this period, widely perceived as threatened by a social degeneracy precipitated by the feminist/'New' woman, the effeminate man and the 'dark savage'. The rising popularity of middle-brow fiction by women authors was frequently seen as symptomatic of a corresponding literary degeneracy. In *Engendering Fictions: The English Novel in the Early Twentieth Century*, Lyn Pykett describes how:

> The rise of male romance in the 1880s was an attempt by male writers, mainly of a conservative bent, to renovate or reinvigorate fiction ... The project was to reclaim the middle-brow popular romance from women writers ... The result was the development by Rider Haggard, G.A. Henty, Robert Louis Stevenson, and Rudyard Kipling (to name only the most well-known exponents) of a masculine aesthetic of the adventure story, centring on action rather than on reflection and introspection, and on codes of male honour, which were to serve as bulwarks against degenerative feminism. As Rider Haggard's *She* so graphically illustrates, the plots and figures of male romance were also, on occasion, deeply misogynistic, defensive reactions to female power and female sexuality.[52]

Such fiction, Pykett adds, 'might also be seen as a homoerotic formation in which (male) writers and readers played out their homoerotic desires'.[53] We know from *Myself When Young: The Shaping of a Writer* that *The Wreck of the Grosvenor* and Robert Louis Stevenson's *Treasure Island* captured du Maurier's childhood imagination and that she enjoyed these stories for boys more than those written for girls (finding *Little Women*, for example, 'rather hard to understand').[54] Adolescence saw her reading books such as *Mr Midshipman Easy* and *With Allenby in Palestine* alongside works by Dickens, Browning and George Eliot.[55] Du Maurier was, then, well read in the sort of masculine romance writing described by Pykett. Seen in this light, *I'll Never Be Young Again* is a book in dialogue with literary history and with the male writer of masculine romance. Its first half skilfully engages with this genre (although its two male protagonists are introspective as well as active); the novel's sea-faring/adventure element should thus be read as a response to the sort of narrative we find in the works of Stevenson and Conrad. The usual dynamic of such a narrative is, however, destabilized in du Maurier's novel by a second half which presents Dick as an inadequate figure when faced by female sexual desire. By the end of the novel, Dick has abandoned his writing career and has implicitly turned his back on a way of understanding himself and his society more fully. Conversely, du Maurier – in re-writing the classic masculine romance (still popular in the 1930s) – was using writing itself to negotiate social constructions of sexual identity.

THE 'OTHER' AND THE 'FOREIGN': *THE PROGRESS OF JULIUS*

Du Maurier's next novel, *The Progress of Julius*, published in 1933, presents the reader with another study of split masculine subjectivity (inflected this time by 'race' and nationality) whilst also carrying the family romance to a shocking conclusion: the father's sexual desire for the daughter results in emotional abuse and murder. It is surprising to find du Maurier using such subject matter at this early stage of her career whilst her own father was still alive (she was only twenty-six when she wrote her third novel), and at a time when such topics were still considered taboo in polite society. (According to Margaret Forster, 'Q', Sir Arthur Quiller-Couch, a near neighbour in Fowey, banned both *I'll Never Be Young Again* and *The Progress of Julius* from his bookshelves and forbade his great-nephew to read them.)[56] Julius's relationship with his daughter, portrayed as an aspect of a life which has chosen to define itself through the will to power, is thus seen in the novel as (disastrously) inflected by a masculine desire for control. Although events are focalized through Julius, his behaviour is not exonerated; instead, it is placed against the broader social backdrop of two class-ridden societies (those of France and England). Julius has apparently broken free from his class origins. However, the word 'chain' is repeated several times in the novel; its final use in relation to Julius's chain of cafés underlines how far he has escaped from what appeared to be his social destiny, although he remains 'chained' to many ideological constructions, including that of the father/daughter romance. The main character, Julius Lévy, has, like Dick in *I'll Never be Young Again*, two father figures. Born in 1860 into a poor family who live in a small village outside Paris, he worships 'grandpère', a Frenchman, Jean Blançard, who makes his living by selling produce on the market, and has a close albeit troubled relationship with 'père', Paul Lévy, an Algerian Jew. (The women of the family, Julius's mother [Louise, daughter to Jean Blançard] and his grandmother, are, by contrast, very shadowy figures when compared with the male characters.) His grandfather is a vigorous, extrovert and patriotic man who delights in getting 'something for nothing' and in making a profit. His father is an introverted, melancholy and artistic figure who plays his flute with long, thin, fingers and who is transformed in the act of playing into 'a magician who called, a white still face of beauty crying in the darkness, a spirit with his hands on the gates of the secret city'.[57] Associated with suffering and with a mysterious spirituality, the father is closer to the literary representation of Jewishness to be found in George Eliot's *Daniel Deronda* than the 'kike' stereotype of Pound's *Cantos*. In this respect, du Maurier's novel is characteristic of what Bryan Cheyette has described as an ambivalence towards Jewishness to be found 'at the heart of domestic liberalism' from the mid-nineteenth century in England and which originated in texts such as Matthew Arnold's *Culture and Anarchy*.[58] This ambivalence expresses itself in a semitic discourse which can be distinguished from the crude anti-semitism to be found in the work of writers such as Ezra Pound and Wyndham Lewis:

> Arnold positioned fixed racial differences between 'Aryans' and 'Semites' as something that should be transcended by his ideal of 'culture'...The accultured 'Jew', in terms of this ambivalent Arnoldian liberalism, is an extreme example of those that may draw closer to 'grace' and 'beauty' by surpassing an unaesthetic, worldly Hebraism.[59]

Paul Lévy's soulfulness links him with the 'accultured "Jew"'; conversely, Julius's delight in making money and gaining power is a trait he shares with his French grandfather (whose name perhaps signifies European 'whiteness') and not his father, who has 'no country', who 'could not earn a sou' and who appears 'a dead thing' (*Julius*, p. 6) by the side of his vital father-in-law. Furthermore, Paul Lévy's sensitivity, dreaminess and passivity link him symbolically with cultural notions of femininity, whilst Jean Blançard's character traits ally him with the 'masculine'. When his grandfather is pleased with Julius, he praises him as a 'real' Blançard; when he is angry with him he roars at him that he is a 'wretched stinking piece of Jew-lust' (*Julius*, p. 7). Identifying with both his grandfather's materialism and resourcefulness and his father's dreamy introspection, Julius's sense of split subjectivity is predicated upon genetic and 'racial' characteristics which are further inflected by notions of gender. In the terms of the binary oppositions set up in Part One of the novel, therefore, to be 'French' is to be properly 'masculine' with a secure identity; to be Jewish is to be 'other' – to be marginalized, feminized and ostracized. It comes as no surprise to the reader, then, that Julius, despite the bond with his father, takes his grandfather as a role model although Jewishness continues to complicate his sense of identity; indeed, du Maurier's portrayal of him in middle age as a successful businessman draws heavily on the 'unaesthetic, worldly Hebraism' that 'the Jew' can also represent within semitic – and anti-semitic – discourse.

Du Maurier's use of dialogue in *Julius* is more skilful than in her first two works and the historical backdrop is convincingly rendered. The story of Julius's early life encompasses the Franco–Prussian war and the siege of Paris, during which his grandfather is shot dead and his mother is murdered by his father in a fit of sexual jealousy. Julius then flees with his mortally ill father to Algiers, where they are granted refuge in a synagogue. Paul Lévy is nursed by the Rabbin but soon dies; his son is thereafter given free board and lodging as a 'child of the Temple'. Julius is reasonably happy in the Temple, but he feels the old excitement return when he goes to the market in Algiers (throughout the novel the market is metonymic of capitalism). Rather than train as a Rabbin he decides to make his way in the world and, at the age of nineteen, he sails for England to make his fortune. His determination to succeed as a restaurateur sharpens his qualities of emotional callousness and financial meanness which become evident in the way he handles his personal relationships. Through his wealth, Julius becomes a force to reckon with in the City and is introduced to the rich Jewish families of London and the aristocracy of the land. The manner in which 'race', class and 'breeding' make up social identity in *fin de siècle* England (and arguably in 1933, when the novel was published) is communicated very clearly in this section of the novel in which 'Jewishness', although part of the fabric of London's cultural and financial life, is represented as 'other':

> he moved amongst men and women who spoke the same language; they held in some queer indefinable fashion his great rapacity towards life, his hunger and his thirst, they did not rest in their lives, but leant out to seize the world with their hands, never satisfied, never appeased, and hiding in the core of their being a seed of loneliness and frustration, a faint far shadow of melancholy madness. (*Julius*, p. 150)

Julius marries a beautiful and intelligent young woman, whom he meets when moving in the upper echelons of Jewish society. It is clear, however, that his motives for marrying her have more to do with expediency than with love:

> Rachel Dreyfus should do. From the little he had seen of her he judged her brain to be just of that intelligence that would not jar – masculine and, thank God, Jewish enough to understand his preoccupation with business; but a good percentage of femininity that would allow her to be subservient and restful. (*Julius*, p. 162)

'Masculinity' for Julius, then, is equated with intellectual sharpness; 'femininity' with passivity;[60] 'Jewishness' is associated with a 'preoccupation for business'. Julius has become, by now, an unsympathetic character (he is an unscrupulous and emotionally sadistic man), the novel evoking the stereotype of the greedy and ambitious Jew in its portrayal of him as a successful business man. Rachel gives birth to a daughter, named Gabriel, in 1895 and Julius is delighted with his family unit: 'There was something pleasing about the possession of a wife and child, they formed another link in a chain of power' (*Julius*, p. 183). Julius has very little to do with his daughter whilst she is growing up, being kept busy by his flourishing business empire, his social life and various mistresses. It is only when he is aged fifty, feeling bored and irritable, that Gabriel has a sudden impact on his life. She has been away at school for some time and Julius returns home one day to hear her

playing his father's flute. The flute, suggestive of his paternal
inheritance, may be seen as metonymic of a different Jewish
identity (or as evoking the 'accultured "Jew"' of semitic discourse),
which has become submerged by his social identity as a ruthless
businessman. However, his recognition of the strong emotional
force of this kind of 'Jewishness' becomes transmuted into a
powerful erotic charge which he interprets as desire for his
daughter:

> he looked at her, her face, her body, her hands on the flute, the
> colour of her hair; he looked at her figure outlined against the
> window, and a fierce sharp joy came to him stronger than any
> known sensation, something primitive like the lick of a flame and
> the first taste of blood, as though a message ran through his brain
> saying: 'I for this – and this for me'.   (*Julius*, pp. 210–11)

Julius develops a 'voracious passion' (*Julius*, p. 213) for Gabriel,
placing Rachel, his wife, in a position of sexual rivalry with her
own daughter, whose precocity adds to her pain. Instead of
sending her away to 'finishing' school, Julius decides to take charge
of the next three years of Gabriel's life and they enter upon an orgy
of spending on hunting, flat-racing and yachting. The novel
carefully avoids any description of actual sexual abuse but it is
clear that Gabriel's playing of her grandfather's flute induces fantasies for Julius which verge on the sexual:

> To Julius with his eyes shut it was like the song that Père had
> sung to him as a child and the whisper that led to the secret city,
> but this was another whisper and another city; this was not the
> enchanted land beyond the white clouds, so melancholy, so
> beautiful, for ever unattainable, a land of promise unfulfilled –
> for there was a sudden swoop and a turn and a plunge into the
> bowels of the secret earth, heart beating, wings battered and
> scorched, and this new-discovered city was one that opened and
> gave itself up to him; there were eyes that welcomed and hands
> that beckoned, all mingled in extravagant confusion of colour
> and scent and ecstasy.
> 'Do you like that, Papa?' said Gabriel, and he was in the room
> again, back in the world, startled as though with the first shock
> of waking, the sight of her standing there so cool and undis-
> turbed jarring upon him who felt dissatisfied and unrefreshed,

an odd taste in his mouth, and a sensation in mind and body that
was shameful and unclean.   (*Julius*, pp. 225– 6)[61]

Their language and behaviour towards each other become that of
lovers rather than parent and child: Julius buys his daughter extravagant presents (a diamond bracelet at one point) and he calls her
'a bitch' when she upsets him. He even thinks of his daughter as a
replacement wife: deciding that Rachel's 'utility was over now' he
is pleased that 'Gabriel would make as good a hostess when she
came out next year' (*Julius*, p. 232). Gabriel, too, is excited by her
father's sophistication and worldly power which make young men
look 'callow and inexperienced' (*Julius*, p. 238); yet the emotional
intensity of their relationship verges on the abusive. Indeed, her
perception of that relationship is expressed through metaphors of
penetration and surfeit:

> She had no will of her own now, no consecutive thought, no
> power of concentration; she was being dashed and hurtled into a
> chaos that blinded her, some bottomless pit, some sweet, appall-
> ing nothingness... He was cruel, he was relentless, he was like
> some oppressive, suffocating power that stifled her and could
> not be warded off; he gave her all these bewildering sounds and
> sensations without pausing so that she was like a child stuffed
> with sweets cloying and rich; they were rammed down her
> throat and into her belly, filling her, exhausting her, making her
> a drum of excitement and anguish and emotion that was grip-
> ping in its savage intensity. It was too much for her, too strong.
>   (*Julius*, pp. 243–4)

Rachel, meanwhile, has developed cancer and when they discuss
possible treatment for her, she intimates that she knows what is
going on. Their apparent refusal to recognize that she understands
leads Rachel finally to despair; she commits suicide by taking an
overdose. Free now to indulge his love for his daughter, Julius feels
reinvigorated and sees Gabriel as 'the ideal companion, the other
self' (*Julius*, p. 254) – just as Janet Coombe saw her son in *The Loving
Spirit*. Even the First World War does not separate Julius and
Gabriel; not only do they enjoy their voluntary work, but Julius
makes a great deal of money out of the war. His Jewishness at this
time preserves him since it provides him with a sense of identity
which is unrelated to nationality: 'England was not his country,

France was not his country' (*Julius*, p. 260). His anguish derives not
from the war, but from his daughter's involvement with other men
and the knowledge that he now bores her. Unable to cope with his
jealousy of her suitors, unable to share her with anyone else, he
arranges a boat trip from Cannes and strangles her with his own
handkerchief whilst she is swimming.[62] The novel thus closes with
an echo of how it began – with a woman as victim in a domestic
murder. Gabriel thereby pays a terrible price for her complicity
with the father and for colluding with the cultural obliteration of
the mother. (Indeed, her behaviour would be seen by feminists
such as Shulamith Firestone and Luce Irigaray as characteristic of
the 'bad faith' which constitutes an inevitable aspect of femininity
within a patriarchal society.) It is assumed by the world that Julius
Lévy's daughter has drowned tragically at sea; the novel ends with
Julius degenerating into a lonely old age and finally dying from a
stroke.

It is perhaps worth pausing here to consider again du Maurier's
portrayal of 'Jewishness' in this novel. It is possible, of course, that
her portrait of Paul Lévy as victim and mysterious 'other' is not
only characteristic of a semitic discourse circulating in England
from the mid-nineteenth century, but that it also unconsciously
reworks what had been the most famous du Maurier 'romance'
so far: her grandfather's best-seller of the 1890s, *Trilby*. George du
Maurier's story of Svengali, the wicked Jewish impresario, took the
world by storm when it was published in 1894. As Brian Cheyette
has noted, George du Maurier's novel expressed nineteenth-
century cultural ambivalence towards the Jewish 'race' in its
starkest form since:

> Svengali is both an outstanding musical genius and a sexually
> rapacious, racialized 'other'. He is, in other words, the extreme
> embodiment of both 'culture' and 'race'.[63]

Arguably, Daphne du Maurier's novel, *Julius*, explores such
ambivalence by splitting Svengali's 'Jewishness' into its component
parts: Paul Lévy's musical gifts place him as the 'accultured "Jew"'
whilst Julius, his son, is presented as racially 'fixed' in his
obsession with wealth and power. Yet his father's identity survives
after his death through the flute music played by Gabriel; it thus
becomes representative, for both the reader and for Julius himself,
of an alternative identity that can be constructed through 'race'.

Since, however, it is one he associates with femininity and power-lessness, he rejects its relevance for himself; instead, its emotional force becomes displaced onto his daughter. Thus, in desiring his daughter, he also expresses a repressed desire for an *alter ego* associated with all that his construction of himself as a 'Jewish' businessman has obscured: beauty, art, spirituality. The 'Jew' in *Julius* is presented through contrasting figures, that of 'the modern alienated artist *and* the incarnation of a corrupt worldliness';[64] he represents 'both the "best" and the "worst" of selves' within the discursive construction of 'Jewishness'.[65] The fact that her main character is haunted by an 'other' 'self' allows du Maurier to experiment with notions of alterity predicated upon 'race', nationality and gender at a time when 'racial' characteristics were becoming increasingly fixed by the discourses of nationalism (par-ticularly that of Germany in the 1930s). This strategy, as we shall see, will be repeated in *The Scapegoat*. Even *within* 'Jewishness', Julius is a stranger to himself: in Kristeva's words, 'Uncanny, foreignness is within us: we are our own foreigners, we are divided'.[66] Further, Rachel's suicide and Gabriel's murder can be metaphorically laid at the door of a masculinity which empowers itself partly through a derogation of the feminine; in murdering Gabriel, Julius murders 'the other self' (*Julius*, p. 254) which is culturally 'feminine' as well as differently 'Jewish'. Nonetheless, the novel could be described as anti-semitic; as Kristeva remarks in *The Powers of Horror*, anti-Semitic representations of 'Jewishness' associate it with a 'desire for what mastery cuts out ... sex tinged with femininity and death'.[67] Furthermore, *Julius* projects incestuous desire upon the 'Jew'. Thus du Maurier uses the figure of Julius to anchor abjection within a body that is both strange and familiar, a strategy she will repeat in her portrayal of the Vicar of Altarnun in *Jamaica Inn*, whose hermaphrodite body becomes the focus for abjection in that novel. Similarly, the body of Rebecca bears traces of Jewishness and 'masculinity', as signifiers of her perversity. As Judith Halberstam notes, 'Gothic anti-semitism makes a Jew a monster with bad blood and it defines monstrosity as a mixture of bad blood, unstable gender identity, sexual and economic parasitism and degeneracy'.[68] Julius is not quite a monster and du Maurier's novel is only liminally Gothic – but it strongly indicates the direction in which her work will develop.

Significantly, years later in the mid 1960s, when writing *Vanishing Cornwall* and remembering the moment of sudden realization –

experienced long ago – that Cornwall was where she would spend
the rest of her life, du Maurier was to recall 'a line from a forgotten
book, where a lover looks for the first time upon his chosen: "I for
this, and this for me" '.[69] In fact, as we have seen, these are the exact
words that spring to Julius's mind when he sets eyes upon his young
adult daughter and realizes how much he desires her. Remarkably,
du Maurier seems to have forgotten that she had herself written this
striking sentence, indicating a curious process of authorial
repression at work. Almost certainly this novel draws upon the
writer's experience of having had a particularly emotionally
demanding father and her own partial complicity with his demands.
A rather casually sinister reference to the intensity of her relationship
with her father occurs in *Myself When Young: The Shaping of a Writer*.
Referring to her early infatuation with her older cousin, Geoffrey,
described as 'My Borgia brother . . ', du Maurier recollects calling out
for her father when coming round from an anaesthetic and
comments: 'So it was not the Borgia brother, but the Borgia father
that the unconscious self demanded' (*Myself When Young*, pp. 109
and 110). Gerald du Maurier is portrayed in his daughter's biography as wanting desperately to be her companion rather than her
father (although as a brother, not as a lover); the innocence of this
desire is, however, undermined rather by the writer's portrait of her
father's jealousy and by the attention du Maurier pays to the despair
her father felt when rejected by his daughters:

> It is the tragedy of every father and every daughter since the
> world began. But he took it harder than most. He brooded upon
> it, and nursed it in his mind. It gave him a little added bitterness
> which was peculiar to him and strangely pathetic.[70]

The presentation of Gerald as a figure of some pathos here
indicates the sentimentalization of the father-daughter relationship
from the eighteenth century onwards. Julius, on the other hand,
demonstrates the dark side of such paternal possessiveness. *Julius*
is an implicit indictment of how the father/daughter romance,
inflected by the changing nature of masculinity itself during the
eighteenth century, and endorsed by the Victorian period's elevation of the family to sacrosanct status, had evolved into a relationship in which the daughter could be quite literally loved to
death. Daphne, a strong character, confronted her father's emotional possessiveness (which may have been the cause of her

mother's remoteness from her[71]) through defiance; Aunt May escaped being possessed by the father only through his death; Gabriel becomes, horrifyingly, victim to the father's will.

It may seem somewhat puzzling that a young woman writer, particularly one so alert to the emotional dynamics of family life, should focalize fictional events through male characters, as du Maurier does in *I'll Never Be Young Again* and *Julius*. Yet this narrative strategy allows her to explore how far changing constructions of both masculinity and femininity are dependent upon one another and how they, in turn, both regulate and are regulated by, the family romance. This emphasis accords precisely with William Patrick Day's claim that 'The thematic focus of the Gothic concerns the nature of masculine and feminine identity and the nature of the family that shapes that identity'.[72] Furthermore, du Maurier's emphasis on the family at this early stage of her writing career exposes how far the marginalization of the mother (a peripheral figure in both *I'll Never Be Young Again* and *Julius*) is integral to patriarchal society, despite its lip-service to the importance of motherhood. Apart from Janet Coombe (whose iconic presence is more effective than her physical one), the mothers in du Maurier's early works are shadowy and ineffectual; they thus resonate interestingly both with the absent or dead mother of the Gothic text and with Irigaray's analysis of the western philosophical tradition as one predicated upon obliteration of the maternal genealogy and transcendance of the female body. The recovery of the lost mother becomes a project for du Maurier in later years; only then did she come to understand how her own mother's emotional remoteness had affected her sense of identity as a child and young woman; only then – as a mother herself – did she come to realize that the threat to the mother is also a threat to the self if one is a woman.

Du Maurier's first three novels, then, can be read as constituting an experiment in the writing of Family Gothic. Margaret Anne Doody has famously commented that 'It is in the Gothic novel that women writers could first accuse the "real world" of falsehood and deep disorder'.[73] In du Maurier's early works, however, the shifting focus between male and female subject positions and the switch between male and female narration allow her to explore both 'masculine' and 'feminine' fears and anxieties concerning the 'disorder' of the world. The presence of the uncanny in these novels signals an ambivalent recognition that the 'other' represents a lack at the heart of the 'self'; moreover this 'other' is frequently 'terrible' because the desire which it inspires is itself of a 'terrible' nature, as in forbidden incestuous love. As Masao Miyoshi suggests, incestuous desire may be of particular significance in Gothic literature in that it redefines the family as a crucible of fear, in which love is transformed into lust, and 'kindness into cruelty'.[74] Arguably, du Maurier's progress between *The Loving Spirit* and *Julius* charts precisely the transformation of 'love into lust' and 'kindness into cruelty'. As David Punter comments: 'what has become increasingly clear about the Gothic in these last few years ... is that part of what it figures is the long-suppressed narrative of child abuse'.[75]

Du Maurier's next step in the exploration of the 'self's' relation to the 'other' takes her into a different kind of writing. Having explored the dynamics of Family Gothic, she now turns to Gothic Romance in order to focus on female subjectivity. Her best-known novels will be dominated by what Alison Light has described as 'the desire to be differently female':[76] they centre on the question 'How can I be a woman without being only a woman?'[77] Part of her answer is to create 'strong' women characters in the novels that follow, but she is also seeking to write romance without writing formulaic women's romantic fiction. She does so by setting her Gothic Romances in a landscape that is both 'romantic' in the modern and popular sense of the word, and 'Romantic', in that it offers a 'free' and oppositional space within which to negotiate questions of gender identity. That space is Cornwall.

3
Cornish Gothic

For du Maurier, the decision in 1929 to live in Cornwall (at the age of 22) marked a significant stage in her writing career. Until then she had struggled to discipline herself to a life of writing while living as part of the family in London and in these circumstances she had found herself prone to distraction and ennui. Going to live in Ferryside, the house her father Gerald had bought in Bodinnick-by-Fowey as a holiday home, seems to have generated a sense of freedom and independence that was to prove very productive. Certainly, in practical terms, the house in Bodinnick offered release from the distractions of family life and the social round of London. While living there she was able to write *The Loving Spirit* and returned to complete her third novel, *The Progress of Julius*. As we have already seen, these novels, along with *I'll Never be Young Again*, experiment with genre and demonstrate the beginnings of a move towards Gothic writing. Du Maurier's sense of identification with Cornwall, we shall argue, developed in such a way that this mode became much more predominant, allowing her to give creative shape to transgressive desires. This new phase of her career was to prove very successful and the publication of *Rebecca* in 1938 consolidated her position as a best-selling author.

Many years later, in a television interview given to Cliff Michelmore when she was seventy, du Maurier was to say that place was very significant to her.[1] Her frequently stated affinity with Cornwall, and the fact that she used Cornish milieux in many of her novels, have ensured her a reputation as a 'Cornish' novelist – indeed the modern-day tourist industry has not been slow to exploit the popularity of 'Daphne du Maurier Country'.[2] Arguably, however, being characterised as a 'Cornish' (in other words, a regional) writer, has had, along with the 'best-seller' tag, an adverse effect on her literary reputation. Regional writing has often been linked with limitation, a kind of parochial concern with matters specific to an area and an emphasis on 'local colour' at the expense of the 'universal' significance which traditional literary

studies used to seek. In the words of Jim Wayne Miller (alluding to
the work of Anatole Broyard):

> Regional fiction is defined in terms of what it is not: it is not about
> big city life, not about life with which the critic is acquainted. It is
> about 'men and women whose existences are more foreign and
> incomprehensible than those of a European peasant'.[3]

The significance of Cornwall in du Maurier's work requires close
examination, inextricably linked as it is with an evolving writing
identity. J. Gerald Kennedy suggests that there may be a correlation
in fiction between an elaboration of place and an autobiographical
project, that 'a writer's fixation with a particular place may signal
the *desire* of autobiography: the longing to reconstruct – albeit in
fictive terms – the relationship between an authorial self and a
world of lived and located experience'.[4] In terms of du Maurier's
evolving writing self, it is perhaps significant that after the initial
The Loving Spirit (which was followed by the cosmopolitan *I'll
Never be Young Again* and *The Progress of Julius*), all but two of her
'Cornish' novels were published between 1934 and 1951. *My Cousin
Rachel* appears to mark the end of the 'Cornish period'. Speaking to
The Cornish Magazine in 1963, du Maurier said, 'What you want to
write about changes with the years. *My Cousin Rachel* possibly
marked the end of a phase.... I cannot see myself settling down
to another Cornish novel'.[5] In fact, two novels, *The House on the
Strand* (1969) and *Rule Britannia* (1972), constitute a revisiting of
Cornwall late in du Maurier's writing career and this is in itself
interesting. It is possible that the traumatic loss of Menabilly, the
house that she had leased for 26 years from the Rashleigh family,
and the subsequent move to the nearby Kilmarth (Menabilly's dower
house) at a time when she had recently been widowed, prompted a
reassessment of the relationship between identity and place.[6]

The initial move to Cornwall appears to have been associated with
the desire, however little articulated at that stage, to establish an
'authentic' voice for herself as a writer. In the first instance this meant
a distancing from the familial creative legacy, the male inheritance.
Both Gerald and George du Maurier (her father and grandfather)
were metropolitan figures whose fame derived from the artistic life
of the capital. Daphne's decamping to Cornwall may be seen as a
positive embracing of the rural rather than the urban, the regional
rather than the metropolitan and the peripheral rather than the

central. Du Maurier is no home-grown regional writer; she was *not*, despite the close identification that now characterizes her reputation, indigenous to Cornwall. The role Cornwall plays in relation to her novels is not the result of deep childhood roots. Any examination of du Maurier's fiction within the framework of regional writing must take this into account. It is rather that she made a deliberate decision to strike into a new space that she believed she could make, imaginatively, her own. Cornwall as it appears in her novels is exactly that imaginative space in which the complex identity matrix of daughter, sister, mother, woman and writer can be explored. In later life, du Maurier herself was to speculate on her own sense of identification with Cornwall. In particular, the two non-fiction books she wrote about the area (*Vanishing Cornwall* [1967], and *Enchanted Cornwall* [1989]) make no pretence at objectivity but offer a personal view of the county and its history that often strays into reflections on herself as writer.[7] These recollections are revealing when read alongside the 'Cornish' novels.

Vanishing Cornwall opens with a story from her childhood. She remembers how, at the age of five, staying on Bookham Common in Surrey, she watched the gardener nail a live snake to a tree. Her admiration for the snake's wildness and 'bravery' prompted her to release the family's two tame pet doves from their cages. Memories of the first childhood trip to Cornwall and subsequent visits become linked with this early experience. Cornwall is perceived as the land of freedom: 'Freedom to write, to walk, to wander, freedom to climb hills, to pull a boat, to be alone' (*Vanishing Cornwall*, p. 6). She describes herself and her sisters as doves freed from the cage of social propriety and expectation: 'The cage was not fastened, and of the three doves I should be the first to fly. The way was open' (*Vanishing Cornwall*, p. 6). The snake's death, however, is an ominous harbinger: Cornwall, as constructed by du Maurier, is a landscape imbued with both temptation and danger, as well as delight. Dona St Columb, in *Frenchman's Creek* (1941), fleeing to Cornwall, likens her need for its space to a linnet's desire to be free of its cage; yet that same freedom delivers a self which is not only adulterous but also potentially androgynous, a self that threatens reputation and domestic stability so that she finally capitulates to the 'cage' of marriage.[8] Du Maurier's novels, which appear to portray Cornwall positively as a place of freedom, space and authenticity, simultaneously portray that very freedom as dangerous in its evocation of an 'other' self that threatens the main character with psychic fragmentation.[9] This presents a paradox, however, since the apparently autonomous act of writing involves an exploration of 'self' which becomes threatening in its movement towards fragmentation: the ultimate incarnation of the dove of freedom in du Maurier's work occurs in the apocalyptic 'The Birds' (1952), a short story set in Cornwall, in which the bird population turns on and destroys the human. Du Maurier's Cornwall is a psychological landscape in which the conscious imagination battles with deeper fears. Because these deeper fears are not excised by the resolution of plot, the desire for freedom and autonomy continues to generate a creative tension in all her work. The statement 'I for this and this for me' – the 'line from a forgotten book' that seemed so apt on visiting Cornwall as a young woman (*Vanishing Cornwall*, p. 6) – holds out the promise of completion and desired authenticity.[10] However, this promise of completion remains unfulfilled in du Maurier's work and the fictional texts demonstrate instead the inherent danger of the fragmentation of the subject in such freedom. The spatial freedom of Cornwall is, then, perceived by du Maurier both as something that enables her to write and as a metaphor for the freedom of writing itself. In writing, she believes, she is able to release 'the boy in the box' and set the dove of imagination free.

Cornwall offers more than just spatial freedom for the writer; the 'Cornish' novels also display a preoccupation with the past. Alison Light suggests that du Maurier's work romanticizes the past, inscribing a nostalgia for 'a noble loftier place where it was possible to live a more expansive and exciting life'. Intent upon categorizing du Maurier as inherently conservative, Light claims that 'hers is a romantic Toryism'.[11] Certainly it is possible to find evidence for such a view in du Maurier's Cornish novels but it is really only *Frenchman's Creek*, the one novel du Maurier would acknowledge as romantic, which allows its heroine to live the carefree life of a pirate and pay only the penalty of having to stop.[12] Although, as the narrator of *Rebecca* says, 'We can never go back again, that much is certain' (*Rebecca*, p. 8), the landscape is represented as embodying the past, a representation that reaches its fullest form in *The House on the Strand*. The cultural geographer Doreen Massey has argued that 'the strategy of radically polarizing time and space, and of defining space by the absence of temporality' is related to 'the broader western mode of dualistic thinking which has been

widely criticized by feminists and linked into the same system of
thought which so sharply distinguishes between masculine and
feminine, defining them through continuous series of mutual oppositions'.[13] In this light, Du Maurier's fictional excursions into the
Cornwall of the past may be seen not only as popular historical
fiction but also as explorations of the complex relationship between
place, time, gender and identity.

In interrogating such oppositions, du Maurier draws upon a
cultural construct of Cornwall as historically unruly and ungovernable, far from the centres of national power: a transgressive
space.[14] Alison Light acknowledges that 'it is not for her
polemical or hortatory powers that her books are remembered,
nor even for her recreation of a convincing past.... Rather it is the
unruly and the ungovernable...which she captures with most
energy and which dominate her novels, almost against her better
judgement, as it were'.[15] The unruly and the ungovernable does
indeed manifest itself time and time again in du Maurier's work
and not only in the Cornish novels. Her sense of identification
with the peripheral culture of Cornwall may be seen as deriving
from her attraction to its strangeness, the 'otherness' of a
landscape permeated by relics of the past and hints of beliefs
alien to the seemingly rational world of the twentieth century.
Her last book, *Enchanted Cornwall* (compiled on her behalf by
Piers Dudgeon towards the end of her life), appears to
acknowledge this: whereas the first two chapters describe her
childhood and discovery of Cornwall, the last three (which focus
on the relationship between the landscape and the novels) are
entitled 'Old Unhappy, Far-Off Things', 'The Calamity of Yes-
terday' and 'Things Unknown'. Quoting Sir Arthur Quiller-Couch
in her introduction, she says, 'All England is a palimpsest'
(*Enchanted Cornwall*, p. 7). This concept of the palimpsestic nature
of place would seem to underlie the appeal of Cornwall to du
Maurier's imagination, deconstructing as it does the place/time
binary. The Gothic elements of du Maurier's work, relocated in a
Cornish milieu, are the primary means by which such a decon-
struction takes place and they develop in powerful ways. The
spatial metaphors of the Gothic are readily assimilated into du
Maurier's writing which is richly informed by her sense of identification with place. Indeed, in one sense du Maurier's retreat to
Cornwall from London may be seen as representing that most
persistent of Gothic tropes: the flight from the patriarchal house.

Yet the *resiting* of Gothic anxieties in a Cornish setting presents an interesting question to the critic and betokens an enduring anxiety about freedom itself.

The concept of Cornwall embraced by du Maurier had already been textualized and assimilated into literary history. As Ella Westland points out, Cornwall has occupied a textual space since the eighteenth century:

> By the 1790s it was no longer necessary to leave Britain in search of a rugged landscape which would inspire ecstasy, tranquillity, sweet melancholy or Gothic horror.... The transformation of Cornwall in the English imagination depended on rocky shores and surging seas taking their place with dark forests and snowy summits as approved sites for romantic sublimity, and literary evidence suggests that this had been achieved before 1800.[16]

As Cornwall afforded 'approved sites for romantic sublimity', du Maurier was able to make a connection between her admiration for the writing of the Brontës and her love of the Cornish landscape. In *Enchanted Cornwall*, she says, 'Cornwall became my text' (p.7). If the embracing of Cornwall was related to an ambivalence towards the paternal creative legacy, the choice of the Brontës as literary forbears may be seen as part of a search for a female writing identity. In *Vanishing Cornwall* she appropriates, in an admirable sleight of hand, the narrative power of the Brontës for herself through the shared terrain of Cornwall: she writes of the similarity between the rocks and stones of the Yorkshire moors 'which became famous as Penistone Crags in *Wuthering Heights*' and those of West Penwith in Cornwall (*Vanishing Cornwall*, p. 161). Noting that the Brontës' aunt and mother came from Penzance, and speculating on how they would have talked of Cornwall to the Brontë children, she claims that the Brontë vision 'was drawn from within, part of the heritage bequeathed to Emily Brontë from the Cornwall she had never seen or known' (*Vanishing Cornwall*, p. 162).[17] It was, of course, only one step from this assertion to the implication that du Maurier, writing from within Cornwall, had access to the narrative power of the Brontës, whose work she absorbed into her own. Her writing life in Cornwall was thus curiously authenticated by the literary genealogy she created for herself. For du Maurier the landscape of Cornwall seemed to authorize and empower her work as a writer, since it linked it with the Romantic and transgressive writing of the Brontës.

TRANSGRESSION AND DESIRE: *JAMAICA INN*

The Brontë influence is readily apparent in the 1936 novel, *Jamaica Inn*.[18] Ironically, much of this novel was written away from Cornwall. Du Maurier had by this time met and married Major Frederick ('Tommy') Browning and had taken up her role as wife of an army officer with its attendant disruptions and relocations. Her sense of identification with Cornwall was perhaps, therefore, all the more poignant at this stage because of her exile from it. Margaret Forster notes that:

> getting away from army life was her prime object throughout 1935. She went down to Fowey as often as possible and even when it poured found the place 'too lovely' and felt better at once. A trip to Bodmin Moor put her in mind of a previous visit with Foy and she began to make notes for the new book she had contracted in February to write – for Victor Gollancz.[19]

The book, of course, was *Jamaica Inn* and the previous visit is described in some detail in *Enchanted Cornwall* (pp. 67–87). Reflecting on this experience, du Maurier writes:

> Like Mary Yellan who, in the novel, comes to Bodmin moor from the tranquil hills and valleys of Helford, I came unprepared for its dark, diabolic beauty. People say that my fictional characters seem to emerge from the places where my stories are set, and certainly when I first set eyes on the old granite-faced Inn itself it made me think that there was a story there, peopled with moorland folk in strange harmony with their background.
>
> (*Enchanted Cornwall*, p. 69)

This reaction appears to have been recollected not so much in tranquillity as in circumstances far removed from the peace and freedom she had enjoyed as a young single woman in Cornwall. The result is a novel that takes du Maurier's work much further into a Gothic mode of writing than her earlier novels had done.[20]

The initial reception of *Jamaica Inn*, however, did not place it as a Gothic novel. Contemporary reviews, reports du Maurier's biographer Margaret Forster, characterized it as a Cornish tale of smugglers and villains, deeming it to be 'all jolly good fun' and 'an exciting brew...just the thing for a late evening's reading'.[21]

Certainly the influence of du Maurier's early reading of boys' adventure stories, in particular the novels of Robert Louis Stevenson, is very apparent in the plot.[22] Several commentators, including Alfred Hitchcock who directed a significantly altered film version, have remarked that it is merely Russell Thorndyke's *Dr Syn* transplanted from the Romney Marshes to Cornwall.[23] More perceptively, Alison Light has recognized its debt to *Wuthering Heights* but is rather dismissive of its more dramatic moments which she sees as placing du Maurier in the Stevensonian line:

> if *Jamaica Inn* rewrites *Wuthering Heights*, it does so in the buccaneering vein of *Treasure Island*. In her preoccupation with the sea, with sailing, piracy, smuggling and shipwreck, du Maurier draws on a 'tushery' and swashbuckling not to be found in the Brontës...[24]

Jane S. Bakerman, more inclined to see the novel in the context of a tradition of women's writing, has, in a 1985 essay on du Maurier's plots, characterized it as a tale of growth to maturity, a *bildungsroman*: its orphaned heroine comes from a sheltered pastoral environment in coastal Helford to face the trials and tribulations associated with Jamaica Inn.[25] All of this is true. What is interesting is the way the novel adopts and adapts these familiar literary forms and absorbs them into the Gothic mode.

The intertextual relationship between *Rebecca* (du Maurier's most famous Gothic novel) and *Jane Eyre* is readily apparent and has recently been explored by Patsy Stoneman; set in the early nineteenth century, before the coasts of Cornwall were policed by officers of the law, *Jamaica Inn* also has many superficial likenesses to the Brontë novels, particularly *Wuthering Heights*.[26] The 'real' Jamaica Inn (for the places exist if not the people) is set high on Bodmin Moor at Bolventor, a place, as du Maurier terms it, of 'dark diabolic beauty'; it would be difficult to find a more 'wuthering' setting. In more profound respects, too, *Jamaica Inn* carries resonances of *Wuthering Heights*. Like Emily Brontë's novel, it is concerned above all with boundaries: boundaries in the landscape give metaphorical expression to boundaries in the psyche and generic boundaries are destabilized as the novel conflates several literary traditions, the most dominant of which is the Gothic. In looking at du Maurier's novel from this perspective, the work of Eugenia C. DeLamotte on nineteenth-century Gothic is particularly useful. In her recent study, DeLamotte suggests that 'Gothic quests' and 'Romantic epiphanies' are 'cognate impulses', aligned as they are respectively to the negative and optimistic sides of Romanticism. She argues that 'boundaries and barriers...are the very stage properties of Gothic romance'; these include 'veils, masks, cowls, precipices, black palls, trap doors, sliding panels, prison walls, castle ramparts' as well as the larger architectural features of Gothic settings.[27] Gothicism is, like Romanticism, she suggests, fundamentally concerned with the boundaries of the self: 'What distinguishes the "me" from the "not-me"?' DeLamotte's is a feminist study and she suggests that:

> because the dividing line between the world and the individual soul has had, from the inception of the Gothic craze, a special relevance to the psychology and social condition of women, this interpretation of the 'deep structures' of Gothicism provides a new explanation of the appeal the genre has always had for women readers and writers.[28]

DeLamotte sees *Wuthering Heights* as a key nineteenth-century text in exploring the boundaries of the self as a Romantic theme. The similarities between *Jamaica Inn* and *Wuthering Heights* are not merely superficial similarities of setting; the later novel also draws on the traditions of Romanticism and Gothicism inherent in the Brontë text in order to explore the boundaries of a *female* self.

As with traditional Gothic tales, the house as place of threat is central to the story. Many of those writing about the Gothic have observed the spatial, architectural character of Gothic tropes – DeLamotte acknowledges the closeness of her own spatial model to that of Eve Kosofsky Sedgwick, for example.[29] While not a grandiose edifice like many of the buildings in earlier Gothic fiction, the 'old granite-faced Inn' (*Enchanted Cornwall*, p. 69) as represented in the novel reverberates with sinister possibilities. Its very name suggests transgression: its exotic connotations link it with the folklore of what was euphemistically known in Cornwall as 'fair trading', with a history of smuggling and wrecking.[30] Its potential irony – nothing could be further from the sub-tropical Caribbean than the blasted heath of Bolventor – also gives a hint of inversion. Both transgression and inversion are crucial elements in the novel. To Mary Yellan, newly arrived on a dark cold night from Helford on the northbound coach which has to make a special stop ('Respectable folk don't go to

Jamaica any more' [*Jamaica Inn* p. 13]), it is a house that 'reeked of evil' and its old signboard makes a 'curious groaning sound like an animal in pain' (*Jamaica Inn*, pp. 27–9). Her sense of the Inn as a place of threat is reinforced by the appearance of the aunt and uncle she has come to live with. These two characters again offer recognizable Gothic types and the scene appears to be set for another reworking of the family romance. Mary's Aunt Patience, her mother's sister, is a 'poor tattered creature' in a state of high nervous anxiety, a shadow of the former 'bewitching creature' (*Jamaica Inn*, p. 19) whom Mary remembers from ten years earlier. The tyrannical father figure, so familiar in Gothic tales, appears in the guise of her uncle Joss Merlyn, 'a great husk of a man, nearly seven feet high' (*Jamaica Inn*, p. 18). To Mary, long without a father and orphaned by the death of her mother (who had single-handedly run the farm at Helford until broken by the loss of its stock through a mysterious sickness), Patience and Joss Merlyn represent surrogate parent figures. Yet the image of gender roles that they offer is repugnant to Mary. Her aunt is cowed into submission by her husband and her life is that of a virtual prisoner within the walls of the Inn. Rather than looking to her as a role model for a different kind of life from the one she had known on the farm, Mary feels a strong desire to protect her from whatever has caused her present state. There is a pervading sense of fear at Jamaica Inn and Patience is consumed by it.

All Gothic texts are characterized by fear (although we may not recognise fear to be their *defining* characteristic as does Ellen Moers).[31] Made of stronger stuff than her aunt, Mary Yellan is no fainting heroine. Throughout the novel she exhibits courage and resourcefulness and frequently expresses a desire for independence in spite of her awareness that for a young and penniless woman the chance of this is remote. Yet she too experiences the fear that pervades Jamaica Inn. What has she to be afraid of? It soon becomes apparent that her uncle is the focus of an easily identifiable transgression. He comes from a long line of lawbreakers (his father was hanged at Exeter for murder and his grandfather was transported for thieving). His cronies who frequent the inn are all associated with anti-social behaviour and a barbaric cruelty that ranges from the callous baiting of the local idiot (*Jamaica Inn*, p. 43) to the deliberate wrecking of ships off the Cornish coast. The latter represents the depth of their depravity; Mary's discovery of this is preceded by other frightening episodes in which she attempts to penetrate the secret of Jamaica Inn. In a classic Gothic trope, for example, she succeeds in gaining entry to a now-abandoned barred room and finds there a length of frayed rope that may or may not be evidence that a dissenter from the group has been murdered. The status of this group of men (there are no women) as social outcasts is graphically represented by their repulsiveness: 'They were dirty for the most part, ragged, ill-kept, with matted hair and broken nails; tramps, vagrants, poachers, thieves, cattle-stealers and gypsies'. The narrative, focalized through Mary, makes much play of the disgust she feels:

> [she] turned sick and nearly faint at the sight of him; and what with the stale drink smell, and the reek of tobacco, and the foul atmosphere of crowded unwashed bodies, she felt a physical disgust rise up in her, and she knew she would give way to it if she stayed there long.   (*Jamaica Inn*, pp. 41–2)

Here Mary Yellan experiences the horror associated with what Julia Kristeva calls abjection; according to Kristeva, feelings of disgust signal the abject. In *Powers of Horror: An Essay on Abjection*, Kristeva argues that the experience of horror is an echo of our early anxieties surrounding the separation from the mother that involve insecurity about materiality and the borders of the self. The abject writ large in social terms, she suggests, is that which:

> disturbs identity, system, order. What does not respect borders, positions, rules. The in-between, the ambiguous, the composite. The traitor, the liar, the criminal with a good conscience, the shameless rapist, the killer who claims he is a savior.... Any crime, because it draws attention to the fragility of the law, is abject, but premeditated crime, cunning murder, hypocritical revenge are even more so because they heighten the display of such fragility.[32]

The band of wreckers that has Joss Merlyn at its centre represents such cultural abjection, by setting itself not only beyond the rule of law but also beyond the bounds of civilized behaviour. The experience of abjection in relation to this band of lawbreakers reaches its climax for Mary in the novel when, forced to accompany them on a wrecking expedition (emblematically on Christmas Eve), she narrowly evades being raped by one of her uncle's cronies by putting up fierce resistance. Du Maurier's text associates her Cornish lawbreakers not with the high adventures of the smugglers in boys' adventure stories but with something much more disruptive. For if *Jamaica Inn* is a *bildungsroman*, it is a female *bildungsroman*, and the exploits of such men are represented as 'otherness' in its most repugnant form and constructed explicitly as involving sexual threat. The language in which this scene is narrated is particularly graphic and violent:

> She moved swiftly, lashing out at him, and her fist caught him underneath the chin, shutting his mouth like a trap, with his tongue caught between his teeth. He squealed like a rabbit, and she struck him again, but this time he grabbed at her and lurched sideways upon her, all pretence of gentle persuasion gone, his strength horrible, his face drained of all colour... as he moved his position and lowered his head she jabbed at him swiftly with the full force of her knee, at the same time thrusting her fingers in his eyes. He doubled up at once, rolling on to his side in agony, and in a second she had struggled from under him and pulled herself to her feet, kicking him once more as he rocked defenceless, his hands clasped to his belly.
>
> (*Jamaica Inn*, p. 162)

Although this is in some ways a classic Female Gothic episode, in which the heroine is under threat from a powerful male, Mary does not experience passive fear. Here it is *the heroine* who inflicts pain by responding to her attacker and Mary's spirited reaction characterizes her as 'unfeminine'. Moreover, du Maurier's writing itself might be seen as 'masculine', drawing more on the style of Hemingway than Radcliffe. Thus the writing itself enacts the disruption of gender boundaries which Mary seeks. What this passage also emphasises is that Mary's involvement with the people associated with Jamaica Inn forces her to acknowledge her own materiality, her female body. Threatened and abused in the wrecking incident, she suffers actual, if not serious, bodily harm. Her relationship to the Merlyn family also leads her to encounter Joss's brother Jem, for whom she feels a strong physical attraction, forcing her to come to terms with a female sexuality she had hitherto denied.

The moor, on the other hand, seems to offer a physical and psychic freedom but this always turns out to be illusory. In spite of Mary's physical robustness she is always defeated by it. Flight, another familiar Gothic trope, involves Mary on several occasions striking out across the moor. In this novel, Cornwall is constructed as two starkly contrasted landscapes: it is made clear from the very start that Bodmin Moor, although only forty miles or so away, is 'a different world' from Helford, the home village from which Mary Yellan has travelled. Helford is remembered for its 'shining waters... green hills and sloping valleys... gentle rain and lush grass' (*Jamaica Inn*, p. 7) whereas Bodmin Moor appears initially 'grey and forbidding' (*Jamaica Inn*, p. 12), its inhabitants behaving in a surly, hostile manner to strangers. Bodmin Moor, Mary soon finds out, is as dangerous as its people: she hears that Matthew Merlyn (her uncle's brother) was drowned in Trewartha Marsh; she puts her own life at risk more than once when she wanders alone on the moor and loses her sense of direction. Yet the moor also seems, in the tradition of Romanticism, to have a sublime aspect:

> the air was strong and sweet-smelling, cold as mountain air and strangely pure. It was a revelation to Mary, accustomed as she was to the warm and soft climate of Helford, with its high hedges and tall protecting trees.   (*Jamaica Inn*, p. 32)

The closeness of 'Gothic quests' and 'Romantic epiphanies' identified by DeLamotte is very apparent here. Placing its heroine in a landscape that holds out the promise of Romantic epiphany (and one that had already entered literary history as such), du Maurier's novel shows clear affinities with the work of the Brontës. Like Emily Brontë's *Wuthering Heights*, *Jamaica Inn* (in DeLamotte's words) makes 'the paradoxical conjunction of transcendent aspiration and Gothic despair... most evident, and, most evidently, a subject of the text itself'.[33]

Already disturbed by the Inn and its people, Mary is disturbed in a different way by the moors. Significantly, she perceives them as unlimited:

> Like an immense desert they rolled from east to west, with tracks here and there across the surface and great hills breaking the sky-line.
>
> Where was their final boundary she could not tell. (*Jamaica Inn*, p. 37)

This landscape is best understood metaphorically; it represents a desire for psychosexual freedom, and an intimation of the possibility of moving beyond a social, gendered identity. The 'strangely pure' air of Bodmin Moor is a revelation in more ways than one; Mary equates the openness of the moors with freedom. In this place 'with no boundary' she articulates a desire that is non-conformist and deviant, a particularly feminine form of transgression in comparison with the law-breaking activities of the men: a desire to transcend the boundaries of her gendered self and to be free of the constraints of femininity. Yet the moors turn out to be the place of greatest danger both physically (as evidenced by the death of the other Merlyn brother) and psychically in the threat of fragmentation that they represent. *Jamaica Inn*'s achievement lies in its use of Gothic writing to interrogate boundaries in such a way as to hold the abject and the sublime in an uneasy balance for much of the narrative and then to demonstrate that abjection and transcendence are in the end relative. Mary Yellan affirms a female heterosexual identity at the end of the novel, having been shown that such intimations of the sublime may be connected with the socially most abject.

Roaming the moors delivers her into the hands of one or other of two men: one is Joss Merlyn's brother, Jem. He is both identified with Jamaica Inn and distanced from it, an ambiguity that is represented at one point in the novel by a clandestine night-time visit to Mary when he speaks to her through the window, an image redolent of *Wuthering Heights*.[34] Jem is a horse thief, a relatively innocuous occupation in the scheme of transgressions set up by the novel. Although apparently no great friend of his brother, his possible involvement in more sinister doings remains in question for Mary, and for the reader, until near the end of the novel. Jem recognizes qualities in Mary which do not conform to the accepted view of femininity: her courage and spirit of independence prompt him to remark, 'If you must be a boy, I can't stop you' (*Jamaica Inn*, p. 195) echoing the words of his brother who tells her, 'They ought to have made you a boy' (*Jamaica Inn*, p. 115). Mary's own dream is to 'save money in some way, and do a man's work on a farm' (*Jamaica Inn*, p. 122). She has, we learn, 'no illusions about romance', since falling in love is merely 'a pretty name' for 'a common law of attraction for all living things' and she has seen how young love in Helford has withered into oppressive marriages. She certainly has no wish to be like her Aunt Patience 'trailing like a ghost in the shadow of her master' (*Jamaica Inn*, p. 139). Her desire for Jem Merlyn is initially purely physical: the shock of realizing that Jem's hands, so attractive to her, are in fact similar to those of his repulsive brother, Joss, forces her to recognize that where boundaries are not actually absent, they are often disturbingly indistinct. She realizes 'for the first time that aversion and attraction ran side by side' (*Jamaica Inn*, p. 126). For there is indeed a sexual dimension to the repugnance that Mary feels towards Joss Merlyn. Her first encounter with him is rendered through a graphic description in which bestial images figure prominently: within the space of two short paragraphs he is variously compared with a horse, a gorilla and a wolf. His appearance, nonetheless, is perceived by her as having degenerated from 'something fine'. Although 'the thought of kissing him revolted her' (*Jamaica Inn*, p. 19) when, much later in the novel, he lays his fingers upon her mouth, she reacts with ambivalence:

> for some reason for ever unexplained, thrust away from her later and forgotten, side by side with the little old sins of childhood and those dreams never acknowledged to the sturdy day, she put her fingers to her lips as he had done , and let them stray thence to her cheek and back again.   (*Jamaica Inn*, pp. 187–8)

Thus the text makes clear that for the female subject the boundary between abjection and desire is intrinsically unstable. When Mary comes upon Jem out on the moor, the description of him establishes his likenesses to his brother:

> He wore a grimy shirt that had never seen a wash-tub, and a pair of dirty brown breeches, covered with horse hair and filth from an outhouse... there was a rough stubble of beard on his jaw. He laughed at her, showing his teeth, looking for all the world like his brother must have done twenty years ago.
> (*Jamaica Inn*, p. 101)

He tells her that he has not washed for three days and orders her to help him fill some water buckets. Far from finding Jem's aspect and behaviour disgusting, Mary finds it attractive – she 'could not help smiling' (*Jamaica Inn*, p. 101). Indeed, his association with the natural and the primitive seems to validate his virility. In this instance, 'filth' represents attraction. rather than abjection. In contrast with Joss, however, Jem is seen for the most part not in the Gothic spaces of the Inn but in the open air, on the moors or in the convivial atmosphere of the fair at Launceston. He is therefore dissociated from the Gothic villain.

The other man whom Mary encounters in her various wanderings on the Moor is the vicar of the nearby village of Altarnun, Francis Davey, who introduces an element of the potentially supernatural into the text. He is weird both in the more modern sense of the word and its older sense of kinship with dark forces. Appearing initially in the guise of a saviour, he is eventually revealed as the master criminal mind behind the wreckers. Francis Davey's nineteenth-century vicar's garments, however, are merely a conventional cover for an identity and a knowledge that threaten anarchy and subversion. He reveals to Mary Yellan his affinity with a pre-Christian, pagan Cornwall (a presence already sensed by her in the landscape) which harbours an ancient knowledge to which he is privy – a link that seems to place him outside contemporary discourses and social constructs. At first, the vicar provokes an ambivalent reaction in her, his albino appearance causing her to see him as a 'freak': 'There was a strangeness about him that was disturbing and pleasant' (*Jamaica Inn*, p. 129). Although Mary is initially drawn to him by his apparent kindness, compassion and air of calm authority, it soon becomes clear to the reader that this quality of freakishness is *signified* by his being an albino rather than *explained* by it. Francis Davey's real 'freakishness' derives from the fact that the sexual characteristics of his body appear indeterminate. His voice, for example, is 'soft and low, like the voice of a woman', his lashes are described as 'fluttering' (*Jamaica Inn*, p. 144); his silence and his gentleness are somehow seen to emasculate him in Mary's eyes: 'He was a shadow of a man .... He had not the male aggression of Jem beside her, he was without flesh and blood' (*Jamaica Inn*, p. 129). Indeed, throughout the novel his effeminacy is clearly counterpointed by Jem Merlyn's aggressive masculine sexuality. It is clear that Mary sees Davey as an hermaphrodite figure and the ambivalence that she feels towards him suggests that he signifies something rather more complex than a grotesque image of self-hatred which is the function Ellen Moers suggests such figures perform in American Female Gothic texts.[35] Clare Kahane has suggested that the hermaphrodite:

[is] in its symbolic dimension a Gothic emblem of that desired transgression of boundaries I experience within the Gothic space.... Especially in a time when the traditional boundaries of sexual identity are in flux, the hermaphrodite, challenging those boundaries by its existence, mirrors both the infantile wish to destroy distinction and limitation and be both sexes – a power originally attributed to the primal mother – and the fear of that wish when it is physiologically realized as freakishness.

Kahane goes on to quote Leslie Fiedler: 'no category of Freaks is regarded with such ferocious ambivalence as the hermaphrodites, for none creates in us a greater tension between physical repulsion and spiritual attraction'.[36] Mary Russo's discussion of freaks in her recent book, *The Female Grotesque*, emphasises the production of freakishness as a cultural phenomenon. For her, 'the freak can be read as a trope not only of the "secret self", but of the most externalized, "out there", hypervisible, and exposed aspects of contemporary culture and of the phantasmatic experience of that culture by social subjects'.[37] Russo draws on the work of Susan Stewart in discussing the physiological freak, asserting that 'the freak of nature' is indeed rather a 'freak of culture', unsettling boundaries. Whereas Siamese twins, for example, problematize the boundary between self and other, the hermaphrodite challenges the boundary between male and female.[38]

Such challenge to boundaries is rather different from that offered by Romantic concepts of transcendence. Davey's identity as a vicar suggests the possibilities of spiritual transcendence He is also closely associated with the moors both in terms of plot (much of the time he is seen travelling across them and indeed he first encounters Mary when she is lost and weary) and in his role as vicar of Altarnun whose beautiful and ancient church is often called 'the Cathedral of the Moor'.[39] He himself acknowledges his own kinship with the moors in terms of their primeval quality: they evoke the time that Mary has already sensed, when 'pagan footsteps trod upon the hills' (*Jamaica Inn*, p. 38). He recognises himself as both 'a freak in nature and a freak in time' (*Jamaica Inn*, p. 243) and interprets Mary's resistance to the constraints of gender in a positive way:

Your revolt and disgust please me the more, Mary Yellan... There is a dash of fire about you that the women of old possessed. Your companionship is not a thing to be thrown aside.

(*Jamaica Inn*, p. 245)

Like the moors, Davey signifies for Mary freedom from the oppression of Jamaica Inn yet the 'freedom' is both illusory and perilous. Davey's strange paintings, which Mary discovers at the vicarage, seem to suggest the uncanny as well as the sublime. The 'green afterglow' in which he has bathed his painting of the interior of his church casts 'a haunting and uncanny glow upon the picture' (*Jamaica Inn*, p. 232). Her subsequent discovery of the drawing that caricatures his congregation as sheep and represents himself as a wolf in the pulpit confirms his aberrant nature.[40] Joss Merlyn may physically resemble the wolf but in Davey, the resemblance runs much deeper. It is no surprise then to the reader to find that Davey has masterminded the wrecking and must indeed, rather than Jem, be the murderer at Jamaica Inn who has killed not only the unknown man earlier in the novel but also Joss and Patience. Francis Davey turns about to be the most abject of all.

In comparison with the albino, sexually ambiguous Davey, Jem Merlyn seems to descend from Heathcliff; his insolence, coarseness and 'rough brutality of manner' (*Jamaica Inn*, p. 64) are associated with an aggressive masculinity which is dangerously attractive to women. He even seems proud of his wife-beating genealogy: 'We Merlyns have never been good to our women' (*Jamaica Inn*, p. 66). Like his Byronic prototype, he appears 'mad, bad and dangerous to know'. In contrast with Davey, he tells Mary, 'Women are frail things... for all their courage' (*Jamaica Inn*, p. 195). Physically, the vicar of Altarnun, with his white hair and colourless eyes, provides an almost photographic negative image of Jem Merlyn who has his brother's dark hair and looks like 'a half-bred gypsy' (*Jamaica Inn*, p. 109); he is visually and sexually an inversion of the Byronic hero.[41] Jem, on the other hand, is associated with a different kind of 'otherness'. Several times the text alludes to his gypsy-like appearance. This not only signals that his nature is, in spite of his roots on Bodmin, itinerant but also hints at a racial 'otherness' not unlike the Jewishness of Julius and the racial indeterminacy of Heathcliff. Judith Halberstam claims that 'the Gothic text plays out an elaborate skin show', arguing that with reference to certain nineteenth-century monsters, skin becomes a kind of metonym for the human: 'its color, its pallor, its shape mean everything within a semiotic of monstrosity'.[42] Du Maurier's earlier novel, *The Progress of Julius*, had traced the history of its eponymous hero who, in spite of his worldly success, remained a perpetual outsider. The use of race to denote 'otherness', while having a long literary history, is

increasingly disturbing to modern-day readers; in the 1930s when
Jamaica Inn was written it was very much part of a discourse of
'otherness' which was to have calamitous results. For Mary Yellan
the wild quality of Jem provokes ambivalence as does the
effeminacy of Davey; in the end the latter proves to be more
unacceptably 'other' to Mary than does the former. Mary's judgement of these two men is one of the key dynamics of the text. For
much of the novel, she believes Davey to be her salvation, someone
whom she can trust, whereas Jem is tainted for her by his kinship
with Joss Merlyn, and in spite of her attraction to him, she remains
wary until the novel's dénouement places him on the side of the
angels. In this way, *Jamaica Inn* exhibits one of the central characteristics of modern Gothics observed by Joanna Russ: the man who
first appears to be sympathetic and protective is really the man who
poses the most threat to the heroine, whereas the 'dark,
magnetic, powerful brooding' male turns out to be the hero.
According to DeLamotte, commenting on Russ:

> The second equation, only vaguely hinted at in earlier Gothic,
> suggests a dissatisfaction with the asexuality of the hero and
> with the asexuality of the image of womanhood to which he
> corresponds in the schizophrenic separation of both the hero and
> heroine from their own passions. The first equation (the identifi-
> cation of apparent hero as secret villain), as earlier Gothic works
> it out, is more thoroughly disguised than the other precisely
> because it more deeply challenges the schizophrenic view in its
> most comprehensive form. The suspicion that the hero is the
> villain, in other words, embodies the writer's suspicion that the
> whole ideology of womanly purity and romantic bliss is a lie.[43]

Davey's affinity with the strangeness of the past introduces a
sense of the uncanny into the novel; confronted by it, Mary is
threatened by the destabilization of boundaries it represents. The
apparent freedom offered metaphorically if not literally by the
moors is now perceived by her as threatening to her sense of self
in a more radical way than the sense of the abject she has earlier
experienced. According to Kristeva, 'The abject is edged with the
sublime. It is not the same moment on the journey, but the same
subject and speech that brings them into being'.[44] In *Strangers to
Ourselves*, Kristeva describes the uncanny as 'the fascinated
rejection of the other at the heart of that "our self"... which

precisely no longer exists ever since Freud and shows itself to be a strange land of borders and othernesses ceaselessly constructed and deconstructed'.[45] Mary's final flight is undertaken under duress with Davey. Heading for the coast, they spend the night near Roughtor, an area Mary thinks of as 'his kingdom'. In her exhausted state Mary seems to see the granite rocks around her transformed into men of a primeval age – 'monsters of antiquity' – who 'spoke in a tongue she could not understand, and their hands and feet were curved like the claws of a bird' (*Jamaica Inn*, p. 254): the doves of freedom have transmuted into something grotesque and threatening. The theme of monstrosity is continued when, pursued by men and hounds, he forces her to climb to the 'great stone slab' (*Jamaica Inn*, p. 257) which is likened to an altar, implying, as in Hardy's *Tess of the D'Urbervilles*, sacrifice. In this text, however, it is not the heroine who is sacrificed to social mores, but the albino vicar, whose freakishness signifies a dangerous subversion of gender codes. The anxieties raised by the text are now transferred to Davey who, put to death by the plot, becomes a textual scapegoat.

Significantly, it is Jem Merlyn, the overtly heterosexual man, who kills Francis Davey, effectively saving Mary from him. The description of Davey's death echoes the bird imagery of *Vanishing Cornwall*: 'He flung out his arms as a bird throws his wings for flight, and drooped suddenly and fell; down from his granite peak to the wet dank heather and the little crumbling stones' (*Jamaica Inn*, p. 258).[46] It also completes his demonization, echoing as it does the fall of Satan. After this plot dénouement Mary Yellan is faced with several choices: she could become a companion to Mrs Bassett, wife of the local squire and magistrate; she could go south, to return to Helford valley for which she has a 'queer, sick longing' (*Jamaica Inn*, p. 259) where she would 'know peace and contentment' again (*Jamaica Inn*, p. 260); or she could go north and throw in her lot with Jem Merlyn who has decided to leave Cornwall. Throughout the novel, Helford has signified a lost wholeness and a dream of potential autonomy, never to be realised. At the end, there is a tacit understanding on Mary's part that a return to Helford would mean in fact an acceptance of domesticity, marriage and allotted social role. Until the very last line of the novel, when she sets 'her face towards the Tamar' (*Jamaica Inn*, p. 267), Mary Yellan implies that she will go south and return home. Her decision to go with Jem means abandoning the domesticity and security that life and marriage in Helford would have offered, and the comfort but servitude of life in the squire's household. It means living like the horse-thief he is, in restless insecurity – a life not considered suitable for a woman. Yet in doing so she is following the physical imperative of sexual desire that, for her, is stronger than the drive towards social conformity. Never can a heroine have had such an odd proposal: 'If you were a man I'd ask you to come with me, and you'd fling your legs over the seat and stick your hands in your pockets and rub shoulders with me for as long as it pleased you' with the rider, 'you're only a woman, as you'd know to your cost if you came with me' (*Jamaica Inn*, p. 265). The import of this choice and decision can, however, only be understood in the light of the third choice that had been offered to Mary Yellan, albeit only implicitly: that of the deepest social nonconformity – the freakishness of breaking the boundaries of sexual identity that the vicar of Altarnun represents. It is this that partially explains the strange pleasure he affords to Mary Yellan, a woman who exhibits qualities in her behaviour, character and values which are conventionally thought to be masculine. This 'choice' is in one sense circumvented by plot, which both criminalizes and erases Francis Davey, but at a metaphorical level its monstrous nature (in social terms) is communicated by the landscape of which he is a part. *Jamaica Inn* can, then, be read as a text that explores transgression both overtly and covertly: the plot centres on the law-breaking activity of smuggling (which is punished); the subtext, however, implies that the ultimate transgression is the breaking of gender boundaries. If we see the novel as a *bildungsroman*, Mary Yellan has effectively redefined, at least for the time being, the boundaries of self. Just as she rejects the uncanny 'otherness' of Davey and the disruption of *sexual* identity it would imply, the novel endorses her choice by making Davey culturally abject. His attempt to induce her to travel the world with him (in what is presented as a grotesque parody of St John Rivers' proposal to Jane Eyre) is the first choice of futures offered to her. She rejects it emphatically.

Ultimately, Davey represents a threat to gendered subjectivity. If ancient Cornwall is seen as a pre-oedipal space in which landscape and people are not differentiated, Davey's uncanniness lies in his challenge to the very categories of modern western thought. The text short-circuits this by placing him back in the modern rational world but making him culturally abject because of his murderous criminal behaviour. In his uncanny aspect, Davey comes close to the sublime but identification with him would mean for Mary abandoning the boundaries that define gender. The text makes Mary's choice easier for her by making the vicar abject because cultural abjection *confirms* the familiar categories that underpin civil society. Culture is shored up by what it abjects; in the Gothic, in the words of Jerrold E. Hogle, 'struggles for cultural definition are what haunt the Gothic most in its anomalous monsters and spectres, as well as in the desires of its heroes and its heroines'.[47] Like the Cornwall it represents, *Jamaica Inn* may be read as a palimpsest. At plot level it inscribes a process of cultural abjection which relates to the period in which it is set, the early nineteenth century: it shows the enforcement of law and order on an unruly periphery. The most powerful anxieties of the text, however, derive from the mid-twentieth century. The 'freakish' Francis Davey is a figure who reflects concerns which the twentieth century had inherited from the *late* rather than the *early* nineteenth century. Mary Russo notes the late nineteenth-century emergence of the freak as cultural spectacle, which results from 'the increasingly codified world of spectacle', 'a world vision that has become objectified'.[48] Lyn Pykett's recent book *Engendering Fictions* develops the work of, among others, Elaine Showalter, in its discussion of the emergence of *fin de siècle* discourses. Describing the degenerationist rhetoric which characterised the period, Pykett quotes Max Nordau who, in his famous *Degeneration* (1893), condemns, among others, those decadent artists for whom 'the highest development of morality consists in renouncing sexuality and transforming oneself into a hybrid hermaphrodite'.[49] The figure of the hermaphrodite as a focus for cultural anxieties, therefore, may be seen in relation to the destabilization of gender boundaries and perceptions of the creative artist at the end of the nineteenth century. These in turn gave rise to the twentieth-century debates about sexual identity which we have outlined in Chapter One. Du Maurier's novel, published in the same year as Djuna Barnes' *Nightwood*, is therefore very much of its own time.

Mary Yellan returns within the boundaries of her own society and her own gender, asserting her materiality and its gender implications. However, although she does this, she remains close to the boundaries by linking her destiny with the liminal figure of Jem. Despite being an inversion of Davey, he is dangerously near to the borders beyond which lies cultural abjection. This allows her to embrace heterosexuality but renounce many of the trappings of femininity. Instead of the young woman of Helford who regards sexual relationships as being for other people, she has become during her stay at Jamaica Inn the heterosexual female subject. If we were to adopt the distinction established by Anne Williams between Female and Male Gothic, the ending of *Jamaica Inn* certainly conforms to one of Williams's characteristics of Female Gothic. 'The female formula', says Williams, 'demands a happy ending, the conventional marriage of Western comedy'.[50] Du Maurier's novel invites us to read *beyond* the ending, however.[51] The affirmative note upon which it ends confirms the power of the Symbolic in a way that is only provisional. Mary Yellan's union with the liminal figure of Jem does not promise a happy ever after. She may shun domesticity but she chooses a sexual conformity that will not necessarily bring happiness. Crossing the Tamar with Jem keeps Mary within a sexually defined self but exiles her from the potentially free space of Cornwall.

'THE BOY IN THE BOX': *THE KING'S GENERAL*

Du Maurier's residence at Menabilly from 1943, a dream fulfilled, appears to have afforded continued inspiration, and the idea of Menabilly seems to have occupied a central place in du Maurier's creative imagination. Her fictional exploration of the house is one of the ways in which she explored her own sense of identification and empathy with it. Menabilly, the du Maurier home in Cornwall for 26 years, and the main inspiration for *Rebecca*'s Manderley, was never owned by du Maurier's family. In 1943, when she signed a twenty-year lease for the house (to be extended in 1963), it belonged to the Rashleighs, as it does today. Her leasing of Menabilly thus commenced five years after the publication of *Rebecca* and was presumably funded, at least to some extent, by money that had accrued from her writing career. In 1943 the then-empty house had no electricity, water or heating and was 'in a fearful state' according to her lawyer, who advised her that she could do no more 'than camp out there occasionally'.[52] She spent many years and thousands of pounds restoring Menabilly (the new roof alone cost £30 000).[53] As a child and young woman she had been fascinated by the abandoned manor house which she had discovered whilst trespassing in its grounds with her sister

Angela.[54] Covered with ivy and hidden in the valley, Menabilly must have seemed an inaccessible and hidden place, full of secrets. Its fairytale quality, which clearly captured the young du Maurier's imagination, is recalled in *Myself When Young*:

> The windows were shuttered fast, white and barred. Ivy covered the grey walls and threw tendrils round the windows. It was early still, and the house was sleeping. But later, when the sun was high, there would come no wreath of smoke from the chimneys. The shutters would not be thrown back, nor the doors unfastened. No voices would sound within those darkened rooms. Menabilly would sleep on, like the sleeping beauty of the fairy tale, until someone should come to wake her.[55]

The King's General (1946) is the first book du Maurier wrote while living at Menabilly and, unlike *Jamaica Inn* and *Rebecca*, it is based on the lives of people who really lived.[56] It is something of a favourite among local people because, of all the Cornish novels, it is the most precisely located in time and place. (In fact du Maurier was disappointed that reviewers did not give her credit for the careful historical research she had undertaken for the novel.)[57] As in *Rebecca*, she uses a female narrator, this time to tell a story in which Menabilly appears as its historical self, sacked and violated in the Civil War. *The King's General*, in regressing to the bleakest period of the house's history, creates not so much an open landscape of transgression or desire (as in *Jamaica Inn* or *Frenchman's Creek*, du Maurier's 1941 fantasy) but one of anxiety. Although the action of the novel ranges across Cornwall and Devon, we are never allowed to escape a sense of confinement: the events are focalized through the crippled female narrator, Honor Harris, who is confined to a wheelchair after a riding accident as a young woman. Ellen Moers argues that one of the defining characteristics of Female Gothic is the grotesque, the distorted body image.[58] In the figure of Honor, the distorted body, rather than representing a loathed 'other', becomes in a strange way empowered by its confinement and speaks for itself. The freakishness is domesticated. Thus a potentially powerful Gothic trope is deflected.

Like the later novel, *The Scapegoat* (1957), *The King's General* appears to resist embracing fully the Gothic mode and operates instead in a liminal area. In *The Scapegoat*, this is the area between the Gothic and the 'realist'; in *The King's General*, it is the area between the Gothic and the historical romance. For if du Maurier's early novels might be described as romancing the family, this one may be seen as romancing the region, in the spirit of Scott's representation of Scotland in the Waverley novels. Du Maurier's novel constructs Cornwall as fiercely independent and resistant to puritan ethics. The very negotiation of the generic boundary, however, is itself interesting, suggesting that it is not always possible to discern where the apparently archetypal familial concerns of Gothic fiction end and broader issues of historically influenced social identity begin. Ian Duncan in his recent study of the Gothic, Scott and Dickens argues that the Gothic

> invokes historical contingency in order to dramatize its reduction under persistent forms of sexual and familial identity.... Through the strategic exoticism of costume and setting we read the figure of the present, and are bound in the spell of simultaneous familiarity and strangeness.[59]

In *The King's General*, however, there is no such subordination of the social and political to the territory of psycho-analysis. Although sexual and familial concerns are played out graphically through the Gothic dimensions of the text, their reciprocal relations with broader social and political formations are never eclipsed. The vexed question of masculinity which is at the novel's core manifests itself in both spheres, and is quite explicitly a theme in a plot which tests 'manhood' in a time of civil war.

The King's General constructs a world which is often verifiable by recourse to historical records and contains much quotidian detail, although du Maurier uses licence in her representation of language and manners. Written in twentieth-century English, it does contain some conspicuous anachronisms, the use of the word 'gerry-mandering', for example, which was a coinage of nineteenth-rather than seventeenth-century politics.[60] A 1962 review of her work in *The Times Literary Supplement* attacked all her historical novels, *The King's General* coming in for particular criticism:

> Miss du Maurier's historical sense is execrable...she has as little sense of the language of her chosen periods as of the probable behaviour, attitudes and outlook of the people who lived in them. Even in *The King's General*, where much historical research

has obviously been undertaken, knowledge and invention have failed to blend, so that though we readily accept that the public events described took place during the Civil War, it is impossible ever to believe the people lived in this period.[61]

The criticisms of this anonymous reviewer fail to recognize the interplay of genres in du Maurier's novel. Her historical romance is infused with Gothic elements and offers a different kind of verisimilitude: it brings into the foreground the cultural bases of familial relationships. Its recourse to the stuff of Gothic fiction, culminating in the walling up of a young man in a secret room in the buttress of the house, is a powerful symbolic representation of such cultural forces at work. Menabilly turns out to be a Gothic edifice in the end, hiding secret fears that lie deeper even than the fear of the opposing army which pervades the novel. In the opening chapter, Honor refers to Menabilly as 'that house of secrets' (*King's General*, p. 15). She then warns the reader early in her narrative that this will be no simple love story: the opening chapters which have told of her courtship by the dashing young soldier, Sir Richard Grenvile, are, as she says, 'but the prologue'. They end with the dramatic riding accident which disables her and she sets the scene for the remainder of the story:

If anyone therefore thinks that a cripple makes an indifferent heroine to a tale, now is the time to close these pages and desist from reading. For you will never see me wed to the man I love, nor become the mother of his children. But you will learn how that love never faltered, for all its strange vicissitudes, becoming to both of us, in later years, more deep and tender than if we had been wed, and you will learn also how, for all my helplessness, I took the leading part in the drama that unfolded, my very immobility sharpening my senses and quickening my perception, while chance itself forced me to my role of judge and witness. (*King's General*, pp. 54–5)

Ostensibly about place and history, *The King's General* also tells another tale, a tale which turns on familial relationships. Honor does not become the mother of Richard's children but she does become a surrogate mother to his son, Dick. Richard is ashamed of the boy because he sees him as effeminate and the complexities of this triangulated relationship find their expression through the Gothic elements in the novel.

However inappropriate the comparison might seem at first, Sir Richard Grenvile is in a direct line of fictional descent from Jem Merlyn. Like the hero of the earlier novel, he exhibits an aggressive masculinity which softens only in relation to the heroine to whom he shows a nurturing side. In many ways this aggressive mascul-inity is even more pronounced in Richard, the cruel streak which it incorporates being given full rein in the context of a civil war. It is further exaggerated by the fact that Richard, in comparison with the marginal criminal figure of Jem, is powerful. For much of the novel he is 'the King's General in the West'. Only towards the end of the story does he become disempowered and indeed, at the very end, a fugitive. He is a figure who instils fear, ruthless to his enemies and given to executing prisoners without compunction. Like Jem he is wayward and arrogant; when Honor first meets him, years before the war, he has just returned from a successful military campaign and he sweeps her forward with him to demand a place at the high table in the celebratory banquet. He is capable of casual personal cruelty, a facet of his character Honor is only too aware of; reminiscing about the past, she recalls:

> I think of the time we were all assembled in the long gallery, and Alice and Peter sang, and John and Joan held hands before the fire – they were all so young, such children . . . . Then Richard, my Richard, broke the spell deliberately with one of his devastating cruel remarks, smiling as he did so, and the gaiety went, and the careless joy vanished from the evening. I hated him for doing it, yet understood the mood that prompted him.
>
> (*King's General*, p. 11)

As with Jem, there are hints of promiscuous behaviour. The 'young kinsman', Jo Grenvile, he admits to a saddened but not surprised Honor, is actually his illegitimate son, conceived while he was living at Killigarth and courting her. Jo's mother was, he acknowledges, 'a dairy-maid at Killigarth. A most obliging soul'. He had discovered Jo the year before on his return from Germany and now 'wouldn't be without him for the world'. He feels no contrition and when Honor remonstrates with him, he merely replies, 'God damn it . . . I didn't ride to see you every day'.

(*King's General*, p. 193)

Honor is, indeed, under no illusions about Richard but loves him nevertheless. In many ways, Richard conforms to the stereotyped hero of women's romantic fiction. He is aggressively masculine yet is also capable of tenderness to the heroine.[62] This is demonstrated at their first meeting, at the banquet in Plymouth when he tends to her after she has had a surfeit of burgundy and roast swan (a menu worthy of any historical romance). Their relationship is terminated by Honor who insists upon the separation after her disabling injury and does not see him again until 1643, when the Civil War throws them together and they meet at Menabilly. In the intervening period she has developed and matured. Coming to terms with her disability, she learns patience and fortitude. She also sets herself the task of developing her mind, an opportunity which would probably have been denied her had she been of sound body. She learns the classics and acquires wisdom along the way. From a young and wilful girl, who was determined to marry Richard Grenvile whatever the opposition, she becomes a cerebral woman who has the judgement to refuse to marry Richard when she meets him again in later life, understanding as she does that he would probably come to resent her were they bound by marriage. In many ways, the young Honor is like Mary Yellan; the middle-aged Honor has not had Mary's liberty to roam the countryside and must seek her freedom through the mind. In so doing, she emphasises her 'freakishness', becoming a cerebral, educated woman at a time when such were rare. In *Enchanted Cornwall*, du Maurier muses on her own sense of identification with this heroine: 'As the drama unfolds Honor Harris becomes an extension of the author, my persona in the past' (p. 151). It seems possible that Honor's physical constraints are a metaphorical expression of constraints that du Maurier, the writer, felt. She explains these in *Enchanted Cornwall* as involving a sense of frustration at being excluded from participation in the events of the past, merely being '"judge and witness", an invalid of time' (p. 152). Specifically, she feels a sense of identification with Honor's powerlessness to save Richard's son Dick:

And when the fate of the young Cavalier – Richard Grenvile's son – is sealed, I feel the shadow of the buttress is upon both Honor and me. Sitting at my typewriter only yards from the site of the airless room I too hear 'the sound of a boy's voice calling my name in terror, of a boy's hand beating against the walls',

and in the pitch-black night, I fancy I can see his ghost, 'vivid,
terrible, accusing'.   (*Enchanted Cornwall*, pp. 151–2)

The historical basis for du Maurier's fancies was an incident dating
back to 1824, when William Rashleigh was making some alterations
to the house. When an apparently redundant buttress was
demolished, a secret room was discovered and in this 'the skeleton
of a young man, seated on a stool, a trencher at his feet, and the
skeleton dressed in the clothes of a Cavalier, as worn during the
period of the civil war' (*Enchanted Cornwall*, p. 145). Such a
powerful Gothic image was apparently the inspiration for *The
King's General*. In the novel, the image is not directly presented,
but it haunts the mind of its narrator, and, it would appear, its
author. Its significance can only be understood in terms of what the
third figure in the triangulated relationship represents.

Dick, the son of Richard Grenvile and Elizabeth Howard, the
woman he married for her money after his estrangement from
Honor, is a disappointment to his father.[63] Dark-haired rather than
red-headed like the rest of the Grenviles, he is effeminate in
appearance. As in *Jamaica Inn*, hands are used synecdochally to
indicate identity: Dick has slender feminine hands, 'too finely slim
for a Grenvile', as Honor says (*King's General*, p. 283). We first see
him aged 14, a shy and unconfident boy whom Richard leaves in
Honor's care while he goes off to fight. Dick is easily frightened
and particularly distressed by the sight of blood, the result, he has
been told, of an incident where his father hit his mother when he
was a baby in her arms. Later, after a lapse of several years and
exile on the continent, he tells Honor of how he has been happy in
Italy, having found a talent for painting and a niche among like-
minded friends. His father, however, had been contemptuous of
his new way of life:

> Painting was womanish, a pastime fit for foreigners. My friends
> were womanish too, and would degrade me. If I wished to live, if
> I hoped to have a penny to my name, I must follow him, do his
> bidding, ape his ways, grow like my Grenvile cousins. God in
> heaven, how I have come to loathe the very name of Grenvile!
>   (*King's General*, p. 282)

There are strong implications that Dick might be homosexual;
certainly his sexuality is ambiguous and he does not measure up

to the model of masculinity espoused and aggressively defended by his father. This is a masculinity which identifies itself powerfully with Englishness and constructs 'foreign' men as effeminate and worthy only of contempt ('Show a frog an English pike and he will show you only his backside' [*KG*, p. 294]). Neither Honor nor the novel itself endorses such a model. Honor defends the boy and is grieved by Richard's treatment of him which exhibits wilful cruelty. When Dick asks at one point, for example, if his father does not have any commands for him, Richard replies, 'Why, yes... Alice Courtney's daughters must have left some dolls behind them. Go search in the attics, and fashion them new dresses' (*King's General*, p. 302). Richard's relationship with his son ends in tragedy; his role in his country's affairs leads to failure and exile.

The novel also offers up another example of ambiguous sexual identity in the shape of the minor characters of the middle-aged Sparke siblings, two sisters and their brother. Resident at Menabilly, taking refuge from the fighting, they provide an almost carnivalesque picture of sexual ambiguity and masquerade:

> Will was one of those unfortunate high-voiced old fellows with a woman's mincing ways, whom I felt instinctively must be malformed beneath his clothes... Deborah made up in masculinity what her brother lacked, being heavily moustached and speaking from her shoes, while Gillian, the younger sister, was all coy prettiness in spite of her forty years, bedecked with rouge and ribbons, and with a thin high laugh that pierced my eardrum like a sword.   (*King's General*, p. 73)

Yet in times of privation, when the house is occupied by the forces of Parliament and its residents are near starvation, they show themselves to be as fully human as anyone else. Will is selfish, concerned only with his own survival but, as Honor relates:

> Deborah, whom I had thought as great a freak in her own way as her brother was in his, showed great tenderness, on a sudden, for all those about her who seemed helpless, nor did her deep voice and incipient moustache discourage the smallest children.
>   (*King's General*, p. 166)

Yet again, the novel domesticates freakishness. The last comment, about the smallest children, suggests that the revulsion from what is deemed to be 'freakish' is acquired, rather than innate.

At first it also appears that the novel will domesticate the Gothic trope of the secret room. Soon dismissing the fear of ghostly presences, Honor discovers the underground passage which links Menabilly to the summer house. It is part of the route by which Jonathan Rashleigh makes clandestine visits in his role of collector for the district, secretly handling precious metals given by local royalist families to boost the King's coffers. Hearing strange sounds in the night in her early days at Menabilly, she spies on the unoccupied room next to her own chamber and observes not a ghost, but a flesh and blood man clad in a crimson cloak, his back turned to her. Determined to find out how he could have had access to the room without going through her own, Honor tenaciously pursues the mystery (as would befit any Gothic heroine) and discovers the secret passage, between Menabilly and the summer house. Jonathan Rashleigh's discovery that she has almost divined his secret is presented in a manner which hints at Gothic horror but then provides a 'rational' explanation:

> even as I watched, I saw, to my great horror, a hand appear from behind a slit in the arras and lift it to one side. There was no time to wheel my chair into the passage, no time even to reach my hand out to the table and blow the candle. Someone came into the room with a crimson cloak about his shoulders, and stood for a moment, with the arras pushed aside and a great black hole in the wall behind him. He considered me a moment, and then spoke. 'Close the door gently, Honor,' he said, 'and leave the candle. Since you are here it is best that we should have an explanation, and no further mischief.'
>
> He advanced into the room, letting the arras drop behind him, and I saw then that the man was my brother-in-law, Jonathan Rashleigh. (*King's General*, p. 110)

The rational explanation, however, hints at the gruesome and, metaphorically, at skeletons in the family closet:

> 'It happened also,' he said in a lower tone, 'that my unfortunate eldest brother was not in full possession of his faculties. This was his chamber, from the time the house was built in 1600 until his death, poor fellow, twenty-four years later. At times he was

violent, hence the reason for the little cell beneath the buttress, where lack of air and close confinement soon rendered him unconscious and easy then to handle.'

He spoke naturally, and without restraint, but the picture that his words conjured up turned me sick. I saw the wretched, shivering maniac choking for air in the dark room beneath the buttress, with the four walls closing in upon him. And now this same room stacked with silver plate like a treasure-house in a fairy tale. (*King's General*, pp. 113–14)

It is this room that provides a useful hiding place for Dick from the enemy during the period of the house's occupation. Only some years later, does Honor see the secret room for herself, and then its full horror impinges on her:

I saw it for the first time, and the last, that secret room beneath the buttress. Six foot high, four square, it was no larger than a closet, and the stone walls, clammy cold with years, icy to my touch. (*King's General*, p. 335)

Significantly, it is Richard who carries her to see the secret room. At the end of the novel the room is the site of the culmination of the vexed relationship between father and son. Suspected of betraying the rebellion, Dick becomes 'scapegoat', ostensibly for the failure of the cause but also for his father's inability to accept him as he is. Threatened by his son's gender ambiguity, Richard denies him. Recounting his family's distinguished history and the valour of his forbears, he pronounces:

'He was a soldier,' they may say. 'The King's general in the west.' Let that be my epitaph. But there will be no other Richard in that book at Stowe. For the King's general died without a son. (*King's General*, p. 318)

The proud intransigence of Richard is counterpointed by Honor's compassionate acknowledgement that the fault is hers and Richard's:

This is our fault, I whispered to myself, not his. Had Richard been more forgiving, had I been less proud; had our hearts been filled with love and not hatred, had we been blessed with greater

understanding.... Too late. Full twenty years too late. And now
the little scapegoat of our sins went bleeding to his doom...
                                    (*King's General*, p. 319)

At this point, Honor withdraws and we as readers never find out
what passes between father and son. Effectively, we share her
sense of impotence. Again, we never see Dick's imprisonment in
the buttress nor know for sure whether he has chosen to sacrifice
himself in this way or whether he has been abandoned by his
father. Whatever the 'truth' might be, what we do see very clearly
is an horrific Gothic trope closing the novel, a trope which makes
concrete du Maurier's metaphor of 'the-boy-in-the-box'. Dick is,
quite literally, a boy in a box. He and the sexual ambiguity he
represents are punished by containment of the most horrific kind
and Honor is powerless to prevent it. Whatever transgressions of
accepted social behaviour are committed during a time of civil war,
the ultimate transgression, it would seem, is the transgression of
gender boundaries. Dick is as culturally abject in this society as the
Vicar of Altarnun in *Jamaica Inn* yet in this novel, such abjection is
presented with sympathy. Rather than being associated with death-
dealing evil, Dick is represented as the scapegoat for the sins of
others. At the very end of the novel, as Honor nears the end of her
life, she speaks with Jonathan Rashleigh about the Grenviles and
says, 'The very least of them showed great courage also' (*King's
General*, p. 346).

Separated by a period of ten years, *Jamaica Inn* and *The King's
General* represent different stages in du Maurier's use of what we
might call Cornish Gothic, just as they represent different stages in
her own life and two different points in history. Why should such a
novel as *Jamaica Inn* have been a best-seller in 1936, mid-way
through what Auden described as a 'low, dishonest decade' and
indeed have remained popular?[64] There has been much work
recently on the relationship between Gothic writing and socio-
political anxieties.[65] Apparently far removed from the 'real'
anxieties of the 1930s – such as unemployment, economic decline
and the rise of Fascism – *Jamaica Inn* would appear at first glance to
be pure escapism, yet it can be seen as inscribing cultural anxieties
concerning identity and difference. The question 'whom can you
trust?' is of central importance and it is significant that when
Hitchcock directed the film version, the plot was changed to make
the local squire the villain of the piece rather than the vicar. The

sense of freakishness was also lost: the squire was a much more conventional villain. A freakish and duplicitously evil vicar was, it would seem, too threatening.

The King's General, written at Menabilly at the end of the Second World War, expresses anxieties about the effects of war on personal relationships and demonstrates the harmful effects of the exaggerated masculinity which it promotes. The novel shows the eventual social, familial and emotional costs for the female subject of choosing the Byronic hero, an aggressively 'masculine' figure, culturally endorsed. Both Jamaica Inn and The King's General represent a Cornwall which is peripheral to England and subversive to concepts of Englishness centred around the South East. The Cornwall of the past in these novels represents the potentially unruly and ungovernable. Jamaica Inn has a fairly precise historical setting: the England of George IV just before the establishment of the coastguard which was to enforce relative law and order around the coasts. Nor is the reader allowed to forget this: Joss mentions King George twice (Jamaica Inn, pp. 26 and 115) and Francis Davey tells Mary that there will soon be men patrolling the coasts and 'a chain across England... that will be very hard to break'(Jamaica Inn, p. 152). In The King's General the Grenviles represent the independent spirit of the west country and much is made of Richard's lineage, including the exploits of his grandfather of the same name who sailed with Drake. At one point Richard has plans for a separatist Cornwall: he wishes to 'hold a line from Bristol Channel to the Tamar, and keep Cornwall for the Prince' (King's General, p. 231). By the end of the novel, however, the harrowing events of the Civil War result in the oppressive rule of Parliament and Richard is in exile in Holland.

Anxieties about the freedom that Cornwall represented to du Maurier continued to surface in her fiction. Only in Frenchman's Creek had she indulged in a fantasy in which her heroine is able with impunity to cross-dress and live out a boys' adventure in a story of piracy. Even here, the novel closes with an acknowledgement that such freedom can be only short-lived: Dona St Columb puts her dress back on and returns to her husband and children. Cornwall, it would seem, could offer to du Maurier a kind of conceptual freedom only. Translated into the practical, such freedom was very circumscribed. Fear of Cornwall succumbing to hegemonic control was very real to her and appeared in a final flourish in her last novel, Rule Britannia (1972), in which a Cornwall of the near future is occupied by American troops and an attempt made at imposing an alien culture. Du Maurier frequently expressed anxiety about the tourist industry, in particular the creeping curse of the caravan.[66] It is ironic, then, that the modern tourist industry has added yet another layer to the 'palimpsest' of Cornwall through its construction of 'Daphne du Maurier country'. It has, for example, created a Jamaica Inn in which the boundary between fact and fiction is destabilized and the casual visitor is encouraged to think that the events of the novel 'really' happened. The visitor can look at a brass plaque in the floor which indicates the spot 'where Joss Merlyn died'.

It is also possible to see all three novels as expressing, however obliquely, anxieties in du Maurier's own life. If we were to look at *Jamaica Inn* in this way, it might be read as a parable of her marriage into the role of itinerant army wife which entailed her own exile from Cornwall as the price to be paid for heterosexual attraction, although it would be a careless reader indeed who would try to establish any simple equation between Jem Merlyn and Tommy Browning. *The King's General*, however, seems to tantalize the reader with the possibility of such an equation between the novelist's husband and the novel's flawed hero. Its dedication reads: 'To my husband. Also a general, but, I trust, a more discreet one'. Certainly there were many anxieties for du Maurier concerning her husband's return from active service. The war had enabled du Maurier to take control of her own life again. The income from her writing had enabled her to lease and restore Menabilly and she had become in all but the legal sense its mistress. As well as offering peace and stability, residence at Menabilly had acquired a symbolic significance for du Maurier. It had come to represent a creative space where the 'boy-in-the-box' could be released (see Chapter 1). The powerful Gothic trope of the boy walled up in the buttress may be seen as representing du Maurier's fears for her creative imagination, her own 'boy-in-the box'.[67]

4

The Secrets of Manderley: *Rebecca*

Gothic fiction over the last two hundred years has given us characters such as Dracula and Frankenstein who have passed into popular culture and taken on an almost mythic dimension.[1] Rebecca, Daphne du Maurier's most famous character, has achieved a similar status. Influenced by *Jane Eyre* (Angela Carter goes so far as to describe *Rebecca* as a book that 'shamelessly reduplicated the plot' of Charlotte Brontë's novel[2]), du Maurier's best-seller, published in 1938, has itself become a strong influence on women's romantic fiction and Female Gothic writing. As Joanna Russ notes in her discussion of popular or 'drugstore' Female Gothic fiction: 'The Modern Gothics resemble...a crossbreed of *Jane Eyre* and Daphne Du Maurier's *Rebecca* and most of them advertise themselves as "in the Du Maurier tradition", "in the Gothic tradition of *Rebecca*", and so on'.[3] The first sentence of *Rebecca*, 'Last night I dreamt I went to Manderley again', a poetic evocation of place, has become one of the most famous opening lines in English fiction.[4] What is it, then, that gives Rebecca her mythic status and Manderley that enduring place in the twentieth-century imagination?

It is the project of this chapter to read *Rebecca* as, above all, a Gothic romance in which the narrator's identity is haunted by an Other, and in which Manderley is seen, like all classic Gothic buildings, to be a house haunted by its secrets. In the second edition of *The Literature of Terror*, David Punter argues that Gothic writers work 'on the fringe of the acceptable, for it is on this borderland that fear resides'. He continues:

> In the best works, the two sides of the border are grafted on to each other: the castle of Udolpho and the house of Bartram-Haugh are reversible medallions, displaying on one side the contours of reality, the detail and structure of everyday life, on the other the shadowy realm of myth, the lineaments of the unacceptable.[5]

Manderley, we would suggest, conforms precisely to this description. Moreover, although *Rebecca* meets Joanna Russ's criterion, which decrees that the secret of the 'Modern Gothic' often 'turns out to be an immoral and usually criminal activity on somebody's part centering around money and/or the Other Woman's ghastly (usually sexual) misbehavior',[6] we shall argue that the secrets of du Maurier's novel are far more profound and disturbing than Russ's words suggest. Rebecca, read as a Gothic rendering of the Other Woman, becomes one of those 'perfect figure(s) for negative identity' which, according to Judith Halberstam, endow certain Gothic texts with the potential for multiple meaning.[7] We shall argue that, in seeming to set up a binary opposition between the narrator and Rebecca, du Maurier's novel in effect explores subjectivity as a spectrum, rather than a position, thus presenting female identity as complex and multifaceted.

Rebecca centres upon a country house inspired mainly by Menabilly although it also draws on memories of Milton in Northamptonshire, where du Maurier had stayed as a child during the First World War. The fact that du Maurier began *Rebecca* in Egypt (her husband having been stationed in Alexandria for almost two years), during a period of temporary exile from her beloved Cornwall, may well have intensified the sense of longing for a lost place that the novel communicates so clearly in its opening pages.[8] It is, however, significant that du Maurier does not draw on historical material connected with Menabilly in her portrait of Manderley. When writing *The King's General* in the mid 1940s she was to use Menabilly's history to construct a detailed picture of a family and its house at a certain historical moment (see Chapter 3); in that novel, locations (as in *Jamaica Inn*) are specific and can be found on a map of Cornwall. By comparison, in *Rebecca* both historical moment and setting are somewhat vague. Du Maurier describes how she decided to set the novel 'in the present day, say the mid-twenties',[9] yet there is no explicit reference in the novel to the larger events of the outside world during that period.[10] Similarly, *Rebecca* communicates no sense of where Manderley is in Cornwall, although most readers assume its site to be that of Menabilly, on the Gribben peninsula, with 'Lanyon' and 'Kerrith' representing Lostwithiel and Fowey respectively. Since du Maurier did not lease Menabilly until 1943 there is a practical explanation for the novel's lack of engagement with Manderley's history. However, as she knew Cornwall well by 1938, its geographical vagueness in the novel seems deliberate and suggestive of a desire to create a 'dream' text rather than a realist one. In *Rebecca*, the approach to the house is constantly linked with entrance into a dark world of forests such that Manderley itself comes to be associated with magic, remoteness and, metaphorically, with entry into the unconscious. On first arriving, the narrator likens the drive to 'an enchanted ribbon through the dark and silent woods, penetrating even deeper to the very heart surely of the forest itself' (*Rebecca*, p. 69), later commenting to Frank (the estate manager) that it reminds her 'of the path in the forest in a Grimm's fairy tale' (*Rebecca*, p. 138). Further references in the novel to myth and fairy tale continue to dislocate expectations of realism that the text seems to set up elsewhere. For example, the valley of salmon, white and gold rhododendrons and azaleas which leads down to the beach is known as the Happy Valley; this spot, which casts its 'spell' over the narrator and which is perceived by her as 'the core of Manderley' (*Rebecca*, p. 115), is thereby associated with the legend of Tristan and Iseult, who are discovered asleep by King Mark 'in the forest of Moroi – the Happy Valley, a sort of paradise for lovers'.[11] Whereas other locations in the novel – Kerrith, the grandmother's house, London, even Monte Carlo – are presented solely in realist mode, Manderley figures as both a 'real' house and the stuff of dreams: 'Last night I dreamt I went to Manderley again'. 'Cornwall', too, functions both as a 'real' place and as a romanticized, Gothic space, the location of Manderley echoing the peripheral siting of Cornwall itself as a potentially wild and ungovernable area. Having set up such a topography in *Rebecca*, du Maurier employs some of the tropes associated with the country house tradition of English writing; for example, control and governance are metaphorically expressed through the disciplining of the land itself – most notably, perhaps, in the representation of Rebecca through the rhododendrons that threaten to overwhelm the drive and which the narrator perceives as 'slaughterous red, luscious and fantastic' and as 'monsters, rearing to the sky' (*Rebecca*, p. 70).[12] Significantly, in the opening dream of the novel, these shrubs, planted by Rebecca, are seen as standing 'fifty feet high', having 'entered into alien marriage with a host of nameless shrubs, poor, bastard things that clung about their roots as though conscious of their spurious origin' (*Rebecca*, p. 6). As we shall see, the threat of illegitimacy and social disruption is an important dimension of the novel's exploration of power relations between men and women.[13] Nevertheless, *Rebecca* undermines the conservative agenda often associated with country house writing, both by its embrace of the Gothic and by a tendency to caricature (seen, for example, in the 'horse and hounds' mentality of the tweedy Beatrice, the louche degeneracy of Jack Favell, the punctilious social behaviour of Colonel Julyan and the sexually inhibited and impoverished English-gentleman figure of Frank Crawley). This inclination to caricature, which inscribes 'Englishness' in the novel in a somewhat parodic manner, is one of the many ways in which the representation of Manderley as the apotheosis of 'English' life is rendered unstable.

Thus, on the one hand the text sets up Manderley as a dream space wherein fantasies can be fulfilled and the object of desire achieved; it thereby constructs the reader as that of women's romantic fiction. Such a reader, however, is invariably puzzled by the unsatisfactory nature of Maxim as the object of desire: for most of the novel, Maxim is a remote and emotionally chilly figure; its opening shows us that he turns into a rather dull invalid. (As Margaret Forster points out, du Maurier herself saw the novel as '"rather grim", even "unpleasant", a study in jealousy with nothing of the "exquisite love story" her publisher claimed it to be'.[14]) On the other hand, the novel simultaneously presents itself as a nightmare space, with the house and the narrator's marriage to Maximilian de Winter full of dark secrets and threatening scenarios. Sometimes this is lightly signalled: 'Like being buried down here?' quips Jack Favell to the young bride, whilst later in the novel Beatrice whispers in her ear 'Why don't you sit down? You look like death' (*Rebecca*, pp. 169 and 236). At other moments, Gothic harbingers are more strongly evident. For example, when she meets him in Monte Carlo, Maxim looks 'medieval in some strange inexplicable way' to the narrator and reminds her 'of a portrait seen in a gallery, I had forgotten where, of a certain Gentleman Unknown' (*Rebecca*, p. 18). The resemblance stays with her, so that later she imagines him as 'cloaked and secret, walk(ing) a corridor by night' and 'standing on the steps of a gaunt cathedral, his cloak flung back'. At one point, alarmed by Maxim's uneasy manner, the narrator even considers the idea 'that perhaps he was not normal, not altogether sane' (*Rebecca*, pp. 21, 42 and 33).[15] Thus *Rebecca*, in presenting Maxim through the eyes of the narrator, encourages us to construct Maxim as both fascinating Gothic villain (in the spirit of Schedoni and Montoni) *and* as the fantasy product of a naive

young mind. For the narrator continually presents her younger self
as one whose values and expectations have been heavily influenced
by popular fiction: 'I thought of all those heroines of fiction who
looked pretty when they cried...'; 'He has kissed me too...Not
dramatic as in books'; 'In books men knelt to women, and it would
be moonlight'; 'In a book or in a play I would have found a
revolver, and we should have shot Favell, hidden his body in a
cupboard' (*Rebecca*, pp. 44, 46, 57 and 343). It is important to
remember that most of the novel's events are focalized through the
eyes of this younger self.

The narrator of *Rebecca* is then, in some ways, a modern Catherine
Morland whose social, intellectual and sexual naivety is painfully
apparent. Her quest must therefore be for knowledge, and the
opening of the novel shows us a woman who eventually gains that
knowledge. Although the narrator, ten years older, presents herself
as dull and 'wrapped in the complacent armour of approaching
middle age', she nevertheless shows herself to be a mature and
reflective woman, who has become 'bold at last' (*Rebecca*, pp. 38
and 13). This opening 'frame' narration, which is typical of Gothic
writing, alerts the reader to the fact there is to be no simple or happy
ending to the plot about to unfold. *Rebecca* is finally concerned less
with presenting a story of romantic love than with showing how,
and at what cost, the transition between ignorance and knowledge
is made in the female subject. Significantly, then, there is much
reference in the text to locks and keys – and to knowledge being
'locked' out of reach. In the opening dream sequence Manderley is
presented as padlocked and chained against intruders – but the
narrator, as a 'spirit', is able to pass through these barriers (*Rebecca*,
p. 5). Conversely, within the plot, nothing on the Manderley estate
is physically barred to the narrator: the West Wing is hers to
discover and even Rebecca's boat-house, which she expects to find
locked, is open to view. At the same time, however, less tangible but
more powerful barriers are put in the narrator's pathway to
knowledge. Maxim, his judgement determined by culturally
endorsed myths, associates sexual experience in women with evil;
he therefore continually surveys the narrator for signs of a fall from
innocence, at times becoming aggressive in his accusations: 'You
had a twist to your mouth and a flash of knowledge in your eyes.
Not the right sort of knowledge' (*Rebecca*, p. 210). Indeed, he
monitors her curiosity and invokes the father/daughter romance
as a cultural endorsement of his over-protectiveness:

'Listen my sweet...A husband is not so very different from a
father after all. There is a certain type of knowledge I prefer you
not to have. It's better kept under lock and key. So that's that.'

(Rebecca, p. 211)

In preserving her innocence and ignorance he wishes to keep her as
a child and this is nowhere more clearly signalled in the text than
when he suggests she go to the Manderley Ball dressed as Alice in
Wonderland. Early in their relationship he makes it clear to her that
he desires her *because* she is not thirty-six and 'dressed in black
satin, with a string of pearls' (*Rebecca*, p. 41), thereby signalling his
anxiety concerning adult female sexuality. In the spirit of Shoshana
Felman's analysis of Balzac's 'Adieu', we might argue that what
Maxim desires is not for the narrator to become knowledgeable,
but for her to acknowledge his wisdom; he does not wish for
cognition in her, but for recognition of the power balance in their
relationship.[16] Free to explore and yet continually held under surveillance, the narrator, like Catherine Morland at Northanger
Abbey, is 'enclosed in openness'[17] and infantilized.

These elements of *Rebecca* evoke, of course, the Bluebeard tale
which has been used as an underpinning narrative of Female
Gothic texts from Charlotte Brontë's *Jane Eyre* to Margaret
Atwood's short story, 'Bluebeard's Egg'. Its continuing importance
as a reference point for Female Gothic writers is, as Anne Williams
has suggested, due to the fact that:

Bluebeard's secret is the foundation upon which patriarchal culture rests: control of the subversively curious 'female', personified
in his wives...[Bluebeard] forbids her the room in order to be
sure that she will open the door, for the contents of the room
represent patriarchy's secret, founding 'truth' about the female:
women as mortal, expendable matter/*mater*....In 'Bluebeard'
narrative techniques subtly but unmistakably side with Bluebeard – not with his habit of murder, to be sure, but with the
unquestioned 'reality' of the male power that makes such murder possible, sometimes even 'necessary'.[18]

As in other founding myths, such as that of Pandora or Adam and
Eve, woman is constructed as 'naturally' curious in the Bluebeard
tale and the story centres on the conflict between the 'irresistible
force of "female" curiosity' and patriarchal law.[19] Like Bluebeard's

bride, the narrator of *Rebecca* is intensely curious. Speculating on the nature of the relationship between Maxim and his dead wife, she suddenly feels 'rather like someone peering through the keyhole of a locked door'; indeed, she recognizes herself as driven by 'a frightened furtive seed of curiosity that grew slowly and stealthily, for all my denial of it' (*Rebecca*, pp. 36 and 127). In a sense, then, in taking his new young bride home to Manderley, Maxim sets the agenda for a revelation of masculine power. This power is demonstrated less through the sadism/masochism dynamic we find in traditional versions of the tale (a dynamic openly articulated in Angela Carter's 'The Bloody Chamber') than through a closing of ranks against the revelation of the murder.[20] Four characters finally harbour the secret of Rebecca's death at her husband's hands, since the narrator and Maxim are well aware that Frank Crawley and Colonel Julyan (the local magistrate), in accepting the doctor's 'explanation' of Rebecca's death when they both suspect Maxim of murder, collude with his crime. To all appearances, the science of medicine, representative of patriarchal discourse, appears to offer the 'key' to the mystery of Rebecca's death: she chose to commit suicide rather than die painfully and slowly from an incurable disease. Yet it is a false key for it does not unlock the whole story. The part that it does unlock, moreover, functions as an alibi which exonerates Maxim from criminal status; it thereby enacts, in miniature, a discursive sanitizing of the violence at the heart of the patriarchal order. Yet ultimately Rebecca has won, as Maxim predicted she would, for the violence was, unbeknown at the time to its perpetrator, orchestrated by a woman who had always done exactly as she pleased. For Rebecca, just as for Richardson's Clarissa, 'death, the most supreme form of self-destruction, serves as a form of recomposition'.[21]

It is Rebecca's wilfulness that drives Maxim to murder and which makes him place her on the side of the devils. Woman, for Maxim, is the Other necessary for the construction of the masculine self;[22] moreover, she is an Other who has two faces: that of demon and that of angel. Thus he construes Rebecca as evil, and the narrator as good and innocent – a bifurcation repeated in Ben's description of Rebecca as giving him 'the feeling of a snake' and of the narrator as having 'angel's eyes' (*Rebecca*, p. 162). Drawing on the work of Simone de Beauvoir, Elisabeth Bronfen notes how, within a patriarchal society, 'Woman comes to represent the margins or extremes of the norm – the extremely good, pure and helpless, or the extremely dangerous, chaotic and seductive'.[23] Maxim's policing of the narrator's understanding and, in particular, his control of her knowledge of female sexual desire, thus signals a need to keep the narrator on the side of the 'angels'. Inevitably, then, in the face of the narrator's continual wish that she were older, her husband pats her head just as he pats that of Jasper, the dog, and continues to treat her as a child, commenting 'It's a pity you have to grow up' (*Rebecca*, p. 57). Not surprisingly, the narrator resents this status and makes frequent reference to 'forbidden' books (*Rebecca*, pp. 30, 97), as if somehow knowledge of adulthood and female sexuality lay in the pages of an inaccessible text, forever out of her reach.

In one sense, however, the book is opened and the secret revealed when Maxim tells his young wife about Rebecca and his murder of her – and the change in the narrator is irrevocable: 'I've grown up, Maxim, in twenty-four hours. I'll never be a child again' (*Rebecca*, p. 276). Their marriage is immediately transformed: they suddenly relate to each other as adult sexual beings (they kiss passionately for the first time) and, in a strange reversal of their former roles, Maxim develops a child-like dependency on the narrator.[24] Furthermore, the narrator finds a new confidence which enables her to run Manderley with the authority she had, till now, lacked: in effect, she becomes more like Rebecca. It gradually becomes apparent that what Maxim most loathed in Rebecca was her chameleon ability to appear 'good' whilst embodying what he perceives as evil; he tells the narrator how living with Rebecca was like 'living with the devil', albeit one with 'a face like a Botticelli angel' (*Rebecca*, pp. 285 and 291). However, the rapid collapse of their relationship forced Maxim to recognize that he married Rebecca because it seemed she would make a good mistress of Manderley: 'I thought about Manderley too much... I put Manderley first, before anything else' (*Rebecca*, p. 286). He was, he acknowledges to the narrator, even prepared to accept a sham marriage when, five days after the ceremony, Rebecca struck a bargain with him, promising to run Manderley in an exemplary fashion so long as she was allowed sexual liberty. The first secret revealed at Manderley, then, is that Maxim murdered his first wife not because her infidelity broke his heart, but because it threatened the integrity of the paternal line: had she really been pregnant by Favell, both Manderley and the de Winter name would have passed to someone else's child, not his own. His act thus exemplifies

Williams's claim that 'women [are] mortal, expendable matter/ *mater*' and illustrates why the polarisation of 'good' and 'bad' women within the bifurcated category of woman as Other is an essential element within the ideology of a patriarchal society. Maxim's worst punishment is not prison or exile, but the loss of his beloved Manderley: with no estate and no heirs to inherit it (the opening of the novel makes it clear that his second marriage will also be childless), the security of Maxim's masculine identity within a class-based, capitalist, patriarchal society is under severe threat (hence, perhaps, his strangely reduced state in the novel's opening pages).

The importance of property, class and lineage as aspects of masculine identity is confirmed by the way in which the novel ends. In discussing the burning of Manderley, Alison Light suggests that it is 'apparently instigated by Mrs. Danvers (although we do not know this for sure; the conflagration is also a kind of spontaneous combustion)'.[25] Other critics make the same assumption, perhaps unconsciously influenced either by the plot of *Jane Eyre* or by Hitchcock's 1940 film version of the novel (Michelle A. Massé, for example, notes that Mrs Danvers 'is of course the major suspect'[26]). In fact, the novel offers strong evidence that the burning of Manderley takes place on the orders of Jack Favell. After the visit to Dr Baker in London with Colonel Julyan, Maxim and the narrator, Favell realizes that he will never be able to prove that Maxim murdered Rebecca. Accusing Maxim of 'a stroke of luck', he makes an ominous threat: 'you think you've won, don't you? The law can get you yet, and so can I, in a different way' (*Rebecca*, p. 386). This conversation takes place at six o'clock in the evening. Significantly he stays behind whilst the others depart; we learn, through Maxim's telephone call to Frank from a restaurant in Soho later during the evening, before the drive back to Manderley, that Mrs Danvers received a long-distance telephone call at about ten past six that evening. Frank informs Maxim (who in turn informs the narrator) that Mrs Danvers had been packing all day and had left Manderley by 6.45 p.m. The narrator immediately assumes that the call was from Favell ('He would tell her what Colonel Julyan said' [*Rebecca*, p. 391]) and jumps to the conclusion that he and Mrs Danvers are plotting a further attempt at blackmail. Maxim, however, has guessed that something might be wrong at Manderley and cancels their original plan to stay overnight in a hotel on the way down. His hunch proves right:

they arrive to find Manderley engulfed by a fire. All the clues point to the fire being started by Mrs Danvers *on the orders* of Jack Favell. Unlike the burning of Thornfield in *Jane Eyre*, an act perpetrated by an 'hysterical' woman, the burning of Manderley is premeditated and signals masculine rivalry (Favell's attempt to blackmail Maxim having failed). The battle between the two men over her dead body is, then, fought through a patriarchal system built on class, property and lineage. Favell alone knows Maxim's secret: that his love of Manderley is greater than that of any woman. Against such considerations, Rebecca herself becomes reduced to the role of catalyst in a masculine struggle for power and social status.

But this is not so for the narrator. For if Rebecca represents one aspect of the feminine 'Other' for Maxim, she is also the narrator's *alter ego*, or double. In obvious ways, she seems to embody all that the narrator is not; the relationship between the two women is one in which, to use Harriet Hawkins's words, 'their counter-images seem photo- negative reversals of each other, or two sides of one coin'.[27] The narrator is plain and socially awkward, with lank hair and sloping shoulders; Rebecca, it seems, was confident, sophisticated and very beautiful. Whereas the narrator is shy and timid, Rebecca was, it appears, well-liked and much admired: 'Someone tall and slim and very beautiful, who had a gift, Beatrice said, of being attractive to people' (*Rebecca*, p. 197). Whereas the narrator is naive, Rebecca was very knowing; indeed, Mrs. Danvers claims that even as a child, Rebecca 'had all the knowledge...of a grown woman' (*Rebecca*, p. 254). Both Mrs. Danvers and Maxim describe Rebecca as clever (*Rebecca*, pp. 254 and 283), but for the former this is part of her charisma, whereas for the latter it is an aspect of her deviancy: 'She was not even normal' (*Rebecca*, p. 283) according to Maxim. Her 'knowledge' is associated both with an ability to control (much is made of her skill in handling difficult horses and her manipulation of people) and with an active, voracious and diverse sexuality. Whereas Rebecca's charismatic sexual identity is associated with the heady scents of the azaleas and with the blood-red rhododendrons of the drive, that of the narrator is linked with the roses that grow beneath the window of her room in the East Wing, flowers which Maxim connects with a domesticated maternal identity: 'I love the rose-garden,' he said: 'one of the first things I remember is walking after my mother, on very small, unsteady legs, while she picked off the dead heads of the roses' (*Rebecca*, p. 81).

These differences between the two women are both signalled and confirmed by their handwriting which, as in Robert Louis Stevenson's *Dr Jekyll and Mr Hyde*, functions 'as a witness to identity'.[28] For Rebecca's uncanny presence in the novel is due not just to other characters' memories of her but to an indelibility which continually surfaces through her signature and the 'curious, sloping letters' (*Rebecca*, p. 62) of her handwriting. The first instance of this occurs in Chapter 4 when the narrator, finding a book of poetry in the glove compartment of Maxim's car, takes it back to the hotel to read. Picking it up later, she notices the dedication:

'Max – from Rebecca. 17 May', written in a curious slanting hand. A little blob of ink marred the white page opposite, as though the writer, in impatience, had shaken her pen to make the ink flow freely. And then as it bubbled through the nib, it came a little thick, so that the name Rebecca stood out black and strong, the tall and sloping R dwarfing the other letters. (*Rebecca*, p. 37)

This is the first of many references to Rebecca's writing that we meet in the novel; always it is associated with 'curious', 'sloping' or 'slanting' letters and with a vibrant vitality: 'How alive was her writing, though, how full of force' (*Rebecca*, p. 62). Her signature which is 'black and strong', suggests extreme confidence, even to the point of aggression:

Max from Rebecca...Max was her choice, the word was her choice, the word was her possession; she had written it with so great a confidence on the fly-leaf of that book. That bold, slanting hand, stabbing the white paper, the symbol of herself, so certain, so assured.   (*Rebecca*, pp. 47–8)

In an attempt to exorcise the powerful presence of Rebecca's writing, and in an episode which portends the end of the novel, the narrator sets fire to the offending page: 'The letter R was the last to go, it twisted in the flame, it curled outwards for a moment, becoming larger than ever. Then it crumpled too; the flame destroyed it. It was not ashes even, it was feathery dust' (*Rebecca*, p. 62)

For a time the narrator lives with the illusion that, by destroying Rebecca's writing, she has taken on her enemy's strength; she, too, is now confident and strong. This state is, however, short-lived –

not surprisingly since, in fact, it is not the destruction of Rebecca's writing but the absorption of the power it signifies which will energize the narrator. Rebecca's presence continues to haunt Maxim's new wife, surfacing in her script and inscriptions of her: the narrator finds Rebecca's handkerchief in the mackintosh she used to wear and it is embroidered with 'A tall sloping R, with the letters de W interlaced. The R dwarfed the other letters'. Later, when she enters Rebecca's bedroom, she sees that her night-dress case is similarly embroidered with 'R d W, interwoven and interlaced. The letters were corded and strong against the golden satin material' (*Rebecca*, pp. 125 and 175). The letter R thus takes on a runic power which derives from its powerful visual impact and its refusal to be destroyed. Whereas the scent of azaleas, which still pervades Rebecca's clothing, signals an adult female sexuality, the dominating R which cannot be burnt away, erased or blotted out, signifies an enduring autonomy. Its disproportionately large and dominant presence is perhaps reminiscent of the famous signature of Elizabeth I, the mark of an unusually powerful woman[29] (interestingly, Clarice, the narrator's maid, remarks of the fancy dress costume that 'It's a dress fit for the Queen of England' [*Rebecca*, p. 220]). It is also possible to see the letter R as an iconic representation of a woman's form, its curved formation and pinched-in waist inscribing an exaggerated femininity on the shape of the female body.[30] Rebecca's writing leaves an indelible trace on Manderley which can only be erased by the destruction of the house itself yet that same writing returns in the text which is *Rebecca* the novel. Not for nothing was her boat called 'Je Reviens'. As Anne Williams has suggested, in Gothic fiction, the ' "other woman" is indeed "the other" – not only female, but a ghost, a revenant';[31] in this novel, however, she surfaces most clearly through her handwriting, a writing which uncannily inscribes the body's presence despite its absence through death.

Yet that very 'absence' becomes problematic when Rebecca's boat is raised and a body found in it, thus casting doubt on the identity of the body in the crypt. What Williams describes as 'that intensely Gothic phenomenon, the sight of a worm-eaten corpse',[32] is denied the reader: instead, we are presented with various scenarios of disintegration.[33] We are thus refused the *point de capiton*, the representation of the body which, in Bronfen's words, 'attempts to attach the dying, decomposing body, destabilizing in its mobility, to a fixed semantic position'[34] and this adds to the novel's

Gothic effect. Mrs Danvers claims that the rocks 'had battered her to bits' so that 'her beautiful face (was) unrecognizable, and both arms gone' (*Rebecca*, p. 178) (although this description presumably refers to the washed-up body which Maxim wrongfully identified as that of Rebecca). Ben suggests that Rebecca has been 'eaten up' by 'the fishes' (*Rebecca*, p. 270); Captain Searle, in charge of raising the dead body from the sea, describes the corpse as 'dissolved, there was no flesh on it' (*Rebecca*, p. 275); the narrator speculates on how sea-water would 'rot' the body (thus merging Rebecca's corpse, appropriately, with that most ungovernable of all elements, the sea). Yet the narrator's final thoughts on Rebecca's body link it not with water, but with dust, and in so doing, associate Rebecca's 'second' burial (which seeks literally to encrypt her ungovernable force) with the end of Dracula, who crumbles to dust at the moment of 'death':

> Ashes to ashes. Dust to dust. It seemed to me that Rebecca had no reality any more. She had crumbled away when they had found her on the cabin floor. It was not Rebecca who was lying in the crypt, it was dust. Only dust.   (*Rebecca*, p. 334)[35]

The apparent finality of this state is, however, undercut by the earlier incident in which the narrator has 'finally' destroyed Rebecca's writing (the dedication in the book of poems), only to find it resurfacing again and again at Manderley. The 'dust' that is Rebecca's body is no more final than the 'feathers of dust' of the burned fly leaf or the ash scattered by the 'salt wind' of the novel's final line.

Interestingly, Rebecca is associated throughout the novel with several characteristics that traditionally denote the vampire: facial pallor, plentiful hair and voracious sexual appetite.[36] And like the vampire, she has to be 'killed' more than once. Indeed, in the plot's excessive, triple killing of Rebecca's body (she was shot; she had cancer; she drowned) and its final encryptment of her corpse, the novel offers both a conservative confirmation of gender values *and* a quasi-parodic version of patriarchy's abjection of the trans-gressive woman.[37] Although Rebecca lacks the requisite fangs and only metaphorically sucks men dry, she can nonetheless be placed within Christopher Frayling's second category of vampires, that of the Fatal Woman, a character whose textual genesis lies in the early nineteenth century. The Fatal Woman, according to Frayling, 'altered the whole direction of the vampire tale' from the mid-nineteenth century onwards; 'sexually aware, and sexually dominant...attractive and repellent at the same time',[38] she is clearly symptomatic of a cultural anxiety concerning adult female sexuality. Seen in this light, Rebecca's literary lineage includes not only Prosper Mérimée's Carmen, but characters such as Poe's Berenice, Gautier's Clarimonde, Le Fanu's Countess Carmilla and Crawford's Verspertilia (who, interestingly for our argument, is used as a metaphor for the creative process).[39] (Norman Collins, who wrote the reader's report on *Rebecca* for Victor Gollancz, drew comparisons between du Maurier's novel and Le Fanu's *Uncle Silas*, published in 1864, but failed to spot its relationship to his 'Carmilla'.[40]) It perhaps goes without saying that such fictional female characters always destroy the men who love them. In the context of culture and history Rebecca may, then, be read as a descendant of the *femme fatale* figure which originated during the nineteenth century and which transmuted into the female vampire in Gothic texts.[41] Like all vampire figures, she is associated with a polymorphous sexuality.

Rebecca's 'monstrous' nature is further inflected by the text's association of her with 'Jewishness'. As both Ken Gelder and Judith Halberstam have noted, the nineteenth-century vampire was often portrayed as having Jewish characteristics; indeed, Halberstam describes modern anti-semitism as 'Gothic' because it condenses various and diverse threats – political, economic and sexual – within the body of the Jew.[42] Rebecca was supposedly based on Jan Ricardo, a 'dark-haired, rather exotic young woman, beautiful but highly strung', according to Margaret Forster,[43] who was once engaged to Major 'Boy' Browning, Daphne du Maurier's husband. However, du Maurier's presentation of Maxim's first wife as a dangerous and beautiful dark-haired woman might well have been unconsciously influenced by the air of anti-semitism prevalent in Europe during the 1930s. It is interesting to note that David Selznick, the producer of Hitchcock's film version of *Rebecca*, is reputed to have had misgivings about the film's title, and to have commented that it would not do 'unless it was made for the Palestine market'.[44] Judith Halberstam argues that 'the nineteenth-century discourse of anti-Semitism and the myth of the vampire share a kind of Gothic economy in their ability to condense many monstrous traits into one body'.[45] We can see this myth and this discourse revived in the twentieth-century creation of Rebecca. Gothic monsters, suggests Halberstam, 'transform the fragments of otherness into one body'.[46] Many anxieties are written on the body of Rebecca.

Against such Gothic evocations of Rebecca as 'Other', however, her writing – as we see it, for example, in the loving dedication to 'Max' and the contents of the morning-room desk – signals not only her vibrant energy, but her ability, during her life, to play an allotted role within the realm of 'everyday legality' and to masquerade effectively as a country house hostess. Rebecca's writing initially appears to tell the tale of an ideal wife, loving towards her husband and the perfect hostess for his elegant country mansion. However, the script itself suggest a different story. The very first reference in the novel to Rebecca's writing indicates her power to name and to possess: only she calls Maxim 'Max' and this is what appears in the inscription on the flyleaf of the book. The narrator's reaction suggests that she is intimidated by the strong personality communicated by the handwriting and that through it she also intuits the power of writing itself. Later, installed at Manderley, the narrator finds herself at Rebecca's writing table:

> But this writing table, beautiful as it was, was no pretty toy where a woman would scribble little notes, nibbling the end of a pen... The pigeon-holes were docketed, 'letters answered', 'letters-to-keep', 'household', 'estate', 'menus', 'miscellaneous', 'addresses'; each ticket written in that same scrawling pointed hand that I knew already... She who sat here before me had not wasted her time, as I was doing... She would tear off sheet after sheet of that smooth white paper, using it extravagantly, because of the long strokes she made when she wrote, and at the end of each of her personal letters she put her signature, 'Rebecca', that tall sloping R dwarfing its fellows.   (*Rebecca*, pp. 90, 92–3)

Here, Rebecca's writing is proof of her efficiency (she runs Manderley like a business), appearing to reinforce the portrait of the ideal wife. Arguably, Rebecca is presented in the tradition of the 'chatelaine' (the word entered the English language in 1855 to mean the powerful mistress of a country house[47]); notwithstanding the mystery of her social background (see note 13), her lineage is clearly not that of the nineteenth-century dependent bourgeois wife. However, the semiotic of Rebecca's handwriting complicates our perception of her function in the novel. The household documents written by her signify both acceptance of a certain social role and the ability to carry it out with verve and sophistication. Yet the manner in which her writing continually irrupts into the text of the novel itself implies a wayward, wilful quality which runs counter to Maxim's idea of the good wife. It is this autonomous energy, implicit in Rebecca's writing, which impresses itself on both the narrator and the reader. Thus, there is a duality in Rebecca's writing, which seems to tell one story but which gives the lie to it in the actual appearance of the writing itself. The activity of writing, then, is seen to be implicated in the production of sexual subjectivity.

Rebecca's handwriting is frequently contrasted with that of the narrator, which is 'small' and 'square' with all the intimations of uniformity, immaturity and social inhibition that this suggests:

> as I wrote...I noticed for the first time how cramped and unformed was my own hand-writing; without individuality, without style, uneducated even, the writing of an indifferent pupil taught in a second-rate school.   (*Rebecca*, p. 93)

Yet it is this narrator, we are asked to believe, who writes the powerful tale of Rebecca; she can, however, only do so by modifying her perception of Rebecca as 'other' and assimilating some of that autonomy. Indeed, we learn at the beginning of the novel that the narrator *has* finally acquired the confidence for which she envied Rebecca as a young woman: 'and confidence is a quality I prize, although it has come to me a little late in the day' (*Rebecca*, p. 13).[48] The conclusion must be that only with Rebecca 'really' dead can she write Rebecca's story, although it is only *through* Rebecca that she can write. Significantly, then, in the final dream of the novel the narrator finds herself writing *as* Rebecca:

> I was writing letters in the morning-room. I was sending out invitations. I wrote them all myself with a thick black pen. But when I looked down to see what I had written it was not my small square handwriting at all, it was long, and slanting, with curious pointed strokes. I pushed the cards away from the blotter and hid them. I got up and went to the looking-glass. A face stared back at me that was not my own. It was very pale, very lovely, framed in a cloud of dark hair. The eyes narrowed and smiled. The lips parted. The face in the glass stared back at me

and laughed. And I saw then that she was sitting on a chair before the dressing-table in her bedroom and Maxim was brushing her hair. He held her hair in his hands, and as he brushed it he wound it slowly into a thick rope. It twisted like a snake, and he took hold of it with both hands and smiled at Rebecca and put it round his neck.

'No', I screamed. 'No. no....'   (*Rebecca*, pp. 395–6)

Whereas the firing of Manderley offers a plot closure which relates the 'story' of the novel to *Jane Eyre*, the dream perpetuates the psychic disruption which Rebecca signifies. It translates into vivid visual terms the buried metaphor of Rebecca's name which, deriving from the Hebrew and meaning 'knotted cord', indicates that – just as a knotted cord should hold firm – so should a woman with the name 'Rebecca' be a firm and faithful wife.[49] The image of the 'knotted cord', evoked also by the interwoven nature of Rebecca's monogram, takes on more negative connotations in the dream, in which Rebecca's hank of hair transmutes into both rope and snake. In a moment of nightmare surrealism, the rope becomes a hangman's noose about Maxim's neck, the comparison with the snake further actualizing Rebecca's sexual treachery and the nature of her threat to Manderley, already presented as a despoiled Eden in the narrator's dream of the novel's opening pages.

Although the narrator harbours a distrust and fear of Rebecca's sexuality, the dream reveals her unconscious identification *with* it. For much of the novel she has consciously wished to be the model wife and hostess she believed Rebecca to have been; yet the mirror image of the dream signals a desire for Rebecca's sexual and *textual* charisma. It is, however, this very charisma that disrupts conventional notions of gender and sexuality, its runic pattern creating a semiotic which disturbs and dislocates the reader's expectations. To some extent the fear and fascination that Rebecca's script holds for the narrator are inflected in the novel by various characters' suspicion of writing: against the importance of writing and script for Rebecca and the narrator (and Mrs Danvers), for example, we have Maxim's airy insistence that 'Writing letters is a waste of time' (*Rebecca*, p. 147), Colonel Julyan's worry that his son will insist on writing poetry (with the implication that he should have been the daughter), and Frank's assurance that he, too, wrote poetry when adolescent but grew out of it: ' "I never write any now" – "Good heavens, I should hope not", said Maxim' (*Rebecca*, p. 308).

Conversely, Mrs Danvers associates Rebecca's writing with her strength and authority, which are coupled with masculinity. Writing itself, then, can destabilize gender boundaries: it represents the threat of effeminacy for men in du Maurier's fictional world, but is associated with strength for women, a strength connected with power, knowledge and visibility (the indelible presence) all of which connote masculinity within the culture of England in the 1930s. The fear and fascination which Rebecca's script holds for the narrator derives from her sense that there are secrets underlying it which might call into question Rebecca's role as the dutiful wife. At some intuitive level, she understands the element of masquerade in social identity.

The Manderley Ball episode foregrounds the concern with masquerade which permeates the novel. In attempting to mimic the apogee of Rebecca's success as society hostess, the narrator finds herself unwittingly caught up in a pretence which provokes a Bluebeard-like anger in Maxim. The costume suggestions that characters make to the narrator – Maxim that she appear as Alice in Wonderland, Lady Crowan that she dress as 'a little Dresden shepherdess' (*Rebecca*, p. 201) and Frank Crawley that she come as Joan of Arc – are significant. They construct her respectively as child-like, pastorally 'pure' and full of virginal integrity; they also indicate an idealized femininity through which the narrator is encouraged to structure her adult female sexuality. Interestingly, costumes chosen by characters other than the narrator are so inappropriate as to suggest that the act of 'dressing-up' also functions as a safe accommodation of what would otherwise be transgressive desire: Giles arrives clothed as an Arabian sheik, Beatrice accompanying him in 'some sort of Eastern get-up'; the utterly conventional Frank Crawley appears in a pirate outfit and that embodiment of conservatism, Colonel Julyan, comes as Cromwell (*Rebecca*, pp. 217, 218 and 306). The narrator, of course, is persuaded by Mrs Danvers that she should appear dressed as one of Maxim's ancestors, Caroline de Winter, 'a sister of Maxim's great-great-grandfather' (*Rebecca*, p. 212), whose portrait is hung in the minstrel's gallery. The picture, by Raeburn, shows a young woman who had been 'a famous London beauty for many years' before her marriage to 'a great Whig politician' (*Rebecca*, p. 212). The subject has beautiful curly hair and her dress is white and has puffed sleeves, a flounce and a small bodice. This becomes the choice of costume for the narrator, for whom it seems to offer a transformation into a beauty and virginal femininity which she thinks Maxim will find irresistible:

> I thought of the soft white dress in its folds of tissue paper, and how it would hide my flat dull figure, my rather sloping shoulders. I thought of my own lank hair covered by the sleek and gleaming curls.   *(Rebecca,* p. 219)

The narrator constructs her transformation as a 'secret' which will delight and surprise Maxim, unaware that the real secret of Manderley, still hidden from her, will render its effect precisely the opposite of that desired. She locks her bedroom door against Maxim whilst dressing and delights in the 'mysterious' rustling sound of tissue paper; she and Clarice talk softly 'like conspirators' and indulge in 'little furtive bursts of laughter' *(Rebecca,* p. 220). Fully costumed, she sees a stranger in the mirror:

> I did not recognize the face that stared at me in the glass. The eyes were larger surely, the mouth narrower, the skin white and clear? The curls stood away from the head in a little cloud. I watched this self that was not me at all and then smiled; a new, slow smile.   *(Rebecca,* p. 221)

Yet the reader knows that this is no stranger. This is Rebecca, who is constantly associated, by the narrator and other characters, with a pale skin and a 'cloud' of hair, the Rebecca who is to appear as the narrator's mirror image in the dream at the novel's end. As readers, then, we can anticipate Maxim's reaction, even before we learn, through the narrator's wretched disappointment, that Rebecca's great triumph was to appear dressed in that very costume at her last Manderley ball.

A sentimental reading of the novel construes Maxim's anger as an expression of his pain on being reminded of past unhappiness and betrayals. However, Rebecca dressed as Miss Caroline de Winter signifies something very different from the narrator dressed as Miss Caroline de Winter. When Rebecca masquerades as Maxim's ancestor, wearing her white dress, she 'puts on' the purity of the virginal young lady, indicating how, more generally, she employs masquerade 'both to hide the possession of a masculinity and to avoid the reprisals expected if she was found to possess it', in Joan Riviere's words.[50] She also uses it to 'disguise bisexual possibilities that otherwise might disrupt the seamless construction of a heterosexualized femininity'.[51] Moreover, the costume allows her to assume, through mimicry, a 'legitimate' place in the de Winter household, foreshadowing her supposed future role as a bearer of Maxim's sons, the inheritors of the Manderley estate. She is thus signalled as the instrument through which the continuation of the patriarchal line is ensured (we have already learnt, through Mrs van Hopper, that Manderley has been 'in his family's possession since the Conquest' [*Rebecca*, p. 19]). Yet, as we have seen, Rebecca's actual behaviour subverts both the patriarchal line and cultural notions of the proper lady. But that secret belongs to her and to Maxim: her appearance at the Manderley Ball as Caroline de Winter is remembered by the local community as a triumph, thus confirming Rebecca's ability to undermine codes of gendered behaviour from within the established order. When the narrator wears the costume, however, the effect is very different. Her lack of knowledge and her innocence (she constantly refers to herself as feeling 'like a child' [*Rebecca*, p. 220] during the episode) signal an ingenuous embrace of what the costume represents – the masquerade of femininity itself. Her overwhelming desire is to please and surprise Maxim by 'dressing up'; she wishes, at this stage, only to delight as object of the male gaze. In that sense, she symbolically enacts what Luce Irigaray defines as women's 'exile from themselves' in the pursuit of 'femininity':

> I think the masquerade has to be understood as what women do in order to recuperate some element of desire, to participate in man's desire, but at the price of renouncing their own. In the masquerade, they submit to the dominant economy of desire in an attempt to remain 'on the market' in spite of everything. But they are there as objects for sexual enjoyment, not as those who enjoy.
>
> What do I mean by masquerade? In particular, what Freud calls 'femininity'. The belief, for example, that it is necessary to *become* a woman, a 'normal' one at that, whereas a man is a man from the outset. He has only to effect his being-a-man, whereas a woman has to become a normal woman, that is, has to enter into the *masquerade of femininity*. In the last analysis, the female Oedipal complex is woman's entry into a system of values that is not hers, and in which she can 'appear' and circulate only when enveloped in the needs/desires/fantasies of others, namely, men.[52]

In dressing as Caroline de Winter, the narrator hopes to please Maxim and further exorcise, or 'blot out' (*Rebecca*, p. 43) the spectre of his dead wife. Ironically, in doing so, she raises Rebecca from the dead with a physical exactitude that is breath-taking (even the sensible Beatrice says 'You stood there on the stairs, and for one ghastly moment I thought...' [*Rebecca*, p. 225]). In this episode, then, du Maurier uses the classic Gothic trope of the portrait 'coming to life', first seen in Walpole's *The Castle of Otranto*, and revived to great effect in works such as Lewis's *The Monk*, J. Sheridan Le Fanu's 'Carmilla' and Wilde's *The Picture of Dorian Grey*. The trope is given a final, ironic twist when, on hearing of Maxim's murder of his 'vicious, damnable' (*Rebecca*, p. 283) wife, the narrator uses the language of portraiture (by now associated with masquerade and deception) to express her sense of reaching the 'truth': 'the real Rebecca took shape and form before me, stepping from her shadow world like a living figure from a picture frame' (*Rebecca*, p. 284). The instability of the portrait's 'meaning', like that of Rebecca's handwriting, thus acts as a signifier of Woman who functions, within patriarchal society, 'as an inessential figure (a disembodied sign without a referent) and as the site of uncanny ambivalence ("Unheimlichkeit")'.[53]

The Manderley Ball provides only one of several key moments in the text when we see a merging of Rebecca and the narrator. In many Gothic novels which feature a double, the plot, whilst being superficially resolved by the death of the second 'self', often presents the narrator as still haunted by the doppelgänger figure (as in, for example, Hogg's *Confessions of a Justified Sinner*). The opening of *Rebecca* shows us an older and a somewhat melancholic narrator, but one empowered by her 'double' and who, far from being haunted, now exudes an understanding of herself and the world about her which has given her strength and self-confidence. The knowledge she craved, it seems, has come to her through marriage – not through Maxim, but through Rebecca. The strange midwife to this transformation, however, is Mrs Danvers, du Maurier's strikingly original addition to the Bluebeard plot. Presented, on the one hand, as a highly efficient housekeeper within the realist mode and on the other as a Gothic Life-in-Death figure (much reference is made to her skeletal appearance and she is always dressed in black), she appears as a quasi-parodic version of Nelly Dean. She is also a grotesquely reductive version of Rebecca, whose pale complexion and skills of household management are embodied in this strange woman who has all the appearance of a revenant. Mrs Danvers is a sinister character suggestive of liminality, transition and the instability of boundaries. The housekeeper is a key figure in the world of the country house, mediating between the social spheres of 'upstairs' and 'downstairs'; in *Rebecca*, Mrs Danvers is also the mediator between the opposing worlds of transgression/conformity, life/death and even 'masculine'/'feminine' (she applauds Rebecca's 'masculine' characteristics and the narrator, upon being telephoned by her, is not sure whether she is listening to a man or a woman, since Mrs. Danvers' voice is 'low and rather harsh' [*Rebecca*, p. 91]). Above all, it is Mrs Danvers who brings Rebecca 'to life' for the narrator, with her constant reference to the 'real' Mrs de Winter and her continual comparisons between Maxim's two wives. In persuading the narrator to dress as Caroline de Winter, she not only endangers the second wife's marriage, but 're-creates' Rebecca at her moment of triumph. Her surveillance of Maxim's new bride (who feels as if she is being continually watched by the housekeeper's dark eyes, sometimes overtly, sometimes secretly, 'her eye to a crack in the door' [*Rebecca*, p. 97]) recalls Madame Beck's surveillance of Lucy Snowe in Charlotte Brontë's *Villette*. In many ways a witch-like figure (the narrator refers at one point to 'playing "Old Witch" with Mrs Danvers', who later arrives to face Colonel Julyan's questioning looking 'shrunken now in size, more wizened' [*Rebecca*, pp. 184 and 355]), she casts a spell over the young wife so as to draw her into the recreation of her dead mistress: 'I feel her everywhere. You do too, don't you?' she says to the frightened young woman (*Rebecca*, p. 181). When Mrs Danvers shows her Rebecca's room in the West Wing, the narrator feels 'like a dumb thing' unable to resist the housekeeper (*Rebecca*, p. 176). Whilst continually pointing out her difference *from* Rebecca, it is Mrs Danvers who draws the narrator into an identification *with* the dead wife. Examples of this abound: in the quasi-erotic scene in which Mrs Danvers displays Rebecca's clothes to the narrator, the young wife is continually urged to touch them and hold them against her own body; the conversation with Mrs Danvers concerning her costume for the Manderley Ball prefaces a scene in which the narrator strangely 'becomes' Rebecca at dinner ('I had so identified myself with Rebecca that my own dull self did not exist' [*Rebecca*, p. 209]); it is Mrs Danvers who orchestrates the narrator's appearance *as* Caroline de Winter/Rebecca; the morning after the fiasco, following an hysterical outburst about her dead mistress, Mrs Danvers tries to seduce the narrator into death itself, almost as if trying to effect a diabolic exchange between the dead and the living: 'It's you that's the shadow and the ghost' she tells the narrator, 'It's you that ought to be lying there in the church crypt, not her' (*Rebecca*, p. 257). The narrator almost capitulates to this notion of herself as a (lesser) aspect of Rebecca ('I should never be rid of Rebecca. Perhaps I haunted her as she haunted me...She was too strong for me' [*Rebecca*, p. 244]).

We noted early in this chapter how Maxim is associated, in the spirit of Bluebeard, with the 'locking up' of knowledge from the narrator. Significantly, Mrs Danvers is both a literal and a metaphorical 'keeper of the keys'. As housekeeper she actually carries a large bunch of keys and refers several times to her ability to unlock rooms within Manderley, the narrator perceiving her 'as though she were a warder, and I in custody' (*Rebecca*, p. 96). Near the end of the novel, in a strange reversal of the usual Manderley hierarchy, Maxim actually asks Mrs Danvers to lock both him and the narrator in their bedroom until the morning, in order to placate Jack Favell, who is concerned that Maxim might 'do a bolt in the night' (*Rebecca*, p. 366) before the trip to London with Colonel Julyan. As 'keeper of the keys', then, Mrs Danvers is, in many ways, a more potent figure than Maxim. She functions as the guardian of the threshold which the narrator must cross in order to reach 'knowledge'; whereas Maxim bars access to Rebecca, Mrs Danvers invites it. This the narrator half intuits: 'She was not dead, like Rebecca. I could speak to her, but I could not speak to Rebecca' (*Rebecca*, p. 251). But that 'knowledge' is not, of course, a simple duplication of Maxim's point of view, constructed from the perspective of the male subject, and one which renders Rebecca as 'evil'. Mrs Danvers, after all, 'adored' Rebecca according to Beatrice and, if Jack Favell is to be believed, became her 'personal friend' (*Rebecca*, pp. 107 and 354). Indeed, there are times when Mrs Danvers herself appears as an aspect of Rebecca: both women are associated with white and black (although the latter is also linked with the colour red) and Rebecca uses the name 'Mrs Danvers' when visiting the consultant in London. Through her ability to almost hypnotize the narrator, Mrs Danvers is associated, as is Rebecca, with 'Jewishness', since nineteenth-century culture frequently represented the Jew as having powers of mesmerism (again, the classic example is Svengali). She functions, therefore, as a figure of liminality who disturbs through her ability to enact the blurring of boundaries. Not only does she blur the boundaries between life/death, respectability/transgression, she also blurs the boundaries of sexual identity itself, making indistinct the cultural lines drawn between masculinity, femininity, heterosexuality, homosexuality and bisexuality. Hence her own uncanniness for, in Shoshana Felman's words, 'what is perhaps most uncanny about the uncanny is that it is not the opposite of what is canny but, rather, that which uncannily *subverts the opposition* between "canny" and "uncanny", between "heimlich" and "unheimlich"'.[54] In unlocking the door to Rebecca, she – far more than Maxim's revelation of the murder – moves the narrator on from her state of naivety. In that sense, the relationship between the three women in the text is more important than the narrator's relationship with Maxim, who indeed appears to many readers as a mere cipher. In making Rebecca 'come to life', Mrs Danvers does not simply reiterate the community's sense of her as a beautiful society 'lady'. Instead, she presents her as a complicated amalgam of gender attributes. On the one hand, she emphasizes her beauty, sensuality and femininity by endowing her fine clothes with a metonymic significance. On the other hand, she stresses Rebecca's power and masculinity, drawing attention not to the 'cloud' of dark hair down to her waist with which other characters associate her, but to the boyish 'crop' she sported in the last few years of her life. What she loved in Rebecca, it seems, was her strength, her courage and her 'spirit', which she associates with masculinity: 'She ought to have been a boy, I often told her that' (*Rebecca*, p. 253). Through Mrs Danvers, we see Rebecca not simply as a 'transgressive' woman, but as one whose desire to please herself entailed refusing to take either romantic love or heterosexual desire seriously ('it was like a game to her' [*Rebecca*, p. 256]). Through Mrs Danvers, then, both reader and narrator perceive Rebecca as a character who rejects cultural definitions of femininity (although able to enact them through masquerade when it suits her) and whose sexual identity is complex and multi-faceted. Mrs Danvers' version of Rebecca thus radically destabilizes Maxim's one-dimensional portrait of his first wife.

We can never know, of course, the 'real' Rebecca: such knowledge is inaccessible, since Rebecca herself is a textual creation constructed as mystery. Indeed, the suspended 'R' of her name and the quasi-illegible 'M' in her engagement diary, by constituting a semiotic of fragmentation and incompleteness within the text, indicate as much. Moreover, the transition from naivety to knowledge on the part of the narrator implies an authorial awareness that sexual identity can never be fully 'known', since it is neither a given, nor a static, state. The opening of the novel shows us a narrator who now realizes that identity continually refashions itself. Seeing herself in a cracked mirror, she believes at one minute that she sees her 'self', 'suspended as it were, in time; this is me, this moment will not pass' but then realizes that this is an illusion, that the 'self' is, in effect, continually in process:

> I say to myself – I am not she who left him five minutes ago. She stayed behind. I am another woman, older, more mature.
>
> (*Rebecca,* p. 49)

The older narrator of *Rebecca* now embraces a far more complex sense of what identity is, and inscribes, through her tale, the complicated matrix of identity that Rebecca represents.

A final, close look at the novel makes us aware that the narrator's identity is also more complex than it might first appear: her representation of herself as committed to romantic, heterosexual love is fissured from the start. For if we accept the iconic significance of rhododendrons and roses in the novel, then we ought to accept that of 'the tiny statue of the naked faun, his pipes to his lips' standing in a clearing made in the rhododendrons which mass against the morning-room window (*Rebecca,* p. 89). The narrator perceives this clearing as 'a little stage, where he would dance and play his part' (*Rebecca,* p. 89). This diminutive figure is, it seems, emblematic of masculinity which, through the words 'stage' and 'part', is also associated with artifice and masquerade. This 'faun' transmutes into a satyr – culturally associated far more closely with licence and male sexuality – by the end of the novel. (Interestingly, in the earlier work, *Julius,* Rachel's awareness of her husband's desire for their daughter translates itself into a perception of him as a satyr.) During their dinner in Soho, before making the trip back to Manderley, the narrator, in planning the changes she will make to the house in the future, thinks: 'That little square lawn outside the morning-room with the statue of the satyr. I did not like it. We would give the satyr away' (*Rebecca,* p. 392). This distaste corresponds to her revulsion from Jack Favell, Rebecca's cousin and lover, whose leering appreciation of the narrator makes her angry and embarrassed. However, in a newspaper report which describes the finding of Rebecca's body, Maxim himself is more directly linked with the mythological figure: 'Maxim sounded vile in it, a sort of satyr' (*Rebecca*, p. 315). There is here an interesting narratorial ambivalence towards male sexuality which we can relate to the narrator's occasional expression of ambivalence towards her marriage. We learn, for example, that she enjoys being on her own and experiences a 'lightness of heart' when Maxim is away (about which she afterwards feels guilty); also that, the evening before the Manderley Ball, she feels much as she did on the morning of her marriage: 'The same stifled feeling that I had gone too far now to turn back' (*Rebecca*, p. 214). These reactions to marriage and male sexuality indicate a sceptical attitude to the fantasies of women's romantic fiction which the narrator, an avid reader of such work, does not overtly admit to herself. Her decision to get rid of the satyr signals an attempt to exorcise what Favell represents; her intuitive understanding of the phallic threat metaphorically embodied in the statue also indicates an awareness that women's romantic fiction does not tell the whole story. As Alison Light notes, *Rebecca* is 'the absent subtext of much romance fiction, the crime behind the scenes of Mills and Boon'.[55] Perhaps the smashing of the cupid ornament was not such an accident after all.

It is possible, of course, to read these ambiguities and tensions within *Rebecca* in relation to biography. Du Maurier, who possessed a boat of her own from the age of twenty-one, arguably projected her restlessness and love of the sea and sailing onto Rebecca, just as she had given them to the character of Janet Coombe in *The Loving Spirit*. Futhermore, Margaret Forster's reading of du Maurier's life as one of repressed desire for other women can be used to interpret *Rebecca* as a novel which offers an anti-heroine who is more attractive than the supposed male object of desire. Such readings, however, fold the novel back into biography and carry the danger of collapsing the instability of Rebecca as sign into biographical speculation concerning du Maurier's 'real' sexual identity. A more fruitful approach is to contemplate the values negotiated over Rebecca's (dead) body. Read superficially, the novel seems to re-establish a cultural order temporarily threatened by the will of a beautiful woman. Yet we see in the opening section of the novel that the narrator herself has not 'abjected' the figure of Rebecca; rather, in accommodating aspects of Rebecca, she has become – like du Maurier herself – a user and controller of signs. This is indicated both by her writing and by the fact that she now reads aloud to

Maxim, who has presumably, like Rochester, been blinded in the fire.[56] She has, moreover, moved beyond her early dreams of romantic love and motherhood. The relationship between the older narrator and Maxim, in exile abroad, is curiously dull and passionless, particularly when compared with the possibilities suggested by Rebecca's sexual energy. The de Winter line, it seems, will come to an end with Maxim, despite the younger narrator's hope that 'We would have children. Surely we would have children' (*Rebecca*, p. 392). This narrator now relates the tale of her love for Maxim de Winter and, recalling her 'dreams', overlays her story with a Gothic patina so as to expose a deep ambivalence about romantic love, heterosexuality and Manderley itself (a place in which she was never at ease, despite her husband's love of it[57]). Claiming that she and Maxim now 'have no secrets from one another' (*Rebecca*, p. 9), the narrator tells a tale which holds the most mysterious 'secret' of all: the nature of female identity. Thus the narrator has no name we can call her own.

Rebecca, that 'perfect figure for negative (female) identity', whose name continually inscribes itself on the reader's imagination, extends the boundaries of identity for the narrator whilst seeming simultaneously to threaten them. Unlike Trilby, who can change into a powerful female presence only through Svengali's manipulation of her, Rebecca's ability to metamorphose and masquerade is her own. Whereas her grandfather's famous novel constructs the mid-Victorian woman's infinite capacity to change as a threat to the men about her,[58] Daphne du Maurier's novel offers a character whose autonomy is both threatening and liberating for the narrator. As her dark double, Rebecca moves from functioning simply as a binary opposite of the second wife's character, to indicating the multiple possibilities inherent in female sexual identity. Thus the element of lesbian desire in the text (commented on by several critics[59]) does not necessarily indicate the 'true' sexual identity of Rebecca (nor that of the narrator nor that of the author). Rather, Mrs Danvers' love for Rebecca and Rebecca's own diverse sexuality function to destabilize the heterosexual desire which drives the plot and which the text (read as women's romantic fiction) seems overtly to celebrate. The triangle of Rebecca, Maxim and the narrator can bear, in interpretative terms, a multiplicity of desires: those of the family romance; the father/daughter romance; incestuous desire; lesbian desire; bisexual desire; heterosexual desire. Similarly Rebecca herself manifests a dynamic multivalent negative alterity: she is whore, lesbian, bisexual, vampire, Jew.[60] The fact that 'Jewishness' and vampirism are almost literally written on Rebecca's body indicates the essential Gothic quality of the novel; for perverse sexuality, in the Gothic, is inevitably 'ascribed to the sexuality of the Other'.[61] Rebecca, like Mr. Hyde, represents 'a composite of a range of alternative identities, identities that...subvert...the unity of the self'. Given the monstrous multiplicity contained by the idea of femininity within the twentieth century, identity itself becomes uncanny, the 'self' haunted by manifold other possible identities.[62] Excess of meaning in the text signifies a fearful plethora of identities within modernity. However, in assimilating aspects of Rebecca, the narrator implicitly rejects the social categorizations which separate the 'bad' from the 'good' woman. 'The doubled subject split between desire and respectability identifies power as the ability to be "radically both"', writes Judith Halberstam.[63] Arguably, this is precisely what the narrator finally achieves. In assimilating the 'disembodied spirit' of Maxim's first wife, the narrator comes to embody aspects of Rebecca's power and confidence. Above all, she writes, and with the maturity and adult sexual identity implied by Rebecca's cursive script rather than with the childish ingenuousness of her former self. In Chapter One we saw how, in letters to friends du Maurier identified, at different points in her life, with both Rebecca and the narrator. Her letters reveal that, having read Jung in the 1950s, she came to identify her creative writing persona with a 'No.2' masculine 'self'. This sense of the writing self as masculine 'Other' can be seen in the inscription of Rebecca's 'masculine' energy through 'those curious, sloping letters' that continually surface in du Maurier's most famous novel, a text in which the transgressions of the 'Other' are both written on the body and are literally embodied in the writing process itself.[64] As we have seen, du Maurier's letters suggest that she moved towards seeing identity as something complex, multiform and fissured, rather than unitary and coherent. Arguably, the writing process itself provided du Maurier with a way of manipulating such multiplicity and of harnessing the potentially destructive aspect of the 'Other' – as it does for the narrator of *Rebecca*. Gothic fiction, as Judith Halberstam notes, 'produces monstrosity as a technology of sexuality, identity and narrative'.[65] In this light, Rebecca can be read as another manifestation of the 'boy-in-the-box': her death within the plot suggests the containment of desire but her 'disembodied spirit', with all its divergent energies, continues to inform the writing process itself. *Rebecca* is the forbidden book for which the narrator was always looking, and which she writes eventually, herself.

5

Foreign Affairs

The two major novels of the 1950s, *My Cousin Rachel* (1951) and *The Scapegoat* (1957), in spite of their differences in setting and period, do have significant similarities. Although the former is an historical novel set in the Cornwall of the early nineteenth century and *The Scapegoat* is set in contemporary rural France, both are first person narratives and in each case the narrator is a man; thus du Maurier in the 1950s reverts to the male narrative persona with which she had experimented in the early novel, *I'll Never be Young Again*. In both novels, too, the notion of 'foreignness' is used to explore divisions within the subject. This is represented in the first novel by the half-Cornish, half-Italian Rachel who is culturally more akin to her Italian mother than her Cornish father. In the second the representation is much more complex as the narrator, John, finds himself the foreigner in a French context where he has unwillingly changed identities with his French double, Jean de Gué. *My Cousin Rachel* echoes both *Rebecca* and *The King's General* in exploring identity through a triangulated relationship, in this case between the narrator (a young man called Philip Ashley), his dead cousin Ambrose and Ambrose's widow, Rachel. In *The Scapegoat*, however, the Gothic trope of doubling, already hinted at in earlier novels, is foregrounded and John, in taking the place of his double, has to negotiate his way through several difficult familial relationships and confront a range of different versions of himself. In both these novels of the 1950s, the adoption of a male narrative persona not only enables du Maurier to explore that masculine side of herself which she had described as 'the boy in the box' but also to explore the fragility of masculinity itself.

'NIGHTMÈRE': *MY COUSIN RACHEL*

My Cousin Rachel was an instant best-seller, described by Victor Gollancz as 'du Maurier bang on form' and selling more in its first year than even *Rebecca*.[1] From du Maurier's own account, the creative drive behind the novel came from her obsessional relationships with

Gertrude Lawrence and Ellen Doubleday. She had already experimented with a further fictional representation of the masculine side of herself in *The Parasites* (1949), a novel about a theatrical family narrated by three siblings (Maria, Celia and Niall) in a manner which indicates that they are three facets of the same psyche. In 1957 she was to write to Maureen Baker-Munton a letter remarkable for its rigorous attempt at self-analysis. Her account of the genesis of *My Cousin Rachel* is worth quoting at length:

> during all those years from '47 to '52, I was neglecting Moper because I was trying to work out the problem of Niall. I had let him swim out to sea once, but the book did not say if he was drowned, and I did not know either. He was not drowned. He came to life again as Philip Ashley in *My Cousin Rachel*, and here I was identifying myself with my boyish love for my father, and my boyish affection for old Nelson Doubleday, and suddenly was overwhelmed with an obsessional passion for the last of Daddy's actress loves – Gertrude – and the wife of Nelson, Ellen. They merged to make the single figure of Rachel, and I did not know if this figure was killing me or not, or if it had killed my father and Nelson. The symbol behind the living woman can either be the Healer, or the Destroyer. In the book I killed both, and Philip Ashley was left to his solitude in his Mena.[2]

Here du Maurier seems to recognize that what she called 'the masculine side' of herself derived from a close identification with her father. This identification, she now realizes, had led her in middle age into 'the obsessional passion' for Gertrude and Ellen. Others have later construed this passion as lesbian desire. Elsewhere, du Maurier describes both Ellen and Gertrude as 'pegs', real people who become invested with significance and used creatively in fiction.[3] Therefore, although it is possible to read the letter to Maureen Baker-Munton as an account of the therapeutic effect of writing the novel, it is equally possible to see du Maurier's relationships with Ellen and Gertrude as part of a process which fed her creative life and moved her into a different phase of her writing career. *My Cousin Rachel* was, she claimed, 'the most *emotionally-felt* book' she had ever written.[4] In contrast with *The Parasites*, *My Cousin Rachel* once again takes up the Gothic mode; its Gothic elements make it more intriguing and more dynamic than the earlier novel and contributed to its success.

My Cousin Rachel was to be the last of du Maurier's 'Menabilly' novels; indeed as we have already noted (see Chapter 3), she still thought in the early 1960s it was the last of her Cornish novels. Although its setting is an unnamed house and estate in Cornwall, it is clear from the letter to Maureen Baker-Munton that du Maurier thought of it as Menabilly. The name of the narrator, Philip Ashley, is a close adaptation of the family name of Menabilly's owners, the Rashleighs, Philip being a common Christian name among them. The topographical features of the Ashley estate, described in some detail, correspond exactly to those of Menabilly and, in contrast with *Rebecca*, there are some real place names, such as Bodmin and Lostwithiel. As in both *Rebecca* and *The King's General*, Menabilly is the site of threat wherein apparent stable established values, enshrined in the house and estate, are seen to be in danger. As in *Rebecca*, the threat is embodied in the figure of a woman. Maxim kills Rebecca because she taunts him with the prospect of another man's son inheriting Manderley and hence breaking the de Winter patriarchal line; Philip, besotted by his dead cousin's widow (the Rachel of the title) willingly hands over his patrimony to her and retrieves it only by knowingly allowing her to go to her death. Whereas the narrator of *Rebecca* changes her image of Rebecca at a certain point in the novel from that of an ideal wife to that of a reviled wicked woman, Philip vacillates in his perceptions of Rachel and the novel ends on a note of uncertainty. Is she a Borgia-like monster who demonstrates the worst of 'feminine' evil that patriarchy can imagine: a wanton profligate who has poisoned her husband? Or is she an innocent and maligned widow, a victim, albeit one who is trying to protect her own interests? The first person narrative viewpoint is tightly controlled so that the reader must attempt to read Rachel through the eyes of Philip Ashley, a young and inexperienced man, aware that his judgement is unreliable.

Du Maurier's return to a male narrative persona in *My Cousin Rachel* signalled a return to a narrative strategy which was to be repeated in the later novels, *The Scapegoat*, *The Flight of the Falcon* and *The House on the Strand*. Du Maurier herself saw these male narrators (along with Dick in *I'll Never be Young Again*) as incarnations of her childhood alter ego, Eric Avon. She comments in *Enchanted Cornwall*:

Philip himself owes much to Eric Avon, a splendid character I invented for myself in early adolescence . . . Eric re-emerged in

different guises as the narrator of five novels I was to write at
long intervals, in the first person, masculine gender...None
resembled Eric very closely, but like him all five personalities
can be seen to be undeveloped, inadequate in some way.
(*Enchanted Cornwall*, p.153)

In *My Cousin Rachel*, as in *Rebecca*, the narrator's older self does not,
after the opening chapters, mediate between the reader and the
younger self of the story. The reader must read between the lines.
The Philip of the story is a young man in his early twenties who
has had a rather unusual upbringing. Orphaned at an early age, he
has been cared for by his cousin Ambrose in an exclusively male
household (Ambrose had dismissed Philip's nurse when he was
three). Philip has absorbed the mild-tempered misogyny of his
cousin ('And now sit back in your chairs and be comfortable,
gentlemen. As there is no woman in the house we can put our
boots on the table and spit on the carpet').[5] Indeed du Maurier
herself refers in *Enchanted Cornwall* to the 'gentlemanly misogyny'
of the Ashley household.[6] The potential dangers of such an
upbringing are identified by Philip's godfather, Nick Kendall,
when he says to Philip: 'There should have been someone in the
house, a housekeeper, a distant relative, anyone. You have grown
up ignorant of women, and if you marry it will be hard on your
wife' (*Cousin Rachel*, p.53). The Ashley household, therefore, has
been a microcosmic if extreme version of the homosocial world
which constructs and shores up masculinity: the encounter with
Rachel is for Philip (as it has indeed been for Ambrose) an
encounter with an unknown 'other'. This novel defamiliarizes femininity for the female reader (as indeed it may have done for the
writer, hence its claimed therapeutic effect); it represents it from
the perspective of a masculinity which has been constructed upon
the exclusion of women. In order to do this, the text presents
Rachel's 'foreignness' as a literal foreignness, her Italian identity,
but a foreignness which is itself inherently ambiguous. For Rachel
is both 'same' (her father was Alexander Coryn of Cornwall, and a
cousin of the Ashleys) and 'other', child of an Italian mother.
Philip's ambivalence about Rachel is summed up in these terms
at the very end of the novel:

I looked on her in profile. She was always a stranger, thus. Those
neat clipped features on a coin. Dark and withdrawn, a foreign

woman standing in a doorway, a shawl about her head, her hand outstretched. But full-face, when she smiled a stranger never. The Rachel that I knew, that I had loved.   (*Cousin Rachel*, p.295)

The plot of the novel is set in motion by the marriage of Philip's cousin Ambrose to Rachel. It comes as a dreadful shock to Philip to find that Ambrose (sent to Italy during the winters for the good of his health) has married his distant cousin, the Contessa Sangaletti, finding her the exception to the rule: 'She is extremely intelligent but, thank the Lord, knows when to hold her tongue. None of that endless yattering so common in women' (*Cousin Rachel*, p.17). Philip's visit to Italy in response to subsequent anguished letters sent by Ambrose (in which he confides his suspicions that Rachel is trying to poison him) confronts him with the 'otherness' of Italy. He notes that 'the valleys were baked brown, and the little villages hung parched and yellow on the hills with the haze of heat upon them' and sees the Arno as 'a slow moving turgid stream' in comparison with the 'blue estuary' of home (*Cousin Rachel*, pp. 20 and 30). He is most struck, however, by a beggar woman who seems to embody the soul of this ancient and alien civilization:

> She was young, not more than nineteen or so, but the expression on her face was ageless, haunting, as though she possessed in her lithe body an old soul that could not die; centuries in time looked out from those two eyes, she had contemplated life so long it had become indifferent to her.   (*Cousin Rachel*, p.30)

Recent theoretical work enables a rethinking of the conflation of individual and national identity. Julia Kristeva in her recent *Strangers to Ourselves* (1991) uses the figure of the outsider to investigate issues of identity, establishing in this book the implicit links between the abjection she had explored in *Powers of Horror* and the way in which we experience foreignness:

> In the fascinated rejection that a foreigner arouses in us, there is a share of uncanny strangeness in the sense of the depersonaliza-tion that Freud discovered in it, and which takes up again our infantile desires and fears of the other – the other of death, the other of woman, the other of uncontrollable drive. The foreigner is within us.[7]

My Cousin Rachel initially enacts such a fascinated rejection of the foreignness embodied for Philip by Rachel. Before he meets her is obsessed by her image, an image which is compounded by his visit to Italy. He thinks of her as old and is shocked when he meets her to find a woman in her thirties; at a much later stage in the novel however his early association of Rachel with the ancient knowledge of Italy is powerfully reinforced when, in delirium, he 'sees' her as the beggar girl. In Philip's mind such knowledge is feared as sinister, a perception which is reinforced by the recurrent motif of poison. Called to Italy by Ambrose's fear that he is being poisoned, he describes the Arno as, 'something to be tasted, swallowed, poured down the throat as one might pour a draught of poison' (*Cousin Rachel*, p.30). Much later, after a nearly fatal illness and fearing himself poisoned, he remembers Rachel's explanation of her knowledge of herbs: 'I learnt them from my mother... We are very old and wise, who come from Florence' (*Cousin Rachel*, p.262).

The novel's use of Italy and the Italian also creates a powerful echo of earlier Gothic novels – Ann Radcliffe's *The Italian* is an obvious example. In the same way that the early chapters of *Rebecca* signal to the reader the Gothic quality of the text (the narrator describes Maxim as looking 'medieval in some strange inexplicable way', for example [*Rebecca*, 18]), the opening chapters of *My Cousin Rachel* create a sense of Gothic mystery in contrast with the descriptions of domestic life in early nineteenth-century Cornwall. When Philip reaches the Villa Sangaletti, its interior is described in a manner which offers an inventory of Gothic features:

> The rooms all led into each other, large and sparse, with frescoed ceilings and stone floors, and the air was heavy with a medieval musty smell. In some of the rooms the walls were plain, in others tapestried, and in one, darker and more oppressive than the rest, there was a long refectory table flanked with carved monastic chairs, and great wrought-iron candlesticks stood at either end.
>
> (*Cousin Rachel*, p.34)

The religious connotations of this description create an atmosphere of the typical Gothic setting of a religious house, even though there is no further evidence that the Villa Sangaletti has been one. The same effect is created by the room where Ambrose died which is described as being 'bare like a monk's cell'.

> (*Cousin Rachel*, p.36)

Philip's encounter with Rachel's friend and lawyer, Rainaldi, also gives us a portrait of a figure from Gothic fiction. He has 'a pale, almost colourless face, and lean aquiline features' and 'something proud and disdainful about his cast of countenance like that of someone who would have small mercy for fools, or for his enemies'. Philip most notices his eyes 'dark and deep-set' (*Cousin Rachel*, p.42). Rainaldi is set up as a potential Gothic villain ('Was it my fancy, or did a veiled look come over those dark eyes?' [*Cousin Rachel*, p.43]). These observations, of course, are Philip's and he is predisposed to be suspicious because of the letter from Ambrose bearing the message: 'For God's sake come to me quickly. She has done for me at last, Rachel my torment. If you delay, it may be too late. Ambrose' (*Cousin Rachel*, p.28). In the event, Rainaldi is only a peripheral figure, for the psychological dynamic of the novel lies in the triangulated relationship between Philip, Rachel and the dead Ambrose. Philip's reading of this dynamic is the real plot of the novel and he is not a reliable reader. For him the reactions of others are as a distorting mirror. He fails to acknowledge, for example, until the end of the book, his powerful resemblance to Ambrose. He notices Rainaldi's dark eyes but fails to recognize the full significance of the fact that they 'at first sight of me startled into a flash of recognition that in one second vanished' (*Cousin Rachel*, p.42). Rainaldi's reaction is, for the reader, the first indication that there is an uncanny likeness between Philip and his dead cousin. Gothic conventions are used at this stage in the novel rather as they are in *Northanger Abbey*, to signal unreliable understanding.

This is particularly the case in relation to Rachel herself. Philip finds her gone when he reaches Florence and continues to construct her in his own imagination as a wicked woman in the Gothic mode. He thinks of Ambrose's last days:

> always within earshot, within sight, was the shadowy hated figure of that woman I had never seen. She had so many faces, so many guises ... Since my journey to the villa she had become a monster, larger than life itself. Her eyes were black as sloes, her features aquiline like Rainaldi's, and she moved about those musty villa rooms sinuous and silent, like a snake.[8]
>
> (*Cousin Rachel*, pp. 49–50)

The young Philip does not recognize the power of his own imagination in constructing this Rachel; when his childhood friend,

Louise, suggests that Rachel might, when married to her first
husband, have had lovers, he dismisses the speculation as the stuff
of fiction and therefore feminine fancy:

> This aspect of my cousin Rachel had not occurred to me. I saw
> her only as malevolent, like a spider. In spite of my hatred, I could
> not help smiling. 'How like a girl,' I said to Louise, 'to picture
> lovers. Stilettos in a shadowed doorway. Secret staircases'.
>
> (*Cousin Rachel*, p.56)

He does not recognise that he has been doing exactly this himself
and his comment about Louise is tantamount to a denial of the
feminine side of himself.

Rachel's arrival in Cornwall marks the beginning of Philip's
encounter with the flesh and blood woman, and it appears initially
to the reader that Philip's Gothic fears and fantasies have been
unfounded and that the novel itself is moving into a different
mode:

> My first feeling was one of shock, almost of stupefaction, that she
> should be so small. She barely reached my shoulder. She had
> nothing like the height or the figure of Louise.
>
> She was dressed in deep black, which took the colour from her
> face, and there was lace at her throat and at her wrists. Her hair
> was brown, parted in the centre with a low knot behind, her
> features neat and regular. The only things large about her were
> the eyes, which at first sight of me widened in sudden recogni-
> tion, startled, like the eyes of a deer, and from recognition to
> bewilderment to pain, almost to apprehension. I saw the colour
> come into her face and go again, and I think I was as great a
> shock to her as she was to me. It would be hazardous to say
> which of us was the more nervous, the more ill-at-ease.
>
> (*Cousin Rachel*, pp.71–2)

The transferral of shock from Philip to Rachel in this passage has
the effect of shifting the Gothic trace of fear and destabilizing any
assumptions we may have made about this relationship. In doing
so, it signals again the powerful uncanny element of Philip's
likeness to Ambrose. The remainder of the novel never loses sight
of the Gothic but uses and destabilizes some of its conventions.
Rachel may or may not be the vulnerable and essentially passive

Gothic heroine trapped in an alien house. (Indeed, for a British reader the house represents a settled rural way of English life and Rachel the alien element.) Philip is not a tyrannical patriarchal figure but one ill at ease with his own adulthood, inexperienced and clearly susceptible to manipulation, a point which Louise perceives. Louise and Philip differ in their reading of Rachel after she has arrived in Cornwall. It is Louise's reading that is more cynical and more mundane: she comes to see Rachel as plotting to exact what benefit she can from the wealth of her husband's family (*Cousin Rachel*, p.247). For Rachel has been left virtually penniless; Ambrose had not signed the will which would have granted her, as his widow, an inheritance.

We are left in no doubt early in the novel that Philip identifies strongly with the estate he has inherited:

> It came upon me strongly and with force, and for the first time since I had heard of Ambrose's death, that everything I now saw and looked upon belonged to me. I need never share it with anyone living. Those walls and windows, that roof, the bell that struck seven as I approached, the whole living entity of the house was mine, and mine alone. The grass beneath my feet, the trees surrounding me, the hills behind me, the meadows, the woods, even the men and women farming the land yonder, were all part of my inheritance; they all belonged.   (*Cousin Rachel*, p.51)

What follows between Philip and Rachel is a complex and ultimately indecipherable mix of sexuality and economics in which the fate of the Ashley estate is at stake. In telling this story, the destabilized conventions of Gothic used in du Maurier's text operate for the feminist reader to query the foundations of patriarchy itself. As Anne Williams points out, Gothic is 'a narrative built over a cultural fault line – the point of conjunction between the discourses of alliance and sexuality, in Foucault's sense of those terms'.[9] In other words, the tension between the family as economic unit and as a set of affective relationships is explored by Gothic texts and the most sinister implications of such tension give rise to the nightmares of Gothic. To look at the Ashley family in Foucault's terms, the 'natural' order of things under the old identity system of alliance should have been for Ambrose to marry and produce an heir into whose hands safe keeping of the house, estate and family wealth would eventually have passed. Given his failure to do that, the heir and surrogate son is Philip. The introduction of Rachel into this equation has a destabilizing effect. It is revealed that she had indeed been pregnant but had miscarried, after which, she confides in Philip, Ambrose 'lost belief' in her and neglected or declined to sign the will in which he had left the property to her for her lifetime (*Cousin Rachel*, p.195). There are thus intimations in the text of an economic dimension to Rachel's presence in Cornwall. The reference to her profile as that stamped on a coin is repeated more than once by Philip and whereas he is conscious of its representation of Rachel as part of the ancient and foreign world of Italy, he seems unaware that his choice of metaphor also suggests possession and exchange. Most significant, however, in exposing the 'faultline' is the repeated reference to Rachel's hands. As in *Jamaica Inn*, hands are used synecdochally; just as Mary Yellan finds Jem's hands fascinating and attractive, Philip is drawn to Rachel's hands. His limited experience of women leads him to compare Rachel's hands with those of the vicar's wife which are 'like boiled hams' whereas Rachel's are 'white and small against embroidery' (*Cousin Rachel*, pp.112 and 129). What he fails to see, but what the reader might, is that hands also signify metonymically the possession and exchange of property. Because of the sexual fascination Rachel holds for Philip, he delivers his paternal inheritance willingly into her hands.

Yet he does so in the implicit belief that he can own her and therefore control her sexuality. After his rejection of the 'Gothic' Rachel of his imagination, he loses his fear of her:

> how could I fear anyone who did not measure up to my shoulder, and had nothing remarkable about her save a sense of humour and small hands? Was it for this that one man had fought a duel, and another, dying, written to me and said, 'She's done for me at last, Rachel, my torment'? It was as though I had blown a bubble in the air, and stood by to watch it dance; and the bubble had now burst. (*Cousin Rachel*, p.79)

Indeed, he becomes captivated by her sense of humour and her physical presence. He succumbs to her femininity. He allows her, encourages her even, to adopt the role of mistress of the estate. The servants fall naturally into the way of calling her the mistress and she involves herself not only in the lives of the tenants (prescribing herbal remedies for their various ills) but in the replanning of the gardens. Although in the former there is the hint of alien and sinister knowledge (which later rouses Philip's suspicions), in the latter the improvement of the estate suggests a commitment to its continuance. This process culminates with the Christmas festivities. Here, Philip and Rachel act out the roles of lord and lady of the manor, bestowing largesse on the tenants at a great Christmas feast complete with giant Christmas tree. It is on this occasion that Philip gives Rachel the pearl collar, a prize item from the family jewels and usually worn by Ashley brides on their wedding day. Although Philip consciously sees this as a gift *to* Rachel, he also implicitly understands it as confirming their relationship. The term collar, rather than necklace, implies shackling and provides an uncomfortable echo of the hanged man described in gruesome detail in the opening chapter when Philip recalls a childhood memory. It also presages the most violent scene in the novel, when Rachel having rejected Philip's assumption that they will become man and wife, incurs his murderous wrath and he attempts to strangle her (*Cousin Rachel*, pp.244–5). The pearl collar, therefore, is a token of patriarchal possession; Nick Kendall's insistence that it be returned to the family jewels only confirms Philip's belief that what he must do is to win Rachel by giving away his inheritance to her. Therefore, when he showers her with all the family jewels on the eve of his birthday the following April, he misunderstands her response. She allows him to make love to her and he assumes that she has accepted him as her husband although he has made no verbal proposal of marriage. The misconception is soon exposed:

> She went on looking at me, incredulous, baffled, like someone listening to words in a foreign language that cannot be translated or comprehended, and I realized suddenly, with anguish and despair, that so it was, in fact, between us both; all that had passed had been in error. She had not understood what it was I asked of her at midnight, nor I, in my blind wonder, what she had given, therefore what I had believed to be a pledge of love was something different, without meaning, on which she had put her own interpretation.   (*Cousin Rachel*, p.243)

Her response has been merely to thank him. Her own 'jewel' does not carry the same significance for her as it does for him and she makes it clear that neither it nor she is to be possessed. And nor does she need to be, for Philip has given away his inheritance to her, without securing her in marriage. This is the turning point for him, as he has hitherto ignored what Ambrose had been trying to tell him.

In attempting to absorb Rachel into a patriarchal structure, Philip has entered into an Oedipal relationship with his dead cousin. For Rachel, as widow of his surrogate father, is in a significant sense a mother figure for Philip. She is indeed at least ten years older than he is and treats him affectionately but as a boy, an intimacy which Philip dares to mistake for something else.[10] His jealousy of Ambrose and Rachel's marriage re-orients itself: no longer jealous of Rachel's place in Ambrose's affections (and of their potential children who would have deprived him of his inheritance), he becomes instead jealous of Ambrose. Philip's Oedipal relationship with Ambrose is signalled in the novel through the uncanny. Not only are there repeated references to the striking likeness between them, but fragments of Ambrose's writing surface insistently in the text. First of all, there are the brief anguished notes from Italy, read by Philip when Ambrose was still alive. After his death, and Rachel's arrival in Cornwall, Ambrose's writing continues to have an uncanny presence in Philip's life, warning him against Rachel.[11] As Philip becomes more and more drawn to her he ignores the warnings that he finds in letters discovered in a book and in an old coat given away to a tenant. Significantly, the letters contain not only Ambrose's suspicions of Rachel's murderous intent but also fragments of warnings concerning the estate:

'I cannot any longer, nay I dare not, let her have command over my purse, or I shall be ruined, and the estate will suffer. It is imperative that you warn Kendall, if by any chance...' The sentence broke off. There was no end to it. The scrap of paper was not dated.   (*Cousin Rachel*, p.146)

Anne Williams points out the role that writing plays in Gothic narratives:

Gothic texts consistently reveal the uneasy compromise made (or imposed) by the Law of the Father on the material conditions of meaning. Writing is inherently a sign of absence, even as it records the signs of a past presence....Gothic narrative conventions (frame and embedded tales, 'found' or translated manuscripts, many narrators) dramatize both the materiality of writing and its implicit inadequacies: its discontinuities, ambiguities, unreliabilities, silences. Many a Gothic plot emphasizes the will, a written text that conveys the 'will' of its writer from beyond the grave, where (particularly interesting in the light of discussions of *écriture*) the author of the words is necessarily absent. Wills are unique in that they become meaningful only after the writer's death. In 'realizing' the desires of the dead, they affirm the Symbolic's investment in its own perpetuation and literalize 'the Law of the Father'.[12]

Philip buries the letter from Ambrose in which he articulates most fully his allegations towards Rachel: her profligacy and the murderous intent he suspects. He buries it in what he considers to be symbolically Ambrose's last resting place. This is beneath a piece of granite that Ambrose had set up on the highest point of the Ashley land which commands a view of the whole estate, claiming that he should be there in spirit after his death rather than in the family vault. Although Ambrose has been buried in the Protestant cemetery in Florence, Philip remembers this claim and buries the letter under the granite slab, in the belief that its contents should die with its writer. This marks his desire to repress such knowledge and to resist the Law of the Father but after his rejection by Rachel, Philip exhumes the letter, now taking its words as truth. This is perhaps the most significant piece of writing in the novel. There is also a will in this text, Ambrose's will, but it is in a sense a false representation of the Law of the Father. Its real significance lies in the fact that Ambrose did *not* sign it; therefore it inscribes Ambrose's original faith in Rachel and it is this that Philip chooses to follow at first. It leads him to give away willingly to her the entirety of his inheritance. Only after her rejection of him as a husband, and hence her own place in the patriarchal order, does he realize the implications of what he has done and begins to see himself as having been tricked. His subsequent acts culminate in what is effectively the murder of Rachel which thus restores his patriarchal inheritance to him and reasserts the social order. In the full knowledge that the bridge over the new sunken Italian garden is unsafe, Philip allows Rachel to go and plunge to her death, an ironically fitting end for this 'foreign' woman who has disrupted the 'natural' order of this English country house.

Ultimately the novel re-enacts the matricide which Luce Irigaray believes to be at the foundations of our culture: 'the whole of our western culture is based upon the murder of the mother'.[13] Philip's return to the Law of the Father (exemplified in the text by Ambrose's writing) revives fully the fear and anxiety he had felt about Rachel before meeting her and leads him inexorably to desire her death. In this, he is doing no more than acting out the fears of patriarchy itself:

> And once the man-god-father kills the mother so as to take power, he is assailed by ghosts and anxieties. He will always feel a panic fear of she who is the substitute for what he has killed.[14]

Such patriarchal repetition is also represented in the text by the Gothic trope of the double, although in this novel this is hinted at rather than foregrounded as in *The Scapegoat*. As we have seen, there are indications that Philip bears a striking resemblance to Ambrose. As Philip's relationship with Rachel reaches crisis point, Philip literally sees himself as Ambrose. Knowing that he has given Rachel everything and that 'nothing remained. Unless it should be fear', Philip puts his hands around Rachel's throat, feeling her 'a frightened bird'; letting her go, he catches sight of his reflection in the mirror in his room: 'Surely it was Ambrose who stood there, with the sweat upon his forehead, the face drained of all colour?' (*Cousin Rachel*, p.244). Again, after his illness and delirium (in which he sees not his own surroundings but Ambrose's bedroom in Italy), he twice looks at the portrait of Ambrose and sees himself:

> I looked over her head, straight at the portrait above the mantelpiece, and the young face of Ambrose staring at me was my own. She had defeated both of us.   (*Cousin Rachel*, pp.278-9)

Examining the role of the double in Gothic fiction, William Patrick Day relates it to the relationship between self and Other. According to Day, the Gothic hero:

> who seeks to dominate his world and acts out the role of sadist, is also inflicting pain and suffering on himself, as all of his actions lead to his own destruction. This internalization of the sadomasochistic pattern is the logical precondition for the Gothic fantasy's repeated use of the double. The self is both sadist and masochist, both dominated and dominator, at once submissive and assertive.

In his discussion of the Gothic hero, Day sees him in relation to a passive heroine 'who accepts domination, accepts the position of masochist, because the assertion of her identity, tied up as it is with the qualities of passivity and respectability, demands she accept this role'.[15] Neither Philip nor Rachel fits comfortably into these roles. It is apparent, however, that Philip's aggressive behaviour towards Rachel occurs at the moments when he most closely identifies with Ambrose, and it is at these moments too that Rachel seems at her most vulnerable: ' "A woman can't suffer twice. I have had all this before." And lifting her fingers to her throat she added, "even the hands around my neck. That too. Now will you understand?" ' (*Cousin Rachel*, p.278). At the very end of the novel, as Rachel lies dying, she sees not Philip but Ambrose:

> She opened her eyes, and looked at me. At first, I think in pain. Then in bewilderment. Then finally, so I thought, in recognition. Yet I was in error, even then. She called me Ambrose. I went on holding her hands until she died.   (*Cousin Rachel*, p.302)

The enigma that is Rachel remains until the end. We never know whether she has murdered Ambrose whose symptoms and death were, Nick Kendall believes, entirely consistent with those of the brain tumour from which Ambrose's father had died. Searching Rachel's room at the very moment when she is visiting the sunken garden, Philip finds two significant letters and the poisonous laburnum seeds catalogued in her desk as botanical specimens. One of these letters shows that, intending to leave England, she has returned the family jewels to the bank in safe keeping for Philip; the other, from Rainaldi, indicates that their relationship had indeed been on a business footing and that she had had a deep affection for 'that boy' (*Cousin Rachel*, p.300). At this point, the final image of Ambrose appears, a drawing in which 'the eyes themselves had a haunted look about them, as though some shadow stood close to his shoulder and he feared to look behind' (*Cousin Rachel*, p.301).

In behaving as Ambrose's double, therefore, Philip does indeed inflict great pain upon himself. In this novel, the embodiment of the Other is itself shifting: apparently located in the foreign, the female and the *unheimlich*, it actually appears as its most destructive in the form of the *heimlich*, where there is most likeness. We know from the opening chapters that Philip has lived a miserable and solitary life since the death of Rachel, consumed by guilt but that he sees his future nonetheless as a solid member of the community. The final sentences of the novel, in uncanny repetition of the logic of patriarchy, echo its opening:

> They used to hang men at Four Turnings in the old days. Not any more though. (*Cousin Rachel*, p.302)

For *My Cousin Rachel* opens in a manner which, echoing *Jamaica Inn*, once again establishes both Cornwall and the past as dark countries: 'They used to hang men at Four Turnings in the old days' (*Cousin Rachel*, p.5). The detailed description of Philip's childhood memory of the corpse on the gallows ('The rain had rotted his breeches, if not his body, and strips of worsted drooped from his swollen limbs like pulpy paper' [*Cousin Rachel*, p.5]) introduces the abject at an early stage and alerts the reader to the possibility that the familial relationship indicated by the title might well be one which is, in true Gothic manner, characterised by evil doing. The hanged man's offence? He killed his wife; she was a 'scold', a woman who talked too much (*Cousin Rachel*, p.7). Indeed, we are left in no doubt as to the portent represented by the corpse: the first chapter ends with the words: 'Had I looked back at you, over my shoulder, I should not have seen you swinging in your chains, but my own shadow' (Cousin Rachel, p.10). What is abject, however, the novel demonstrates, has its origins deep within the self.

In inscribing the murder of the mother, therefore, *My Cousin Rachel* in some respects conforms to what Anne Williams characterizes as Male Gothic: 'Male Gothic is a dark mirror reflecting patriarchy's nightm*ère*'.[16] Philip's own nightmare is represented through his dream in delirium:

> I was standing on a bridge, beside the Arno, making a vow to destroy a woman I had never seen. The swollen water passed under the bridge, bubbling, brown, and Rachel, the beggar girl, came up to me with empty hands. She was naked, save for the pearl collar round her throat. Suddenly she pointed at the water and Ambrose went past us, under the bridge, his hands folded on his breast. He floated away down the river out of sight, and slowly, majestically, his paws raised stiff and straight, went the body of the dead dog after him. (*Cousin Rachel*, p.259)

In parodic fashion, Philip's dream makes visual his deepest fears. The dark waters of the Arno are suggestive of the Styx, signifying death. His attempt to control Rachel's sexuality is graphically represented by the naked Rachel wearing only the pearl collar. Rachel's appearance as the beggar girl not only asserts her affinity with the ancient knowledge of old Italy but also indicates her economic status, the empty hands echoing the recurrent hand imagery. Most graphically of all, Philip's own sexuality is represented by the dog floating away after the dead Ambrose. Dreaming, Philip sees his devotion to Rachel as dog-like and his sexual desire, represented four times over by the phallic images of the dog's 'stiff and straight' paws, as an object of ridicule.

The opening of *My Cousin Rachel* (and its echo at the very end) might suggest an emphasis on horror that would categorize the novel, in Anne Williams' terms, as male rather than female:

> Male Gothic conventions imply that the focus of horror is not merely 'the female' in general, but more specifically, her most mysterious and powerful manifestation as mother or potential mother. In the light of Kristeva's analysis of horror, therefore, we can see that Male Gothic conventionally echoes that primitive anxiety about 'the female', specifically the mother. The gruesome physical materiality of Male Gothic horror expresses 'the abject', the 'otherness' of the *mater*/mother who threatens to engulf the speaking subject.[17]

'Female Gothic,' on the other hand, 'creates a Looking-Glass World where ancient assumptions about the "male" and the "female"...are suspended or so transformed as to reveal an entirely different world, exposing the perils lurking in the father's corridors of power'.[18] Rachel's resistance to Philip's attempts to contain her (most graphically symbolized by the pearl collar) seem to indicate that *My Cousin Rachel* also falls into the 'female' category. Indeed, the radical ambiguity of *My Cousin Rachel* results in its subversion of the dichotomy between Male and Female Gothic, a subversion which is, we suggest, related to du Maurier's experimentation with gendered subject position. Williams identifies differences in Male and Female Gothic at the levels of narrative technique, assumptions about the supernatural and plot. *My Cousin Rachel* follows the Female convention of restricted point of view – but that point of view is masculine rather than feminine; it

eschews the use of the supernatural or apparent supernatural,
hinting only at the uncanny. Like Male Gothic, it has a tragic plot
and uncertain closure; it offers physical horror to the reader, but
through Philip's memory or imagination rather than direct
description. The ultimate horror for the feminist reader lies in
Philip's own subjectivity. If we acknowledge and recognize this,
then Rachel emerges as victim who is the scapegoat which ensures
the restitution of patriarchal inheritance. Philip pays for this
through a lifetime of guilt:

> No one will ever guess the burden of blame I carry on my
> shoulders; nor will they know that every day, haunted still by
> doubt, I ask myself a question which I cannot answer. Was
> Rachel innocent or guilty? Maybe I shall learn that too, in purg-
> atory.   (*Cousin Rachel*, p.7)

THE STRANGER IN THE MIRROR: *THE SCAPEGOAT*

Du Maurier's 1957 novel *The Scapegoat*, as its title suggests, takes up
the theme of the scapegoat and develops it further. In doing so, it
draws on two important dimensions of du Maurier's own sense of
identity in middle age. One is her French ancestry and the other is
the insight gained from her discovery of the works of Jung in the
1950s. Ironically perhaps, du Maurier's most Jungian novel takes us
right back again into the heart of the family romance. Du Maurier's
fascination with things French derived from a keen awareness of, if
problematic relation with, her sense of family identity. We have
already seen how she rejected her metropolitan background in
favour of a particular affinity for Cornwall; this was complicated
by an enduring identification with the French ancestry she equated
with a paternal inheritance of creativity. Her sense of the French
influence in her life seems to have become more powerful as she
got older. In a letter to her young friend Oriel Malet, for example,
she invokes George du Maurier's book *Peter Ibbetson*, a best seller of
the 1890s:

> I have been looking into my grandfather's *Peter Ibbetson* again,
> and it's queer how he had these same feelings about forebears
> that I have – an almost agonized interest – and how part of his

dream in the book was to *become* them in the past, and how they became *him* in the future.[19]

Du Maurier became more and more inclined to cite her French ancestry when discussing her own characteristics. In an interview given to Cliff Michelmore in 1977, for example, she invoked it to explain her 'carefulness' with money; Oriel Malet recalls a conversation early in her friendship with the writer in which she self-mockingly acknowledged her particular affinity with her son, Kits: 'Ah, one's *son* . . . it's my French blood, I expect'.[20] If her self-identification with Cornwall appears to have been part of her quest to discover an authentic self, her appeals to her French ancestry can be seen in the same light.

Before she wrote *The Scapegoat*, du Maurier had represented France and Frenchness through the biographical family saga *The du Mauriers* (1937) and in the novels *I'll Never be Young Again* (1932) and *Frenchman's Creek* (1941). In 1963 she was to publish *The Glass Blowers*, a novel based on the family history of the du Mauriers in the French Revolution.[21] None of these could be described as a Gothic text. In the early novels, France is represented as an 'otherness' embodying both excitement and danger, whether it be the site of dissolution and excess as in the Paris of the picaresque *I'll Never be Young Again*, or the home territory of the seductive pirate in *Frenchman's Creek*. In the latter, du Maurier achieves an identification to some extent between France and Cornwall, by making her French pirate a Breton and a representative of the periphery with all its latent unruliness. This, according to du Maurier 'the only one of my novels I am prepared to admit is romantic' (*Enchanted Cornwall*, p. 89), continues to offer Cornwall as a site of transgression. Interestingly, perceptions of the French pirate as degenerate are focused through the eyes of the Englishmen in the novel who are themselves represented parodically as decadent or merely selfish and stupid. His very Frenchness signifies an alarming degeneracy to English eyes, exemplified by Lord Godolphin's remark that ' "these foreigners are half women, you know" ' (*FC*, p. 222). The novel does not endorse the English stereotype of the decadent Frenchman, however, presenting the French pirate rather as refined and artistic.[22] In these early novels, the representations of Frenchness incorporate the kind of cultural stereotypes described by Phillippe Sollers:

'Too French' means: love affairs, libertinism, witticisms, fickle-
ness, lack of substance and seriousness, fashion, petite Parisian
women, economic incompetence, Pigalles, Folies-Bergère, Mou-
lin-Rouge, banks of the Marne, Impressionism, the tradition of
the eighteenth century, too frivolous, too much froth and bub-
ble...[23]

Such cultural stereotypes, as this quotation implies, have strong *fin
de siècle* overtones and became another dimension of the anxieties
concerning degeneracy within English culture during this period.
Du Maurier's 1957 novel, *The Scapegoat*, negotiates the tension
between such stereotypes and her own sense of French identity
through the classic Gothic convention of the double.

Set entirely in modern-day France, the plot of *The Scapegoat* turns
on one premise: that it is possible for one person to so resemble
another that he may take the other's place without even his closest
family suspecting the switch. Once this premise is accepted – and
as Karl Miller has pointed out in his book on doubles, technically
the difficulties of managing the double (in particular his arrival or
debut) are very daunting[24] – the novel proceeds in a determinedly
'realist' mode. Gothic tropes are constantly domesticated to present
a detailed portrait of French provincial life and the complexities of
a dysfunctional family. Unlike well known novels in this sub-group
of the Gothic (e.g. *Confessions of a Justified Sinner* or *Dr Jekyll and Mr
Hyde*) du Maurier's work deliberately eschews the supernatural
and demonic.[25] An English academic specializing in French
history, John, who narrates his own story, meets his double, the
Comte Jean de Gué in Le Mans on his way home from a working
holiday. Jean appears to be everything John is not: French, stylish
in a slightly debauched way and encumbered with family and
financial problems – in contrast with the emotionally isolated John
who at the time of the meeting is contemplating the worthlessness
of his arid life of study. Jean drugs John in a hotel room and,
having switched all their belongings, disappears, leaving John to
be collected the next day by the family chauffeur and taken back to
the Chateau St Gilles. Quite literally stepping into the shoes of his
double, he there finds himself confronted with a messy tangle of
family and financial involvements including a pregnant wife, a
disgruntled brother with whose wife he seems to be having an
affair, a bedridden mother, a sister who does not speak to him and
a ten-year-old daughter who projects herself as a religious

visionary. In addition, there is attached to the chateau, a *verrerie*, an old-fashioned glass-making concern, which is in severe financial difficulties. A visit to the local town complicates matters further, as not only does John discover the extent of the family's financial difficulties, including a marriage settlement which ties up his wife's substantial fortune (unless she produces a male heir or dies), but also another woman who is, to use an old-fashioned term, Jean de Gué's 'mistress'. Further developments reveal the source of the feud between Jean and his sister, Blanche, to date back to the war, when Jean and co-resistance workers murdered Blanche's fiancé, the manager of the verrerie, on the grounds that he was a collaborator. The untimely death of the wife, Françoise, solves the financial problems, facilitating the reconciliation and healing that John, during his short time in the role as head of this family, seeks to bring about. In so doing, he finds new dimensions to himself and a new meaning in his own life. This is cut short, however, by the reappearance of the real count who not only demands to resume his own identity but reveals that he has disposed of all John's worldly goods and connections whilst in London. The novel ends with John setting off for the monastery, the Abbaye de la Grande-Trappe, which he had been contemplating visiting at the opening of the story. This time, presumably, it is for good.

Thus *The Scapegoat* develops further the Gothic trope of the double that haunts *My Cousin Rachel* and like the earlier novel, explores it in relation to national identity. Homi Bhabha, in a recent book, *The Location of Culture* (1994), has argued that it is the experience of postcolonialism which has led to an examination of the figure of the outsider as a focus for understanding that national identity is constructed through narration, or, in other words, that nation or culture is 'the subject of discourse and the object of psychic identification'.[26] Bhabha draws upon the work of, among others, Julia Kristeva in *Strangers to Ourselves* (1991), whose argument that 'foreignness' is a projection of 'the strange within us' is so apposite to *My Cousin Rachel*.[27] The following passage from Kristeva's book describes what *The Scapegoat* enacts through its narration:

> Living with the other, with the foreigner, confronts us with the possibility or not of *being an other*. It is not simply – humanistically – a matter of our being able to accept the other, but of *being in his place*, and this means to imagine and make oneself other for

oneself....Being alienated from myself, as painful as that may
be, provides me with that exquisite distance within which perverse pleasure begins, as well as the possibility of my imagining
and thinking, the impetus of my culture. Split identity, kaleido-
scope of identities: can we be a saga for ourselves without being
considered mad or fake? Without dying of the foreigner's hatred
or of hatred for the foreigner?[28]

In a particularly apposite disquisition on the question 'Might
Culture be French?', Kristeva also makes a statement which would
appear to sum up even more specifically the project of *The
Scapegoat*:

There are foreigners who wish to be lost as such in the perverse-
ness of French culture in order to be reborn not within a new
identity but within the enigmatic dimensions of human experience that, with and beyond belonging, is called freedom.[29]

At the end of the novel, John sets off for the Abbaye, having lost
everything but 'with and beyond belonging', possessing a freedom
he had not had before. Du Maurier herself appears to have believed
that she had written a novel about different aspects of the self:

Actually, in *Scapegoat*, I've tried to say too many things at once.
How close hunger is to greed, how difficult to tell the difference,
how hard not to be confused, how close one's better nature to
one's worst, and finally, how the self must be stripped of everything, and give up everything, before it can understand love. But
one can't tell that to the ordinary reader. He that has ears to hear,
let him hear.[30]

Indeed, the text constantly hints at the idea that John and Jean
represent two aspects of the same man. In the opening chapter,
before meeting Jean, John reflects on 'the self who clamoured for
release, the man within'.[31] When the two meet, the uncanny resemblance is demonstrated in a mirror image:

it showed us plainly enough to be standing together, straining,
anxious, searching the mirrored surface as though our lives
depended upon what it had to tell. And the answer was no
chance resemblance, no superficial likeness to be confounded

by the different colour of hair or eyes, by the dissimilarity of
feature, expression, height, or breadth of shoulder: it was as
though one man stood there.   (*Scapegoat*, p.13)

Bhabha's words can illuminate the metaphorical import of this
passage:

This image of human identity and indeed, human identity as
image – both familiar frames or mirrors of selfhood that speak
from deep within Western culture – are inscribed in the sign of
resemblance.

The *double* image in the mirror here signifies an internal alterity: a
refracted image of a subject which is not unitary. This is what
Bhabha calls the 'spatialization of the subject', or 'doubling'.[32] For
Kristeva, such internal alterity may be described in the Freudian
vocabulary of *heimlich* and *unheimlich*. According to Freud, the
heimlich in signifying 'friendlily comfortable' carries with it the
implication of 'concealed, kept back from sight'; his concept of the
uncanny is 'that class of the frightening which leads back to what is
known of old and long familiar.' Kristeva points out that 'Freud
noted that the archaic, narcissistic self, not yet demarcated by the
outside world, projects out of itself what it experiences as dangerous or unpleasant in itself, making of it an alien *double*, uncanny
and demoniacal'.[33] Kristeva goes on to argue that the uncanny was
the way in which:

Freud introduced the fascinated rejection of the other at the heart
of that 'our self,' so poised and dense, which precisely no longer
exists ever since Freud and shows itself to be a strange land of
borders and othernesses ceaselessly constructed and deconstructed.

Freud, claims Kristeva, 'teaches us to detect foreignness in ourselves'.[34] Thus, as we have argued in Chapter 2, the foreigner
becomes a figure of cultural abjection.

Jean de Gué may therefore be seen as the foreignness within the
English John, embodying as he does many of the cultural
stereotypes of Frenchness. John describes himself as 'a law-abiding,
quiet, donnish individual of thirty-eight' (*Scapegoat*, p.9); he lives a
solitary life with no ties and his life is of the imagination. Yet at the

opening of the novel, just before his meeting with Jean, he reflects on the inadequacy of his 'library knowledge' and 'tourist's gleanings' of France. In spite of his perfect command of the language, his sense of foreignness is acute, as is his desire to 'break the barrier down', but, he concludes, 'I should never be a Frenchman, never be one of them' (*Scapegoat*, p.8). Jean de Gué is the genuine article; an aristocrat with a penchant for good living, he has just returned from a visit to Paris to resume a provincial life he finds uncongenial. Whereas John is characterized by restraint, Jean's hallmark is excess, from the 'hair-raising ride' he gives John in his own solid Ford Consul, to the sexual entanglements which become apparent as the novel progresses. Jean is self-indulgent where John is ascetic and repressed, his sexual experience limited to casual, unsatisfying encounters during the War. Jean is greedy and careless, his prodigality having forced the family business and fortunes into apparent terminal decline. In assuming Jean's social identity, John is forced to confront the implications of such otherness.

The world that John enters has all the potential ingredients of a Gothic novel, yet the narrative remains resolutely 'realist'. The Gothic genre as a literature of terror is intrinsically the inscription of the *unheimlich*, the uncanny which terrifies just as it leads back 'to what is known of old and long familiar'. Family relationships are portrayed in the Gothic in threatening ways, often evoking repressed incestuous desire.[35] Such desire is represented in *The Scapegoat* as containable (just) within the bounds of normality. Jean's idolization of his daughter and her excessive love for him may have resulted in a somewhat spoilt child, but we have only the word of Charlotte (the rather malicious servant) that the relationship has been unhealthily intense. Jean has not slept with his sister , but with his brother's wife. He has killed not his father but his sister's fiancé. And so on. Furthermore, John's intervention in Jean's world steers those relationships away from excess and places them back firmly within the bounds of the socially acceptable. The castle of St Gilles then, is more a French Northanger Abbey hiding nothing more unusual than a family history of greed, jealousy and sibling rivalry rather than a Udolpho with its darker secrets. As in Charlotte Brontë's novel, *Jane Eyre*, there is certainly a woman in the attic yet this is no mad woman but the ageing *comtesse* willingly abdicating her role in the household as she struggles with despair and morphine addiction. As in *Jane Eyre*, the grotesque form of the woman in the attic has her opposite in the intense, religious child, Marie-Noel. Yet Jean's daughter is no Helen Burns, burning with an angelic zeal and fated to suffer an early, martyred death but a flesh and blood child, prone herself to jealousy and even more prone to histrionic excesses in her expressions of religious fervour. The Chateau St Gilles is located in an everyday France, firmly rooted in time and place. Some of the names have been changed but it could probably be found on the map from the precise references to actual places; there is also much descriptive detail of a rural way of life with its markets and shoots and small towns. The novel presents a pastoral society which is under pressure in the post-war world, a society very precisely located in time, in the mid-1950s when the legacy of war is part of people's personal history. The test of what it meant to be truly 'French' during this time of crisis has had outward and visible effects on personal lives, effects that John uncovers. The relationships in this world are circumscribed by history but also by money, which in its turn is related to questions of responsibility and inheritance. This is a world of contracts and bank managers, recognizably 'real' in the mid-twentieth century. The family business of the verrerie (based on that of du Maurier's own ancestors) is struggling to survive in the face of mass production and modern business methods.[36] Even John's solution to its problems, turning to the making of trinkets for tourists rather than practical goods, is one which acknowledges the economic realities of the time.

The identity of John's double, Jean de Gué, is shown to be that of a man who is selfish, greedy and carelessly cruel. He has had the power to wreck the lives of those closest to him. Not surprisingly, John does not like what he finds, yet cannot dissociate himself from the other:

> What was happening, then, was that I wanted to preserve Jean de Gué from degradation. I could not bear to see him shamed. This man, who was not worth the saving, must be spared. Why? Because he looked like me?   (*Scapegoat*, p.99)

What he finds he must do is to recuperate the image of Jean through kinder, altruistic behaviour, to undo the harm done. He tries to treat the wife considerately, he gently but firmly rebuffs the advances of the brother's wife, he attempts a reconciliation with the sister. In fact, the project of the novel, in terms of its plot, is to restore family and tradition, an achievement which is symbolically represented by the descent of the old *comtesse* from her tower room in order to direct a lavish and traditional funeral for Franoise like that she had organized for the old *comte*. The stability of the family is further ensured by the conciliatory gesture to the brother Paul of giving him a different role in the family business; the fifteen years' silence maintained by the sister, Blanche, towards Jean (because of his part in the murder of her fiancé) is broken down and charge of the verrerie given to her.

But what of John? In what sense is he the 'scapegoat' of the title? In general usage, a scapegoat is one who innocently bears the blame of others. There is a Christian dimension to the concept of the scapegoat in the doctrine that Christ was the God-man who died to atone for the sins of all mankind. The Catholic resonances of the novel appear to sustain this reading of John's role: that he, the innocent man, suffers for the sins of his double. This is symbolically enacted in the scene where John deliberately burns his hand in a bonfire to avoid being exposed in the following day's shoot as an impostor because of his ineptitude with a gun. In echoing the references to Joan of Arc, 'the half-boy with her pure, fanatic's eyes'(*Scapegoat*, p.6) in the opening pages, this representation of martyrdom by burning also reminds the reader of the issue of nationality: Joan of Arc is after all a *national* heroine, put to death by the English. The return of Jean makes it appear that John has lost everything, but is this true? The relationship he enjoys with Jean's Hungarian 'mistress', Béla, seems to suggest that in this aspect of his change of social identity, he finds a freedom in a liminal state which is beyond identity itself:

Anonymity closed in upon me. I was on a border-sea between two worlds. The narrow island that once confined me had slipped away, rock-bound and isolated; the crowded continent waiting to receive me, vociferous, demanding, was momentarily out of sight. Wearing another skin had spelt release, yet bondage too. Something had been resurrected but was also spent. If the claims could be forgotten and the oblivion kept, which man should I be, myself or Jean de Gué?   (*Scapegoat*, p.143)

It transpires, not surprisingly, that Béla is the only person not deceived by the switch and it is to her that John at the very end of the novel admits that his sense of failure has now been transformed into love. Rather than this being the end, he believes, it might be the beginning. Seen in Christian terms, John has lost everything worldly but found himself: he has been redeemed.

The Catholic dimension of the novel is one which du Maurier seemed to be aware of : she comments to Oriel Malet, 'Re *Scapegoat*, I know that has been written from a sort of spiritual awareness, which is why the people are *not* Pegged'.[37] Her interest in the life of St Thérèse de Lisieux surfaces in the text in relation to the daughter, who is given a copy of *The Little Flower* as a gift and who likes to think of herself as becoming like the saint. Again, the use of use of St Thérèse, famous for 'the little way', defuses some of the Gothic potential of the text.[38] In the traditional Gothic text, Catholicism was part and parcel of an exotic European setting (French, Spanish or Italian), an alien 'other' in the British Protestant imagination.[39]

The Christian aspects of the text might also be seen to relate to du Maurier's new-found interest in the works of Jung. Du Maurier's discovery of Jung seems to have given her a conceptual framework through which to understand her own creativity. Jungian influences are apparent in *The Scapegoat*, particularly the idea of 'the shadow', the unconscious part of the self which complements the ego. Looked at from this perspective, John and Jean function as each other's shadows but it is only John who comes to terms with this and moves through what Jung called 'individuation' towards a sense of wholeness. While du Maurier might have written *The Scapegoat* with Jung's ideas in mind, such a model provides only partial answers for the critic. Most significantly, perhaps, it does not acknowledge the gender dimensions of the text.

The relationships which John finds himself drawn into are inevitably gendered relationships. The plot of the novel allows him to exercise a patriarchal role which his solitary life had hitherto denied him. In bringing about reconciliation in the de Gué household, he is restoring the family as a patriarchal unit; the identity he adopts, neither his nor Jean's, is one of benevolent paternalism. The result is distinctly conservative, represented through recognizable stereotypes of women. The clinging, sickly wife is contrasted with the sensual, understanding (and, interestingly, foreign) mistress, for example, and the sexually voracious sister-in-law is set against the religious, apparently frigid, sister. The Gothic trace in the text takes on a more *unheimlich* aspect if its representations of femininity are looked at more closely. In this respect, the polarity of the old mother and the child is particularly interesting. Both are described as versions of the double. On first seeing the child, John's description is emotional:

> It stared up at me with enormous eyes and close-cropped hair, and I felt sick because it was replica of Jean de Gué, and therefore in fantastic fashion of a self long buried in the past and so forgotten.   (*Scapegoat*, p.59)

His earlier encounter with the mother had produced a similar uncanny mirroring effect, even more strikingly described through a distinctly Gothic trope:

> She held out her arms, and drawn to her like a magnet I went instinctively to kneel beside her chair, and was at once caught and smothered, lost in the mountain of flesh and woollen wraps, feeling momentarily like a fly trapped in a great spider's web, yet at the same time fascinated because of the likeness, another facet of the self, but elderly, female and grotesque.   (*Scapegoat*, p.40)

These female versions of the double force John to confront the feminine within himself, which has been repressed and long-forgotten. The materiality of the mother which John finds *heimlich* is also *unheimlich* in its monstrosity. Interestingly, whilst Jean has disempowered his mother by encouraging her morphine addiction, John brings her down from her attic room and into the life of the chateau, hence recognizing the importance of the role of the mother figure. However, from another perspective, John's fear of being trapped in an ageing female body, 'like a fly trapped in a great spider's web', vividly expresses the author's fear of growing older. The liberation which John undergoes through his encounter with his own 'foreigner within' is an aspect of the therapeutic process that writing was for his creator. As in *Rebecca*, it would seem, the figure of the double becomes refracted into a multiplicity of possible identities.

The most positive representations of femininity in the novel are outside the family circle. One is the sexually active woman, the loving and intuitive Béla with whom John forms an intimate relationship which transcends his assumed identity. (Béla, it is revealed at the end of the novel, is the only person who recognized that he was not Jean.) The other is the apparently marginal figure of the older peasant woman, Julie, who is often observed at a distance by John:

> I watched her feed some rabbits in a hutch, talking to them all the while. I thought of the comtesse at the chateau feeding sugar to the terrier dogs. Suddenly it seemed to me that both women were strong, virile, tender, fundamentally the same; and yet one of them had grown awry, twisted, and in a strange way maimed, and it was because of something within herself that had never flourished.   (*Scapegoat*, p.167)

Recounting an episode during the war when she had helped a young German soldier who was likely to get into trouble, Julie says:

> I thought of my own two boys, André who was a prisoner and Albert who was killed, and there was this boy of the same age standing there, far from his home, asking me, who could have been his mother, to clean the stain on his jacket. Of course I cleaned it for him ... It made no difference to me whether he was German or Japanese or had fallen from the moon ... when war comes to one's own village, one's own doorstep, it isn't tragic and impersonal any longer. It is just an excuse to vomit private hatred. That is why I am not a great patriot.
>   (*Scapegoat*, p.169)

Julie's perspective on nationality and foreignness is reminiscent of Virginia Woolf's statement, 'As a woman I have no country'.[40] The authentic *French* identity which du Maurier appears to be seeking is shown in *The Scapegoat* to be found not in the cultural stereotypes of Frenchness which Sollers identifies but in a different one: that of the idealized stoical peasant woman. This appears to be a self-image that du Maurier felt she could adopt for her later years. In a letter to Oriel Malet in 1965 she was to lament her ageing looks and to remark:

> The only way to treat it, is to think I'm a throwback to old glass-blowing provincial *aïeux* – you know how peasants etc. get very old and wrinkled by forty and bent, and in shawls, carrying pails of water to cows! Maybe I'd better go the whole hog, and start to dress like that, it would be in keeping![41]

Thus it would seem that in the search for authenticity through nationality, another dimension of identity is discovered, that female identity which accepts ageing and asserts that it has no country, that in a sense it is always the outsider.

The Scapegoat was written during a period which had witnessed an increasing rigidification of gender roles in the aftermath of World War Two. As men had returned to civilian life at the end of the war, women had been encouraged to move back into the domestic sphere. For du Maurier, this period coincided with her own progress towards middle age, which brought with it a deeper awareness of the self's complexity. The *writing* identity, her Jungian 'No. 2', she had come to see as masculine and she made this more and more explicit through her writing by adopting male personae. (In the 1960s she was to write two more novels with a male first person narrator – *The Flight of the Falcon* [1965] *and the House on the Strand* [1969].) In *Julius*, du Maurier had used Jewishness to signify 'otherness' and, as we have seen, there is a trace of this in *Rebecca* too. There is no trace, however, in *My Cousin Rachel* and *The Scapegoat* which were written in a post-war, post-holocaust context where such usage could only have been construed as anti-Semitic. *My Cousin Rachel* draws instead upon Gothic conventions in setting up Italy as the location of an exotic 'otherness' but *The Scapegoat*, through its engagement with 'Frenchness', presents a more complex picture. During the fifties, as the letters to Oriel Malet illustrate, du Maurier was fascinated by the implications of her French ancestry for her own sense of identify. This sense of 'foreignness' within parallels her awareness of the masculine writing identity within her female 'self'. Unlike Jewishness in the early novels, it is acknowledged through the trope of the double as part of the self, what Kristeva would call, 'the strange within us'. In *The Scapegoat*, du Maurier's male English narrator encounters not only his French double but a range of versions of that double in Jean de Gué's familial 'selves'. The novel interrogates these French identities, exposing the inadequacies of various stereotypes of Frenchness. Du Maurier's writing of the novel may be seen as part of a process of 'othering' versions of the self, the kind of revisionism discernible in the letters to Oriel Malet when she analyses her passion for Ellen and Gertrude as the creation of 'pegs' (see Chapter 1). The novel thus follows in the tradition of nineteenth-century texts (most notably *Dr Jekyll and Mr Hyde*) which inscribed imaginatively the process of what nineteenth-century medicine called '*dédoublement*', the ascribing of negative attributes to other selves. The positive aspects of a female sexual identity are represented in the novel by Béla, foreign to both John and Jean and increasingly inaccessible as a self-image for the older du Maurier. The male narrator, John, rejects a sexual identity at the end of the novel when he sets off to embrace the monastic life in the Abbaye de la Grande-Trappe. Du Maurier, searching for a post-menopausal self-concept, seems to find the best hope in the stoical wisdom exemplified by the old peasant woman, Julie.

6
Murdering (M)others

The Flight of the Falcon (1965), although one of du Maurier's lesser known novels, is perhaps her most ambitious. Set in contemporary Italy, it attempts to contextualize the dynamics of familial relationships within the patriarchal cultural inheritance of Europe. In so doing, it offers the reader a text in which the conventions of Gothic fiction are used self-consciously within a 'realist' framework that furnishes constant reminders of the traumatizing effects of World War Two. Those critics of du Maurier who have categorized her as merely a writer of popular fiction expressing a nostalgic yearning for the past, might well find such categorization difficult to apply in relation to this novel.[1] Likewise, the recent dismissal of her as 'an agreeable writer of agreeable fiction but not a serious author' sounds particularly hollow.[2]

Indeed, du Maurier herself seems to have been aware, as she was with *The Scapegoat*, that she was trying to work on several levels. Contemplating *The Flight of the Falcon*'s American publication, she commented to Oriel Malet in a letter, 'I'm afraid people are not going to understand it at all'.[3] Such fears seem to have been well-founded, for when *Good Housekeeping* bought it for serialization, significant revisions were demanded, including a rewriting of the ending. Du Maurier, perceiving herself to be 'on the slide', wanted to maximize her earnings. She was also distracted because her husband was seriously ill. Therefore she concurred.[4] In an earlier letter to Malet, she had commented, 'I know it has some 'Deeper' Thought layers, but I'm sure Victor has not spotted them, and just thinks it's a suspense story, the ignorant old man'.[5] Commenting on the reviewers' response to the novel, Margaret Forster writes:

> Unlike the disappointing reception of certain other novels – such as *Hungry Hill* – the less than enthusiastic response for this one did not disturb her. On the contrary, the American serialization rights and the fact that the Literary Guild took the novel when

Double-day published it made her consider it quite a triumph. She also felt that in some way she had scored over reviewers because they had indeed 'missed the point'. So did almost everyone she knew who read it, but that made her more amused than depressed – it was quite a new experience to be thought obscure.[6]

Undoubtedly there are Jungian resonances in this late novel, evidence of the influence of du Maurier's reading of Jung's work in the 1950s which is also discernible in *The Scapegoat*. There is again the pairing of characters, although this time they are long-lost brothers rather than doubles in the more unlikely, and indeed uncanny, sense as John and Jean are. Again there is the weaving of Christian iconography into a tale that attempts to show that the unconscious as well as the conscious element of the individual mind is part of an historical process. It is this that du Maurier explores in her 'allegory', as Forster describes it.[7] The writing of her 'Urbino book' (Urbino appears as Ruffano in the novel) was not an easy project. Writing to Malet, du Maurier comments:

> I have to study the plans and postcards of Urbino, and the books about the University there, day after day, so that I could, in a way, find my way blindfold about the place!... then when I come to outline the story I find the first suspense idea, and the *son et lumière*, all become involved with deeper levels – I mean, there has to be an explanation of *why* the person directing the acting in the *son et lumière* (a professor at the University), begins to make it all come real to himself, and to the students etc, etc, what is his deep unconscious motive in wanting to re-enact history, and the wicked Duke. So it's much more difficult than I thought, hence the slowness of the notes.[8]

In *The Flight of the Falcon*, du Maurier's abiding interest in the relationship between the past and the present reaches its most complex expression. As in *My Cousin Rachel* and *The Scapegoat*, she again adopts an 'undeveloped, inadequate' male narrative persona (see Chapter 5) in the figure of Armino Fabbio. Armino is a tour guide in his early thirties who reawakens his past as 'Beo' (short for 'Il Beato'), younger son of Aldo Donati, pre-war Superintendent of the Ducal Palace at Ruffano.

The novel opens in contemporary Rome where Armino is passing through with a tour. A chance encounter with a woman vagrant stirs memories of his past. She reminds him of his childhood nurse, Marta; this evokes memories of the altar-piece in San Cipriano, a church in his home town of Ruffano, which to his childish eyes had seemed to represent Marta looking on at the raising of Lazarus. Such images are inextricably linked with memories of his brother, Aldo, whom he believes dead, killed as a fighter pilot in World War Two. After the vagrant is found murdered, Armino becomes convinced that she was indeed Marta. He believes himself to be in part responsible for her death because on impulse he had placed a 10 000 lire note in her hand, which had presumably supplied the motive. He abandons his clients to return to Ruffano for the first time since he had left it during the war, in the company of his widowed mother and her German Commandant lover, his father having died in an Allied prison camp. He soon becomes involved in the life of the university and is shocked to find that his brother, far from being dead, has returned to become Director of the Arts Council. Likewise, Aldo is astounded to find that his younger brother, whom he believed dead, has come back. Aldo is preparing for Ruffano's annual festival and plans to re-enact the exploits of the notorious fifteenth-century Duke Claudio, 'the Falcon'. It soon becomes apparent to Armino that Aldo's commitment to verisimilitude in the staging of the festival is excessive and, perceiving him to be rousing the students to engage in genuine street fighting, he suspects that his brother might be verging on insanity. He believes himself to be wanted by the Roman police for Marta's murder and, fearing arrest, allows Aldo to have him smuggled out to the coast. There, a series of clues culminate in the discovery that Aldo is not his true brother but had been adopted at birth. He deduces, wrongly, that Aldo has murdered Marta to silence her, and returns to Ruffano. There, he tells Aldo that he knows the truth about his birth and that he understands why he killed Marta. Armino then joins Aldo for his reckless chariot ride through the streets of Ruffano. After this, the Gothic setting comes into the foreground as Aldo retreats into the ducal palace and is chased by Armino up a 'twisting spiral' to the top of one of the towers. Here they have their last encounter before Aldo attempts his re-enactment of the Falcon's climactic 'flight'. This, however, is undertaken alone by Aldo only after he has told Armino that Marta had been his real mother but that he had not, in any literal sense, murdered her; nor is Armino any longer a suspect as an arrest had been made in

Rome. Instead of pulling the rip-cord on his parachute, Aldo kicks free of his harness and allows himself to plunge to his death. The novel closes with Aldo's obituary, which refers to Armino's staying on in Ruffano to continue his older brother's work with orphaned students.

In keeping with its project to explore the links between past and present, the novel's plot allows the juxtaposition of characteristically Gothic motifs with a narrative set in a recognisably 1960s Italy, complete with Vespas.[9] The ancient university of Ruffano has acquired a new faculty of Commerce and Economics and the city is now a busy place where the new clashes with the old. There is rivalry in the university between this new faculty and the old-established Arts Faculty, the former perceiving itself as the epitome of the modern world in comparison with what it sees as outmoded Arts. Ruffano's other famous feature is the Ducal Palace, and this is the focus of the novel's Gothic aspect. Here the Italy of the novel is that old Italy, redolent of darkness and mystery, of the Gothic tradition, an Italy already encountered in du Maurier's fiction in *My Cousin Rachel*. The dark spaces of the Ducal Palace with its secret passages and stairways, its dynastic portraits, are an ever-present reminder of the sinister world of Duke Claudio's Ruffano, a world of dreadful atrocities perpetrated on the whim of the Duke. It is within the walls of the Ducal Palace that Aldo meets in secret with his band of acolytes who, dressed in Renaissance costume, appear to bring the past to life. Orphaned children of war, now young men, they act out the part of 'lost boys' in this sinister never-never land.[10] Twelve in number, they provide a disturbing and parodic echo of the apostles. The Palace remains unchanged in the heart of modern day Ruffano, representing a barbarous past which has never gone away. In the text, it represents the Gothic space wherein the nightmares/nightmères of the family romance are played out.

The reading of the past is problematized in the novel. Aldo believes Duke Claudio to have been a man of great culture whose aim was to teach a lesson to his hypocritical and philistine contemporaries, a view endorsed by Italian manuscripts he has read in Rome. Armino, on the other hand, reads the account of a nineteenth-century German scholar who describes the appalling cruelty of the Duke, including the immolation of an unfortunate link-boy who had forgotten to kindle the lights. Du Maurier's text here evokes the horror characteristic of many Gothic novels in its ghastly description of the boy's death:

He was seized by the Falcon's bodyguard, who enveloped the wretched lad in sear-cloth coated with combustibles, and after setting fire to his head drove him through the rooms of the ducal palace to die in agony."

According to one version of Claudio's story, the Duke threw himself from a high tower in the belief that he could fly; in the German account, he had been set upon and killed by the townsfolk after many of them had been trampled underfoot when he had driven eighteen horses through the town. Whereas Armino thinks of the Duke as a ruthless and probably insane tyrant, Aldo seems to see him as a kind of Nietzschian figure, innately superior to his fellow human beings, 'beyond good and evil', and not to be judged by the same standards. Aldo quotes Nietzsche to Armino just before their chariot ride at the end of the novel: 'He who no longer finds what is great in God will find it nowhere; he must either deny it or create it'. (*Flight of the Falcon*, p. 273) The language of Nietzsche, whose vision of the 'superman', the *übermensch*, was appropriated by the Nazis, is also the language of 'the German Commandant' (from whom Armino gained his proficiency in German). It is also, however, the language of the German historian of the Falcon, who condemned his barbaric behaviour. The evocation of Nietzsche's *übermensch* is a reminder of Aldo's earlier self in the Italian Fascist Youth organization. Thus, the parallel presents itself as not merely one man's revisiting of an earlier barbaric history, but as part of a much more comprehensive historical trajectory.

Indeed, the question of the relationship between 'civilization' and 'barbarism' runs through the novel. At the beginning, Armino equates culture and civilization with Italy; he nicknames his American tourists 'barbarians' and reflects that 'these people were running wild on pasture land and prairie when we were ruling the world from Rome' (*Flight of the Falcon*, p. 8). The dark side of such an inheritance, however, is encapsulated in his response to two of his English tourists when they voice concern over the vagrant who turns out to be Marta: 'In the city of the emperors oxen, cats, children and the aged receive their just reward. The old woman is lucky in that refuse is no longer fed to the lions' (*Flight of the Falcon*, p. 13). The barbarism that is war, however, is much more recent history for all the characters in the novel. Aldo makes the link between the history of the twentieth century and that of the fifteenth:

Renaissance man tortured and killed without compunction...
but usually he had a motive. Someone had done him a wrong,
and he acted from revenge. A mistaken motive, possibly, but that
is open to argument. In our time men have killed and tortured
for their own amusement.   (*Flight of the Falcon*, p. 198)

Du Maurier's novel destabilizes the apparent binary between
civilization and barbarism, echoing Walter Benjamin's insight that
'there is no document of civilization which is not at the same time a
document of barbarism'.[12] It does this through interleaving various
layers of history. Links with the fifteenth century are established
through the Gothic dimension of the novel. As David Punter points
out:

Gothic ... is intimately to do with the notion of the barbaric....
Time and time again, those writers who are referred to as Gothic
turn out to be those who bring us up against the boundaries of
the civilized, who demonstrate to us the relative nature of ethical
and behavioural codes, and who place, over against the conventional world, a different sphere in which these codes operate at
best in distorted forms.[13]

Twentieth-century history is ever-present in the 'realist' framework, the 'conventional world' in which, we are reminded, the
horrific and barbaric have happened only recently on a large
scale. There are frequent references to what both Armino and
Aldo see as their mother's betrayal of them and their dead father;
Aldo describes her as seeing herself as 'the spoils of victory'
(*Flight of the Falcon*, p. 116). In mentoring his orphaned young
men, Aldo has seen them as surrogates for a young brother he
presumed dead; it is now they who aid and abet him in stirring
up the university world of Ruffano. In the same way, his own
experience as a wartime pilot may be seen in relation to the
execution of his final feat as the Falcon. He admits to Armino
that his plane's destruction and his near death was, for him, a
transcendent experience:

The point was that at the moment of impact, when she was hit – I
was climbing at the time, and I knew what it was – the explosion
and my release in the sky, happened almost simultaneously, and
the moment of triumph, of ecstasy, was indescribable. It was

death and it was power. Creation and destruction all in one. I
had lived and I had died. *(Flight of the Falcon*, p. 125)[14]

His attempt to recreate it at the end of the novel proves fatal. Du
Maurier herself, in changing the working title of her novel from *The
Night the Falcon Fell*, was aware of the ambiguity of the word
'flight'.[15] As well as echoing the recurrent bird imagery in other
work by du Maurier (see Chapter 3), it also has a Jungian
resonance, implying the transcendence which the bird symbolizes.
Jung's *Man and his Symbols* (published posthumously in 1964) notes
the appropriation by the shaman in primitive societies of bird
costumes to symbolize his power:

> At the most archaic level of this symbolism we again meet
> the Trickster theme. But this time he no longer appears as a
> lawless would-be hero. He has become the shaman – the medi-
> cine man – whose magical practices and flights of intuition
> stamp him as a primitive master of initiation. His power resides
> in his supposed ability to leave his body and fly about the
> universe as a bird.[16]

This shaman is a masculine figure, a cultural construct of
patriarchy. The description of Aldo as would-be shaman fits very
well; we never know if he had deluded himself into thinking that
he could actually fly. For the reader, however, 'flight' may have
other connotations: one can be in flight *from* something. How does
this apply to Aldo? At the level of plot, the answer lies in the
history of the family. Yet at a deeper level, one that du Maurier
may or may not have been aware of, the answer lies at the heart of
European culture itself. What *The Flight of the Falcon* demonstrates
is the cost at which patriarchal lines are preserved, the cultural
matricide that Irigaray identifies and that du Maurier had already
explored in *My Cousin Rachel*. For Irigaray, Western culture has
been predicated upon a masculine subjectivity which relegates the
feminine maternal to the status of inchoate matter out of which the
male must, through a painful and complex process, rise; in Plato's
terms this is his journey out of the cave and into the light.[17] The
western iconography of flight is a cultural expression of this masculine subjectivity. If Aldo's flight into air may be seen in these
symbolic terms, his deliberate plunge to earth can be viewed as a
final acknowledgement of the maternal.

Armino's recognition of Marta in Rome starts a process whereby
a family history of secrets and guilt (the characteristic subject
matter of the Gothic novel) is uncovered. This history centres on
the parentage of Aldo who had returned to Ruffano after the war to
reinstate the Donati family as custodians of the city's history.
Armino, on the other hand, is a dispossessed figure, as his professional requirement to be always on the move indicates. He makes
frequent reference throughout the novel to his nomadic childhood,
trailed about Europe by his mother to live in various hotels first
with her German and then an American lover. Even after coming to
rest in Turin when his mother remarries, he can not reclaim his
identity as Aldo has done. He adopts the name of his stepfather
who pays for an education which takes him further from his roots
as he becomes a speaker of several languages and embarks upon a
peripatetic career. An adolescence spent in close proximity to what
he perceives as his mother's sexual promiscuity (he refers to her as
a 'beautiful slut' [*Flight of the Falcon*, p. 33]) has given him a
mistrust of women. This mistrust, verging on misogyny, at times
manifests itself as physical revulsion. On one notable occasion,
while waiting in the flat of a woman he has met in Ruffano (Carla
Raspa), he goes into the bathroom and, seeing some stockings
soaking in the bidet, is overcome by nausea:

> The disorder, the intimacy, reminded me of hotel bedrooms long
> ago, in Frankfurt and other cities, when side by side with my
> mother's underwear, similarly washed and rinsed, would be
> male socks and handkerchiefs, toothbrushes and hair-
> lotion... The stench of lust pursued me across Germany to Turin.
> It followed me still.   (*Flight of the Falcon*, p. 222)

Carla Raspa's attempt to seduce Armino meets with a slap in the
face. Indeed, Armino perceives her active and assertive sexuality as
monstrous, comparing her with both a 'praying mantis' and a
vampire (*Flight of the Falcon*, pp. 88 and 161–2). His memories of
his nurse, Marta, are rather different. If he has come to see his
mother as a whore figure, he associates Marta in his memory with a
more pure maternal femininity. Marta had been, like her biblical
namesake, Martha, dedicated to a life of domestic service: 'she who
had been clean, fastidious, forever washing, pressing, folding
clothes and fresh linen and laying them away in closets' (*Flight of
the Falcon*, p. 86). Thus he has constructed these two mother figures,

the real and the surrogate, as patriarchy's two polarities of femininity. This is disrupted for him by the 'huddled, drunken figure' with 'the sour, stale smell' Marta had become (*Flight of the Falcon*, p. 86).

Aldo's assertion of patriarchal values takes a different turn. Unable to live in the old family home, he has tried to recreate it in a house in the same street, the Via dei Sogni (literally, 'street of dreams'). Armino's first visit to this house has an uncanny effect on him as he finds all the furniture and belongings from his old home arranged there. Aldo has not married and lives alone with a male servant (a former wartime subordinate); his relationship with the Rector's wife, it transpires as the novel progresses, while deriving from love on her side, is based only on expedience on his. Aldo's attitude to women is in its own way as misogynist as Armino's; he excludes women from active participation in the festival, for example, and he comments that Livia Butali, the Rector's wife, wants 'the same thing' as Carla Raspa but is less honest about it. Aldo's contempt for women is matched by his respect, even reverence, for his paternal lineage.

At the level of plot, the novel unlocks a secret which appears to hold the key to Aldo's present behaviour. As first person narrator, it is Armino who has gradually to discover this secret so that it can be unfolded to the reader. The secret, of course, is that Aldo is not who he thinks he is: he is not his father's son. This secret is revealed to Armino on his return to Ruffano through pieces of writing: a double baptismal entry for Aldo in the church's records, a letter in an old book in the library. In a novel where name and identity are issues, the unknown name of Luigi Speca emerges persistently from these fragments of text to haunt Armino. Its significance is only comprehended by him towards the end when he meets a nun from Ruffano's orphanage who, by disclosing the identity of Speca, provides the final clue to Aldo's identity. Not a doctor who had restored a sickly Donati firstborn to health as Armino had conjectured, he is instead the former superintendent of the orphanage who had supplied a replacement for the dead child. The patristic text in this novel, while *appearing* to disrupt patriarchal lines, could be seen to reinforce them. Aldo is, in his own terms, an impostor: Armino is the only rightful heir to the Donati name. His revelation to Armino, just before the chariot ride, that he has known this since the previous November helps to make sense of his behaviour in connection with the Falcon and the festival. Armino retrieves a narrative of family through one set of written texts; Aldo attempts to recreate history by interpreting another set, the written accounts of the Falcon. Aldo might therefore be seen as attempting to compensate for his own sense of dispossession at the familial level through his apparent affinity with Duke Claudio.

The relationship between the two brothers is also of key importance here. Armino, the younger, has grown up in the shadow of his brother. As children, Aldo (eight years his senior) had always been dominant and Armino's adult life has been haunted by his memory of Aldo. The initial encounter with Marta in Rome prompts nightmares for Armino in which he is transported back in dream to 'that nightmare world where Aldo was my king' (*Flight of the Falcon*, p. 17). Armino's nightmare focuses on the altar-piece in San Cipriano in Ruffano and introduces the Lazarus motif into the novel:

> The picture was of the Raising of Lazarus, and out of a gaping tomb came the figure of the dead man, still fearfully wrapped in his shroud – all save his face, from which the bindings had somehow fallen away, revealing staring, suddenly awakened eyes, that looked upon his Lord with terror. The Christ, in profile, summoned him with beckoning finger. Before the tomb, in supplication and distress, her arms bowed, her flowing garment spread, lay a woman, supposedly the Mary of Bethany who, often confused with Mary Magdalena so adored her master. But to my childish mind she resembled Marta.
>
> (*Flight of the Falcon*, p. 16)[18]

The dream prompts Armino to remember the games inflicted on him by Aldo in which, locked in the linen cupboard for a tomb, he was forced to play Lazarus. Aldo's role, however, was more ambiguous. He sometimes appeared as Christ who 'beckoned me with a smile' and sometimes 'wearing the dark shirt of the Fascist Youth organization to which he belonged and armed with a kitchen fork, he would represent Satan, and proceed to jab me with his weapon' (*Flight of the Falcon*, p. 17). Who is Lazarus in the novel? This is not clear; believing each other dead, both brothers are Lazarus-like for each other. The function is relational. Indeed, by the end of the novel the two have effectively changed places: the dispossessed younger son assumes the civic role of his brother and thus appears set to perpetuate the Donati lineage and its role in the affairs of Ruffano. Aldo suffers the ultimate dispossession of death. Thus the succession of the Falcon's brother, Carlo the Good, to the Dukedom after Claudio's death is echoed in the events of the present day. For Aldo and Armino, however, the exchange takes place symbolically before this, in the chariot ride. Throughout the novel, Armino has alluded to himself as courier and often whimsically describes himself as a charioteer (for example, reflecting on his profession while in Rome he asks himself, 'Why was I doing this? What urge drove me, like a stupefied charioteer, on my eternal, useless course?' [*Flight of the Falcon*, p. 12]). The masquerade element in the novel, associated with the Gothic space of the palace, is in evidence here. Armino is dressed by Aldo in a blonde wig and saffron-coloured tunic to represent Duke Claudio, the Falcon, during the chariot ride. Thus attired, he looks feminine; Jacopo's observation that Armino looks like his mother forces him to recognize the origin of his identity as material, maternal form, repressed both intellectually and culturally. At this point in the novel, that origin returns to haunt him as physical likeness in an 'uncanny familiarity', a collapse of the *unheimlich* into the *heimlich*.[19] Thus his homecoming to Ruffano is shown to be a 'homecoming' in this Freudian sense too. When asked by Armino who would have played the Falcon had he not returned to Ruffano, Aldo replies, 'I intended to drive alone... [t]here were no couriers five centuries ago. The Falcon was his own charioteer'. In a moment of uncharacteristic self-assertion, Armino replies, 'very well... then today you can be mine' (*Flight of the Falcon*, p. 270).

From a Jungian perspective, it is possible to see Aldo and Armino as each other's shadows (like John and Jean in *The Scapegoat*), and this, indeed, may have been what du Maurier intended. Each is, in his own way, inadequate but the death of Aldo will, the end of the novel suggests, be in several ways the making of Armino. In childhood, Aldo's dominance had been dependent on Armino's submission; in adulthood, the relationship seems have perpetuated itself as the charismatic Aldo sweeps a reluctant Armino along in his plans. The subsequent and final feat that Aldo attempts to perform places him back in the role of the Falcon and recalls the other vision of Armino's initial nightmare in Rome:

The altar-piece became associated with another picture, this time in the ducal palace in Ruffano... It had for subject the Temptation and showed Christ standing on the Temple pinnacle.

The artist had composed the Temple to resemble one of the twin towers of the ducal palace... Furthermore, the face of Christ... had been drawn by the daring artist in the likeness of Claudio, the mad duke named the Falcon, who in a frenzy had thrown himself from the tower, believing, so the story ran, that he was the Son of God.   (*Flight of the Falcon*, p. 18)

Just as accounts of the Falcon's end differ, the meaning of Aldo's flight is unstable. If, as Armino believes at one point, he is mad, has he in some sense become the Falcon? Is he deluded that he is Christ but succumbing to the temptation of the Devil, and believing that he can actually fly? Or does he believe that his suicide will teach the people of Ruffano a lesson in the way that his followers' humiliation of senior members of the university was designed to teach them a lesson? More personally, does he make a tragic but rational choice to kill himself because he cannot live with the knowledge that he is not Donati's son and, perhaps even more significantly, the knowledge that his brother knows this? Or does he genuinely believe that he is an impostor and must make way for this brother? Or does he believe that, the supports of his social identity shaken, he must in some Nietzschian manner make his own destiny, hence his quotation of Nietzsche to Armino before the chariot ride? Certainly, his behaviour has had much of the Nietzchian about it in its rejection of mediocrity. Setting himself above the ordinary people of the town and university, his flight could be seen as an outward and visible sign of the 'will to power'. However, his motive remains as impenetrable to the reader as it does to the narrator, Armino. Whatever his motivation, his death is reminiscent of the Vicar of Altarnun's in *Jamaica Inn* (see Chapter 3). For a moment he is apparently on the edge of transcendence, flying Icarus-like in the winged apparatus: 'the feathers, silver in the sunlight, turned to gold'. Then 'he threw himself clear, spreading his arms wide like the wings he had discarded, then bringing them to his side, he plummeted to earth and fell, his body, small and fragile, a black streak against the sky' (*Flight of the Falcon*, p. 282). 'Explanations' of his suicide in terms of the Gothic plot are all plausible. Yet in a sense, his self-inflicted death also marks symbolically not only the futility of denial of the material origins of being, but also a positive recognition of the maternal in these terms.

At the top of the tower (a high place reminding the reader of the painting of Christ's temptation), Aldo tells Armino that he, Aldo, is not their father's son: he is actually the illegitimate son of Marta and his paternity is unknown. His denial of the literal murder of Marta is all the more convincing because of his admission that he was nonetheless responsible for her death:

> Yes, I killed her ... but not with a knife – the knife was merciful. I killed her by despising her, by being too proud to admit the fact that I was her son. Wouldn't you say that counts as murder?

He describes how 'She kept her secret until that birthday evening in November, when on a sudden lonely drunken impulse she revealed the truth' (*Flight of the Falcon*, p. 279). Armino in turn recognizes that he too is guilty in the same way of murdering his mother, having refused contact with her when she was dying of cancer. (Francesca Donati suffers the same fate that would have befallen Rebecca had Maxim not murdered her: cancer of the womb. This is perhaps a symbolic representation of the opprobrium and punishment visited by society upon promiscuous women.) Both admissions echo the reflection of Armino upon the statuette of the Virgin Mary in San Cipriano: 'It seemed to me then that the Mother played a sorry part in her Son's story' (*Flight of the Falcon*, p. 266). Thus the mother figure takes centre stage again and Marta's central significance in the text becomes clear. The polyvalence of her name becomes fully apparent here: Marta/ Martha/ mater/ matter/ martyr.[20] From a figure of cultural abjection, the despised 'refuse' in Rome, she is reconstructed in Armino's memory as a Martha figure but then comes to represent what, in Irigaray's terms, is martyred in the process of establishing and sustaining patriarchy within western culture. According to Irigaray, mythology legitimizes and confirms such cultural constructions:

> It is Apollo, the farsighted one who is always already speaking, who first commanded the murder of the mother. Thus wiping away, denying, the illegitimacy of his own birth? Blood shed to confirm that he belongs to the law of the father alone. Necessary sacrifice to order in the home. Apollo–the brother, in God, of Athena. Patriarchal right/ blood ties. Orestes who slits his mother's throat, takes refuge in the temple of the God who is subject to the wishes of Zeus alone. The women who cry out for revenge are thrown out of the temple as if they were bringing in filth.[21]

Marta, similarly banished from the holy place, is both exile and martyr in this Irigarayan sense. She is absorbed within the discourse of Christianity which recurs so frequently and so powerfully in the text, but in such a way as to question the very foundations of that patriarchal culture of which Christianity is a cornerstone. What is so significant is that both brothers recognize the martyrdom of Marta; thus the binaries which separated her and the other mother figure, Aldo's adoptive mother and Armino's natural one, break down.

Thus from one perspective, Aldo's death-dealing flight could be seen as an assertion of patriarchy and his sacrifice to it. His death allows the true son of the father to take his rightful role. At the level of plot, *The Flight of the Falcon* is a typical Gothic narrative, ending with the assertion of a true heir. Emblematically, however, Aldo's suicide is an acknowledgement that the cultural forces which had shaped his identity are based on the murder of the mother; his death is therefore a sacrifice to an individual and collective guilt. Aldo's confession to his brother confirms his recognition of personal guilt; du Maurier's text cumulatively asserts the collective guilt. Her ambitious novel attempts to show in Jungian terms the link with the past through which individual destinies are part of a collective history but it also succeeds in inscribing in popular fiction some of the insights that can be found in Virginia Woolf's 1938 essay, *Three Guineas*.[22] Woolf's work makes a clear connection between the excesses of fascism and the logic of patriarchy as experienced at a domestic level. Later scholarship has also made the link between masculine gender subjectivity and Nazi ideology.[23] Du Maurier's novel, published twenty years after the end of the war, depicts a Europe with the scars of its traumatic recent past still visible but demonstrates that these must be viewed as part of a much longer historical process. It shows that they are the product of a patriarchal construction of the mother. If masculinity is predicated upon the rejection of the mother, the price is paid in the widest possible cultural terms; such barbarism persists down the ages.

The Flight of the Falcon is the culmination of Daphne du Maurier's mature phase as a novelist and it is the last Gothic novel she wrote. It seems that this so-called 'agreeable writer of agreeable fiction' was able to represent some of the most intractable problems of twentieth-century history in a manner which was accessible to a wide range of readers. Undoubtedly, her own personal anxieties are located in her text too. It is probably no coincidence that

Armino, walking around the snow-covered streets on his first evening in Ruffano, describes himself as a 'disembodied spirit' (*Flight of the Falcon*, p. 38), but in many ways his other self, Aldo, is closer to the disruptive spirit of the imagination to which du Maurier had given this name in her letters. Aldo is the supreme exponent of 'gondalling', one who allows the imagination to take hold to such an extent that it is no longer possible for him to distinguish between what is a creation of the imagination and what is the everyday world. *The Flight of the Falcon* allows du Maurier to write out her anxieties about the destructive force of the imagination while locating them in a much wider set of cultural anxieties. The masculine writing identity enables her to examine the very character of masculinity itself. The answers she finds are far from reassuring and her Gothic plot forces the reader to pursue the origins of horror. The later short story, 'Don't Look Now' (1971) turns its focus on to the inadequacies of masculine subjectivity. Distilled into the short story form at which she had become adept, it is the climax of her career as a Gothic writer.

DEATHS IN VENICE: 'DON'T LOOK NOW'

In spite of the enduring popularity of Hitchcock's 1940 film, most people recognize *Rebecca* (1938) as a Daphne du Maurier novel. Fewer people know that du Maurier wrote the short story 'Don't Look Now' on which Nicholas Roeg's 1973 film – described in *The Second Virgin Film Guide* as one of his 'finest and most accessible' works – is based.[24] The story, published in 1971, opens with a conversation between John and his wife, Laura, who have come on a short holiday to Venice. They are there in order to try to recover some sense of normality following the loss of their five-year-old daughter, Christine, who has died from meningitis. The plot which follows is effectively simple: John and his wife meet Scottish twin sisters in their sixties, one a retired doctor, the other blind, who are also tourists in Venice. The blind sister is psychic and claims to have had a vision of the couple's dead daughter, which she communicates to Laura. Laura believes this and gains comfort and happiness from it; John is annoyed and upset by the claim. A strange incident occurs: one evening, walking in the narrow streets of Venice, they hear a strangled cry; John then catches sight of what looks like a little girl, wearing a pixie hood, who seems to be trying to escape from something or someone by jumping from boat to boat in the canal. Unnerved by this, and made anxious by the sisters, John tries to engineer their outings so that they avoid the two women but, by coincidence, it seems, they keep meeting them in different parts of Venice. The couple receive a telegram from their son's school, informing them that he has suspected appendicitis and may have to be operated upon; Laura catches a flight to Gatwick; the plan is that John will follow her by car and boat. After seeing his wife safely off in the airport launch, however, John thinks he sees her, looking distressed, travelling on a vaporetto with the two sisters. Convinced that she has been abducted by the women, he reports his wife as a missing person to the police in Venice. Whilst at the police station he learns that two murders of a particularly horrible nature have recently been committed. Later, telephoning his son's school in England, he discovers that his wife has arrived there safely. Meanwhile, the two sisters have been arrested for the abduction of his wife. He makes a formal apology to both the police and the two sisters, at which point the psychic sister goes into a trance-like state. Returning from the police station to his hotel, John loses his way amongst the labyrinthine streets of Venice and comes upon the pixie-hooded figure he saw earlier. Again she seems to be running for her life; this time he follows her, assuming she is fleeing from the murderer since he spots a man in pursuit. Anxious to protect her, he follows the child into a room in a building and locks the door behind him, against the pursuing male. He turns to reassure the 'child'; her pixie-hood falls away from her head and he is faced with the unveiled, monstrous spectacle of a 'thick-set dwarf woman'[25] with long grey hair and a huge head who draws a knife on him. The story closes with his consciousness fading as the blood runs from his body, the knife having pierced his throat.

The setting for du Maurier's short story follows the conventions of the classic Gothic tale which frequently uses Italian cities as sites for the exotic, the sinister and the transgressive. Du Maurier's Venice represents the precariousness of 'normality': a holiday resort, it is nevertheless haunted by death. In 'Don't Look Now' the city appears warm and sheltered by day but this 'bright facade' (p. 25) gives way to an 'altogether different' place at night with the long narrow boats on the dank canals looking 'like coffins' (p. 19). Indeed, John himself perceives it as a dying city, sinking down into its own waters, doomed to become eventually 'a lost underworld of stone' ('Don't Look Now', p. 26). Like the city of Thomas Mann's *Death in Venice*, it is a site of death, decay and degeneration. Yet, as a place famous for its tradition of masquerade, Venice is also associated with carnival. However, the festive inversions typical of carnival survive in this story only in grotesque form in the figure of the dwarf-woman murderess who dresses as a child. Correspondingly, the city's very brilliance is predicated upon a dark underside which invites a descent into horror, suggested by the labyrinth of narrow canals which John negotiates so well at first but in which he eventually loses his way and, finally, his life. In her short story, du Maurier seems to draw on both the Venetian tradition of carnival and, more generally, the post-Enlightenment fascination with masquerade itself. Terry Castle suggests in her introduction to *The Female Thermometer: Eighteenth-Century Culture and the Invention of the Uncanny* that it was 'the Enlightenment rigidification of conceptual hierarchies and atomized view of personal identity' that made masquerade so popular in – and so unsettling to – eighteenth-century England. She continues:

> With its shocking travesties and mad, Dionysiac couplings, the masquerade represented a kind of 'uncanny space' at the heart of eighteenth-century urban culture: a dream-like zone where identities become fluid and cherished distinctions – between self and other, subject and object, real and unreal – temporarily blurred.[26]

Like Anne Williams, then, Terry Castle sees the Enlightenment as necessarily *having created* its own darkness and uncanny spaces: arguably, Romanticism further developed this culturally created sense of the uncanny in its rendering of the Gothic, whilst Freudian discourse later duplicated its narrative and epistemological strategy.[27] Correspondingly, du Maurier's tale draws both on Freudian discourse and on a post-Romantic sense of the grotesque as strange and uncanny. This mode of the grotesque, as Mary Russo points out, 'is associated with Wolfgang Kayser's *The Grotesque in Art and Literature*, with the horror genre, and with Freud's essay "On the Uncanny"'.[28] In differentiating between the comic grotesque (associated with carnival) and the grotesque as uncanny, she asserts that the latter:

is related most strongly to the psychic register and to the bodily as cultural projection of an inner state. The image of the uncanny, grotesque body as doubled, monstrous, deformed, excessive, and abject is not identified with materiality as such, but assumes a division or distance between the discursive fictions of the biological body and the Law.[29]

'Don't Look Now', we suggest, both presents and implicitly interrogates a Freudian analysis of an identity in crisis. It also constructs the uncanny figure of the dwarf (like that of Rebecca) as polymorphous and multivalent; as in *Rebecca*, this character functions as a 'perfect figure for negative identity'.[30] Through the dwarf du Maurier is able to explore yet again her continuing preoccupation with identity.

A Freudian reading illuminates some aspects of the story. In its use of eyesight/blindness and fear of madness as recurrent motifs, du Maurier's tale, like E.T.A.Hoffmann's *The Sandman*, lends itself to a Freudian approach which reads such motifs as expressing fear of death and castration. Like Hoffmann's story, du Maurier's tale is concerned to explore estrangement and alienation; it is, ironically, John's fidelity to the realm of 'everyday legality' or the Law (represented in 'Don't Look Now' by the discourses of medicine and patriarchy) which prevents him from understanding Venice and its signs and which leads directly to his ghastly death in a room somewhere in the back alleys of the city. As the place of escape from death and self-interrogation, Venice becomes the location of John's confrontation with both. Because he refuses the latter, he invites the former.[31] However, integral to this process of denial is the role played by the elderly twin sisters, whose 'uncanniness' is linked to both the everyday unusual (they are identical twins) and the 'supernatural' (the blind twin is 'psychic'). Their physiological 'doubleness' which disturbs the eye (and the 'I' of John) is offset, though, by the differences between them: one sister, rather masculine in dress, is a retired doctor who practised in Edinburgh and is often described as 'active'; the other is blind, psychic and invariably passive except when she goes into trance or pronouncement. They both are, and are not, 'identical': one appears to suggest the *heimlich*; the other the *unheimlich*. John's reaction to these sisters veers between extremes: sometimes he credits them with evil power (at one point he perceives the blind sister as a Gorgon-like figure who fixes him with her sightless eyes ['Don't

Look Now', p. 14]); at other times he dismisses them as merely eccentric and interfering. His rejection of the sisters can be read as a rejection of death itself; his inability to accept fully his daughter's death is signalled by the fact that his attempts to return life to 'normal' are fated to failure, indicated by his 'seeing' the dwarf woman as a five-year-old girl. His efforts to make the hotel room like home – an assertion of the *heimlich* in the face of the unknown – involves the repression of his and Laura's experience of death and suffering. However, the repressed, as Freud pointed out, has a habit of returning. Consequently, even within the supposedly safe confines of the hotel room, the radio song 'I love you Baby . . . I can't get you out of my mind' evokes the presence of the dead daughter. Further, John's determination to avoid meeting the sisters leads him, uncannily, to the very restaurant near the church of San Zaccaria where the sisters have also chosen to eat. Explained in terms of Freud's repetition–compulsion principle, this element of *unheimlich* in du Maurier's story signals repression – in this case the repressed fear of death – which is projected by John onto his environment. John's tendency either to dismiss or domesticate the strange can be seen as a denial mechanism; this, in turn, leads him into errors of judgement, the most grave of which brings about his own death. Such an interpretation of 'Don't Look Now', of course, turns John into a case study of psychological malfunction and the story into a cautionary tale in which the elements of Gothic and masquerade can be best interpreted through the discourse of Freudian psychoanalytic theory.

This reading, however, also constructs the sisters as merely an adjunct to the central story of John's psyche and its mechanisms of repression. The text itself, though, allows the sisters to function in a much more complex way than this might suggest; its meaning(s) cannot be contained by the Freudian frame. Within its first few pages the tale allows the women a multiplicity of imaginary roles. ' "Don't look now", John said to his wife, "but there are a couple of old girls two tables away who are trying to hypnotise me" ' ('Don't Look Now', p. 7); Laura and John then amuse themselves, barely suppressing their hysteria, by speculating on what the twins might 'really' be. The list includes middle-aged transvestites, murderers, hermaphrodites, retired schoolmistresses and lesbians. John, relieved that his wife is smiling and laughing again, recognizes this fantasizing as a healing process which has 'temporarily laid' the 'ghost' of their dead daughter ('Don't Look Now', p. 8). Within the first few pages, then, the story both appropriates and travesties the transgressive and supernatural elements found in Gothic writing. However, what the reader is soon allowed to see, which John cannot, is that his own 'psychic' powers, perceived by the blind twin, which he refuses to acknowledge, mark him as the third 'weird' sister. This denial of supra-rational knowledge, outside the realm of 'everyday legality', goes hand in hand with a denial of that side of himself which he perceives as 'feminine'; for example, he finds it difficult to handle his emotions on hearing his wife's voice on the telephone from England – 'shame upon shame, he could feel tears pricking behind his eyes' ('Don't Look Now', p. 44). Laura's natural wish to grieve for her daughter and to preserve her memory (even through the agency of the blind sister's psychic powers) is deflected by her husband's supposedly superior knowledge of what is best for her in her current emotional state of mind, but the story itself shows this knowledge to be both fallible and inadequate in the face of death.

John's 'superior' knowledge emanates from a subject position constructed through age, nation, class and gender. His confidence that he is right derives from his identity as a well-educated, upper-middle-class English male of the mid twentieth century and he dislikes or dismisses anything which threatens that sense of self. He is part of an episteme which frames 'knowledge' within certain accredited discourses; he negotiates Venice by map; he accepts his doctor's medical opinion of what Laura 'needs'; he is deeply suspicious of anything beyond the rational and the logical: 'There was something uncanny about thought-reading, about telepathy. Scientists couldn't account for it, nobody could...'('Don't Look Now', p. 13). This sense of identity valorizes and defines itself *against* the feminine. So John perceives women and children as needing his protection; to a certain extent he infantilizes his wife (offering, for example, to buy her things to cheer her up) and seems to concur with their doctor's advice, the language of which construes women as 'other': 'They all get over it, in time. And you have the boy' ('Don't Look Now', p. 10). He deals with his wife's very different approach to life largely by ignoring it: 'John *knew* the arrival of the telegram and the foreboding of danger from the sisters was coincidence, nothing more, but it was pointless to start an argument about it' ('Don't Look Now', p. 27; our italics). John's rationality is, then, based on what feminist theorists have defined as an exclusion model: 'reason, conceptualized as transcendence, in practice (comes) to mean transcendence of the feminine, because of the symbolism used'.[32] It is also typical of Enlightenment epistemology which, as Terry Castle suggests, defines itself through a 'rigidification of conceptual hierarchies and (an) atomized view of personal identity'.

However, the sisters impinge upon John's confidence in himself and provoke an ambivalent reaction: he thus describes them variously as 'the old dears', 'two old fools', 'frauds', and 'a couple of freaks'('Don't Look Now', pp. 13, 14, 23 and 24). His attitude to them derives from a construction of masculinity which is complemented by its binary opposite of a weak and dependent femininity and which consigns the older woman to the category of the grotesque – a category which is, nevertheless, as Mary Russo has pointed out, 'crucial to identity-formation for both men and women as a space of risk and abjection'.[33] John thus finds the masculine appearance and apparent self-assuredness of one of the sisters threatening to his own 'manhood':

> He had seen the type on golf-courses and at dog-shows – invariably showing not sporting breeds but pugs – and if you came across them at a party in somebody's house they were quicker on the draw with a cigarette-lighter than he was himself, a mere male, with pocket-matches. ('Don't Look Now', p. 9)

The blindness of the other sister, then, symbolically demonstrates the fear of castration that John feels in the presence of the twins. Dismissive of the sisters' 'knowledge' of his child's death at first, John's confidence in his ways of 'knowing', and hence in himself, are gradually undermined as the sisters appear to be more in the right as the story proceeds; he correspondingly demonizes them, referring to them at one point as 'those diabolical sisters' ('Don't Look Now', p. 39). He is finally thrown into crisis by the fact that they are proved publicly right and he is proved wrong (they have not abducted his wife; she is safe in England). Significantly, it is at this point that his feelings of paranoia and hysteria, indicative in classic Gothic texts of masculine and feminine anxiety respectively, force him to reflect on the fact that he might be going mad.[34] He is at that moment of hesitation diagnosed by Tzvetan Todorov as central to such literature:

> [E]ither he is the victim of an illusion of the senses, of a product of the imagination – and laws of the world then remain what

they are; or else the event has taken place, it is an integral part of reality – but then this reality is controlled by laws unknown to us.[35]

Rejecting his vision of the vaporetto (and with it the possibility of 'reading' the uncanny and 'laws unknown'), John chooses to 'contain' the experience within the discourses he recognises as valid: 'The only explanation was that he had been mistaken, the whole episode an hallucination. In which case he needed psycho-analysis, just as Johnnie had needed a surgeon' ('Don't Look Now', p. 45). Typically, then, John pathologizes a state of consciousness (even his own) which is outside the scheme of everyday legality, just as he goes on to pathologize the blind sister's trance-like state as epilepsy. Du Maurier's story thus throws into doubt the adequacy of a Freudian psychoanalytic reading, since John himself, in recognizing that he might be a suitable case for such treatment, thereby defines it as a dominant discourse which is part of the very episteme the tale sets out to destabilize. In this sense, the story accords with Jacqueline Howard's definition of Gothic writing as a 'metadiscourse' which works 'on prior discourses which embed values and positions of enunciation of those values'.[36]

The horror of the tale's end revives certain Gothic conventions in such a way as to confirm the reader's sense, set up by the text's insistent reference to his mistakes, that John is constantly prone to error. The most chilling example of this occurs when the pixie-hood, misconstrued by John as a child's garment, drops to reveal a 'creature' of 'hideous strength':

> The child struggled to her feet and stood before him, the pixie-hood falling from her head on to the floor. He stared at her, incredulity turning to horror, to fear. It was not a child at all but a little thick-set woman dwarf, about three feet high, with a great square adult head too big for her body, grey locks hanging shoulder-length, and she wasn't sobbing any more, she was grinning at him, nodding her head up and down... The creature fumbled in her sleeve, drawing a knife. ('Don't Look Now', p. 55)

The veil which obscures the beauty of the eighteenth-century Gothic heroine is here grotesquely travestied. In fact, the 'pixie-hood' bears more resemblance to the sinister cowl of Gothic fiction which often drops to reveal a similarly murderous intent, as in Ann Radcliffe's *The Italian* (1797):

> The monk... advanced, till, having come within a few paces of Vivaldi, he paused, and, lifting the awful cowl that had hitherto concealed him, disclosed – not the countenance of Schedoni, but one which Vivaldi did not recollect ever having seen before! ... the intense and fiery eyes resembled those of an evil spirit, rather than of a human character. He drew a poniard from beneath a fold of his garment, and, as he displayed it, pointed with a stern frown to the spots which discoloured the blade.[37]

The puzzling 'doubleness' of the twins, then, gives way finally to the sinister 'doubleness' of the dwarf whose childish clothes veil an aged murderess. John has fled from a male figure who, it turns out, was probably a policeman, when he should have fled the female dwarf – an interesting variation on the classic Gothic 'pursuit' scene.

The figure of the dwarf woman is richly suggestive and one which enables du Maurier to explore powerful emotions such as intense fear and the desire for revenge. As a focus for revenge, the dwarf-as-child can be read as problematizing twentieth-century sentimental narratives of the nuclear family. Certainly, in metaphorically presenting the 'child' as dangerous, du Maurier's story is typical of many mid twentieth-century Gothic texts which interrogate the parent/child relationship and the 'innocence' of the young. Seen as a child (which is how John sees her, to his cost), she acts out the daughter's repressed feelings of hatred for the father within the family romance. She is both the unspoken narrative of Christine's (the dead daughter's) tale and, arguably, the avenging daughter of the father/daughter dyad within the modern family. As we have seen, the father/daughter romance significantly informed du Maurier's own life as well as her early fiction.[38] 'Don't Look Now' is one of several stories in the Gollancz 1971 collection (originally published as *Not After Midnight*) which suggest the author's continuing interest in the family romance; 'A Border-Line Case', for example, is a disturbing tale which deals with a young woman's brief love affair with an older man who turns out to be her father.

If, however, we adopt an Irigarayan perspective, the dwarf woman can be interpreted more broadly as an avenging figure who emerges from the dark corners of the Platonic cave or the well-lit Enlightenment mansion. Marianne DeKoven, summarising Irigaray's work, notes that:

> In its compulsion to repress the maternal origin, masculine (self-) representation defines (refines) itself in opposition to maternal materiality as pure intellect, ideality, and reason.[39]

As we have seen, John does indeed define his identity in this way, in opposition both to the superstition and irrationality that the twin sisters seem to represent and to his own wife's 'emotional' nature. In this light, John's death in the labyrinthine ways of Venice may be read as a manifestation of patriarchal anxiety: John is killed by the 'phallic' mother.[40] That is, he is killed by what has been repressed within Western culture, a system whose values have constructed his own. As we have seen, according to Irigaray, the symbolic order involves a failure to represent the mother tantamount to matricide. Irigaray states:

> And once the man-god-father kills the mother so as to take power, he is assailed by ghosts and anxieties. He will always feels a panic fear of she who is the substitute for what he has killed. And the things they threaten us with! We are going to swallow them up, devour them, castrate them... That's no more than an age-old gesture that has not been analysed or interpreted, returned to haunt them.[41]

Du Maurier's association of women in 'Don't Look Now' with intuition, emotion and the uncanny is not, therefore, any more than is Irigaray's philosophy, a repetition of the classic equation that the feminine *equals* the irrational and the emotional; nor is it a prescription *for* female irrationality. Rather, as Margaret Whitford suggests in discussing the work of Irigaray,

> to say that rationality is male is to argue that it has a certain structure, that the subject of enunciation which subtends the rational discourse is constructed in a certain way, through repression of the feminine.[42]

What Irigaray explores in her work, and what – one might argue – is implicit in du Maurier's story, is a proposal for 'the *restructuring* of the construction of the rational subject';[43] like Irigaray's work, 'Don't Look Now' can be read as exposing the supposedly neutral discourses of science and medicine as discourses of the *masculine* subject.[44] Read in this manner, the dwarf woman's act of plunging a knife into John's throat can be seen as retribution for the old woman's death in *The Flight of the Falcon*, published in 1965. For in that novel Marta, we remember, died twice: she was stabbed to death in the streets of Rome but Aldo's refusal to acknowledge her existence as his mother, as he later confesses to his brother, also 'killed' her.

However, the dwarf, like Venice itself, is a site of shifting meaning. She represents fear and terror as well as an avenging horror. For not only can she be read as the ultimate nightmare of patriarchy – the death-dealing figure of the avenging mother – but she may also be seen as a focus for masculine revulsion from the aged female body, a culturally constructed revulsion internalized by women as a terror of the ageing process itself. For the 'child' of John's imagination transmutes, in an instant, into the shrunken crone, with shoulder-length 'grey locks', who grins at her victim. The dwarf, in this reading, is a cackling hag whose physical presence bespeaks the horrors of old age for the woman writer and reader. Du Maurier was 63 years old when she wrote 'Don't Look Now' (the same age as the twin sisters in the tale); her anxiety about ageing is apparent in a letter written to Oriel Malet in 1965:

> Kits, when he was here, took some photographs of me, and also a proper photographer came from St. Ives to do me too... But they make poor Tray look just like an old peasant woman of ninety – *far* older and more wrinkled than Lady Vyvyan, and I nearly cried when I saw them. I know I am lined, but I had not realized how badly! And the awful expression on my face, like a murderess.[45]

There is an echo of *The Scapegoat* here, in that du Maurier sees herself as 'an old peasant woman of ninety', although in the 1957 novel this image of ageing is presented more positively – as a metaphorical transition into a simple way of life characterized by moral integrity. In a novel published a year after 'Don't Look Now', du Maurier again managed to construct the ageing process optimistically. *Rule Britannia* (1972) is dominated by the character of an unconventional octogenarian, a retired actress named 'Mad' (short for 'Madam') who rules over an equally unconventional household comprising six adopted unruly boys and her grand-daughter, Emma.[46] Supposedly based on the actress Gladys Cooper, Mad, who wears a Chairman Mao cap and who strides about the Cornish countryside, in fact bears a close resemblance to du Maurier herself who, in her seventies, 'looked eccentric and sometimes, in spite of her frailty, a touch threatening', according to Margaret Forster.[47] She would, apparently, eat her meals quickly:

> then was capable of leaving the table abruptly and marching off. In her thick jacket and the postman-style cap to which she had become attached she looked as though she had settled into one last part and didn't care what anyone thought.[48]

Comic and resolutely non-Gothic, *Rule Britannia* is an entertaining but odd and unconvincing work, 'the last and the poorest novel (du Maurier) ever wrote' according to Forster.[49] It is, nevertheless, interesting when read as an almost jaunty attempt to construct old age as a positive phase in a woman's life. In her darker moments, however, du Maurier saw old age in entirely negative terms. In a letter written to Oriel Malet in 1956 (when she was only 49 years old), du Maurier refers to herself as 'your foolish old Granny Tray'.[50] 58 years old and postmenopausal when she wrote the letter concerning her appearance to Oriel Malet, she saw herself as ageing rapidly.[51] Known for her beauty and vitality when young, she now felt herself to be asexual and potentially monstrous ('like a murderess'). The very grounds of her identity seemed to be shifting beneath her. In this, she was not unusual. Simone du Beauvoir, born a year after du Maurier, records in her book *Old Age*, published in 1970, how common it is for old people to have a distorted view of their body image, seeing themselves as grotesque or even as subhuman: Swift, for example, projected his disgust at his ageing body on to the Struldbugs and Picasso portrayed himself when old as 'a withered shrunken old man or even a monkey'.[52] This de Beauvoir attributes to the low status accorded to the old in modern Western societies.

On the one hand, then, 'Don't Look Now' can be seen as expressing not only a masculine revulsion from the older woman, but also the feminine fear of *becoming* that grotesque figure. On the other hand, du Maurier's tale becomes a warning against a gender-based complacency, vindicating as it does the wisdom of 'old women' (the twins) rather than that of its more youthful male 'hero' through whom all the events are focalized. Thus du Maurier's story perfectly captures the precarious status of the aged woman in Western society as one which slides between that of wise seer and death-dealing grotesque: the dwarf woman, like the freak of Russo's enquiry,

> can be read as a trope not only of the 'secret self', but of the most externalized 'out there', hypervisible, and exposed aspects of contemporary culture and of the phantasmatic experience of that culture by social subjects.[53]

Noting that old people often dissociate their 'real' selves from their mirror reflections, de Beauvoir describes old age as having 'an existential dimension' since 'it changes the individual's relationship with time and therefore his relationship with the world and with his own history'.[54] The 'real' 'self', at such a time, can seem to become an 'Other' which is trapped within a decaying husk of a body which strangely continues to identify the individual; by the same token, the body itself may be perceived as monstrous and 'otherized' as irrelevant to the 'real' 'self'. This experience seems to be one that du Maurier suffered in old age and her fears and anxiety transmute themselves into Gothic tropes in her work. Only her writing seemed to guarantee the continuance of an 'authentic' identity.

Yet the work itself was becoming increasingly difficult to sustain. In the absence of fresh inspiration, du Maurier turned from fiction to biography, writing two books on the Bacon brothers which were published in 1975 and 1976. After the mid 1970s the only works to appear until the time of her death were reprints and newly edited collections of stories and autobiographical pieces written years earlier. The final and tragic subtext of 'Don't Look Now' is, then, the decline and death of the creative self. For with the death of John, we see also the death of du Maurier's writing persona, that 'masculine' side of herself which she associated with mental energy and the creative imagination. John's psychic powers, perceived by others but unacknowledged by himself, can be seen to represent the writer's intuitive understanding of life. In this bleak reading, the hideous figure of the dwarf is a grotesquely parodic version of the bent and shrunken older woman who kills the 'boy-in-the-box'. Age destroys not only youth and beauty, but mental ability and imaginative gifts – or so it seemed to du Maurier. Yet the 'boy-in-the-box' has, in this narrative, a feminine side – for John's psychic gifts are associated with that repressed imaginary identified with the feminine by Irigaray. In what is probably her last successful piece of fiction, du Maurier interrogates the nature of that inner self, so vital to her sense of identity, and destabilizes those boundaries which had for so long separated her 'masculine' writing persona from her social and public identity as a woman. Faced, however, with the death of that inner self, du Maurier seemed to lose the will to live and went into a long decline, dying in 1989.[55]

As in her most successful works, then, such as *Rebecca* and *The Scapegoat*, du Maurier uses Gothic conventions in 'Don't Look Now' to explore not just the notion of the supra-rational, but the social construction of identity. In this complex short story, du Maurier uses the Gothic tropes of the monstrous body, veiling, freakishness and masquerade in order to interrogate the uncanny nature of identity itself. A story based on *mistaken* identity, it can be read as interrogating gender as a form of masquerade, old age as a culturally constructed state of 'freakishness', the happy nuclear family as anodyne myth and rationality as a post-Enlightenment mental strait-jacket. As such, it is a classic piece of Gothic writing, emblematic of modernity in its anguished engagement with ways of knowing and ways of being.

Endword

Daphne du Maurier's fiction, written over a period of some 40 years, charts the progress of an evolving writing self. In 1977, twelve years before she died, she wrote 'All autobiography is self-indulgent'.[1] Her autobiographical writings are therefore confined to the 1977 *Myself When Young* and the various fragments (which she described as being about 'the conscious self, the person who is Me'),[2] collected together with 'The Rebecca Notebook' and published as *The Rebecca Notebook and Other Memories* (1981). For readers of du Maurier's work, the dichotomy between the conscious 'self' of autobiography and the 'imagination' which she sees as generating the fiction, is not so apparent, however. The 'disembodied spirit' and 'boy-in-the box', identified so clearly in her self-analysis are, as we have seen, central to the fiction. The anxieties which they generate provide much of the creative tension in her best work. As du Maurier grew older, their meaning became differently inflected in her work, so that by 1965 in *The Flight of the Falcon*, the 'disembodied spirit' had become externalized into a male fictional character whose inadequacies are a major feature of the novel.

The most significant way in which the 'disembodied spirit' found expression in Daphne du Maurier's fiction was through Gothic writing. In considering du Maurier as a Gothic writer, we have not found it possible to categorize her work as either distinctively 'Female' Gothic or 'Male' Gothic according to the characteristics established by critics such as Anne Williams and Jaqueline Howard. We have concluded that this very distinction is itself highly problematic. Du Maurier's own sense of identity, as we have seen, involved a negotiation between what she perceived as the male and female aspects of herself in a continually self-conscious performative process of gender identification. Her Gothic writing is a way of transcribing this process; hence it seems to resist identifying itself as characteristically Female or Male. It is likely that Gothic writing appealed to her because of the very fact that it destabilizes all kinds of boundaries. The destabilization of gender boundaries is therefore reflected in du Maurier's writing itself. However, her Gothic writing did develop in such a way as to constitute a critique of masculinity and femininity; in this respect she was able to express creatively and intuitively through fictional writing the kinds of insights developed later by the feminist philosopher Irigaray. This in itself might well constitute a different kind of 'Female Gothic'.

Du Maurier's fiction also destabilizes generic categorization. The novels variously draw upon the family saga, boys' adventure stories, the psychological novel, realist fiction, the picaresque, women's romantic fiction and historical romance. Some of her novels, *The King's General, My Cousin Rachel* and *The Scapegoat* for example, may be described as being only liminally Gothic. Even *Rebecca*, widely acknowledged as a Gothic classic, works partly through its manipulation of its readers' awareness of the conventions of other genres. Not all of du Maurier's novels are Gothic, or even liminally Gothic. *Hungry Hill* (1943) is a family saga and she wrote two historical romances, *Mary Anne* (1954) and *The Glass Blowers* (1963) (based upon her own ancestors), as well as the historical fantasy, *Frenchman's Creek* (1941). *The Parasites* (1949) is a subtle psychological study of family life and fragmented identity. The late novels, *The House on the Strand* (1969) and *Rule Britannia* (1972) both operate more in the fantasy mode, although there is certainly scope for an examination of Gothic influences on the former. Interestingly, none of these novels is (with the exception of *Frenchman's Creek*) among her most popular. There are various reasons for the success of *Frenchman's Creek*, including its escapist appeal in a time of war and its very specific local setting. However, it has perhaps done considerable harm to du Maurier's literary reputation, giving rise to a belief that she is no more than a writer of escapist fiction. It has been the project of this book, however, to argue that du Maurier's best work is that which uses the Gothic to powerful effect. Moreover, it is this work which retains its popular appeal. Du Maurier wrote within the parameters of popular fiction and indeed her work continues to sell well. Her plots are strong and all her work is characterized by a vigorous narrative drive. She was not an innovator in terms of style or structure. She was not a modernist. Her great strength was that, using recognizable popular forms, she was able to explore through Gothic writing the anxieties of modernity in the kind of fiction many people find accessible. Here lies the secret to the compulsive quality of her best novels and the explanation for their enduring popularity.

Notes and References

1 A 'Disembodied Spirit': Writing, Identity and the Gothic Imagination

1. Ronald Bryden, 'Queen of the Wild Mullions', *The Spectator*, 20 April 1962 pp. 514–15.
2. Neil Spencer in a feature on critics' favourite summer reading, *The Observer Review*, 4 August 1996, p. 16.
3. *The Times*, 6 August 1996 p. 1. The four other women in the Royal Mail series of stamps were Dorothy Hodgkin, Margot Fonteyn, Elisabeth Frink and Marea Hartman.
4. Margaret Anne Doody, *Frances Burney: The Life in the Works* (New Brunswick, New Jersey: Rutgers University Press, 1988) p. 9.
5. See, for instance, Linda Kauffman, *Discourses of Desire: Gender, Genre and Epistolary Fiction* (Ithaca and London: Cornell University Press, 1986); Sidonie Smith, *A Poetics of Women's Autobiography* (Bloomington: Indiana University Press, 1987); Leah D. Hewitt, *Autobiographical Tightropes* (Lincoln: University of Nebraska Press, 1990); Sidonie Smith, *Subjectivity, Identity and the Body: Women's Autobiographical Practices in the Twentieth Century* (Bloomington and Indianapolis: Indiana University Press, 1993); Leigh Gilmore, *Autobiographics: A Feminist Theory of Women's Self-Representation* (Ithaca and London: Cornell University Press, 1994) and Laura Marcus, *Autobiographical Discourses: Theory, Criticism, Practice* (Manchester and New York: Manchester University Press, 1994).
6. Janice Morgan, 'Subject to Subject/Voice to Voice: Twentieth-Century Autobiographical Fiction by Women Writers' in Janice Morgan and Colette T. Hall (eds), *Redefining Autobiography in Twentieth-Century Women's Fiction* (New York and London: Garland Publishing Inc., 1991) p. 6.
7. Judith Kegan Gardiner, 'On Female Identity and Writing by Women', Elizabeth Abel (ed.), *Writing and Sexual Difference* (Brighton: Harvester Press, 1982) p. 184. This chapter first appeared in article form in *Critical Inquiry* Vol.8, No.2 (1981) pp. 347–61.
8. Ibid., p. 187.
9. Angela du Maurier, Daphne du Maurier's older sister, also notes in *Old Maids Remember* that 'there was a very special affinity between our father and Daphne' (London: Peter Davies, 1966) p. 138.
10. Margaret Forster, *Daphne du Maurier* (London: Chatto & Windus, 1993) p. 18.

190   *Notes and References*

11. Daphne du Maurier, *Myself When Young: The Shaping of a Writer* (1977; London: Arrow Books, 1993) p. 51.
12. Ibid., p. 19.
13. Oriel Malet (ed.), *Daphne du Maurier: Letters from Menabilly – Portrait of a Friendship* (London: Weidenfeld & Nicolson, 1993) p. 120.
14. In his essay 'Family Romances' Freud states that it is common for the child to fantasize replacing 'both parents or... the father alone by grander people'; such 'replacements' signal both the child's wish to be of higher social standing/greater worth and an infantile regression to the stage when 'his father seemed to him the noblest and strongest of men and his mother the dearest and loveliest of women'. Peter Gay (ed.), *The Freud Reader* (London: Vintage, 1995) p. 300.
15. Margaret Forster, *Daphne du Maurier*, p. 17. The quotation is taken from a letter written to Ellen Violett in August 1949.
16. Ibid., pp. 156 and 227. A sentence from one of du Maurier's letters to Ellen Doubleday (wife of her American publisher), quoted by Forster in her biography of du Maurier, would seem to confirm at least one of these identifications: 'You are the mother I always wanted' (p. 238). 'Ferdy' was the French teacher with whom she formed a close emotional bond while at school in France.
17. Ibid., p. 228.
18. Ibid., p. 222.
19. Ibid., p. 235.
20. Ibid., p. 232.
21. Ibid., p. 276.
22. The extracts from du Maurier's letters to Ellen Doubleday certainly suggest that her relationships with both Ellen and Gertrude Lawrence were intense and romantic. However, du Maurier's craving for a physical closeness to both women might well have derived as much from her need for a mother figure (see Forster, pp. 227, 228 and 238) as from sexual desire for another woman. Undoubtedly du Maurier's relationships with other women during her life were more complex than was suggested by the 'closet-lesbian' view of her embraced by several reviewers of Forster's biography.
23. Oriel Malet (ed.), *Letters from Menabilly*, p. 33.
24. Emily Brontë, *Wuthering Heights* (with introduction by Daphne du Maurier) (London: Macdonald, 1955) p. ix.
25. Oriel Malet (ed.), *Letters from Menabilly*, p. x.
26. We owe this idea to Scott McCracken.
27. Oriel Malet (ed.), *Letters from Menabilly*, p. 178.
28. Ibid., p. 111.
29. Ibid., p. 133.
30. Margaret Forster, *Daphne du Maurier*, p. 421.
31. Oriel Malet (ed.), *Letters from Menabilly*, pp. 111–12.
32. Margaret Anne Doody, *Frances Burney*, p. 216.
33. Oriel Malet (ed.), *Letters from Menabilly*, p. 54.
34. Ibid., pp. 106–7.

35. Oriel Malet has told us that she herself asked Daphne du Maurier to destroy her own part of the correspondence, being later embarrassed by some of her youthful confessions. This was done, a fact she new slightly regrets, as they would have been helpful when editing *Letters from Menabilly*. She has also told us that to the best of her knowledge she has no unpublished letters from du Maurier. (interview with Oriel Malet, 6 November 1995).

36. The phrase is contained in a letter to Ellen Doubleday dated 10 December 1947 (Margaret Forster, *Daphne du Maurier*, p. 221).

37. Margaret Forster, *Daphne du Maurier*, p. 428.

38. The letters between Daphne du Maurier and Ellen Doubleday are owned by Ellen Violett, a daughter of Ellen Doubleday by her first marriage (Ellen Doubleday always kept carbon copies of her corrrespondence, so both sides of the exchange are held by Ellen Violett). She allowed Margaret Forster access to selected letters and gave her permission to quote extracts from them in her biography of du Maurier, but then donated them to Princeton University Library, where they remain sealed to scholars, at her discretion, until 2003.

39. 'Don't Look Now' was published by Victor Gollancz Ltd in 1971 in the collection *Not After Midnight*.

40. Alison Light, *Forever England: Femininity, Literature and Conservatism Between the Wars* (London: Routledge, 1991) p. 165.

41. Oriel Malet (ed.), *Letters from Menabilly*, pp. 162–3. According to Malet (p. x), 'Main' here means 'Of major importance'; 'menace' means an attractive person, or someone to whom one is attracted. 'Moper' was the family nickname for du Maurier's husband in his later years.

42. Daphne du Maurier, *The Flight of the Falcon* (1965; Harmondsworth: Penguin Books Ltd, 1969) p. 38.

43. Daphne du Maurier, *Myself When Young*, p. 53.

44. Diana Fuss, *Identification Papers* (New York and London: Routledge, 1995) p. 2. She also notes, on the same page, that 'Identification is the psychical mechanism that produces self-recognition. Identification inhabits, organizes, instantiates identity. It operates as a mark of self-difference, opening up a space for the self to relate to itself as a self, a self that is perpetually other. Identification, understood throughout this book as the play of difference and similitude in self–other relations, does not, strictly speaking, stand against identity but structurally aids and abets it'.

45. Mary Mason's words are cited by Janice Morgan in the essay referred to in Note 6.

46. Jonathan Dollimore, *Sexual Dissidence: Augustine to Wilde, Freud to Foucault* (Oxford: Clarendon Press, 1991) p. 26. See pp. 3–81 for Dollimore's discussion of 'depth' and 'surface' models of identity, for which he takes Gide and Wilde respectively as paradigmatic figures.

47. Judith Butler, *Gender Trouble: Feminism and the Subversion of Identity* (London: Routledge, 1990) pp. 24–5.

48. Ibid., p. 6.
49. Daphne du Maurier, *September Tide* (1948); revised version by Mark Rayment (London: Samuel French, 1994) p. 34.
50. Janice Morgan, 'Subject to Subject/Voice to Voice' in Morgan and Hall (eds.), *Redefining Autobiography in Twentieth-Century Women's Fiction*, pp. 11 and 15.
51. Martha Vicinus, 'Distance and Desire: English Boarding School Friendships 1870–1920' in Martin Bauml Duberman, Martha Vicinus and George Chauncey, Jnr (eds), *Hidden from History: Reclaiming the Gay and Lesbian Past* (1989; London: Penguin Books, 1991) p. 213.
52. Lillian Faderman, *Surpassing the Love of Men: Romantic Friendship and Love Between Women from the Renaissance to the Present* (1981; London: The Women's Press, 1985) p. 311.
53. Ibid., p. 311.
54. Esther Newton, 'The Mythic Mannish Lesbian: Radclyffe Hall and the New Woman' in Martin Bauml Duberman, Martha Vicinus and George Chauncey, Jr (eds), *Hidden from History*, p. 287.
55. Richard von Krafft-Ebing, *Psychopathia Sexualis with Especial Reference to the Antipathetic Sexual Instinct* (1886) trans. F.J.Rebman (Brooklyn: Physicians & Surgeons Book Co., 1908) p. 355. Quoted in Carroll Smith-Rosenberg, 'Discourses of Sexuality and Subjectivity' in Duberman, Vicinus and Chauncey (eds), *Hidden from History*, p. 270.
56. Lillian Faderman, *Surpassing the Love of Men*, pp. 470–1.
57. See Lillian Faderman, pp. 341–4. See also Alexandra Warwick's 'Vampires and the empire: fears and fictions of the 1890s' in Sally Ledger and Scott McCracken (eds), *Cultural Politics at the Fin de Siècle* (Cambridge: Cambridge University Press, 1995) pp. 202–20, for an interesting essay on how the changing representation of the vampire in nineteenth-century texts reflects a growing anxiety about the 'masculinization' of women in their transition from angels of the hearth to 'wandering' New Women.
58. Carroll Smith-Rosenberg, 'Discourses of Sexuality and Subjectivity: The New Woman 1870–1936' in Duberman, Vicinus and Chauncey (eds), *Hidden from History*, p. 272.
59. Esther Newton, 'The Mythic Mannish Lesbian', in Duberman, Vicinus and Chauncey (eds), *Hidden from History* p. 291.
60. Sandra Gilbert, 'Costumes of the Mind: Transvestism as Metaphor in Modern Literature' in Elizabeth Abel (ed.), *Writing and Sexual Difference* (Brighton: Harvester Press, 1982) p. 206. The phrase is cited by Esther Newton in 'The Mythic Mannish Lesbian', p. 289.
61. Esther Newton, 'The Mythic Mannish Lesbian' in Duberman, Vicinus and Chauncey (eds), *Hidden from History* p. 285.
62. See Lillian Faderman, *Surpassing the Love of Men*, pp. 314–15.
63. Oriel Malet, *Letters from Menabilly*, p. 133. The letter was written in January 1962.
64. Ed Cohen, 'The double lives of man: narration and identification in late nineteenth-century representations of ec-centric masculinities'

in Ledger and McCracken (eds), *Cultural Politics at the Fin de Siècle*, p. 108. Cohen points out that Freud's observation of male 'inverts' leads him to conclude that, since the masculine male invert usually desires a man with feminine mental traits, then his nature is essentially bisexual rather than homosexual. Interestingly, Cohen links this sense of doubleness within the self to the split subjectivity apparent in many representations of masculinity in late nineteenth-century texts.

65. Angela du Maurier, *Old Maids Remember* (London: Peter Davies, 1966) p. 55.

66. Martha Vicinus, 'Distance and Desire' in Duberman, Vicinus and Chauncey (eds), *Hidden from History*, p. 228.

67. Deirdre Beddoe, *Back to Home and Duty: Women Between the Wars 1918–1939* (London: Pandora Press, 1989) p. 9.

68. Ibid., p. 26. Plot synopses of both these novels can be found in Nicola Beauman, *A Very Great Profession: The Woman's Novel 1914–1939* (London: Virago, 1983) pp. 73–7.

69. Arabella Kenealy, *Feminism and Sex Extinction* (T.Fisher Unwin, 1920) p. 74. Quoted in Lyn Pykett, *Engendering Fictions: The English Novel in the Early Twentieth Century* (London: Edward Arnold, 1995) p. 37.

70. Jane Lewis, *Women in England 1870–1950* (Brighton: Wheatsheaf Books Ltd, 1984) pp. 81 and 116.

71. See Daphne du Maurier, *Gerald: A Portrait* (London: Victor Gollancz Ltd, 1934) p. 154 for the du Maurier family's attitude to 'the stable' (it was the young author's open acknowledgement of her father's infidelities which shocked readers when the book was first published) and Margaret Forster, *Daphne du Maurier*, chapters 4 and 5, for Daphne du Maurier's affair with Carol Reed.

72. See, for example, Oriel Malet (ed.), *Letters from Menabilly*, p. 21 and Margaret Forster, *Daphne du Maurier*, pp. 101 and 180.

73. Daphne du Maurier, *Myself When Young*, p. 22.

74. Janet Sayers, *Sexual Contradictions: Psychology, Psychoanalysis, and Feminism* (London and New York: Tavistock Publications Ltd, 1986) pp. 173–4.

75. Judith Butler, *Gender Trouble*, p. 51.

76. A whole page of the 11 May 1927 issue of *Punch* is devoted, in mildly satirical spirit, to the ways and places in which women might wear trousers. This is reproduced, in part, on the cover of Jane Lewis's *Women in England: 1870–1950*.

77. Quoted in Margaret Forster, *Daphne du Maurier*, p. 222.

78. Margaret Forster, *Daphne du Maurier*, p. 418.

79. See Margaret Forster, *Daphne du Maurier*, p. 417. Compare also Judith Butler's remark that 'The constitutive identifications of an autobiographical narrative are always partially fabricated in the telling' (*Gender Trouble*, p. 67).

80. The very writing of such novels may have been for du Maurier, as for Dorothy Strachey when she wrote *Olivia*, 'a process of mourning, an attempt to sustain desire by narratively

194

incorporating the Other who has been lost.' (Diana Fuss, *Identification Papers*, p. 133.)

81. Ibid., p. 140.
82. Daphne du Maurier refers to her grandfather as 'a bohemian at heart on the fringe of High Society' in her introduction to *The Young George du Maurier: A Selection of his Letters 1860–1867* (London: Peter Davies, 1951) p. ix.
83. Judith Butler, *Gender Trouble*, p. 17.
84. Daphne du Maurier, *The Rebecca Notebook and Other Memories* (1981; London: Arrow Books, 1993) p. 49.
85. Andrew Michael Roberts, The *Novel : A Guide to the Novel from its Origins to the Present Day* (London: Bloomsbury, 1994) p. 136 and Richard Kelly, obituary on Daphne du Maurier, The *Independent*, 21 April 1989, p. 17.
86. See, for example, Tania Modleski, ' "Never to be Thirty-six years old": *Rebecca* as Female Oedipal Drama', *Wide Angle*, 5:1 (1982) pp. 34–41 (later revised as Chapter 3: 'Women and the Labyrinth' in Tania Modleski, *The Women Who Knew Too Much: Hitchcock and Feminist Theory* (New York and London: Routledge, 1988); Yves Alion, '*Rebecca*', *Revue du Cinéma*, 442 (1988) p. 37; Mary Ann Doane, '*Caught* and *Rebecca*: The Inscription of Femininity as Absence', in Constance Penley (ed.), *Feminism and Film Theory* (New York and London, Routledge and BFI Publishing, 1988) pp. 196–215; Ed Gallafent, 'Black Satin: Fantasy, Murder and the Couple in "Gaslight" and "Rebecca"', *Screen*, 29: 3 (1988) pp. 84–103; Karen Hollinger, 'The Female Oedipal Drama of *Rebecca* from Novel to Film', *Quarterly Review of Film and Video*, 14: 4 (1993) pp. 17–30; Noël Herpe, '*Rebecca*: Une esquisse du procès de l'idéalisme', *Positif*, 389–90 (1993) pp. 112–14; Alison Light, 'Gothic *Rebecca*: Hitchcock's Secret', *Sight and Sound*, 6: 5 (May 1996) pp. 29–31.
87. Allan Lloyd Smith, 'The Phantoms of *Drood* and *Rebecca*: The Uncanny Reencountered through Abraham and Torok's "Cryptonymy"', *Poetics Today*, 13: 2 (Summer 1992) pp. 285–308.
88. See Roger Bromley, 'The gentry, bourgeois hegemony and popular fiction: *Rebecca* and *Rogue Male*', in P. Humm, P. Stigant and P. Widdowson (eds), *Popular Fictions: Essays in Literature and History* (London: Methuen, 1986) pp. 151–72 and Alison Light, ' "Returning to Manderley": romance fiction, female sexuality and class', *Feminist Review*, 16 (Summer 1984), later revised and incorporated as part of the section on du Maurier's work in Light's *Forever England: Femininity, Literature and Conservatism between the Wars* (London: Routledge, 1991).
89. Alison Light, ' "Returning to Manderley" – romance fiction, female sexuality and class', *Feminist Review*, 16 (Summer 1984). This essay was later reprinted in Terry Lovell (ed.), *British Feminist Thought: A Reader* (Oxford: Basil Blackwell Ltd, 1990) pp. 325–44, where the phrase 'a displaced aristocrat' can be found on page 339. Light's mistaken perception of du Maurier's background as an aristocratic one has been repeated by several critics, including (most recently)

Janet Harbord, who describes what she terms 'the outing of du Maurier' as 'wholly unremarkable in the way that it delivers one more aristocratic figure to the history of lesbianism alongside Vita Sackville-West, Virginia Woolf, Radcliff (sic) Hall and others'. ('Between Identification and Desire: Rereading *Rebecca*', *Feminist Review* No 53 Summer 1996 p. 106)

90. Alison Light, *Forever England*, p. 156.
91. Ibid., p. 194. Note 66 to Light's chapter on du Maurier in *Forever England* reads: 'Such is the power of names that I assumed her to be "a displaced aristocrat" in my article of 1984, "Returning to Manderley"' (p. 258).
92. Ibid., p. 156.
93. We owe this information to Oriel Malet who has also noted in a letter to us that du Maurier 'was *certainly* left in *all* her ideas, tho' refusing to be definitely associated with one party' (correspondence dated 13 March 1996).
94. Oriel Malet (ed.), *Letters from Menabilly*, pp. 67 and 253.
95. Ibid., p. 254.
96. Margaret Forster, *Daphne du Maurier*, p. 388.
97. Malcolm Kelsall, 'Manderley Revisited: *Rebecca* and the English Country House', *Proceedings of the British Academy*, 82 (1993), p. 310. This article was originally given as the British Academy Warton Lecture in 1992. In it, Kelsall argues that Manderley draws on the reader's 'instinctive memory of some image of a Renaissance house' and is thus a 'folk icon lodged in the imagination of the race' (pp. 314–15).
98. Oriel Malet (ed.), *Letters from Menabilly*, p. 136.
99. See Daphne du Maurier, *Gerald: A Portrait* (London: Victor Gollancz, 1934) pp. 262, 263, 278 and 288.
100. Margaret Forster, *Daphne du Maurier*, p. 424.
101. Judith Butler, *Gender Trouble*, p. 55.
102. See Marjorie Garber, *Vice Versa: Bisexuality and the Eroticism of Everyday Life* (London: Hamish Hamilton, 1995) p. 43.
103. McAleer quotes a statement by a library assistant in Chelsea taken from the Tom Harrisson Mass Observation Archive held by the University of Sussex ('Reading' Box 8 File C [14 July 1943]): 'I get in forty new books every four weeks for the twopenny library, but as you can see from the shelves, most of them are out, so there's never much of a choice. The men all choose those detective stories or the Wild West sort of thing, but the women are always asking for a really nice novel: Vicki Baum or Daphne du Maurier – they've both been very popular'. Joseph McAleer, *Popular Reading and Publishing in Britain 1941–1950* (Oxford: Clarendon Press, 1992) p. 91.
104. The Penguin imprint of *Rebecca*, first published in 1962, for instance, carries the blurb 'There are said to be three books that every woman reads: *Jane Eyre*, *Gone With the Wind*, and *Rebecca*. And who can say how many men have read them all?' Later, other publishers who bought the paperback rights for *Rebecca* commissioned covers for the novel which suggest that the targeted reader was, and continues

to be, one who enjoys women's romantic fiction and who may well also be a 'fan' of what has been defined by American critics as 'drugstore Gothic'. The Arrow paperback edition of the novel, for example (first published in 1992), features a young and vulnerable woman standing in front of a rather mysterious-looking building and staring into the distance in what seems to be a state of sadness and emotional confusion. The 1975 Pan cover for the novel, in contrast, is much more historically specific, portraying the narrator sporting a neat 1930s hairstyle and wearing a 'Peter Pan' blouse suggestive of the period. The Arrow cover clearly aligns the novel with the Gothic genre, although the words 'Her world-famous bestseller of romantic suspense', printed on the front cover, characterize it as Female Gothic.

105.   Judith Halberstam, *Skin Shows: Gothic Horror and the Technology of Monsters* (Durham and London: Duke University Press, 1995), pp. 127–36.

106.   Joanna Russ, 'Somebody's Trying to Kill Me and I Think it's My Husband: The Modern Gothic', *Journal of Popular Culture* 6: 4 (1973) pp. 666–91; Margaret Anne Doody, 'Deserts, Ruins and Troubled Waters: Female Dreams in Fiction and the Development of the Gothic Novel', *Genre* 10 (Winter 1977) pp. 529–72; Coral Ann Howells, *Love, Mystery and Misery: Feeling in Gothic Fiction* (London: University of London, Athlone Press, 1978; reprinted with fresh preface in 1995); Sandra M. Gilbert and Susan Gubar, *The Madwoman in the Attic: The Woman Writer and the Nineteenth-Century Literary Imagination* (New Haven and London: Yale University Press, 1979); Claire Kahane, 'Gothic Mirrors and Feminine Identity', *The Centennial Review* 24: 1 (Winter, 1980) pp. 43–64) (reprinted later in revised form in Shirley Nelson Garner, Claire Kahane and Madelon Sprengether (eds), *The (M)other Tongue: Essays in Feminist Psychoanalytic Interpretation* [Ithaca: Cornell University Press, 1985]); Tania Modleski, *Loving with a Vengeance: Mass-produced Fantasies for Women* (1982; London and New York: Routledge, 1988) – see chap. 3, 'The Female Uncanny: Gothic Novels for Women'; Juliann E. Fleenor (ed.), *The Female Gothic* (Montreal: Eden Press, 1983); Frances L. Restuccia, 'Female Gothic Writing: "Under Cover to Alice"', *Genre* 18 (Fall 1986) pp. 245–66; Kate Ferguson Ellis, *The Contested Castle: Gothic Novels and the Subversion of Domestic Ideology* (Urbana: University of Illinois Press, 1989); Eugenia C. DeLamotte, *Perils of the Night: A Feminist Study of Nineteenth-Century Gothic* (New York and Oxford: Oxford University Press, 1990); Michelle A. Massé, *In the Name of Love: Women, Masochism, and the Gothic* (Ithaca: Cornell University Press, 1992); Susan Wolstenholme, *Gothic (Re)Visions: Writing Women as Readers* (State University of New York Press, 1993); Jacqueline Howard, *Reading Gothic Fiction: A Bakhtinian Approach* (Oxford: Clarendon Press, 1994) – see chap. 2, 'Women and the Gothic'; Anne Williams, *Art of Darkness: A Poetics of Gothic* (Chicago and London: University of Chicago Press, 1995). See also Mary Jacobus's *Reading Woman: Essays in Feminist Criticism*

(1986; London: Methuen, 1987); and *Women's Writing* 2: 1 (1994): Special Issue on Female Gothic Writing.

107. Elaine Showalter, *Sisters' Choice: Tradition and Change in American Women's Writing* (Oxford: Clarendon Press, 1991) p. 127.
108. Ibid., p. 129.
109. Robert Miles, *Ann Radcliffe: The Great Enchantress* (Manchester: Manchester University Press, 1995). See also his *Gothic Writing 1750–1820: A Genealogy* (London: Routledge, 1993).
110. Eugenia C. DeLamotte, *Perils of the Night: A Feminist Study of Nineteenth-Century Gothic* (New York and Oxford: Oxford University Press, 1990) p. 25.
111. Ibid., p. 186 and Anne Williams, *Art of Darkness: A Poetics of Gothic* (Chicago and London: University of Chicago Press, 1995) p. 103.
112. See Tania Modleski, 'The Female Uncanny: Gothic Novels for Women' (Chap. 3) in *Loving with a Vengeance: Mass-produced Fantasies for Women* (New York and London: Routledge, 1982) for a good early essay on this kind of fiction.
113. Anne Williams, *Art of Darkness*, p. 102.
114. Ibid., pp. 103–4.
115. Ibid., p. 139.
116. Ibid., p. 140

2 Family Gothic

1. Elisabeth Bronfen, *Over Her Dead Body: Death, Femininity and the Aesthetic* (Manchester: Manchester University Press, 1992) p. 26.
2. William Patrick Day, *In the Circles of Fear and Desire: A Study of Gothic Fantasy* (Chicago and London: The University of Chicago Press, 1985) p. 19.
3. See John Matthews, 'Framing in *Wuthering Heights*' in Patsy Stoneman (ed.), *New Casebooks: Wuthering Heights* (London: Macmillan, 1993) pp. 54–73, for an interesting essay which considers the notion of boundaries and the sites of division (including that between 'self' and 'other') in Emily Brontë's novel.
4. Judith Halberstam, *Skin Shows: Gothic Horror and the Technology of Monsters* (Durham and London: Duke University Press, 1995) p. 13.
5. Cf. Robert Miles who, in *Gothic Writing, 1750–1820: A Genealogy* (London: Routledge, 1993), argues that 'the Gothic is a discursive site [and] "carnivalesque" mode for representations of the fragmented subject' (p. 4) and Jerrold E. Hogle who, in 'The Gothic and the "Otherings" of Ascendant Culture: The Original *Phantom of the Opera*', *South Atlantic Quarterly*, 95:3 (Fall 1996) pp. 821–846, suggests that Gothic writing 'comes to expose the basic nature of the culturally-determined "deadlock of desire", the social and then psychological instability that perpetually threatens the dissolution of the middle-class "fragmented subject"' (p. 828). See also Patrick William Day who claims in his book, *In the Circles of Fear and Desire:*

A Study of Gothic Fantasy (London and Chicago: University of
Chicago Press, 1985), that nineteenth-century Gothic texts
'addressed those parts of the...reader's inner life that were dis-
ordered or fragmented, giving expression, not to their ideal or their
best self, but to their fears and anxieties about their own fragility
and vulnerability' (p. 10).

6. The phrase 'the family romance' owes its provenance, of course, to
    Freud's brief essay 'Family Romances', which was written in 1908,
    and which was entitled in the German, 'Der Familienroman der
    Neurotiker'. As Peter Gay notes, the translation of this phrase into
    'the family romance' suggests that such a 'story' is not confined to
    neurotics and also that it transmutes the notion of the family 'novel'
    (with its nineteenth-century 'realist' associations) into a genre closer
    to fantasy. See, Peter Gay (ed.), *The Freud Reader* (London: Vintage,
    1995) pp. 297–8.

7. Recent critical works which deal with the father/daughter
    relationship (some of which examine incestuous bonds) include:
    Judith Lewis Herman with Lisa Hirschman, *Father-Daughter Incest*
    (Cambridge, MA: Harvard University Press, 1981); Mary Poovey,
    'Fathers and Daughters: The Trauma of Growing Up Female' in
    Women and Literature 2 (1982) pp. 39–58; Lynda E. Boose and Betty
    S. Flowers (eds), *Daughters and Fathers* (Baltimore: John Hopkins
    University Press, 1989); Patricia Yaeger and Beth Kowaleski-
    Wallace (eds), *Refiguring the Father: New Feminist Readings of
    Patriarchy* (Carbondale and Edwardsville: Southern Illinois Uni-
    versity Press, 1989); Patricia Meyer Spacks, 'Fathers and Daughters:
    Ann Radcliffe' in *Desire and Truth: Functions of Plot in Eighteenth-
    Century English Novels* (1990) (Chicago and London: University of
    Chicago Press, 1994) pp. 147–74; Susan Allen Ford, ' "A name more
    dear": Daughters, Fathers, and Desire in *A Simple Story*, *The False
    Friend* and *Mathilda*' in Carol Shiner Wilson and Joel Haefner (eds),
    Re-visioning Romanticism: British Women Writers 1776–1837 (Phila-
    delphia: University of Pennsylvania Press, 1994) pp. 51–71. See also
    Marianne Hirsch, *The Mother/Daughter Plot: Narrative, Psycho-
    analysis, Feminism* (Bloomington: Indiana University Press, 1989).

8. Daphne du Maurier, *Gerald: A Portrait* (London: Victor Gollancz,
    1934) p. 44. Page references hereafter in the text.

9. Janet Todd, *Sensibility: An Introduction* (London: Methuen, 1986) p. 18.

10. Margaret Anne Doody, *Frances Burney: The Life in the Works*, p. 24.

11. Margaret Forster, *Daphne du Maurier* (London: Chatto & Windus,
    1993) p. 12.

12. Ibid., pp. 63 and 94.

13. Gérard Lauzier's film, *Mon Père Ce Héros* (starring Gérard
    Depardieu and made in 1991), is a romantic comedy which subtly
    reveals the sexually ambiguous nature of the father–daughter rela-
    tionship. As such, it is evidence both of the continuing existence of,
    and interest in, this particular aspect of the family romance.

14. Anne Williams, *Art of Darkness: A Poetics of Gothic* (Chicago and
    London: The University of Chicago Press, 1995) p. 32.

15. The short stories du Maurier was also writing at this time are similarly structured. Some of these early stories were collected together with others and published by Victor Gollancz in 1980 under the title *The Rendezvous and Other Stories*.

16. Anne Williams, *Art of Darkness*, p. 22.

17. Ibid., pp. 22 and 241.

18. Ibid., p. 245. The previous lines draw their material from the chapter entitled 'The Mysteries of Enlightenment; or Dr. Freud's Gothic Novel' in Williams pp. 239–48.

19. Ibid., p. 248.

20. Ibid., p. 242.

21. Jerrold. E. Hogle, 'The Gothic and the "Otherings" of Ascendant Culture' p. 825. (For another interesting analysis of the limitations of psychoanalytic readings of Gothic texts, see Judith Halberstam, *Skin Shows: Gothic Horror and the Technology of Monsters* [Durham and London: Duke University Press, 1995].)

22. Ibid., p. 825.

23. The other two are waste and the signs of sexual difference which, as Elizabeth Gross points out, roughly correspond to anal and genital erotogenic drives, whereas food corresponds to the oral drive. See Elizabeth Gross, 'The Body of Signification' in John Fletcher and Andrew Benjamin (eds), *Abjection, Melancholia and Love: The Work of Julia Kristeva* (London and New York: Routledge, 1990) p. 89.

24. Jerrold E. Hogle, 'The Gothic and the "Otherings" of Ascendant Culture', p. 842.

25. The phrase is from the poem 'Self-Interrogation' which can be found in Janet Gezari (ed.), *Emily Jane Brontë: The Complete Poems* (London: Penguin Books, 1992) pp. 23–4.

26. See Heather Glen's excellent introduction to the Routledge 1988 edition of *Wuthering Heights* for a fuller discussion of the discourses which feed into Brontë's novel (pp. 1–33).

27. Margaret Forster, *Daphne du Maurier*, p. 77.

28. Ibid., p. 77.

29. Ella Westland, 'The passionate periphery: Cornwall and romantic fiction' in Ian A. Bell (ed.), *Peripheral Visions: Images of Nationhood in Contemporary British Fiction* (Cardiff: University of Wales Press, 1995) pp. 153–72.

30. Daphne du Maurier, *The Loving Spirit* (London: Arrow, 1994) p. 351. Page references hereafter in the text.

31. Alison Light, *Forever England: Femininity, Literature and Conservatism Between the Wars* (London: Routledge, 1991) p. 167.

32. Lyn Pykett, 'Gender and Genre in *Wuthering Heights*: Gothic Plot and Domestic Fiction' in Patsy Stoneman (ed.), *New Casebooks: Wuthering Heights*, p. 95.

33. Alison Light, *Forever England*, p. 167.

34. During the first few decades of the twentieth century, popular fiction constantly represented the lives of professional unmarried women as emotionally unfulfilling. For example, Winifred Ashton's popular novel, *Regiment of Women*, published in 1915, has one

character retort to another: 'When youth is over what is the average
single woman, a derelict, drifting aimlessly on the high seas of
life... she's a failure, she's unfulfilled' (quoted by Lillian Faderman
in *Surpassing the Love of Men: Romantic Friendship and Love Between
Women from the Renaissance to the Present* [1981; London: The
Women's Press, 1991] pp. 342–3).

35.   Christine Bridgwood, 'Family Romances: the contemporary
      popular family saga' in Jean Radford (ed.), *The Progress of Romance:
      The Politics of Popular Fiction* (London and New York: Routledge &
      Kegan Paul, 1986) p. 176.
36.   Ibid., p. 178.
37.   In Freudian terms Joseph would be seen as suffering from an
      inability to free himself from his mother. Freud saw the daydreams
      resulting from such an attachment 'as the fulfilment of wishes and
      as a correction of actual life. They have two principal aims, an erotic
      and an ambitious one – though an erotic aim is usually concealed
      behind the latter too' (Peter Gay [ed.], *The Freud Reader* [London:
      Vintage, 1995] p. 299). Freud explored the 'erotic aim' behind such
      fantasies more fully in his essays which offer theories of infantile
      sexuality and analyses of hysteria, dreams and slips of the tongue.
38.   Sigmund Freud, 'On the Uncanny', reprinted in extract form in
      Victor Sage (ed.), *The Gothick Novel* (London: Macmillan 1990) p. 86.
39.   Shoshana Felman, *What Does a Woman Want? Reading and Sexual
      Difference* (Baltimore and London: The Johns Hopkins University
      Press, 1993) p. 63.
40.   Ibid., p. 64.
41.   Ibid., p. 64.
42.   Daphne du Maurier, *Rebecca* (London: Arrow Books Ltd, 1992) p.
      211.
43.   Daphne du Maurier, *I'll Never Be Young Again* (1932; London,
      Arrow Books: 1994). Page references hereafter in the text.
44.   Alison Light, *Forever England*, p. 169.
45.   Ibid., p. 168. In an interview given in 1977, du Maurier
      acknowledged that she had been influenced by Hemingway in
      writing *I'll Never be Young Again* (Banner Films, 1977).
46.   As Alison Light notes, Hesta's beret links her with Michael Arlen's
      best-selling novel of 1924, *The Green Hat* (*Forever England*, p. 169).
      According to Light, Arlen's novel was a 'sex novel' of the sort
      popular in the late 1920s, a term used 'to describe the new fiction
      which set out to explore feminine sexuality and was seen either as a
      decadent symptom of the post-war malaise or as a sign of modern
      emancipation from the past' (*Forever England*, p. 255). Claud
      Cockburn discusses Arlen's novel in *Bestseller: The Books that
      Everyone Read 1900–1939* (London: Sidgwick & Jackson, 1972),
      describing the narrator as 'an outsider' and the heroine as
      'Bohemian and very much at odds with her environment' (p. 167).
      Billie Melman devotes a chapter to *The Green Hat* in her *Women and
      the Popular Imagination in the Twenties: Flappers and Nymphs* (London:
      Macmillan Press, 1988), noting that the heroine rebukes the narrator

for his 'fanciful, superficial writing' (p. 73) and that she 'is assimilated to the male narrator's literary *alter ego*' (p. 74). Even these brief references suggest parallels between Arlen's book and *I'll Never Be Young Again* and provide some evidence that *The Green Hat* had a considerable influence on du Maurier's writing of her own novel.

47. Margaret Forster, *Daphne du Maurier*, pp. 79–80.
48. Eve Kosofsky Sedgwick, *Epistemology of the Closet* (1990; Harmondsworth: Penguin Books, 1994) p. 188. See pp. 19–21 for her definition of 'homosexual panic'.
49. Ibid., p. 188.
50. See Jonathan Dollimore, *Sexual Dissidence: Augustine to Wilde, Freud to Foucault* (Oxford: Clarendon Press, 1991) pp. 304–5.
51. Daphne du Maurier, *Enchanted Cornwall* (London: Michael Joseph/Pilot Productions, 1989) p. 153.
52. Lyn Pykett, *Engendering Fictions: The English Novel in the Early Twentieth Century* (London: Edward Arnold, 1995) p. 67.
53. Ibid., p. 67.
54. Daphne du Maurier, *Myself When Young: The Shaping of a Writer* (published by Victor Gollancz Ltd in 1977 as *Growing Pains: The Shaping of a Writer*) (London: Arrow Books, 1993), pp. 28, 29 and 40.
55. Ibid., pp. 47–9.
56. Margaret Forster, *Daphne du Maurier*, p. 97.
57. *The Progress of Julius* was reprinted by Arrow Books in 1994 as *Julius*. All page references, including this one to page 6 of the novel, are to this edition. The Estate of Daphne du Maurier reduced much of what it saw as the anti-Semitic language of the novel (originally published by Heinemann in 1933) for the 1994 Arrow edition.
58. Bryan Cheyette, *Constructions of 'The Jew' in English Literature and Society: Racial Representations, 1875–1945* (Cambridge: Cambridge University Press, 1993) p. xi.
59. Ibid., p. 5.
60. This gendering of characteristics reflects Freud's conservative notions of the masculine and the feminine. For example, in his essay 'The psychogenesis of a Case of Homosexuality in a Woman' (1920), Freud notes that although his patient does not look 'masculine' in appearance, 'some of her intellectual attributes could be connected with masculinity; for instance, her acuteness of comprehension and her lucid objectivity' (quoted in Lillian Faderman, *Surpassing the Love of Men:Romantic Friendship and Love between Women from the Renaissance to the Present* [1981; London: The Women's Press, 1985] p. 324). Interestingly, in *Gerald: A Portrait*, du Maurier describes her father as having a 'definite feminine strain' in his nature (p. 233) in so far as he loved gossip, intrigue and drama; she is careful, however, to state that although he was 'feminine' he was 'not effeminate' (p. 233). In the same work, Viola Tree (Beerbohm Tree's daughter) is presented as having an 'almost masculine intelligence' (p. 236).

61.   Whereas the language in *I'll Never be Young Again* shows the influence of Hemingway, the writing here suggests that of D.H. Lawrence.

62.   Julius's jealousy, his racial 'otherness', and the introduction of a handkerchief into the plot seem to suggest the influence of Shakespeare's *Othello* on du Maurier's creative imagination.

63.   Brian Cheyette, *Constructions of 'the Jew' in English Literature and Society*, p. 6.

64.   Ibid., p. 9.

65.   Ibid., p. 12.

66.   Julia Kristeva, *Strangers to Ourselves*, trans. Leon S. Roudiez (New York: Columbia University Press, 1991) p. 181.

67.   Julia Kristeva, *Powers of Horror: An Essay on Abjection*, trans. Leon S. Roudiez (New York: Columbia University Press, 1982) p. 180.

68.   Judith Halberstam, 'Technologies of Monstrosity: Bram Stoker's *Dracula*' in Ledger and McCracken (eds), *Cultural Politics at the Fin de Siècle*, p. 252.

69.   Daphne du Maurier, *Vanishing Cornwall* (Harmondsworth: Penguin Books, 1967) p. 6

70.   Daphne du Maurier, *Gerald*, p. 255.

71.   Forster claims that Muriel du Maurier's angry silences and emotional distance from her middle daughter expressed jealousy of her husband's love for Daphne (*Daphne du Maurier*, pp. 63–4).

72.   William Patrick Day, *In the Circles of Fear and Desire: A Study of Gothic Fantasy* (Chicago and London: The University of Chicago Press, 1985) p. 5.

73.   Margaret Anne Doody, 'Deserts, Ruins and Troubled Waters: Female Dreams in Fiction and the Development of the Gothic Novel', *Genre* No. 10 (1977) p. 560.

74.   Masao Miyoshi, *The Divided Self: A Perspective on the Literature of the Victorians* (London: University of London Press, 1969) pp. 11–12. Quoted in Eugenia C. DeLamotte, *Perils of the Night*, p. 22.

75.   David Punter, 'Contemporary Scotish Gothic: An Essay on Location' (*Gothic Studies*, forthcoming).

76.   Alison Light, *Forever England: Femininity, Literature and Conservatism Between the Wars* (London and New York: Routledge, 1991) p. 166.

77.   The question is one posed by Terry Brown in a chapter entitled 'Feminism and Psychoanalysis, a Family Affair?' in *Discontented Discourses: Feminism/Textual Intervention/Psychoanalysis* (Urbana and Chicago: University of Illinois Press, 1989) p. 34.

3   Cornish Gothic

1.   Interview with Cliff Michelmore, *The Make-Believe World of Daphne du Maurier* (Banner Pictures, 1977).

2.   This is the title of a book by Martyn Shallcross, *Daphne du Maurier Country* (St Teath: Bossiney Books, 1987). The Tourist Information Centre at Fowey offers 'Discover Daphne du Maurier Country'

guided walks to visitors, and a visit to Jamaica Inn will clearly
demonstrate a process of 'Disneyfication' at work.

3. Jim Wayne Miller, 'Any Time the Ground is Uneven: The Outlook
for Regional Studies and What to Look Out For' in W.E. Mallory
and P. Simpson-Housley (eds), *Geography and Literature: A Meeting
of the Disciplines* (Syracuse: Syracuse University Press, 1987) p. 2.

4. J. Gerald Kennedy, 'Place, Self and Writing', *The Southern Review*
(Baton Rouge), 26:3 (1990) p. 512.

5. Quoted in Martyn Shallcross, *Daphne du Maurier Country*, p. 85.

6. Margaret Forster describes how Philip Rashleigh took a long time to
make up his mind about the repossession of Menabilly and how in
the end du Maurier 'was forced to capitulate, or lose Kilmarth too –
"My landlord has dealt his blow ... I must take it as a challenge ... it
is a bit like the breakdown of a marriage without the finality of
death or even the disturbance of divorce"' (Margaret Forster,
Daphne du Maurier [London: Chatto and Windus, 1993] p. 358).

7. Daphne du Maurier, *Vanishing Cornwall* (Harmondsworth: Penguin,
1967); *Enchanted Cornwall*, ed. Piers Dudgeon (London: Penguin in
Association with Michael Joseph / Pilot Productions, 1989). Page
references hereafter in the text.

8. Daphne du Maurier, *Frenchman's Creek* (1941; London: Arrow
Books, 1992) p. 20.

9. Alison Light comments, 'The heaviest of du Maurier's debts to the
Brontës was to a romantic tradition which centred on feeling and
which claimed the importance of romantic love as a potentially
dangerous place where the individual, and especially the woman,
might get taken "beyond herself", uncover hidden desires and
often destructive wants' (Alison Light, *Forever England: Femininity,
Literature and Conservatism between the Wars* [London: Routledge,
1991] p. 161).

10. Du Maurier herself had used this line in *The Progress of Julius*: it is
spoken by Julius when he experiences a sense of epiphany on
seeing his daughter playing the flute (*Julius*, p. 211). See Chapter 2.

11. Alison Light, *Forever England*, p. 156.

12. Interview with Cliff Michelmore, *The Make-Believe World of Daphne
du Maurier* (Banner Pictures, 1977). Although set in the past,
Frenchman's Creek is arguably very much a novel of its time. The
liberty experienced by Dona St Columb reflects the increased liberty
enjoyed by women in the war years. It also offers a romantic escape
from the real hardships of war. A letter in the Malet collection also
suggests that du Maurier based her pirate on Christopher Puxley,
with whom (according to Margaret Forster) she had a close relationship (Oriel Malet [ed.], *Daphne du Maurier, Letters from Menabilly*
[London: Weidenfeld & Nicolson, 1993] p. 134. Margaret Forster,
Daphne du Maurier, pp. 168–70).

13. Doreen Massey, *Space, Place and Gender* (Cambridge: Polity Press,
1994) p. 6.

14. This construct continues to emerge: in 1996, the BBC showed *The
Lord of Misrule*, a 1995 television film which superimposed a

political comedy (in the form of a plot involving the blackmail of the government by an eccentric and wayward ex-Lord Chancellor) upon ancient Cornish carnivalesque rituals of misrule. It was filmed in Fowey.

15. Alison Light, *Forever England*, p. 157.

16. Ella Westland, 'The Passionate Periphery' in Ian Bell (ed.), *Peripheral Visions: Images of Nationhood in Contemporary British Fiction* (Cardiff: University of Wales Press, 1996) p. 154.

17. Du Maurier, however, is not the only writer to claim the Brontë sisters for Cornwall. A.L. Rowse, the historian, does exactly the same in a 1991 article: 'The Brontës were Cornish on their mother's side, Irish on their father's – pure Celts, we may say. Yorkshire annexed them.' ('Cornwall in History and Literature', *Contemporary Review*, 1991, Sept., pp. 159–60).

18. Daphne du Maurier, *Jamaica Inn* (1936; London: Arrow Books, 1992). Page references hereafter in the text.

19. Margaret Forster, *Daphne du Maurier*, p. 118. Foy was Foy Quiller-Couch, daughter of the famous novelist and academic.

20. The Arrow edition of *Jamaica Inn* describes it as 'this famous gothic masterpiece' in its cover blurb.

21. Margaret Forster, *Daphne du Maurier*, p. 122.

22. Du Maurier gives an account of her early reading in *Myself When Young* (London: Arrow Books, 1993), first published as *Growing Pains: The Shaping of a Writer* (London: Gollancz, 1977).

23. John Russell Taylor, *Hitch: the Life and Work of Alfred Hitchcock* (London: Faber & Faber, 1978) p. 160.

24. Alison Light, *Forever England*, p. 165.

25. Jane S. Bakerman, 'Daphne du Maurier' in Jane S. Bakerman (ed.), *And then there Were Nine . . . More Women of Mystery* (Bowling Green, OH: State University Popular Press, 1985) pp. 18–19.

26. Patsy Stoneman, *Brontë Transformations: The Cultural Dissemination of Jane Eyre and Wuthering Heights* (Hemel Hempstead: Harvester Wheatsheaf, 1996).

27. Eugenia C. DeLamotte, *Perils of the Night: A Feminist Study of Nine-teenth-Century Gothic* (New York and Oxford: Oxford University Press, 1990) p. 19.

28. Ibid., p. 23.

29. Ibid., p. 13.

30. For an account of 'fair trading' around Fowey see John Keast, *The Story of Fowey* (Redruth: Dyllansow Truran, 1950) pp. 101–4 and Chapter 14 of *Vanishing Cornwall*.

31. Ellen Moers, *Literary Women* (1976; London: The Women's Press, 1978) p. 90.

32. Julia Kristeva, *Powers of Horror: An Essay on Abjection*, trans. Leon S. Roudiez (New York: Columbia University Press, 1982) p. 4.

33. Eugenia C. DeLamotte, *Perils of the Night*, pp. 122–3.

34. For a discussion on the significance of windows in *Wuthering Heights*, see Dorothy Van Ghent's essay on Brontë's novel in *The*

English Novel: Form and Function (1953; New York: Harper & Row, 1967) pp. 187–208.
35. Ellen Moers, *Literary Women*, p. 109.
36. Clare Kahane, 'The Gothic Mirror' in Shirley Nelson Garner, Clare Kahane and Madelon Sprengnether (eds), *The (M)other Tongue: Essays in Feminist Psychoanalytic Interpretation* (Ithaca and London: Cornell University Press, 1985), p. 347.
37. Mary Russo, *The Female Grotesque: Risk, Excess and Modernity* (London, Routledge, 1994), p. 85.
38. Ibid., p. 79.
39. For the Cornish reader it would perhaps come as no surprise when Davey is revealed as a demonic figure since associated with Altarnun is the story of 'Peter the Devil', a seventeenth-century deacon of the church who became notorious for his evil behaviour (Beryl James, *Tales of the Saints' Way* [Redruth: Dyllansow Truran, 1993] pp. 22–3).
40. There are carvings of sheep on the pew ends at the church at Altarnun, a feature of which du Maurier was perhaps aware.
41. Again, there is an echo of Heathcliff, who is described by Lockwood in the opening chapter of *Wuthering Heights* as being a 'dark-skinned gypsy in aspect' (Emily Brontë, *Wuthering Heights* [1847; Oxford: Oxford University Press, 1995] p. 3).
42. Judith Halberstam, *Skin Shows: Gothic Horror and the Technology of Monsters* (Durham and London: Duke University Press, 1995) pp. 6–7.
43. Eugenia C. DeLamotte, *Perils of the Night*, p. 160.
44. Julia Kristeva, *Powers of Horror: An Essay on Abjection*, p. 11.
45. Julia Kristeva, *Strangers to Ourselves*, trans. Leon S. Roudiez (New York: Columbia University Press, 1991) p. 191.
46. Francis Davey's plunge to earth is echoed in the 1965 novel, *The Flight of the Falcon* when one of its central characters, Aldo, deliberately sabotages his own staged flight as part of a festival recalling medieval events, and falls to his death.
47. Jerrold E. Hogle, 'The Gothic and the "Otherings" of Ascendant Culture: The Original *Phantom of the Opera*' in *South Atlantic Quarterly* 95:3 (Fall 1996) p. 826.
48. Mary Russo, *The Female Grotesque*, p. 79.
49. Lyn Pykett, *Engendering Fictions: The English Novel in the Early Twentieth Century* (London: Edward Arnold, 1995) p. 30.
50. Anne Williams, *Art of Darkness: A Poetics of Gothic* (Chicago: University of Chicago Press, 1995) p. 103.
51. Rachel Blau DuPlessis in *Writing Beyond the Ending* (Indiana: University of Indiana Press, 1985) identifies the attempts of women writers to question narrative forms as being connected to the movement towards women's emancipation in the late nineteenth and early twentieth centuries. This called into question political and legal forms related to women's social role.
52. Daphne du Maurier, *The Rebecca Notebook and Other Memories* (1981; London: Arrow, 1993) p. 126.
53. Margaret Forster, *Daphne du Maurier*, p. 317.

54.   Anyone wishing to have sight of Menabilly today would also
        probably have to trespass. It is hidden from the road and its present
        owner, Sir Richard Rashleigh, does not appear to welcome
        enquiries from those interested in its former occupant. A letter to
        him from the writers requesting a brief visit remained unanswered.
55.   Daphne du Maurier, *Myself When Young* (London: Arrow Books,
        1993) p. 117 (first published as *Growing Pains: The Shaping of a Writer*
        [London: Victor Gollancz, 1977]). This description recalls the
        opening sequence of *Rebecca* in which Manderley is described by
        the narrator as if seen in a dream: 'No smoke came from the
        chimney, and the little lattice windows gaped forlorn' (p. 5).
56.   There is a tablet in memory of Robert and Honor Harris in Tywar-
        dreath church.
57.   Her sources included the memoirs of Honor Harris and papers
        made available to her by the Rashleigh family, the owners of
        Menabilly.
58.   Ellen Moers, *Literary Women* (1976; London: The Women's Press,
        1978) p. 108.
59.   Ian Duncan, *Modern Romance and Transformations of the Novel* (Cam-
        bridge: Cambridge University Press, 1992) p. 26.
60.   Daphne du Maurier, *The King's General* (1946; London: Arrow
        Books, 1992) p. 296. Page references hereafter in the text.
61.   *The Times Literary Supplement*, 19 October 1962, p. 808.
62.   For a discussion of the conventions of popular romantic fiction, see
        Tania Modleski, *Loving with a Vengeance: Mass-Produced Fantasies for
        Women* (1982; London: Methuen, 1984) pp. 35–58.
63.   It is perhaps no co-incidence that du Maurier chose the name 'Dick'
        for three of her male characters, in *I'll Never be Young Again* and *The
        House on the Strand* as well as this one. All of these men have
        difficulty in adjusting to their social and sexual roles.
64.   Like much of du Maurier's work, it has never been out of print and
        several adaptations have been made of it, including a television
        mini-series shown in 1982. The Auden quotation is from 'September
        1, 1939' (W.H. Auden, *Selected Poems*, ed. Edward Mendelson
        [London: Faber and Faber, 1979] p. 86).
65.   For example, Robert Miles, *Gothic Writing: A Genealogy 1750–1820*
        (London: Routledge, 1993) and Jerrold E. Hogle, 'The Gothic and
        the "Otherings" of Ascendant Culture': *The Original Phantom of the
        Opera* in *South Atlantic Quarterly* 95:3 (Fall 1996) pp. 157–171.
66.   See, for example, Chapter 15 of *Vanishing Cornwall* (pp.197–8).
67.   See Margaret Forster, *Daphne du Maurier* (Chapters 12 and 13) for an
        account of this period of du Maurier's life.

4 The Secrets of Manderley: *Rebecca*

1.   See William Patrick Day, *In the Circles of Fear and Desire: A Study of
        Gothic Fantasy* (Chicago and London: The University of Chicago
        Press, 1985) p. 3.

2. Angela Carter, *Expletives Deleted* (1992; London: Vintage, 1993) p. 163. See Patsy Stoneman, *Brontë Transformations: The Cultural Dissemination of 'Jane Eyre' and 'Wuthering Heights'* (London and New York: Prentice Hall/Harvester Wheatsheaf, 1996) pp. 99–104, 106–8 and 148–50 for an analysis of the influence of Charlotte Brontë's *Jane Eyre* on du Maurier's *Rebecca*.

3. Joanna Russ, 'Somebody's Trying to Kill Me and I Think It's My Husband: The Modern Gothic', in Juliann E. Fleenor (ed.), *The Female Gothic* (Montreal: Eden Press, 1983) p. 31. Originally published as an article in *Journal of Popular Culture* Vol. 6 No.4 pp. 666–91. Victoria Holt's *Mistress of Mellyn*, published in 1961, is a good example of the type of 'crossbreed' defined by Joanna Russ in this article. Set in nineteenth-century Cornwall, with a governess for its heroine, Holt's novel draws heavily on both *Jane Eyre* and *Rebecca*. Its dénouement, in which the heroine almost suffers the fate of being entombed alive in the forgotten priest hole of the country house owned by her employer, perhaps also owes something to du Maurier's *The King's General*.

4. Daphne du Maurier, *Rebecca* (London: Arrow, 1992) p. 5. All page references, which appear hereafter in the text, are to this edition. *Rebecca* was first published by Victor Gollancz in 1938.

5. David Punter, *The Literature of Terror*, Volume 2 (Second edition) (London and New York: Longman, 1996) p. 189.

6. Joanna Russ, 'Somebody's Trying to Kill Me and I Think It's My Husband: The Modern Gothic' in Fleenor, p. 33.

7. Judith Halberstam, *Skin Shows: Gothic Horror and the Technology of Monsters* (Durham and London: Duke University Press, 1995) p. 22.

8. The first quarter of *Rebecca* was written in Alexandria between July and mid December of 1937. The rest of the novel, completed by April 1938, was written at 'Greyfriars', a house in Church Crookham, near Fleet, Hampshire, where her husband was stationed from the beginning of 1938. See Margaret Forster, *Daphne du Maurier*, pp. 123–35 for an account of du Maurier's time in Alexandria.

9. Daphne du Maurier, *The Rebecca Notebook and Other Memories* (1981; London: Arrow, 1993) p. 10.

10. Beatrice's supposition that Communists scuppered Rebecca's boat may be seen to reflect a British inter-war anxiety about the spread of socialism. However, the text's quasi-parodic representation of 'Englishness' in Maxim's sister warns us that we should not take her fears seriously; significantly, the narrator dismisses them as unfounded.

11. Daphne du Maurier, *Enchanted Cornwall* (ed. Piers Dudgeon) (Harmondsworth: Penguin Group in association with Michael Joseph/Pilot Productions, 1989) p. 106.

12. Interestingly, in her poem 'The Dancer' written during the 1930s (which may in part seek to evoke memories of Isadora Duncan), H.D. uses the rhododendron as an image to convey the integrity and sexual presence of the woman artist.

13. Class is an important aspect of this, as Light so persuasively argues in ' "Returning to Manderley" – Romance Fiction, Female Sexuality and Class' in Terry Lovell (ed.), *British Feminist Thought: A Reader* (Oxford: Basil Blackwell, 1990) (originally published in *Feminist Review* 16, 1984), but it cannot tell the whole story. Interestingly, despite Maxim's grandmother's belief that Rebecca had 'the three things that matter in a wife...breeding, brains, and beauty' (p. 284), Rebecca's social class is not entirely clear from the novel. Light assumes that it is her 'aristocratic lineage (which) allowed her a passionate and equal sexuality' (as distinct from the 'bourgeois model of femininity' available to the narrator [Lovell (ed.), p. 328]), whereas Michelle A. Massé, in speculating that Rebecca was married for her money, opens up the possibility that the marriage, combining aristocratic status with *nouveau riche* wealth, was one of expediency for both parties (as she points out, 'Manderley's splendor is very recent') (*In the Name of Love: Women, Masochism, and the Gothic* [Ithaca and London: Cornell University Press, 1992] p. 181).

14. Margaret Forster, *Daphne du Maurier* (London: Chatto and Windus, 1993) p. 137.

15. In this respect, Maxim foreshadows the character of Aldo in du Maurier's later novel, *The Flight of the Falcon*, published in 1965.

16. Shoshana Felman, *What does a Woman Want?: Reading and Sexual Difference* (Baltimore and London: The Johns Hopkins University Press, 1993) p. 36.

17. The phrase is Paul Morrison's and is taken from 'Enclosed in Openness: *Northanger Abbey* and the Domestic Carceral', *Texas Studies in Literature and Language* 33 :91 (1991) pp. 1–23.

18. Anne Williams, *Art of Darkness: A Poetics of Gothic* (Chicago and London: The University of Chicago Press, 1995) pp. 41, 43 and 46.

19. Ibid., p. 42.

20. But compare Michelle A. Massé's analysis, which foregrounds sadism/masochism, in a reading of *Rebecca* as 'a beating fantasy' in which the narrator longs 'for the power of the beater whilst claiming the blamelessness of the beaten' (*In the Name of Love: Women, Masochism and the Gothic* [Ithaca and London: Cornell University Press, 1992] p. 191).

21. Elisabeth Bronfen, *Over her Dead Body: Death, Femininity and the Aesthetic* (Manchester: Manchester University Press, 1992) p. 150.

22. Compare Elisabeth Bronfen in *Over Her Dead Body*: 'Woman functions as a sign not only of the essence of femininity but also of the Other in whose mirror or image masculine identity and creativity finds its definition' (p. 209).

23. Ibid., p. 181.

24. Compare Hitchcock's film of the novel, in which the narrator is kept in an infantilized state through, for example, continued emotional dependence on Maxim and exclusion from the trip down to London to investigate the nature of Rebecca's visit to Dr Baker.

25. Alison Light, ' "Returning to Manderley" – Romance Fiction, Female Sexuality and Class' in Terry Lovell (ed.), *British Feminist*

Thought: A Reader (Oxford: Basil Blackwell, 1990) p. 338. She later notes, however, in an article on Hitchcock's film of *Rebecca*, that 'du Maurier involves Rebecca's incestuous cousin in the arson, and lets Mrs Danvers disappear' ('Gothic *Rebecca*: Hitchcock's Secret', *Sight and Sound* 6:5 [May 1996] p. 30).

26. Michelle A. Massé, *In the Name of Love*, p. 189.
27. Harriet Hawkins, *Classics and Trash: Traditions and Taboos in High Literature and Popular Modern Genres* (Hemel Hempstead: Harvester Wheatsheaf, 1990) p. 144.
28. Judith Halberstam, *Skin Shows*, p. 60.
29. We owe this point to Peter Childs.
30. We owe this idea to Michael Parker. Compare Allan Lloyd Smith's comment that ' "R" might encompass the idea of a hanged person, as well as the sexual innuendo of a female body (sloping in Rebecca's monogram), with spread legs suggesting availability' in 'The Phantoms of *Drood* and *Rebecca*: The Uncanny Reencountered through Abraham and Torok's "Cryptonomy"', *Poetics Today* 13: 2 (1992) p. 304. These different reponses to Rebecca's initial could be construed as different masculine readings of the sign 'woman'.
31. Anne Williams, *Art of Darkness*, p. 69.
32. Ibid., p. 73.
33. Rebecca's body – to use Tania Modleski's words – 'becomes the site of a bizarre fort/da game'. (Tania Modleski, *The Women Who Knew Too Much: Hitchcock and Feminist Theory* [London and New York: Routledge, 1988] p. 49.) Modleski uses this phrase to describe the manner in which representations of Rebecca are played out on the narrator's body, but it is just as appropriate to describe the absence/presence of Rebecca's (dead) body.
34. Elisabeth Bronfen, *Over Her Dead Body*, p. 53.
35. Compare the death of Dracula: 'It was like a miracle; but before our very eyes, and almost in the drawing of a breath, the whole body crumbled into dust and passed from our sight'. Bram Stoker, *Dracula* (1897; Harmondsworth: Penguin Books, 1993) p. 484. See also Bronfen, citing the work of Robert Hertz, on primary and secondary burial, in *Over Her Dead Body*, pp. 103, 177, 199 and 295.
36. See Ernest Jones, 'On the Vampire' in Christopher Frayling, *Vampyres: Lord Byron to Count Dracula* (1991; London: Faber and Faber, 1992) p. 409.
37. It is perhaps worth noting here how, in many Gothic texts, certain revenants (such as vampires) can be eliminated only by being 'killed' three times. See, for example, J. Sheridan Le Fanu's 'Carmilla' (1872) in which an 'old woodman' describes how revenants who had troubled a village were 'extinguished in the usual way, by decapitation, by the stake, and by burning' (*In a Glass Darkly* [Stroud, Gloucestershire: Alan Sutton Publishing, 1990;1993] p. 303).

38. Christopher Frayling, *Vampyres: Lord Byron to Count Dracula* (London: Faber & Faber, 1992) pp. 68 and 71–2.
39. Ibid., pp. 48–9, 54–6 and 56–7.
40. Norman Collins's reader's report for *Rebecca* is held by Victor Gollancz Ltd, who kindly allowed us access to it. Collins notes, in particular, the effective characterization of Mrs Danvers, who is compared to the 'terrifying' old woman in Le Fanu's novel.
41. The changing representation of the vampire in nineteenth-century texts also, according to Alexandra Warwick, reflected a growing anxiety about the 'masculinization' of women in their transition from angels of the hearth to 'wandering' New Women. See Alexandra Warwick, 'Vampires and the empire: fears and fictions of the 1890s' in Sally Ledger and Scott McCracken (eds), *Cultural Politics at the Fin de Siècle* (Cambridge: Cambridge University Press, 1995) pp. 202–20.
42. See Ken Gelder, *Reading the Vampire* (London and New York: Routledge, 1994) pp. 13–17 and Judith Halberstam, *Skin Shows: Gothic Horror and the Technology of Monsters* (Durham and London: Duke University Press, 1995) pp. 86–106; and 'Technologies of Monstrosity: Bram Stoker's *Dracula*' in Ledger and McCracken (eds), *Cultural Politics at the Fin de Siècle*, pp. 248–66.
43. Margaret Forster, *Daphne du Maurier*, p. 91.
44. Martyn Shallcross, *The Private World of Daphne du Maurier* (1991; London: Robson Books, 1993) pp. 69–70.
45. Judith Halberstam, *Skin Shows*, p. 88.
46. Ibid., p. 92.
47. *The Shorter Oxford English Dictionary* Vol. I (Oxford: Clarendon Press, 1973) p. 318.
48. Compare the version contained in the original epilogue: 'and I – rather too late in the day – have lost my diffidence, my timidity, my shyness with strangers' (*The Rebecca Notebook and other Memories*, p. 44).
49. Charles Johnson and Linwood Sleigh, *The Harrap Book of Boys' and Girls' Names* (1962; London: Harrap, 1973) p. 173. The entry for the name also notes that its first bearer, who was the wife of Isaac and the mother of Jacob and Esau, was 'noted for her great beauty'.
50. Joan Riviere, 'Womanliness as a Masquerade' in Victor Burgin, James Donald and Cora Kaplan (eds), *Formations of Fantasy* (London and New York: Methuen, 1986) p. 38. This essay was first published in *The International Journal of Psychoanalysis* 10 (1929).
51. Judith Butler, *Gender Trouble: Feminism and the Subversion of Identity* (New York and London: Routledge, 1990) p. 47. See also pp. 46–54.
52. Margaret Whitford (ed.), *The Irigaray Reader* (1991; Oxford: Blackwell, 1994) pp. 135–6. The section from which this extract is taken, entitled 'Questions', is reprinted from *This Sex Which Is Not One*, trans. Catherine Porter with Carolyn Burke (Cornell University Press, 1985).
53. Elisabeth Bronfen, *Over Her Dead Body*, p. 66. See also Tania Modleski, *The Women Who Knew Too Much: Hitchcock and Feminist*

Theory (New York and London: 1988) p. 54, for a brief discussion of the Manderley Ball scene in Hitchcock's film of *Rebecca* in relation to Irigaray's concept of masquerade. Janet Harbord also touches an femininity as masquerade in 'Between Identification and Desire: Rereading *Rebecca*', *Feminist Review*, No. 53, Summer 1996, p. 101.

54. Shoshana Felman, *What Does a Woman Want?*, p. 65.
55. Alison Light, '"Returning to Manderley" – Romance Fiction, Female Sexuality and Class' in Terry Lovell, *British Feminist Thought: A Reader* (Oxford: Basil Blackwell, 1990) p. 341.
56. As several critics have noticed, early notes towards the novel contained an epilogue, which presented 'Henry' as 'crippled', 'maimed' and 'scarred'. See Daphne du Maurier, *The Rebecca Notebook and Other Memories* (1981; London: Arrow, 1993) pp. 34 and 44.
57. See Mark Girouard's comment in *Life in the English Country House: A Social and Architectural History* (New Haven and London: Yale University Press, 1978) that 'Country houses could project a disconcerting double image – relaxed and delightful to those who had the *entrée*, arrogant and forbidding to those who did not' (p. 242). As the anonymous reviewer of the Penguin imprint of *Rebecca* remarked in 1962, 'social insecurity is not necessarily trivial and may be the proper stuff of nightmares' ('Archangels Ruined', *The Times Literary Supplement* 3,164, 19 October 1962) p. 808.
58. See Nina Auerbach, *Woman and the Demon: The Life of a Victorian Myth* (Cambridge, Massachusetts and London: Harvard University Press, 1982) pp. 15–22, for an interesting analysis of Trilby as 'an image of infinite change' (p. 18).
59. See, for example, Tania Modleski, *The Women Who Knew Too Much: Hitchcock and Feminist Theory* (New York and London: Routledge, 1988) p. 51; Karen Hollinger, 'The Female Oedipal Drama of *Rebecca* from Novel to Film', *Quarterly Review of Film and Video* 14: 4 (1993) p. 24; Mary Wings, 'Rebecca Redux: Tears on a Lesbian Pillow' in Liz Gibbs (ed.), *Daring to Dissent: Lesbian Culture from Margin to Mainstream* (London: Cassell, 1994) pp. 11–33; Alison Light, 'Gothic *Rebecca*: Hitchcock's Secret', *Sight and Sound* 6: 5 (May 1996) pp. 29-31; Janet Harbord, 'Between Identification and Desire: Rereading *Rebecca*', *Feminist Review*, No. 53, Summer 1996, pp. 95-107.
60. Compare Judith Halberstam on Mr Hyde, *Skin Shows*, p. 77
61. Ibid., p. 68.
62. Ibid., pp. 75 and 77.
63. Ibid., p. 69.
64. See Allan Lloyd Smith, 'The Phantoms of *Drood* and *Rebecca*' pp. 301–2 for a rather different reading of the significance of Rebecca's handwriting. Compare also Judith Halberstam's comment on *Dracula*: 'The activities of reading and writing...in this novel...are annexed to the production of sexual subjectivities.' ('Technologies of Monstrosity: Bram Stoker's *Dracula*' in Ledger and McCracken (eds), *Cultural Politics at the Fin de Siècle*, p. 251.)

65. Judith Halberstam, 'Technologies of Monstrosity: Bram Stoker's *Dracula*' in Ledger and Mc Cracken (eds), *Cultural Politics at the Fin de Siècle*, p. 263.

5 Foreign Affairs

1. Margaret Forster, *Daphne du Maurier* (London: Chatto and Windus, 1993) pp.255–6.
2. Letter to Maureen Baker-Munton (4th July 1957) reproduced in full in Margaret Forster, *Daphne du Maurier*, pp. 420–5. Forster points out that the letter was written shortly after du Maurier's husband, referred to as 'Moper', had had a nervous breakdown and du Maurier herself was struggling to avert her own breakdown.
3. Oriel Malet, *Daphne du Maurier: Letters from Menabilly – Portrait of a Friendship* (London: Weidenfeld & Nicolson, 1993) pp.80 and 133.
4. Ibid. p.80.
5. Daphne du Maurier, *My Cousin Rachel* (1951; London: Arrow, 1992) p.12. Page references hereafter in the text.
6. Daphne du Maurier, *Enchanted Cornwall* (ed. Piers Dudgen) (Harmondsworth: Penguin Group in Association with Michael Joseph/Pilot Productions, 1989) p.153.
7. Julia Kristeva, *Strangers to Ourselves* (trans. Leon S. Roudiez) (New York: Columbia University Press, 1991) p.191.
8. The image of Rachel as 'a snake' is reminiscent of Ben's description of Rebecca (*Rebecca*, p.162) which is echoed in the narrator's dream at the end of *Rebecca* when, looking in the mirror, she 'becomes' Rebecca, her hair 'twisted like a snake' (*Rebecca*, p.396).
9. Anne Williams, *Art of Darkness: A Poetics of Gothic* (Chicago: Chicago University Press, 1995) p.95.
10. In *Enchanted Cornwall*, du Maurier describes Philip's love for Rachel as 'an odd, almost child-like infatuation, unquestioning, adoring, the son looking for his mother'. (*Enchanted Cornwall*, pp.154–5). This is an interesting reversal of the relationship between Maxim and the narrator in *Rebecca*, where the husband behaves more like a father.
11. In contrast with the representation of Ambrose's writing, where the signified has priority, Rachel's writing is described as handwriting. Here, Philip searches for Rachel's identity, but finds, enigmatically, only signifiers: 'I looked at the handwriting on the folded paper. I don't know what I thought to see. Something bold, perhaps, with loops and flourishes; or its reverse, darkly scrawled and mean. This was just handwriting, much like any other, except that the ends of the words tailed off in little dashes, making the words themselves not altogether easy to decipher.' (*My Cousin Rachel*, p.57)
12. Anne Williams, *Art of Darkness*, pp. 66–7.
13. Luce Irigaray, 'Women-mothers, the silent substratum', in Margaret Whitford (ed.), *The Irigaray Reader* (Oxford: Blackwell, 1991) p.47.
14. Ibid., p.49.

15. William Patrick Day, *In the Circles of Fear and Desire: A Study of Gothic Fantasy* (Chicago and London: University of Chicago Press, 1985) p.19.
16. Anne Williams, *Art of Darkness*, p.107.
17. Ibid., pp. 105–6.
18. Ibid., p.107.
19. Oriel Malet (ed.), *Letters from Menabilly*, p.131.
20. Interview with Cliff Michelmore (Banner Films, 1977) and Oriel Malet (ed.), *Letters from Menabilly*, p.3.
21. Daphne du Maurier, *The du Mauriers* (London: Gollancz, 1937); *The Glass Blowers* (London: Gollancz, 1963); *Frenchman's Creek* (London: Gollancz, 1941); *The Scapegoat* (London: Gollancz, 1957). All references to the latter in this chapter are from the Arrow edition (London, 1992).
22. The artistic drawing talents of Jean-Benoit Aubéry echo those of du Maurier's grandfather, George du Maurier, the famous illustrator, while his role as a pirate offers a reminder of Gerald's most famous stage role as Captain Hook in J. M. Barrie's *Peter Pan*.
23. Phillipe Sollers, *Théories des Exceptions*, cited in John Lechte, *Julia Kristeva* (London: Routledge, 1990) p.13.
24. Karl Miller, *Doubles: Studies in Literary History* (Oxford: Oxford University Press, 1985) p.14.
25. The 1962 *Times Literary Supplement* review of du Maurier's work states that 'the best quality of this book is, surprisingly, its "realism"', although it does place it in the tradition of the 'demoniac' novel, claiming that 'it is almost consistently in this field that Daphne du Maurier has chosen to write her novels'. The anonymous reviewer believes that du Maurier has 'in her more trivial books got the heart of the matter in her. Twice, in *Rebecca* and in *The Scapegoat*, her talent rose to meet the better potentialities of her favourite genre' (*The Times Literary Supplement*, 19 October 1962) p.808.
26. Homi Bhabha, *The Location of Culture* (London: Routledge, 1994), p. 153.
27. Julia Kristeva, *Strangers to Ourselves*, p.191.
28. Ibid., pp. 13–14.
29. Ibid., pp. 147–8.
30. Oriel Malet (ed.), *Letters From Menabilly*, pp. 80–1.
31. Daphne du Maurier, *The Scapegoat* (1957; London: Arrow, 1992) p.9. Page numbers hereafter in the text.
32. Homi Bhabha, *The Location of Culture*, p.49.
33. Julia Kristeva, *Strangers to Ourselves*, pp. 182–3.
34. Ibid., p.191.
35. Classic examples are Radcliffe's *The Italian*, Walpole's *The Castle of Otranto* and Lewis's *The Monk*.
36. Du Maurier is drawing on her own family history here: her French antecedents were glass blowers.
37. Oriel Malet (ed.), *Letters from Menabilly*, p.80.

38. Du Maurier's letters to Oriel Malet indicate that St Thérèse of Lisieux and 'the little way' had captured her imagination. See Oriel Malet (ed.), *Letters from Menabilly*, pp.195, 196–7, 199, 207, 211, 274 and 276.
39. For a full discussion of this, see Ian Duncan, *Modern Romance and Transformations of the Novel: The Gothic, Scott and Dickens* (Cambridge: Cambridge University Press, 1992); and Victor Sage, *Horror Fiction in the Protestant Tradition* (London and Basingstoke, Macmillan, 1988).
40. Virginia Woolf, *Three Guineas* (1938; Oxford: Oxford University Press, 1992) p.313.
41. Oriel Malet, *Letters from Menabilly*, p.194.

6 Murdering (M)others

1.   Most notably, Alison Light. See, for example, Alison Light, *Forever England: Femininity, Literature and Conservatism Between the Wars* (London: Routledge; 1991) p. 156.
2.   This comment was attributed to Quentin Bell in an article in *The Times* discussing the inclusion of du Maurier in a set of special stamps celebrating 'great twentieth-century women'. (*The Times,* 6 August 1996).
3.   Oriel Malet (ed.), *Daphne du Maurier: Letters from Menabilly – Portrait of a Friendship* (London: Weidenfeld & Nicolson, 1993) p. 177.
4.   Margaret Forster, *Daphne du Maurier* (London: Chatto & Windus, 1993) p. 337.
5.   Oriel Malet (ed.), *Letters from Menabilly*, p. 176. 'Victor' was du Maurier's publisher, Victor Gollancz.
6.   Margaret Forster, *Daphne du Maurier*, pp. 337–8.
7.   Ibid., p. 337.
8.   Oriel Malet (ed.), *Letters from Menabilly*, p. 167.
9.   The 'Vespa' was an Italian motor scooter particularly popular amongst the young in the 1960s in a number of European countries.
10. There is a curious resonance here. The 'lost boys' in J.M. Barrie's *Peter Pan* were based on cousins of du Maurier, the children of Gerald's sister, Sylvia Llewelyn Davies.
11. Daphne du Maurier, *The Flight of the Falcon* (1965; Harmondsworth: Penguin, 1969), p. 129. Page references in the text hereafter.
12   Walter Benjamin, *Illuminations: Essays and Reflections* (ed. and with an introduction by Hannah Arendt; trans. Harry Zohn) (1968; New York: Schocken Books, 1969) p. 256.
13. David Punter, *The Literature of Terror*, Vol.2, *The Modern Gothic* ([2nd edn] London: Longman, 1996) pp. 183–4.
14. This is a multivalent image. Reminiscent of Yeats's 'lonely impulse of delight', to a Freudian reader it might also suggest sexual release. ('An Irish Airman Foresees his Death' [1919], in W. B. Yeats, *Collected Poems* [London: Dent, 1990] p. 184.)

15   Oriel Malet (ed.), *Letters from Menabilly*, p. 169.

16.   Carl Jung, *Man and his Symbols* (1964; London: Picador, 1978) p. 147.

17.   Irigaray's account of this is to be found in the 'Plato's *Hystera*' section of Luce Irigaray (trans. Gillian C. Gill), *Speculum of the Other Woman* (1974; Ithaca and New York: Cornell University Press, 1985) pp. 243–364.

18.   The distinction made here between Mary of Bethany and Mary of Magdalena is interesting as it seems to be related to cultural stereotypes of women. Whereas Mary of Magdalena was a reformed prostitute, Mary of Bethany, who was supposed to have anointed Jesus's feet, was a much more mystical figure.

19.   This moment in the novel recalls the intrusion of the *unheimlich* into *The Loving Spirit* connected to Joseph's intense relationship with his dead mother and his death-dealing failure to sustain a satisfactory relationship with any other woman.

20.   See Anne Williams: 'One might generalize that within the Symbolic, mothers (matter/*mater*) are "horrible" and fathers are "terrible"' (*Art Of Darkness: A Poetics of Gothic* [Chicago: University of Chicago Press, 1995] p. 77)

21.   Luce Irigaray, *Marine Lover of Friedrich Nietzsche* (New York: Columbia University Press, 1991) p. 100.

22.   Virginia Woolf, *Three Guineas* (London: Hogarth, 1938).

23.   Marianne DeKoven cites the work of Klaus Thewelweit whose book *Male Fantasies* Vol. 1: *Women, Floods, Bodies, History* was written at about the same time as Irigaray was writing *Speculum of the Other Woman*. Dekoven states: 'Thewelweit historicizes Irigaray's deconstructed metaphysics, discovering it first in narratives written by Nazi soldiers, then reconstructing in its light the entire history of bourgeois culture... The written texts of these Nazi men reveal versions of self and attitudes towards femininity that Thewelweit does not find an exception to, or a pathological distortion of, some more benign norm, but rather an extreme point *within* a continuum of characteristic masculine gender subjectivity in a patriarchal culture. The texts construct a self rigorously defended, armored, rigidified – a self in terror of dissolution in the "abyss" associated with sexuate women and vaginal fecundity.' Marianne Dekoven, *Rich and Strange: Gender, History, Modernism* (Princeton: Princeton University Press, 1991) pp. 33–4.

24.   James Monaco, James Pallot and BASELINE, *The Second Virgin Film Guide* (London: Virgin Books, 1993) p. 220.

25.   Daphne du Maurier, 'Don't Look Now', *Don't Look Now and Other Stories* (Harmondsworth: Penguin Books, 1973). p. 55. This collection was originally published by Victor Gollancz in 1971 under the title *Not After Midnight*. Page numbers hereafter in the text.

26.   Terry Castle, *The Female Thermometer: Eighteenth-Century Culture and the Invention of the Uncanny* (New York and London: Oxford University Press, 1995) p. 17.

27. See Chapter 2 for a brief summary of Anne Williams' work on the Gothic, the Enlightenment and the uncanny.
28. Mary Russo, *The Female Grotesque: Risk, Excess and Modernity* (New York and London: Routledge, 1994) p. 7.
29. Ibid., p. 9.
30. Judith Halberstam, *Skin Shows: Gothic Horror and the Technology of Monsters* (Durham and London: Duke University Press, 1995) p. 22.
31. Nicolas Roeg's film emphasizes this by adding a scene in which John (in the film a restorer of old buildings) almost falls to his death while working on a project in a Venetian church. It is perhaps worth recalling here that du Maurier's first novel, *The Loving Spirit*, took its title from a poem by Emily Brontë entitled 'Self-Interrogation'.
32. Margaret Whitford, *Luce Irigaray: Philosophy in the Feminine* (London and New York: Routledge, 1991) p. 58.
33. Mary Russo, *The Female Grotesque*, p. 12.
34. Eve Kosofsky Sedgwick, *The Coherence of Gothic Conventions* (1980; London and New York: Methuen, 1986) pp. v–xiii.
35. Quotation from Tzvetan Todorov, *The Fantastic: A Structural Approach to a Literary Genre* (1973) in Linda Ruth Williams, *Critical Desire: Psychoanalysis and the Literary Subject* (London: Edward Arnold, 1995) p. 95.
36. Jacqueline Howard, *Reading Gothic Fiction: A Bakhtinian Approach* (Oxford: Clarendon Press, 1994) p. 45.
37. Ann Radcliffe, *The Italian* (Oxford: Oxford University Press, 1991) p. 318.
38. See Chapter 1 and Chapter 2, first and third sections.
39. Marianne DeKoven, *Rich and Strange: Gender, History, Modernism* (Princeton, New Jersey: Princeton University Press, 1991) p. 30.
40. We are grateful to Clare Hanson for pointing out this connection to us.
41. Margaret Whitford (ed.), *The Irigaray Reader* (1991; Oxford: Blackwell, 1994) pp. 49–50.
42. Margaret Whitford, *Luce Irigaray: Philosophy in the Feminine*, p. 53.
43. Ibid., p. 53.
44. This reading, whilst drawing on the work of Luce Irigaray, clearly refutes Jacqueline Howard' s recent assertion that French feminist interpretations of Gothic fiction tend to collapse women's writing into *écriture féminine* (*Reading Gothic Fiction*, p. 55) and that they fail to acknowledge how differently individual women write; it also counters her complaint that feminist readings of Gothic works tend to universalize women as victims (*Reading Gothic Fiction*, p. 56).
45. Oriel Malet (ed.), *Letters from Menabilly*, p. 194.
46. The novel was published by Victor Gollancz in 1972. The latest edition was published by Arrow Books in 1992; interestingly its cover features not the old Mad, but her young granddaughter, Emma, gazing out of a window in what looks like a state of emotional expectation. The cover is thus designed to appeal to a reader of women's romantic fiction (who is likely to be rather

puzzled by the bizarre plot of this novel); it is yet another example of the way du Maurier's works have been marketed within a particular generic category.

47.   Margaret Forster, *Daphne du Maurier*, pp. 382 and 412.

48.   Ibid., p. 412.

49.   Ibid., p. 383.

50.   Oriel Malet, *Letters from Menabilly*, p. 80. 'Tray' was one of du Maurier's several nick-names.

51.   Several letters in this volume refer to 'C. of L.' (an abbreviation for 'the change of life' or the menopause) and its effects on du Maurier's sense of self.

52.   Simone de Beauvoir, *Old Age* (translated by Patrick O'Brian) (1970; Harmondsworth: Penguin Books, 1977) pp. 340 and 374. *Old Age* was published in France in 1970 as *La Vieillesse*.

53.   Mary Russo, *The Female Grotesque*, p. 85.

54.   Simone du Beauvoir, *Old Age*, p. 15.

55.   See Part Five, entitled 'Death of the Writer', in Forster's biography for an account of this period of du Maurier's life.

Endword

1.   Daphne du Maurier, *Myself when Young* (1977; London; Arrow Books, 1993) Author's Note.

2.   Daphne du Maurier, *The Rebecca Notebook and Other Memories* (1981; London: Arrow Books, 1993) p. 49.

Select Bibliography

PRIMARY TEXTS

Works by Daphne du Maurier

The Loving Spirit (London: William Heinemann, 1931; London: Arrow Books 1994)
I'll Never Be Young Again (London: William Heinemann, 1932; London: Arrow Books 1994)
The Progress of Julius (London: William Heinemann, 1933; reprinted as *Julius* by Arrow Books in 1994)
Gerald: A Portrait (London: Victor Gollancz, 1934)
Jamaica Inn (London: Victor Gollancz, 1936; London: Arrow Books, 1992)
The du Mauriers (London, Victor Gollancz, 1937)
Rebecca (London: Victor Gollancz, 1938; London: Arrow Books, 1992)
Frenchman's Creek (London: Victor Gollancz, 1941; London: Arrow Books, 1992)
The King's General (London: Victor Gollancz, 1946; London: Arrow Books, 1992)
September Tide (1948) Revised version by Mark Rayment (London: Samuel French, 1994)
My Cousin Rachel (London: Victor Gollancz, 1951; London: Arrow Books, 1992)
The Scapegoat (London: Victor Gollancz, 1957; London: Arrow Books, 1992)
The Glass Blowers (London: Victor Gollancz, 1963)
The Flight of the Falcon (London: Victor Gollancz, 1965; Harmondsworth: Penguin Books, 1969)
The House on the Strand (London: Victor Gollancz, 1969; London: Arrow Books, 1992)
Vanishing Cornwall (London: Victor Gollancz, 1967; Harmondsworth: Penguin Books, 1972)
Rule Britannia (London: Victor Gollancz, 1972; London: Arrow Books, 1992)
'Don't Look Now' and Other Stories (Harmondsworth: Penguin Books, 1973) Originally published by Victor Gollancz in 1971 under the title *Not After Midnight*.
Myself When Young: The Shaping of a Writer (London: Arrow Books, 1993) Originally published by Victor Gollancz in 1977 as *Growing Pains: The Shaping of a Writer*.
The Rendezvous and Other Stories (London: Victor Gollancz, 1980)
The Rebecca Notebook and Other Memories (London: Victor Gollancz, 1981; London: Arrow Books, 1993)

Enchanted Cornwall, ed. Piers Dudgeon (London: Michael Joseph/Pilot Productions Ltd, 1989)
Daphne du Maurier: Letters from Menabilly – Portrait of a Friendship ed. Oriel Malet (London: Weidenfeld & Nicolson, 1993)

Works Edited and Introduced by Daphne du Maurier

Brontë, Emily *Wuthering Heights* (with introduction by Daphne du Maurier) (London: Macdonald, 1955)
Du Maurier, George *The Young George du Maurier: A Selection of his Letters 1860–1867* ed. Daphne du Maurier (London: Peter Davies, 1951)

Other Primary Texts Used

Auden, W.H. *Selected Poems* ed. Edward Mendelson (London: Faber & Faber, 1979)
Brontë, Emily *Wuthering Heights* (1847; Oxford: Oxford University Press, 1995)
Carter, Angela *Expletives Deleted* (1992; London: Vintage, 1993)
Doolittle, Hilda *H.D.: Selected Poems* ed. Louis L. Martz (New York: New Directions Books, 1988)
Du Maurier, Angela *Old Maids Remember* (London: Peter Davies, 1966)
Hogg, James *The Private Memoirs and Confessions of a Justified Sinner* (1824) ed. Carey, John (Oxford and New York: Oxford University Press, 1991)
Holt, Victoria *Mistress of Mellyn* (1961; London: Fontana, 1963)
Le Fanu, *Uncle Silas* (1864) ed. McCormack, W.J. assisted by Swarbrick, Andrew (Oxford: Oxford University Press, 1981)
—— *In a Glass Darkly* (1872) introd. by McCormack, W.J. (Stroud, Gloucestershire: Alan Sutton Publishing Ltd., 1990)
Lewis, Matthew *The Monk* (1796) ed. Anderson, Howard; introduction and notes by McEvoy, Emma (Oxford and New York: Oxford University Press, 1995)
Radcliffe, Ann *The Italian* (1797) ed. with an introduction by Garber, Frederick (Oxford and New York: Oxford University Press, 1968; 1991)
Stoker, Bram *Dracula* (1897) ed. with introduction and notes by Hindle, Maurice (Harmondsworth: Penguin Books, 1993)
Walpole, Horace *The Castle of Otranto* in *Three Gothic Novels* introd. by Praz, Mario (Harmondsworth: Penguin Books 1968; 1986)
Woolf, Virginia *Three Guineas* (1938) (Oxford: Oxford University Press, 1992)
Yeats, W.B. *Collected Poems* (London: Dent, 1990)

SECONDARY SOURCES

Secondary Sources on Daphne du Maurier, Her Life and Work (Including Reviews and Interviews)

Anon, 'Archangels Ruined', *The Times Literary Supplement* No.3, 164, 19 October 1962 p. 808

220 *Bibliography*

Bakerman, J.S. 'Daphne du Maurier' in Bakerman, J.S. (ed.) *And Then There Were Nine..More Women of Mystery* (Bowling Green, OH: Bowling Green State University Popular Press, 1985) pp. 12–29

Bromley, Roger 'The gentry, bourgeois hegemony and popular fiction: *Rebecca* and *Rogue Male*' in P. Humm, P. Stigant and P.Widdowson (eds) *Popular Fictions: Essays in Literature and History* (London: Methuen, 1986) pp. 151–72

Bryden, Ronald 'Queen of the Wild Mullions', *The Spectator*, 20 April 1962, pp. 514–15

Forster, Margaret *Daphne du Maurier* (London: Chatto & Windus, 1993)

Harbord, Janet 'Between Identification and Desire: Rereading *Rebecca*', *Feminist Review*, No. 53 (Summer 1996) pp. 95–106

Kelly, Richard 'Dame Daphne du Maurier' (obituary) *The Independent* 21 April 1989

Kelsall, Malcolm 'Manderley Revisited: *Rebecca* and the English Country House', *Proceedings of the British Academy*, 82 (1993) pp. 303–15

Light, Alison ' "Returning to Manderley": romance fiction, female sexuality and class', *Feminist Review*, No.16 (Summer 1984). This essay was later reprinted in Terry Lovell (ed.), *British Feminist Thought: A Reader* (Oxford: Basil Blackwell Ltd, 1990) pp. 325–44. It was also revised and incorporated as part of the section on du Maurier's work in Light's *Forever England* (see below)

——*Forever England: Femininity, Literature and Conservatism Between the Wars* (London: Routledge, 1991). See Chap. 4, 'Daphne du Maurier's romance with the past', pp. 156–207

Michelmore, Cliff *The Make-Believe World of Daphne du Maurier* (Banner Pictures, 1977) (interview)

Shallcross, Martyn *Daphne du Maurier Country* (St Teath: Bossiney Books, 1987)

——*The Private World of Daphne du Maurier* (London: Robson Books, 1991)

Smith, Allan Lloyd 'The Phantoms of *Drood* and *Rebecca*: The Uncanny Reencountered through Abraham and Torok's "Cryptonomy" ', *Poetics Today* 13:2 (Summer 1992) pp. 285–308

Westland, Ella 'The passionate periphery: Cornwall and romantic fiction' in Ian A. Bell (ed.) *Peripheral Visions: Images of Nationhood in Contemporary British Fiction* (Cardiff: University of Wales Press, 1995) pp. 153–72 (includes discussion of du Maurier's work)

Wings, Mary 'Rebecca Redux: Tears on a Lesbian Pillow' in Gibbs, Liz (ed.), *Daring to Dissent: Lesbian Culture from Margin to Mainstream* (London: Cassell, 1994) pp. 11–33

Secondary Sources on Film Versions of du Maurier's Work (Including Reviews)

Alion, Yves '*Rebecca*', *Revue du Cinema* No.442 (1988) p. 37

Doane, Mary Ann '*Caught* and *Rebecca*: The Inscription of Femininity as Absence', pp. 196–215 in Constance Penley (ed.), *Feminism and Film Theory* (New York and London: Routledge and BFI Publishing, 1988) pp. 196–215

Gallafent, Ed 'Black Satin: Fantasy, Murder and the Couple in *Gaslight* and *Rebecca*', *Screen* 29:3 (1988) pp. 84–103

Herpe, Noël '*Rebecca*: Une esquisse du procès de l'idéalisme', *Positif* No.389–90 (1993) pp. 112–14

Hollinger, Karen 'The Female Oedipal Drama of *Rebecca* from Novel to Film', *Quarterly Review of Film and Video* 14:4 (1993) pp. 17–30.

Light, Alison 'Gothic *Rebecca*: Hitchcock's Secret', *Sight and Sound* 6:5 (May 1996) pp. 29–31

Modleski, Tania ' "Never to be thirty-six years old": *Rebecca* as Female Oedipal Drama', *Wide Angle* 5:1 (1982) pp. 34–41 (later revised as Chapter 3 'Women and the Labyrinth' in *The Women Who Knew Too Much: Hitchcock and Feminist Theory* (New York and London: Routledge, 1988).

Secondary Sources on the Gothic

Day, William Patrick *In the Circles of Fear and Desire: A Study of Gothic Fantasy* (Chicago and London: The University of Chicago Press, 1985)

DeLamotte, Eugenia C. *Perils of the Night: A Feminist Study of Nineteenth-Century Gothic* (New York and Oxford: Oxford University Press, 1990)

Doody, Margaret Anne 'Deserts, Ruins and Troubled Waters: Female Dreams in Fiction and the Development of the Gothic Novel', *Genre* Vol.10 (Winter 1977) pp. 529–572

Duncan, Ian *Modern Romance and Transformations of the Novel: The Gothic, Scott and Dickens* (Cambridge: Cambridge University Press, 1992)

Ellis, Kate Ferguson *The Contested Castle: Gothic Novels and the Subversion of Domestic Ideology* (Urbana: University of Illinois Press, 1989)

Fleenor, Juliann E. (ed.) *The Female Gothic* (Montreal: Eden Press, 1983)

Frayling, Christopher *Vampyres: Lord Byron to Count Dracula* (1991; London: Faber & Faber, 1992)

Gelder, Ken *Reading the Vampire* (London and New York: Routledge, 1994)

Halberstam, Judith *Skin Shows: Gothic Horror and the Technology of Monsters* (Durham and London: Duke University Press, 1995)

Halberstam, Judith 'Technologies of monstrosity: Bram Stocker's *Dracula*' in Ledger and McCracken (eds) *Cultural Politics at the Fin de Siècle* (Cambridge: Cambridge University Press, 1995) pp. 248–66

Hogle, Jerrold E. 'The Gothic and the "Otherings" of Ascendant Culture: The Original Phantom of the Opera ', *South Atlantic Quarterly*, 95:3 (Fall, 1996) pp. 157–71

Howard, Jacqueline *Reading Gothic Fiction: A Bakhtinian Approach* (Oxford: Clarendon Press, 1994)

Howells, Coral Ann *Love, Mystery and Misery: Feeling in Gothic Fiction* (London: University of London, Athlone Press, 1978; reprinted with new preface in 1995)

Kahane, Claire 'Gothic Mirrors and Feminine Identity', *The Centennial Review* 24:1 (Winter, 1980) pp. 43–64

—— 'The Gothic Mirror' in Garner, Kahane and Sprengnether (eds), *The (M)other Tongue: Essays in Feminist Psycholanalytic Interpretation* (Ithaca: Cornell University Press, 1985)

Massé, Michelle A. *In the Name of Love: Women, Masochism, and the Gothic* (Ithaca: Cornell University Press, 1992)

Moers, Ellen *Literary Women* (1976; London: The Women's Press, 1978). See Part I, Chapter 5, 'Female Gothic'

Miles, Robert *Gothic Writing: A Genealogy 1750–1820* (London: Routledge, 1993)

—— *Ann Radcliffe: The Great Enchantress* (Manchester: Manchester University Press, 1995)

Modleski, Tania *Loving with a Vengeance: Mass-produced Fantasies for Women* (1982; London and New York: Routledge, 1988). (See Chap. III, 'The Female Uncanny: Gothic Novels for Women')

Punter, David *The Literature of Terror* (Second edition) Vols. 1 and 2 (London: Longman, 1996)

Punter, David, 'Contemporary Scottish Gothic: An Essay on Location', *Gothic Studies* (forthcoming).

Pykett, Lyn 'Gender and Genre in *Wuthering Heights*: Gothic Plot and Domestic Fiction' in Patsy Stoneman (ed.), *New Casebooks: Wuthering Heights* (London: Macmillan, 1993) pp. 86–99

Restuccia, Frances L. 'Female Gothic Writing: "Under Cover to Alice"', *Genre* Vol.18 (Fall 1986) pp. 245–266

Russ, Joanna 'Somebody's Trying to Kill Me and I Think It's My Husband: The Modern Gothic', *Journal of Popular Culture* 6:4 (1973) pp. 666–91. Reprinted in Fleenor (ed.), *The Female Gothic* (Montreal: Eden Press, 1983)

Sage, Victor *Horror Fiction in the Protestant Tradition* (London and Basingstoke: Macmillan, 1988)

Sage, Victor (ed.), *The Gothick Novel* (London: Macmillan, 1990)

Sedgwick, Eve Kosofsky *The Coherence of Gothic Conventions* (1980; London and New York: Methuen, 1986)

Warwick, Alexandra 'Vampires and the empire: fears and fictions of the 1890s' in Ledger and McCracken (eds) *Cultural Politics at the Fin-de-Siècle* (Cambridge: Cambridge University Press, 1995) pp. 202–20

Williams, Anne *Art of Darkness: A Poetics of Gothic* (Chicago and London: The University of Chicago Press, 1995)

Wolstenholme, Susan *Gothic (Re)Visions: Writing Women as Readers* (State University of New York Press, 1993)

Women's Writing 2:1 (1994) Special Issue on Female Gothic Writing edited by Robert Miles

Secondary Sources: General

Abel, Elizabeth (ed.), *Writing and Sexual Difference* (Brighton: Harvester Press, 1982)

Auerbach, Nina *Woman and the Demon: The Life of a Victorian Myth* (Cambridge, Massachusetts and London: Harvard University Press, 1982)

Bakerman, J.S. (ed.), *And Then There Were Nine.. More Women of Mystery* (Bowling Green, OH: Bowling Green State University Popular Press, 1985)

Beauman, Nicola *A Very Great Profession: The Woman's Novel 1914–1939* (London: Virago Press Ltd., 1983)

Beauvoir, Simone de *Old Age* (1970) trans. by O'Brian, Patrick (Harmondsworth: Penguin Books, 1977)

Beddoe, Deirdre *Back to Home and Duty: Women Between the Wars 1918–1939* (London: Pandora Press, 1989)

Bell, Ian (ed.), *Peripheral Visions: Images of Nationhood in Contemporary British Fiction* (Cardiff: University of Wales Press, 1995)

Benjamin, Walter *Illuminations: Essays and Reflections* ed. and with an introduction by Arendt, Hannah; trans. Zohn, Harry (New York: Schocken Books, 1969)

Bhaba, Homi *The Location of Culture* (London: Routledge, 1994)

Blau DuPlessis, Rachel *Writing Beyond the Ending* (Indiana: University of Indiana Press, 1985)

Boose, Lynda E. and Flowers, Betty S. (eds) *Daughters and Fathers* (Baltimore: Johns Hopkins University Press, 1989)

Bridgwood, Christine 'Family Romances: the contemporary popular family saga' in Jean Radford (ed.), *The Progress of Romance: The Politics of Popular Fiction* (London & New York: Routledge & Kegan Paul, 1986)

Bronfen, Elisabeth *Over Her Dead Body: Death, Femininity and the Aesthetic* (Manchester: Manchester University Press, 1992)

Brown, Terry *Discontented Discourses: Feminism/Textual Intervention/Psychoanalysis* (Urbana and Chicago: University of Illinois Press, 1989)

Burgin, Victor and Donald, James and Kaplan, Cora (eds), *Formations of Fantasy* (London and New York: Methuen, 1986)

Butler, Judith *Gender Trouble: Feminism and the Subversion of Identity* (London: Routledge, 1990)

Castle, Terry *The Female Thermometer: Eighteenth-Century Culture and the Invention of the Uncanny* (New York and London: Oxford University Press, 1995)

Cheyette, Bryan *Constructions of 'The Jew' in English Literature and Society: Racial Representations, 1875–1945* (Cambridge: Cambridge University Press, 1993)

Cockburn, Claud *Bestseller: The Books that Everyone Read 1900–1939* (London: Sidgwick & Jackson, 1972)

Cohen, Ed 'The double lives of man: narration and identification in late nineteenth-century representations of ec-centric masculinities' in Ledger and McCracken (eds.), *Cultural Politics at the Fin de Siècle*, pp. 85–114

DeKoven, Marianne *Rich and Strange: Gender, History, Modernism* (Princeton: Princeton University Press, 1991)

Dollimore, Jonathan *Sexual Dissidence: Augustine to Wilde, Freud to Foucault* (Oxford: Clarendon Press, 1991)

Doody, Margaret Anne *Frances Burney: The Life in the Works* (New Brunswick, New Jersey: Rutgers University Press, 1988)

Duberman, Martin Bauml, Vicinus, Martha and Chauncey, George, Jnr (eds), *Hidden from History: Reclaiming the Gay and Lesbian Past* (1989) (London: Penguin Books, 1991)

Faderman, Lillian *Surpassing the Love of Men: Romantic Friendship and Love Between Women from the Renaissance to the Present* (1981) (London: The Women's Press, 1985)

Felman, Shoshana *What Does a Woman Want: Reading and Sexual Difference* (Baltimore and London: Johns Hopkins University Press, 1993)

Fletcher, John and Benjamin, Andrew (eds), *Abjection, Melancholia and Love: The Work of Julia Kristeva* (London and New York: Routledge, 1990)

Ford, Susan Allen, ' "A name more dear": Daughters, Fathers, and Desire in *A Simple Story*, *The False Friend* and *Mathilda*' in Carol Shiner Wilson and Joel Haefner (eds), *Re-visioning Romanticism: British Women Writers 1776–1837* (Philadelphia: University of Pennsylvania Press, 1994) pp. 51–71

Fuss, Diana *Identification Papers* (New York and London: Routledge, 1995)

Garber, Marjorie *Vice Versa: Bisexuality and the Eroticism of Everyday Life* (London: Hamish Hamilton, 1995)

Gardiner, Judith Kegan 'On Female Identity and Writing by Women', *Critical Inquiry* 8:2 (1981) pp. 347–361. Reprinted in revised form in Abel, Elizabeth (ed.), *Writing and Sexual Difference*, pp. 177–91

Garner, Shirley Nelson, Kahane, Claire and Spregnether, Madelon (eds) *The (M)other Tongue: Essays in Feminist Psychoanalytic Interpretation* (Ithaca: Cornell University Press, 1985)

Gay, Peter (ed.) *The Freud Reader* (London: Vintage, 1995)

Gezari, Janet (ed.), *Emily Jane Brontë: The Complete Poems* (London: Penguin Books, 1992)

Gilbert, Sandra and Gubar, Susan *The Madwoman in the Attic: The Woman Writer and the Nineteenth-Century Literary Imagination* (New Haven and London: Yale University Press, 1979)

Gilbert, Sandra 'Costumes of the Mind: Transvestism as Metaphor in Modern Literature' in Abel, Elizabeth (ed.), *Writing and Sexual Difference*, pp. 193–219

Gilmore, Leigh *Autobiographics: A Feminist Theory of Women's Self-Representation* (Ithaca and London: Cornell University Press, 1994)

Girouard, Mark *Life in the English Country House: A Social and Architectural History* (New Haven and London: Yale University Press, 1978)

Glen, Heather (ed.) *Wuthering Heights* (London: Routledge, 1988); introduction pp. 1–33

Gross, Elizabeth 'The Body of Signification' in John Fletcher and Andrew Benjamin (eds), *Abjection, Melancholia and Love: The Work of Julia Kristeva* (London and New York: Routledge, 1990) pp. 80–103

Hawkins, Harriet *Classics and Trash: Traditions and Taboos in High Literature and Popular Modern Genres* (Hemel Hempstead: Harvester Wheatsheaf, 1990)

Heath, Stephen 'Joan Riviere and the Masquerade' in Burgin, Donald and Kaplan (eds), *Formations of Fantasy* pp. 45–61

Herman, Judith Lewis with Hirschman, Lisa *Father-Daughter Incest* (Cambridge, MA: Harvard University Press, 1981)

Hewitt, Leah D. *Autobiographical Tightropes* (Lincoln: University of Nebraska Press, 1990)

Hirsch, Marianne *The Mother/Daughter Plot: Narrative, Psychoanalysis, Feminism* (Bloomington: Indiana University Press, 1989)

Irigaray, Luce *This Sex Which Is Not One* trans. Catherine Porter with Carolyn Burke (Ithaca: Cornell University Press, 1985)

Irigaray, Luce *Speculum of the Other Woman* (1974) trans. Gill, Gillian C. (Ithaca: Cornell University Press, 1985)

Irigaray, Luce, *Marine Lover* (New York: Columbia University Press, 1991)

James, Beryl *Tales of the Saints' Way* (Redruth: Dyllansow Truro, 1993)

Johnson, Charles and Sleigh, Linwood *The Harrap Book of Boys' and Girls' Names* (London: Harrap, 1962; 1973)

Jung, Carl *Man and his Symbols* (1964) (London: Picador, 1978)

Kauffman, Linda *Disourses of Desire: Gender, Genre and Epistolary Fiction* (Ithaca and London: Cornell University Press, 1986)

Keast, John *The Story of Fowey* (Redruth: Dyllansow Truran, 1950)

Kennedy, J. Gerald 'Place, Self and Writing', *The Southern Review* (Baton Rouge) 26:3 (Summer 1990)

Kristeva, Julia *Powers of Horror: An Essay on Abjection* translated Leon Roudiez (1980; New York: Columbia University Press, 1982)

Kristeva, Julia *Strangers to Ourselves* translated Leon S. Roudiez (New York: Columbia University Press, 1991)

Lechte, John *Julia Kristeva* (London: Routledge, 1990)

Ledger, Sally and McCracken, Scott (eds), *Cultural Politics at the Fin-de-Siècle* (Cambridge: Cambridge University Press, 1995)

Lewis, Jane *Women in England 1870–1950* (Sussex: Wheatsheaf Books Ltd., 1984)

Lovell, Terry (ed.), *British Feminist Thought: A Reader* (Oxford: Basil Blackwell, 1990)

Mallory, W.E. and Simpson-Housley, P. (eds), *Geography and Literature: A Meeting of the Disciplines* (Syracuse: Syracuse University Press, 1987)

Marcus, Laura *Auto/biographical Discourses: Theory, Criticism, Practice* (Manchester and New York: Manchester University Press, 1994)

Massey, Doreen *Space, Place and Gender* (Cambridge: Polity Press, 1994)

Matthews, John 'Framing in *Wuthering Heights*' in Patsy Stoneman (ed.), *New Casebooks: Wuthering Heights* (London: Macmillan, 1993) pp. 54–73

McAleer, Joseph *Popular Reading and Publishing in Britain 1941–1950* (Oxford: Clarendon Press, 1992)

Melman, Billie *Women and the Popular Imagination in the Twenties: Flappers and Nymphs* (London: Macmillan Press, 1988)

Miller, Jim Wayne 'Any Time the Ground is Uneven: The Outlook for Regional Studies and What to Look Out For' in W.E.Mallory and P.Simpson-Housley (eds), *Geography and Literature: A Meeting of the Disciplines* (Syracuse: Syracuse University Press, 1987)

Miller, Karl *Doubles: Studies in Literary History* (Oxford: Oxford University Press, 1985)

Modleski, Tania *Loving With a Vengeance: Mass-produced Fantasies for Women* (New York and London: Routledge, 1982)

—— *The Women Who Knew Too Much: Hitchcock and Feminist Theory* (New York and London: Routledge, 1988)

Moers, Ellen *Literary Women* (1976) (London: The Women's Press, 1986)

Monaco, James, Pallot, James and BASELINE *The Second Virgin Film Guide* (London: Virgin Books, 1993)

Morgan, Janice 'Subject to Subject/Voice to Voice: Twentieth-Century Autobiographical Fiction by Women Writers' in Morgan and Hall (eds), *Redefining Autobiography in Twentieth-Century Women's Fiction* (see below)
—— and Hall, Colette T. (eds), *Redefining Autobiography in Twentieth-Century Women's Fiction* (New York and London: Garland Publishing Inc., 1991)

Morrison, Paul 'Enclosed in Openness: *Northanger Abbey* and the Domestic Carceral', *Texas Studies in Literature and Language* 33:91 (1991) pp. 1–23

Newton, Esther 'The Mythic Mannish Lesbian: Radclyffe Hall and the New Woman' in Duberman, Vicinus and Chauncey (eds), *Hidden from History* pp. 281–293

Penley, Constance (ed.), *Feminism and Film Theory* (New York and London: Routledge and BFI Publishing, 1988)

Poovey, Mary *The Proper Lady and the Woman Writer: Ideology as Style in the Works of Mary Wollstonecraft, Mary Shelley, and Jane Austen* (Chicago and London: The University of Chicago Press, 1984)
—— 'Fathers and Daughters: The Trauma of Growing Up Female' in *Women and Literature* Vol.2 (1982) pp. 39–58

Pykett, Lyn *Engendering Fictions: The English Novel in the Early Twentieth Century* (London: Edward Arnold, 1995)

Radford, Jean (ed.), *The Progress of Romance: The Politics of Popular Fiction* (London & New York: Routledge & Kegan Paul, 1986)

Roberts, Andrew Michael *The Novel: A Guide to the Novel from its Origins to the Present Day* (London: Bloomsbury, 1994)

Riviere, Joan 'Womanliness as Masquerade' in Burgin, Donald and Kaplan (eds), pp. 35–44

Rowse, A.L. 'Cornwall in History and Literature', *Contemporary Review* Sept. 1991 pp. 157–60

Russo, Mary *The Female Grotesque: Risk, Excess and Modernity* (London: Routledge, 1994)

Sayers, Janet *Sexual Contradictions: Psychology, Psychoanalysis, and Feminism* (London and New York: Tavistock Publications Ltd., 1986)

Sedgwick, Eve Kosofsky *Between Men: English Literature and Male Homosocial Desire* (New York: Columbia University Press, 1985)
—— *Epistemology of the Closet* (1990: Harmondsworth: Penguin Books, 1994)

Showalter, Elaine *Sisters' Choice: Tradition and Change in American Women's Writing* (Oxford: Clarendon Press, 1991)

Smith, Sidonie *A Poetics of Women's Autobiography* (Bloomington; Indiana University Press, 1987)
—— *Subjectivity, Identity and the Body: Women's Autobiographical Practice in the Twentieth Century* (Bloomington and Indianapolis: Indiana University Press, 1993)

Smith-Rosenberg, Carroll 'Discourses of Sexuality and Subjectivity' in Duberman, Vicinus and Chauncey (eds), *Hidden from History*, pp. 264–280.

Spacks, Patricia Meyer *Desire and Truth: Functions of Plot in Eighteenth-Century English Novels* (Chicago and London: University of Chicago Press, 1990)

Spencer, Jane *The Rise of the Woman Novelist: From Aphra Behn to Jane Austen* (Oxford: Blackwell, 1986)

Stoneman, Patsy (ed.), *New Casebooks: Wuthering Heights* (London: Macmillan, 1993)
—— *Brontë Transformations: The Cultural Dissemination of 'Jane Eyre' and 'Wuthering Heights'* (Hemel Hempstead: Harvester Wheatsheaf, 1996)
Taylor, John Russell *Hitch: The Life and Work of Alfred Hitchcock* (London: Faber & Faber, 1978)
Todd, Janet *Sensibility: An Introduction* (London: Methuen, 1986)
Van Ghent, Dorothy *The English Novel: Form and Function* (1953; New York: Harper and Row, 1967)
Vicinus, Martha 'Distance and Desire: English Boarding School Friendships 1870–1920' in Duberman, Vicinus and Chauncey (eds), *Hidden from History*, pp. 212–29
Whitford, Margaret (ed.), *The Irigaray Reader* (1991; Oxford: Blackwell, 1994)
Whitford, Margaret *Luce Irigaray: Philosophy in the Feminine* (London and New York: Routledge, 1991)
Williams, Linda Ruth *Critical Desire: Psychoanalysis and the Literary Subject* (London: Edward Arnold, 1995)
Wilson, Carol Shiner and Haefner, Joel (eds), *Re-visioning Romanticism: British Women Writers 1776–1837* (Philadelphia: University of Pennsylvania Press, 1994)
Yaeger, Patricia and Kowaleski-Wallace, Beth (eds), *Refiguring the Father: New Feminist Readings of Patriarchy* (Carbondale and Edwardsville: Southern Illinois University Press, 1989)

Index

split subjectivity/fragmented
identity 5, 7, 13, 32, 45, 51, 53,
55, 67, 126
Spregnether, Madelon 196n, 205n
Stein, Gertrude 16
Stevenson, Robert Louis 52, 53, 70,
109
Dr Jekyll and Mr Hyde 147,
157
Stewart, Susan 80
Stigant, P. 194n
Stoker, Bram (*Dracula*) 99, 111,
209n, 211n
Stoneman, Patsy 71, 197n, 199n,
207n
Strachey, Dorothy 193n
sublime, the 81, 82, 85
Svengali 4, 59, 121, 125

Taylor, John Russell 204n
Thackeray, William 33
Thérèse de Lisieux 154, 214n
Thewelweit, Klaus 215n
Thorndyke, Russell 71
Times Literary Supplement, The
(anonymous review) 213n
'Tod' (Miss Maud Waddell) 4
Todd, Janet 32, 198n
Todorov, Tzvetan 179
Torok, Maria 22, 194n, 209n
Tree, Beerbohm 201n
Tree, Viola 201n
Tristan and Iseult 101
Trollope, Anthony 33

Ulrich, Karl Heinrich 15
uncanny, the (*unheimlich*) 32, 35,
42, 43, 60, 62, 81, 82–3, 84, 85,
119, 126, 135, 142, 150, 151, 155,
175–7
Urbino 160

vampire figure
in *Rebecca* 111–13
associated with
'Jewishness' 112, 126
in *The Flight of the Falcon* 166
Van Ghent, Dorothy 204n
Vaughan, Tom 24
Vicinus, Martha 14, 15, 17
Violett, Ellen 191n
Vyvyan, Lady Clara 183

Walpole, Horace 119
The Castle of Otranto 213n
Warwick, Alexandra 210n
Weldon, Fay 29
Wells, H.G. 38
West, Mae 18
Westland, Ella 38, 69
Whitford, Margaret 182, 210n
Widdowson, P. 194n
Wilde, Oscar 48, 119
Williams, Anne 27, 28, 29, 30, 34,
35–6, 86, 104, 107, 110, 136, 138,
143, 144, 175, 187, 196n, 197n,
198n, 199n, 205n, 208n, 209n,
212n, 215n
Wilson, Carol Shiner 198n
Wilson, Harold 23
Wings, Mary 211
Wolstenholme, Susan 27, 196n
Woolf, Virginia 195n
Mrs Dalloway 40
Orlando 16
Three Guineas 172, 214n
World War Two 157, 159, 161
written texts (their significance in
Gothic narratives) 139–40,
162–3, 167

Yaeger, Patricia 198n
Yeats, W.B. 214n